PETALUMA SLOUGH

A Novel

Kenneth J. Nugent

ISBN: 1544215940
ISBN 13: 9781544215945

Dedicated to Charlene.

We'll always have Plattsburgh.

CONTENTS

CALIFORNIOS
Autumn 1845

Rancho Arroyo de San Antonio graced a Pacific coastal valley of near-biblical promise. For thousands of years, its Mediterranean climate nurtured the delights of aboriginal man, large animals, and delicate creatures of spectacular beauty. A tidal slough connected the valley to the ocean via San Francisco Bay. Juan Miranda had built a family adobe on a low rise in the unspoiled hills west of the brackish slough. Bricks of mud, manure, and straw—stacked block upon block—formed symmetrical rectangles to wall off the chaos of wild man and animal. The home staked his dominance over the land and anchored the Miranda cattle ranch. While his wife, Luz, waited outside the adobe for relief from an overdue *carreta*, Juan lay dying in their darkened bedroom. The mudbrick walls he built to project his might, separated him from his last moments in paradise.

Luz paced beyond the commotion of animal enclosures. A lone horseman approached from over a rise. He slumped forward, giving the walking horse the bit. Their swerving track alarmed quick-footed quail. Coveys, flushed from tall grasses, cross-stitched the path.

"Speak," she shouted at her son, throwing up her hands. "What have you heard?"

An off-balance wave greeted her cry. The rider sat back. "Men." Sweat-matted hair swung behind as he dismounted. Gravity pulled him down off the saddle. "I heard men on horseback."

"Only men? I instructed you to report to me when you heard squealing from an ox-drawn wagon. You have the gall to ride back here to tell me you only heard men?"

The sighting of an enormous carreta coming down the rise would herald deliverance for Juan.

"That's what I said." He leaned on the shoulder of the horse. "Men."

"It can't only be men. Must be the *escolta* riding ahead of the carreta. How many are in the escort?"

"Who knows? Could have been riders, or it might have been workers stomping mudbricks at the hacienda. I don't know. The wind blows here and there. Sound carried on the wind is confusing.… Maybe I was mistaken."

A twitchy thumb scratched his cheek. It nudged a kerchief slanted across his left eye socket. Years earlier, while rounding-up cattle for the fall matanza slaughter, a misdirected lariat snared both a wild bull and Teodoro's forearm. The violent jolt crushed his eye and tore off his arm below the elbow. Slathered hot-pitch applied to the amputation had cauterized the darkened stump— and the remaining days of his life.

"Stop fretting," he said. "The sound came from over there." Teodoro aligned his appendage with the distant construction site of a massive adobe. Even in its unfinished state, they referred to the assembled mudbricks and redwood posts as "the palace," the largest private building in Alta California.

Hammer strikes and ripped wood carried on the winds from the hacienda to Luz. Incessant noise from mallet, chisel, and saw drummed her head. Sometimes the construction sounded as though it were nearby, pounding a stake barricade that closed around her life. Other times, the racket faded to a buzz, an impossible distance away. The staccato beat haunted with the antithetical perceptions of time moving too fast, and of time moving too slow. She jammed her hands against the sides of her ears. "How can you listen for anything over that commotion? Go back and yell at the riders to hurry and bring up the carreta."

"In a minute. Right now, I drink." He pinched the center of his mouth with his thumb and index finger. A boozy laugh spit between his lips. "Women should close their mouths and open their ears when men tell them not to worry. The soldiers know we're here."

Twenty miles to the east of the Miranda rancho, past the hacienda, Sonoma Pueblo ascended on the Mission San Francisco Solano ruins. A one-night ride to their south, another pueblo, formed on the Mission San Rafael de Arcángel vestiges, slumped from years of near-abandonment. The padres had built it as an *assistencia*, a warmer, backup medical facility, for the inhospitable Mission Dolores in Yerba Buena. Luz had pledged to bring her husband to what remained of the mission before he died.

If the itinerant priest there determined Juan's soul had not yet left his body, he could administer the end-of-life sacrament of Extreme Unction. With holy oil on his right thumb, she expected the priest to make a cross on Juan's forehead and chant, "*Si vivis, ego te absolvo a peccatis tuis. In nomine Patris et Filio et Spiritus Sancti, amen.*" The Latin prayer translated to, "If you are living, I absolve you from your sins. In the name of the Father and of the Son and of the Holy Ghost, amen."

If they are living, Catholic rituals secured the anointed a place in heaven. Without the blessing, the sin-stained dead faced eternity in purgatory or hell.

"Your father's safety depends on the escolta to get him to the mission while he still breathes."

3

"Maybe I detected something else—other men coming. Maybe it was pitter-patter of quail. I'm tired and it's not important. Generalissimo Vallejo will provide the carreta."

Luz coughed the Don's name, as if she expelled an inhaled bug. "Then Don Guadalupe's men had better hurry."

Generalissimo Mariano Guadalupe Vallejo, commander of the revolutionary Republic of Mexico, controlled the province that included their rancho. Since the day of her daughter's shotgun marriage, Vallejo's name on Luz's lips never rose above the basest civility.

"I trust him," said Teodoro.

"I don't. He steals our time."

"Squawk, squawk. *Ow!*"

Luz seized Teodoro's sideburns and tugged straight to her shoulders. "Speak up. You slur your words."

"Let go." Throwing back its head against the bridle restriction, the horse nickered away from her taunt.

"Well?"

"They're coming—ow!" Luz yanked another quick pull of his hair. Teodoro pulled on the reins from a crabbed position. "I heard the carreta, too. Okay? Let go." She pressed her forehead against him. Brandy vapors that clung to his goatee crunched her nose, adding to the menace of Luz's demeanor.

"I don't hear them." Dominant traits of their diluted African ancestry cured richer in her dark flesh tone than it colored Teodoro's complexion. Gritty perspiration worked up from his meandering ride smeared her brow. "Boy, are you certain the sounds are from the soldiers *and* from the carreta?"

She released him from a submissive crouch to cup her hand to her ear. No whistle of salvation—no squeals from overheated wooden hubs—threaded through the construction din. Her son's rheumy eye avoided her gaze. He swayed on the bridle for support and redirected his mother's attention to northern autumnal hills. "*Si, cierto.* They're coming. Maybe from that direction."

Emerald trains of grasses, ornamented with brilliant lupine and mustard blossoms, had parched over the rainless summer months to lighter chestnut browns. Dry season left the slopes scraggled. Deep-green beards of oak and alder crowded the ravines.

"That devil will be to blame if your father dies before he gets to the mission."

"Shhh," said Teodoro, pushing up a smile.

"Don't smile at me like a cornered possum. No. You will not quiet me—nor will Vallejo. He treats us like savages."

An index finger wavered across his lips. "We're too close to home. Others might hear. My wife is learning to yowl like you."

Since the time of his horrendous disfigurement, Vallejo inveigled Teodoro with a special credit at his liquor *pulperia* in Sonoma. He provided free anodyne to relieve his pain.

Said Vallejo, "It would make my heart happy to imagine you as the son I've never had." Addiction to the generalissimo's benevolence grew in equal measure to Vallejo's secret entreaties. Although he never joined Teodoro in alcoholic drink, they talked in confidence, one better-bred gentleman to another, Vallejo asking for incidental considerations. "Persuade your mother to be more cooperative. Remind her territory affairs are not women's concern. Please do me that very small service, and I will do everything I can to retain your title to the Miranda rancho after Juan dies."

Emboldened by the promise, Teodoro gloated at Luz with a lazy smile. "Has your hearing dried, too? Listen harder. They're coming. The carreta *and* the escolta are coming." A goatskin of strong brandy aguardiente appeared from under his poncho. "Here, lap some up." The uncorked bag sagged across his short limb. "It'll make you sweeter."

Luz slapped his face with a swiping, knuckled backhand. Frontier-hardened strength still banded her sinew. "Remember your place," she said.

The skin slipped from his grasp, sloshing to the ground. He swung up his club-like stump. The marrow throbbed as if hot razors sliced and seared where blood pulscd at its end. "Soon, this is *my* place." A blackened cigarillo fumbled between his teeth. The juice extracted from the spongy leaves quelled his pain. Teodoro bent toward the skin for more relief. "You will never hit me again. This is my place." He stumbled forward a half step and swiped twice at the alcohol bladder before he clutched its neck. Lifting it to his lips, he squeezed. Noisy gulps forced the burning liquid down his throat. "If you can't accept that," he croaked, "then you can argue with the generalissimo. But I warn you, your quick anger may vex him. He'll take this rancho back if you are not respectful."

Teodoro grew bolder while Juan weakened. Prompted by Vallejo, he challenged his mother's presumption to the family head.

Vallejo exercised ultimate control over life and death in the region. He manipulated men, divided loyalties, and allocated land to increase his power. The borders he drew for Rancho Arroyo de San Antonio—a minor concession for Vallejo—marked one of the smaller ranchos on the *Frontera del Norte*. Tule marshes on its eastern border abutted the sprawling *Rancho Arroyo Lema,* Vallejo's property.

"Shush!" Turning toward her idle oxcarts by the adobe, Luz said, "If my strong son were here, we would be on our way using one of those. I wouldn't be wasting your father's last breaths with you." Referring to his younger brother, Mariano, as her "strong son," drew cruel attention to Teodoro's diminished capabilities. Unlike Teodoro, Mariano drove her carretas. That choice no longer remained. Mariano had ridden north to attack Indian camps around the geysers. Vallejo's genocidal raids kept him away for several days.

Teodoro endured his mother's derisions as often as he had suffered illusory pain from his lost limb. She meant her stings to remind him of her anger. Both knew it. His handicaps left him unable to manage their cattle enterprise. Without an able male heir to run the ranch, widowhood might leave Luz at Vallejo's mercy and devious benevolence.

Teodoro fretted his father's death more than Luz dreaded the loss of her husband. If the family shunned him, he could neither support his wife and children, nor assume the more demanding patriarchal mantle. The family's unspoken measure of his leadership—of his manliness—narrowed to see if he got their father to the mission alive.

Their destiny depended on securing reliable transportation to San Rafael. They had none on the Miranda Rancho. Single axle carretas provided adequate drayage for delivering their short decks of hides to the slough. They could not haul an oversized load the long distance to San Rafael.

Luz had ridden to Sonoma and demanded from Vallejo his largest, and most valuable, twin-axle carreta to carry her family to the Pueblo. She put Vallejo on notice: "Juan stood by you through your insurrections. Your troops would find it unforgiveable if you withheld your best carreta from their dying comrade."

More than a decade after the revolutionary government seized Alta California from the Spanish Empire, the government in Mexico City called on Vallejo's troops to settle the remaining Mexican frontier. Juan supported Vallejo in conquest and stood by him during five insurrections. With Juan and his small cadre of trusted men, Vallejo imposed his authority. They faced challenges from native and foreign foes on their frontier: incorporated Russians clung barnacle-like to jagged coastal settlements, powerful British ships sailed to the bay from Fort Vancouver, American trailblazers poured into unpopulated valleys, and thousands of native peoples, whose ancient homelands Vallejo intended to seize by callous force and deception, refused to surrender. Vallejo buttressed his loyal troops with the northern adobe stronghold. A "palace" built to declare his might and increase his fortune. The bulwark rose unmatched from San Diego to Sonoma.

As she waited, perils of Vallejo's treachery nagged at Luz as much as the journey's nocturnal dangers. *What will happen to me if Don Guadalupe withheld his carreta?*

"Prepare," she said to Teodoro. "I don't want to leave the family, but we must get on *Camino de San Rafael*."

Mules brayed in the corral next to the mustang paddock. The draft animals shared twin enclosures with sturdy oxen. Either of those forms of propulsion could transport Luz and her husband without help from Vallejo—if they traveled only with Teodoro.

Night crept a few hours away. Predators, too treacherous for a one-armed escort to hold off alone, awakened from their lairs. Although Vallejo had pledged to send his finest soldiers and their sharpest blades with the cart to defend her family from the wild, Luz erred in relying on her tormentor's arsenal.

Latino gentleman of Vallejo's pedigree never demeaned a lady in person—even if she were a *mestiza*. He relied on other channels to convey demeaning rebukes. She knew that if Vallejo reneged on his promise, he intended the slight as an unspoken edict to the pueblo: the days of spousal privilege for Luz Miranda had ended.

Other threats to Luz, dangers more tangible than Machiavellian intrigues, mounted on her knot of worries. By now the pumas glided noiseless as smoke, shadowing hillside contours in the twilight. Invisible, they waited in ambush to take physical form in a frenzy of artery-puncturing carnage. Luz believed that at night uprooted Indians turned from obsequious foragers into highway marauders. They leapt from covered bear-trap holes to assail travelers.

Juan had advised Luz when they planned for his final hours, "Stop worrying of *Indios*. Those docile animals shouldn't be your primary concern. Nor should the puma hold you back. I have confronted clawed-beasts, even bear, in my travels. They're wiser than men are in the night. Be patient. They'll retreat off the road and let you pass. The threat is *El Toro*. The bull will block your way. We brought the beast to the new world. He learned to act like us. Be on guard. He won't retreat. And he won't allow you escape. No, he *will* gore you. Full-sized Criollo bulls are far more dangerous than the grizzlies. Look what they did to our son."

Despite her husband's counsel, Luz feared each predator that might lurk along the overnight passage. She reserved her utmost terror for the thick-furred grizzlies. At the height of the Great Smallpox Plague, she saw dislocated bears rake claws through a mass grave where Mexicans interred Indians who died of European diseases. One hungry bear foraged from the loose soil cap the bent leg of a ten-year-old boy. To Luz's unutterable horror, the limb belonged to a live child. The dying boy's weak cries resounded in her ears, as if they joined with wails from his decimated Indian people. She made no effort to save the child. Furtive, brown eyes of grizzlies and Indians marked her perfidious witness.

Years later, her apprehensions flared anew. A pockmarked merchant sailor delivered a message to the rancho from the Presidio. Juana Briones, her sister-in-law, sent the sailor to find her. He relayed Juana's warning of a vision.

"A grizzly bear spoke to Señora Briones in a dream. The animal prophesied vengeful bears from the East would come to devour your adobe, your children, and the land where you live."

Without questioning, Luz nodded and made the sign of the cross. She asked the sailor to carry a message to Juana when his trading vessel returned to the Yerba Buena cove. "My dearest sister-in-law, Señor Miranda is at the final judgment."

She repeated her dictation, allowing the sailor to memorize each word. "I beg you to meet with me at the San Rafael Pueblo. Bring comfort to my dying husband."

Juana and Luz had shared powerful bonds before they married the Miranda brothers. Their Africans ancestors mined Spanish colonial silver. After generations of racial intermarriage, society categorized the women in the *Indios casta*. They began their lives together at Villa de Branciforte, a settlement near Mission Santa Cruz. Both brother-husbands served in the army commanded by Vallejo.

Juana, a respected and sought-after Curandera folk-healer, gained a land grant in Yerba Buena despite a separation from her abusive husband. That rare acquisition by a quasi-unmarried woman inspired Luz to establish her own powerful, Latina matriarchy. Now Vallejo, the society's alpha bull, blocked her road to independence.

Will the carreta come in time?

She prayed. "Damn the soul of Don Guadalupe. Forgive me Santa Maria, but damn him to burn in Hades' hottest fire. And damn his bastard children."

Throughout that morning, puffs separating Juan's cracked lips slowed. When the brass clock in the main room chimed twice, Luz stepped from the deathwatch to outside the adobe. She spied a sullen rider and a sea of tipsy grasses waving back from *el Llano de los Petalumas*—armed, serious men, leading a grande carreta, had not arrived.

Along the Sierra Range, a five-day ride away, golden nuggets wider than hardtack balanced lazy as turtles on sun-bleached rocks. Other placers rolled in torrents of melted snow. Even more gold, glittering, ground and compressed up between the warp of two continents—an empire-building treasure of precious flakes— lay in dried streambeds undiscovered by white men. The transformative power of the metal poised to infect the world.

As if in a game of craps, where gods tossed lots upon the green landscape of California's gambling table, Providence, fate's stickman, readied to call the point. A tumble of golden dice aligned the destinies of Luz Miranda and generations that followed.

BANISHED

The Petaluma "palace" embodied Vallejo's expanding power and authority. Its proximity to where international trading schooners landed, and the toil of Indian slaves within its warrens, produced extraordinary wealth for Vallejo. He summoned Teodoro Miranda to meet him there in his upstairs quarters, above where enslaved women wove blankets.

When Teodoro arrived, Vallejo set Plutarch's classic *Parallel Lives* aside on a candle stand table. He wiped the book cover with a chamois cloth.

"Please sit. I was just dreaming of the Roman Empire. Inspiring. Have you read of the great Romans?"

"I don't read."

Both knew he knew. "Oh. I would love to share with you stories of their genius. That's a lesson for another occasion. At present, we have vital matters to discuss."

Rhythmic battening, from looms in the quarters below, softened to a slower beat vibrating the floor.

Teodoro put aside his liquor skin. The bladder squatted on the history book. "Are we to discuss tomorrow's march to San Rafael?"

"Not just about the journey. That is a small matter. The time has come for us to consider your future." Vallejo cleared his throat and wiggled a finger. Teodoro slid the liquor sack off the leather-covered book, setting it on his legs.

"I have decided not to send my carreta," said Vallejo.

A gasp drew tantalizing brandy vapors from his lap into Teodoro's sinuses, teasing inside his cheeks. "Mother is depending on you to deliver the wagon tomorrow."

"And for two days after that. Three full days? Three productive days without that wagon? It will slow the south wing completion. You can see the work I'm doing here. The rancho can't grow in these cramped spaces. My workers need to pick up the pace of construction. Your mother's whimsies inconvenience me. And they are a threat to our prosperity."

"Of course, the carreta is not a worry of mine. I have no need for it." Teodoro leaned forward. "It's for Father's benefit."

"That would be fine if the journey were his idea."

"I want—" Teodoro sought strength from the liquor bag warming his thighs. He savored its relaxing fumes. "My *father* wanted a final blessing at the mission. The family expects me to lead them. They're like children without my guidance. I will come back to Petaluma as the Miranda rancho head."

"Exactly. I will secure that future for you. That's why we are having this little talk. Understand me. I would drain my veins for *mi amigo*. However, Juan did not petition his dearest, lifelong friend. Your mother came here flapping her wings like a mockingbird. Squawking, squawking, and squawking. Her agitation would have embarrassed your father."

"She's an old, stupid woman."

"She's an old *bird*. Knock sense into her—knock it in hard. Let Juan die like a man. Quietly. At home, in the world he created.

Men choose how they live. They decide how they die. He's not a woman. Women lay down like grass in a hard wind. This foolish journey was her idea. Has your mother heeded nothing I suggested for you to tell her?"

"She told me her request is not for her convenience, but it is for your benefit."

"My benefit? Nonsense. How could that be?"

"Mother believes respecting Father is a sign of loyalty to all who carry swords for Mexico. She says the men in the barracks love Father. They expect you to love him, too."

"Seditious words—from whomever speaks them."

"Those are her beliefs not mine. I am not her. Look at my flesh. It's pale."

"You are your father's son. Thank God you have his *testículos*, too."

"You won't suffer mother's nonsense from me."

"Have soldiers been to your rancho and visited your father while he has been ill?"

"Those who fought the insurrections hold a vigil at the adobe. They have not forgotten what Ortega did to Father, how he brought him down. Ortega debased their uniform and their loyalty."

"Never mention that name. Ortega is dangerous. Do the soldiers blame me for his villainy?"

"I don't."

"Yes, of course, *you* do not. Do the soldiers? I'm the one who drove Ortega from the territory. The troops must appreciate that, too."

"I guess."

"Well they should have no resentments then. Let her take your father in one of his own single-axle carretas. After all, I gave him the rancho, so those carretas are as good as mine."

"She wants the largest of your two-axle wagons so there's enough space to carry our family. Your soldiers suggested that to her."

"The soldiers can't possibly support her crazy notions."

"They're contriving a show to make her feel better. The angrier they appeared, the happier Mother seemed."

Teodoro waited for Vallejo's reaction. He did not respond with his usual prompt assertions. Clatter in the weaving room below halted. The ceiling beams quieted until a book slammed above the Indian women. Legs on a chair scratched across the rough floor planks.

"I'll release the large wagon," grumbled Vallejo. Heavy boots clomped in wide circles. "The pueblo may mock me—think I'm too kind with my accommodations. They'll be right. But I will suffer their slings because I am doing it so Juan doesn't have to listen to her squawk. And you make sure you let the soldiers know that was my reason. Do you hear me?" He dropped into a seat. "Go alone with them to San Rafael. No one else from your family. None of the others. They have designs on your birthright. No more passengers than you and your parents may go on my wagon. That's everyone. Not one person more."

"I hear what *you* say." Teodoro sat back and brushed dried clay off his knee. "But my mother has never cared for what I say."

"It's time she listened. I'm an old fool. Perhaps, I should keep my suspicions to myself. Nevertheless, my love for your father won't permit it. Rumors abound. Evil ones intend to steal the rancho from my friend's firstborn while you are grieving. I have to think about your future."

"You wouldn't let that happen to me." His short arm flopped, slapping against his ribs as though a rodent gnawed at its stub.

"Listen to my words." Vallejo squeezed Teodoro's stump in a hard grip. Unanchored muscles, seeking a tendon, twitched in his hand. "Even a good man can talk nonsense on his deathbed. He can bestow his property upon those who don't have a birthright to his legacy. Schemers surely plot to trick your father at the end. Remember, no one other than you should whisper in his ear. Keep the others away."

Vallejo released the stump with a shove.

Teodoro nodded in agreement. Brandy squirted from the skin into his mouth, slopping his cheek. "We'll move faster without them, especially with Captain Salvador leading us."

"That giant wagon comes back in three days."

"The soldiers *de escolta* have been ordered, yes? We need—*Mother* needs their escort for her protection on the journey."

"Yes. Yes. This is paramount. The carreta must arrive and return safely. Then as if to insult me further, your mother insists I also send my best Kanaka to go with it. No savages. She declined my alternative offer of many Indian workers, as many as she wants. I sacrifice much for her comfort. Why is she so quarrelsome?"

Vallejo knew the answer: Indians were not strong enough drivers to right an imbalanced wagon. Giant carretas required men with extraordinary brute strength to stabilize their shifting centers of gravity. Axles often collapsed from pressures on their wooden hubs. Repairs took the labor of at least four Indians, or a single Kanaka, to lift the load, pull the broken shaft, and slide a spare axle into place. Such individual feats required men with Kanakas' mighty profiles: solid heads, stout, sloped shoulders and squat, barrel legs powered by explosive hearts. A properly driven grande carreta required the anatomy assembled in the brawn of Kanaka Hoku. His arms hung as if watermelons wedged them from his torso.

"Mother is too foolish to appreciate the finest soldiers from the barracks—our best men—would be there to assist." Teodoro winked. "Squawk. Squawk."

"Your mother irritates like fly-sores. She whined that all hope would be lost if an axle splintered. I'm to listen to the opinion of a woman who thinks Indios could not repair a broken axle and get the carreta to San Rafael in time? My God."

"Squawk, squawk."

"Normally, I would not dignify such a barrage of nonsense with an appropriate answer. As a compassionate gentleman, I relented. The weak man in me offered the services of my Kanaka Hoku."

"And soldiers.… Mother will welcome the soldiers. I only have my musket."

"Tolerate the odor of the one savage. I send it to appease that woman, my son. The Kanakas *are* pigs. Do not worry, his stench will get lost among the oxen."

"Island mongrels disgust me as much as the Indios." Teodoro sneered. "Our mighty escolta will keep him on the path."

"Push the animals on," said Vallejo. "Remember, that carreta comes back in three days."

"And the soldiers?"

"Make the load light. Speak up to your mother. Show her men don't ask foolish questions." He raised his hand in salute. "Long live the head of Miranda Rancho."

A cockeyed grin spread across Teodoro's cheeks. He rose on unsteady legs, holding up the liquor bladder. "To my rancho."

Vallejo pushed the bag into his chest. "And to our destinies. Three days. Go! I am now forced to involve my Kanaka in our new plans."

Guiding Teodoro on the exterior staircase steps, he called for Hoku to meet him in his quarters. Instructions he gave Hoku differed from the itinerary Luz had demanded. First, he was to deliver an extra-large cargo of hides to the slough landing. Second, once the peons had refitted the wagon bed, he must proceed with the empty carreta to Miranda Rancho and arrive by nightfall, not midday. Then lastly, he should be prepared to leave soon after for the San Rafael pueblo.

Hoku's head dropped. "Overnight and alone, Generalissimo?"

"My troops are rounding up northern belligerents. That is more important to the pueblo. I have no brave Mexicans to spare for three days."

Hoku rotated his palms up and looked over his brow. "Weapons?"

"I'll entrust you with more lances than you need to protect Señor Miranda. Included with the handsome knife you carry, two pikes should be plenty."

"There's work in the forest before the rains."

"I know. I know. We must both sacrifice. Choose wisely. I'm offering you a chance to earn a place for your people here. Besides, I send you with the carreta you work best. It will keep you safe. Great Roman General Cincinnatus would envy a war chariot like that."

The knife to which Vallejo referred, an ivory-handled flensing blade, Hoku had received as a gift from a whaling captain in Lahaina, Maui, where he spent his youth. He slept with the razor-edged knife strapped to his leg. Moreover, he used the extolled "war chariot" daily in his work. The oversized lorry hauled sectioned redwood logs.

Hoku stared through Vallejo, hiding his skepticism. Inscrutability had been his best defense since arriving in Alta California. It kept his intentions from Mexicans—and from Vallejo, in particular.

Few of Vallejo's schemes remained secret from Hoku. Neophyte Indian women, who wove blankets below Vallejo's quarters, spied for Hoku as they had spied for him when Teodoro had a meeting with Vallejo. Before the next day, they would report to Hoku what they heard. Whenever the generalissimo had visitors in Petaluma, the Indian women slowed the transverse of their shuttles and listened to the parlor floor above them. Between each row of batten taps, they judged the warp and weft of unseen men he entertained, monitoring their voices and movements. Vallejo regaled those who brought the latest news from south of the bay. He encouraged them to share with him what they had learned of Monterey and Mexico City government intrigues.

The women once overheard Vallejo discuss the merits of Sandwich Islander men with an English trapper. The guest flattered Vallejo, calling him the son of Cortes, "Last of the conquistadores."

"My Kanakas are lazy and good-natured, akin to a mixed breed of Indios and Negroes."

"Magnificent creatures," said the trapper. "Bodies so impressive, yet their spirits are broken and compliant."

"Childlike. Don't be unduly enthralled. They're not rational. No morality." Vallejo paused long enough for the inquisitive women to assume he waggled his finger. "I'm always on lookout for an unfortunate *perro* that Kanakas might have scalded and scraped. Dog loin tempts Kanakas as sweet cream cake entices Spanish padres. It's not that I think darker mestizos haven't earned their place in our society. They have. We need them to breed more strong backs."

Vallejo offered figs, oranges, and grapes from a fruit bowl. "Nevertheless, our superiority gives us the right, the duty—No! The *burden* to command them. I have the bloodline to do that."

He often reminded anyone who listened that he descended from the purest race of Criollo Spanish, the ruling Iberian Peninsula class at the caste pinnacle. "As for the Indios, well, none of them handle my citrus. They're vile. Very low. My daughters picked these fruits."

"Your fruits are splendid." Spritz from a ripped orange that the trapper sectioned with his thumb perfumed through the floorboards. "Indios are undisciplined. I've seen them rooting on the ground when I crossed the Sacramento Valley."

"Diggers." Vallejo set the bowl aside. "They should be grateful for the wise European hand on the whip. We've won nothing from the mongrels that Spain hadn't already discovered, improved, or discarded. Same would be true if English, Dutch, or Portuguese landed on these shores before Spain."

"Here, here," said the trapper. "We gave them our high culture. And they offer us in return meager potatoes, cacao, tobacco, and wasted land to graze cattle."

Vallejo talked as if his head shook in agreement. "Indios are savage without the restraint of our guns. They will remain so forever."

The loom operators had an image of Vallejo's face glowing crimson as he laughed. "How dull am I? Ay, ay, ay. I speak the obvious to you. My babbling is an old washerwoman's prattle. Of course, you agree. The Romans passed down our common values. That legacy girds our loins. Indios have no history."

Vallejo solicited the trapper to bring him a leather-bound book. "Here, this is our backbone. Literature. It's from my modest athenaeum at the Sonoma pueblo. Have you studied the Roman rulers? You must. The good emperors have taught me much wisdom. I filled my library with their biographies and with other liberal ideas. Voltaire and Rousseau!"

"Does not that jeopardize your relations with the missionaries? Papists don't condone enlightenment," said the trapper.

"Let the devil take them."

La Casa Grande, his home residence on the plaza in Sonoma, housed the most extensive book collection in the territory. It included many philosophical books condemned by Papal Rome and the federal government. The illegal acquisition of his library resulted in his excommunication from the Catholic Church. "I'll keep my twelve thousand tomes."

The trapper laughed. "It does wonders for the soul of a man to spit in the eye of Pope Gregory."

"Stay with us awhile. Don't leave until I have had the honor of entertaining you at the Independence Day bull-bear fights. Here in Alta California you will not only read of past great civilizations, you'll experience the greatest one. This is the epoch of Spanish culture. It's no wonder Californios share a great love and respect for one another. I would sacrifice my life for any of my brothers. Selflessness is the duty of a *seigneur*, a nobleman …"

"—I say are you listening?" Vallejo's slap stung the muscular shoulder of Hoku. The women weaving below heard Vallejo's boot stomp on their ceiling. "Boy! Wake up. Pay attention to me."

The sharp blow startled Hoku's thoughts back to the present from his daydream. His overlord's face had moved closer.

"Understand what I am saying." Vallejo made sure he had Hoku's eyes on him. "This is your moment of acceptance. When you return in no more than three days with my wagon—three days—I'll reward you with a cow, a calf, and land near the hot springs mill. Three days." He held up his three outer fingers. "Do you hear me? You must arrive in San Rafael before Señor Miranda dies. And shield him from all disturbances, especially from his children. Those are your most important instructions."

Hoku grunted.

"Return in three days. Deliver Miranda alive to the old mission. And, except for Teodoro, the Miranda runts may not leave the rancho."

"Phooey," he wished to tell Vallejo. "*Haoles* should care for their sick." If he protested, he'd lose the offer of a modest land grant. And more annoying to Hoku, he'd give up his outbuilding room, forcing him to sleep in the hacienda south fields.

Before sunrise the next morning, workers assembled in the unfinished quadrangle to breakfast on hot corn and nut mush. Mexicans separated the Indian men who worked on the construction from those who would go with Hoku to the boat landing. After eating, they stacked a triple load of oozing rawhide skins layered on the carreta. Bags of tallow filled the empty spaces.

Hoku started the wagon from the hacienda at dawn. Sullen workers followed. Heavy wheels crunched the sloping road. The eastern valley crest blazed a golden corona behind them. Sunlight passed through millions of leaves bleeding a lime glow into the air. Birds, awakened from their cover, climbed to the sky. Backlit flutters radiated translucent as the iridescent wings of dragonflies. On the lower grassland, steers rose and meandered. Crawling masses blotted miles of the valley a dark indigo, resembling the easy drift of cumulus shadows viewed from a mountainside. Sweet clover, chest-high wild oats, and herbs perfumed the trail shoulders. A network of creeks, which in winter boiled with salmon bursting from deep shadow to flashes of vermilion light, had dried to graveled gullies by summer.

Where the crew rendezvoused with waiting coastal trading ships, scows heeled on muddy embankments. River rot suspended on the slow-moving morning air. Deckhands hailed the cargo arrival. They threw the plank for the slave laborers to carry the load on their heads. By late afternoon, the Indians finished hauling aboard the ship hides the Yankee traders called, "California Dollars." They returned to the hacienda without Hoku.

The transfer dragged on longer than anticipated. He had miles to travel alone with animal skin odors attracting predators as the daylight shortened. High in the fall sky, charcoal strands of waterfowl flew southeast before the arrival of seasonal storms. Their thin undulations floated light as spider webs blown from wind-tossed branches. To the west, jewel box shimmers of yellows, blues, and greens crowned the heavens. White tapers of low marine clouds billowed through a mountain gap.

Hoku drew deep breaths and shouted to no one since at that leg of the journey no one accompanied him. "Ha! Ha! If you act stupid, then you are stupid. Like the Mexicans! And stupid things will happen to you."

Mucus dripped into his throat from the chill. He spit and considered the dangers before him—and those he left at the pueblo if he turned back. His voice grew hoarse. "Only a fool would return to the hacienda."

Stones clattered on the wagon planks. He grabbed one, snapping the projectile at the lead beast. The carreta sped from the heave of six spooked oxen until they resumed a walking pace, following the *Paso del Estero de Petaluma*. Three roughhewn logs bound their horns. The giant innocents resembled twinned cross-bearers on the road to Golgotha.

Hoku used stones and a sharpened goad to work the beasts. He preferred to control them with the hardwood *punta de buey*, instead of the leather lash cracked by the Mexicans. When the team stride slowed, he jabbed a flank. Five other mates lurched to the quickened steps that matched the sinless animal whose pierce wound trickled his side. With his arms draped over the prod resting across his shoulders, the oxen tracked the stick movement beneath his bulrush hat, paying no attention to his grumbles.

The wagon passed the primary Miwok encampment. A stub of the Indian culture survived there as drifters. Terrified flight from the infernal squeal scurried adults into tule *Kotcha* huts. When uneven wheels rumbled loud against hard clay, it reminded them of invaders who hunted their people at night.

Myths evolved from the terror reinforced by the conquerors. Spanish had warned the Indians that the carreta transformed into a death-cart after dark with a skeletal driver, *Nahualli*, and two boney oxen. They howled across their despoiled Eden at a pitch higher than overheated axles. Tragedy pursued anyone who looked at the wagon.

Indian camp children had not yet invested their lives in their elders' apprehensions. They greeted Hoku with giggling excitement when his carreta approached. Malnourished boys and girls, naked but one, sprang from their huts and scurried to catch the empty cart. Flea welts peppered their lean trunks. They raced to clutch the solid rims. Rotation jerked their wiry bodies up the four-wheeled carousel and spilled them to the carreta rear. Tumblers rolled. Their gleeful peals drowned under the screeching.

One by one, the children scurried back to the warmth of the hamlet. A lone girl, with breasts of a child budding into adolescence, followed Hoku's cart. She stayed ten silent paces behind the carreta.

Taller than most Indian girls Hoku had seen, he assumed she straggled from the Cainamero people in the region north of Sonoma. Vallejo's ally, Chief Solano, of the powerful Suisunes, kidnapped well-formed Cainameros. He and Mexican raiders sold the statuesque women to Russians at Fort Ross.

It surprised Hoku an unaccompanied girl from that tribe wandered alone.

Her parents must have perished protecting her. She dare not follow me much farther.

Hoku pondered the hapless child and the futility of his efforts for Vallejo. He yelled, "No good spirits remain at Mission San Rafael, if there ever were any there. Stupid Mexicans filled the cemetery with Indios who died of their good spirits."

The last time Hoku passed the ruins, the mission reminded him of a shark-stripped whale carcass. Vallejo had plundered to his Petaluma rancho the best fruit and animals farmed by the padres.

Alta California casts dangerous incantations, thought Hoku. *It's like the honeyed smell of women's sun-warmed hair.* His adopted home held irresistible powers to corrupt men who could never escape its hold. "This land is strong sex," he shouted.

The girl examined the back of Hoku's wide head. His heavy-muscled shoulders rose to meet it. She wondered if either he had no neck, or he hid a lamb under his shirt. He couldn't rotate his head without his upper body following his ears.

"The land makes men *loco*," Hoku rambled. "Look at these valleys. Look at these mountains. Mexicans think they own them. They believe they're masters of all life on them. Bah! Pieces of paper are what they own. Mexicans see animals as wealth and men as animals. The land will change them. The land *is* changing them. They think they're changing the land. They think they control destiny. *Owhyee* knows only gods make a difference—not man."

Hungry and chilled because of the late start, he couldn't allow the vagabond girl-child to delay him further. Hoku turned, waving his hat. He yelled over the wooden axles' unearthly pitch. "Go back." His voice boomed, as if carronades fired from the rear of his throat. "Cainamero! Owhyee will never return me to my islands. If the spirit is pleased, Owhyee may bring me a rancho. Do not get in my way."

She sat on the earth. Wind ruffled her double apron, rabbit-skin loincloth. The breeze exposed the swell of her adolescent hips. Doe-like eyes stared into his face. She regarded him as if she knew him.

Do I want to frighten her off, or steal a chance to eye her? Hoku hesitated. *Or is she stealing my thoughts?* He bellowed, again, intending to startle her. "Run. Now!"

She did not flinch. He grabbed a stone and side-armed it behind the wagon. It skidded to her feet.

Her eyes opened wider. She snorted and picked up the warning. Uncrossing her legs, she glided back into a stand. Her mouth bent to a scowl.

Hoku swallowed.

Her bare foot stamped once on the ground. She lofted the stone at him underhanded.

Hoku caught it in his meaty palm. They stared at each other until she surprised him with an impish giggle. He turned on his heel, sniffing his fist before rifling the stone up the road. The projectile missed the snout of the lead, but the ox understood its intent. He started the carreta toward their destination.

Sea breaths, visible as spreading low clouds to the west, filled Hoku's nostrils. He inventoried early-evening stars and recounted lessons passed from his seafarer ancestors. Hoku had experienced in Alta California that when night fog settled in the valley bowl, darkness obliterated visual perspective. Mist hid everything but the ground on which you stood.

Sighs from the earth, many octaves below the axles' falsetto, caught his attention. He sharpened his hearing to a precise lower point. Hoku placed the prod on a snout. The carreta paused.

"Young girl. Hear our mother. Listen."

The girl blinked at the word *mother*. She lowered her head.

Hoku closed his eyes. "That rhythm." He whispered, "That. Hear? Tick. Tick. Hear that sound?"

Hypnotic susurrus from rustling browned grasses filled the air.

He pushed back his hat. "The oats. Listen. The tick slows. That's the voice of Mother Earth." Hoku's face warmed, as if he heard a lullaby. "A time has come. A time has come."

The girl pulled her hand across her opposite wrist to ward off the chill made worse when they stopped. Hoku opened his eyes to her lip shivering distress. His muscled torso prevented him from crossing his arms or reaching his shoulders; instead, he shimmied around his bulk to imitate her shivers. "Are you cold?"

Cautious eyes stared from under her black, chopped bangs.

He snatched a heavy linen tarp from the cart and threw it at her feet.

The girl sat straight on the road.

Hoku grumbled, "You have the brain of a mollusk." He walked in front of her and fixated on the crown of her head. Feminine scalp-scents rose deep into his lungs. Young breasts upwelled from under her folded arms. A warm shaft of lust seized him. He longed to press his forehead atop hers, to inhale her gentle exhalations, to feed on her spirit.

Hoku plucked the fabric and draped its corner on her shoulder. He cursed as he trod to the carreta. When he reached the cart, he turned to see she had wrapped herself in the material. A sudden strong feeling of excitement went up his neck. The flesh of oxen shuddered behind him. One tremulous quiver followed the other. A zephyr's tingle leapt from him to wither to wither.

"A time has come." Hoku's blunt fingers fanned the air. "Mother Earth carries her children—you and me—through heaven. We are in heaven. Look around. Smell. Feel. Listen. Mother Earth whispers lessons. You must listen, Cainamero. She cools. Feel the sound? Feel it. Tick. Tick. Tick. See? Do you feel the sound now?"

He listed to his side, eyes closed, concentrating on hums rising from the ground. "Our time is measured. Tick, tick, tick. Mother reminds her children our time is measured."

Bright pinpricks of Venus and Saturn appeared low in the west, signposts that harvest should have ended. Daylight hours had shortened. The rainy season arrived soon. Rain made mud. Soaked ruts became an impossible mire of clay, sucking boots from cart drivers' feet.

Hoku's concentration faded from cool seasonal changes to his hot yearnings for the girl's skin. He contemplated what he glimpsed of her soft, virginal belly, how her acorn-brown flesh rose and fell along its irresistible line of declivity; the supple bend of her knee; her compliant demeanor, and his desire to smother his loneliness deep between her breasts. Though he knew it taboo to hold children to him, he thought, *She has come of age. Did she not display women's comforts?*

Across the llano, fields bristled with autumn flowers. Life swayed in their timeless rhythm.

Fate meant for me to have her. I can take her, and then leave her to return to safety where she belongs.

Amid his temptations, Hoku wrestled to concentrate on the threats they approached. In not far-off, forbidden places skulked insatiable pursuers of meat. They waited without a sound. Sense of their hunger prickled his skin. Within dark woods stalked the invisible puma; the predacious black bear, king of shadows; the almighty, male grizzly and, within the shortest striking-distance, the hungriest of flesh lusting hunters, the persistent yearnings of man.

Shocked that his caution had returned to his craving distractions, Hoku threw another projectile. This one sailed with near-lethal vehemence. *Thwack!* It ricocheted off the hip of the lead ox.

The girl piped a whistle deep in her throat as if she deciphered his stirring.

Could she read my secrets? My desires? Did she know the conversations my spies overheard? Could she sense my years of humiliation, too? Does she know of the monster Ortega?

He spun toward her, clutching at his stomach. "Ortega—his name makes me vomit."

Inscrutable eyes stared back in silence. Hoku spread his arms to the side. "Is it fair I am here and cold because of him? Am I a fool?"

The stiff tarp, gathered around the girl's face, slipped to her bosom. Good white teeth heightened the allure of her unexpected smile.

Hoku lowered his voice. "Yes, you are right. I *am* a fool."

Neither Hoku nor the girl knew that fate, not foolishness, had set them on their heading a decade earlier. Their path began when the federal government in Mexico sponsored a colony of more than 200 men, women, and children to build a pueblo north of the Sonoma Mission San Francisco Solano. The "Hijar-Padres Cosmopolitan Company" included teachers and artisan workers from Mexico City. The colonists' allegiance lay with the Mexican president, not with Vallejo and not with the Californios Governor in Monterey.

Among the selected emigrants was a Catholic priest who had renounced his vows, Leonito Antonio Duque de Ortega. A sequence of deceits aligned his destiny with those of Hoku and the Cainamero girl.

To Vallejo and the Alta California Governor, the newcomers' landing meant they intended to usurp the Californios's semifeudal way of life and replace it with central governance from the Mexican capital. They planned to appoint their own administrators.

Vallejo defied the orders he received and withheld his military support. It exposed the settlers to Indian attacks. The desperate colonists prepared to rebel. Before they could retaliate, Ortega determined Vallejo had the fighting advantage, and he betrayed his compatriots' intentions.

"Generalissimo," Ortega confided to Vallejo, "Mestizos, the dirty city street people, are about to revolt. You and your fellow Californios are their targets. These are their plans …."

Vallejo seized their weapons before they struck. The Governor in Monterey deported their leaders. Ortega's treachery gained him the high position of *mayordomo* at the Sonoma pueblo. The appointment pushed out Juan Miranda, who had been mayordomo for five years.

Ortega solidified his position as Vallejo's unscrupulous foil while he seized church property from the control of Mission San Francisco Solano. Everyone suspected that if he had an inclination, Vallejo could have had Ortega kill his opponents for a trifle. Ortega began each day with drafts of barrel-drawn brandy at his adobe. He leered from his building across the road at the dilapidated mission. Vallejo encouraged humiliation of the church's authority. Ortega gloried in bragging to the affronted priest that he had forced himself on every woman in the pueblo—sometimes on the cool altar slab of the desecrated church.

Hoku turned to the silent girl. "When the generalissimo traveled, I helped the priest put up signs around the plaza in the dark. They read, 'Death to Ortega!'"

Bending forward, Hoku spat on his sandals. The sputum brought back memories of a warm pee-rope splashed across his instep.

"Ortega found I made fermented-root *okolehao*. That bad monster wet me up my leg to the sheath of my knife. He demanded that

I buy my spirits from his store. A gang of men, including Teodoro Miranda, the son of the man we are supposed to be saving, laughed while they watched him do it to me."

Hoku could not utter the most persistent humiliation to the girl, or to anyone. After Ortega emptied his bladder and stuffed his protuberance into his pants, he delivered a permanent stain. Its soil remained after Hoku scrubbed urine off his legs with river rocks. Ortega took in Hoku's mortification. He tilted his head back, and squinted over his horse-lip curl at the Kanaka warrior's feet.

"Coward," he said.

Hoku petitioned the Indian girl as if her innocence gave her power to rain righteous condemnations on the unscrupulous. "And lie down with *wahine?* Kanaka had to pay Ortega. Though I paid him with our best tobacco from Dry Creek, the land of your people, he took the first taste of wahine I wanted—after taking my good tobacco. I sent off my dear brother Naukane with same good tobacco under his dead testicles. He warned me before he died of loneliness, 'Go with the Britishers. Fort Vancouver is colder than Alta California, but Owyhee brothers have their own village there. Three years' work with Britishers and Kanaka can sail home. Here the Mexicans trap us."

Her head cocked to the side.

"Why do I tell you this? I tell you this because that smelly pig, Ortega, eventually lay on the wrong wahine," said Hoku. "Her name is Francesca Miranda. She lives where we go, at the rancho with her children. I know Vallejo made Ortega marry the pregnant girl." Hoku tapped his finger on his temple. "Otherwise, Juan Miranda would have killed him and anyone who supported Ortega, including Vallejo. He could do it. I believe if Miranda didn't pursue his revenge, the evil pissed by Ortega would have destroyed the whole pueblo."

Vallejo had ordered Ortega to his hacienda when Francesca showed early signs of pregnancy after her rape. Vallejo screamed at him. "Juan Miranda has Cassius's lean and hungry look—and I'm his Julius Caesar."

Ortega's deeper voice responded. "His women have made him frail. He weeps like a cloistered nun."

"Your depravity has jeopardized my authority. I should throw you into the bear pit. Fortunately, for you, you're more valuable to me alive. I need to convince Juan your intentions with his daughter were chaste."

"Challenge him to come for me," said Ortega. "I'll be the last one to see him."

"If your death helped me, I would. But he'd direct his fury toward me next. You'll do as I tell you."

Heavy furniture moved and rusted chest-hinges creaked above the weaving room ceiling. "Take this land grant I carved out for you and the Miranda girl. It's a small rancho."

Though modest, the property he offered held importance to Vallejo. Its strategic location, where Arroyo de San Antonio flowed into the slough, presented sweeping views of approaching watercraft. Ranchers could signal an alarm if hostile boats sailed up the creek to the hacienda.

"Outside of this room," Vallejo said to Ortega, "we'll call the exchange my wedding present. But its purpose is to save your neck. I want you to leave the pueblo. Go occupy the rancho with your whore-bride for a few weeks. Before that sorry, bastard child is born, I'll order you to drive my cows north to the Britishers."

"That won't be necessary. People forget."

"I don't forget. I don't forgive. Never come back."

When Ortega married and then days later crossed into the Oregon Territory, Vallejo further appeased Juan's murderous anger. He helped him to apply in the territory capital of Monterey for new ownership of Rancho Arroyo de San Antonio. They did not expect any objections. Mexican law voided a land grant if the owner left Alta California. The Governor accepted his claim, but didn't sign the deed before his political opponents ousted him from office.

Fate intervened. Vallejo's duplicity, Ortega's depravity, and the confusion of whether the rancho belonged to Ortega or Miranda, evolved into a muddled custody battle after the United States won sovereignty of California.

DIGGERS

Smoke sailed above chimneys on the horizon. Crooked elbows crinkled and fanned eastward from the Miranda's rancho. Their appearance carried away dark reminiscences of Ortega from Hoku's consciousness. He no longer threatened him. Only Vallejo could hurt Hoku now. His presence loomed everywhere, even beyond the reaches of his heart-shaped cattle brand. Vallejo's fiefdom stretched beyond the peaks dissolving in lavender hues. The land was his and his word was law. Government writ, secured and filed in Mexico City, bolstered the generalissimo's presumption of his divine right to sovereignty.

Unlike the indigenous peoples, each succeeding invader drafted new documents that self-validated their control over the valley. Neither language nor imprimatur on papers mattered. At nightfall, the province reverted to the realm of the feral. The conquerors held precarious dominion over their fellow man, but none over primal nature. Interlopers changed, as did each of their foreign drafts. Pulp they felted into embossed paper disintegrated with their legacies. Nations rose. Nations fell. The circle turned. And the land they called Petaluma remained.

Where the snaking courses of the creek straightened, Hoku stopped to refresh the oxen. Brooding eyes of paired *ojo de agua* ponds stared back at him and the girl. They supplied sweet water to centuries of travelers who trekked on the *Dos Piedras*—Two Rock path—which connected Bodega Bay and the inland valleys.

Purple stemmed berries flamed with fall colors and spread from the watering holes. Above them, grapes hugged tree trunks. The wild interwoven fruit crept to the edge of cultivated orchards that marked the last mile to the adobe. Hoku restarted the team and stripped thick handfuls of burnished grape leaves as he passed. He slipped them under his shirt. Large, waxy textures delighted his skin.

The Indian girl followed, padding silent as mist.

A fence built of branches double-lashed with rawhide straps formed one side of a pen holding a score of nervous sheep. It drew them to the adobe front yard where a Mexican girl stuck a wooden *pala* inside an oven. She flipped rows of blackened tortillas, stirring the sea-moistened air with the tang of burned oak.

Hoku's innards rumbled as tense faces watched him. A dozen adults, adolescents who held croupy babies, and quiet children stood beside the warm *hornos*. Dried mud caked the boys' legs.

Hoku glanced back at the downcast Indian girl's head. *Pay no attention. They're giving me that look, too—as if I'm a Digger.*

"Shhh," he hissed at fussy chickens before the oxen. In pidgin Spanish, he called out, "Señora Miranda." A blunt-eared dog returned the hail with a dismissive bark. Condemnatory eyes by the oven followed him. No one acknowledge his call. His closed expression hid his increasing anger.

They have as much Indios and African blood as Spanish blood, probably more. They look at us the same way Vallejo regards them. Let it pass. Stick to your business. Shut your brain, Hoku. Let it pass.

"Señora Miranda," he called out again. His unusual Polynesian dialect spooked a twitchy tailed mustang. The stallion galloped his frantic mares circling inside the paddock. Fine dust they raised settled on Hoku's tattooed forearms. He halted the carreta and motioned to the girl to wait with the rig.

Quiet roared in his ears as he walked by a grain mill. Hooves from stoical burros scored a halo around its abrasive wheel. He looked up from the ground and a woman appeared under the adobe eaves. Her dark form melded into its blue, shell-plastered walls.

Hoku slid closer while she waited. Her complexion had the duskier African tints of Portuguese sailors in Lahaina. A netted bun gathered her hair. Her chin tilted higher. Hoku imagined she had once been a señorita with unmatched feminine grace. A rancher's life on the frontier had replaced her youthful allure with a prideful, steel mask.

He avoided her eyes. "Señora Miranda?"

Absence of teeth puckered her mouth. Her lower lip burrowed beneath the upper. "Vallejo sent you here unaccompanied?" Tight lines in the corners bracketed her frown.

He braced against the strain in her voice. "Yes Señora."

Callused peasant hands rested across her abdomen, clutching a ladle. Two arthritic fingers fused in a hook. "No one else? No soldiers? No escort? No one?"

"The Indios girl."

"It stays outside." Luz pivoted to the open door. "Follow me." A faded red brooch, the color of dried peppers bundled on the wall, clasped her lace rebozo around her shoulders. Juan had given her the elegant pin in 1810, on the autumn day they married at Santa Clara Mission.

Hoku lowered his hat to his belt. A lion's mane of thick, matted hair sprang out full.

Luz rustled away. "You speak Spanish, yes?"

He waited at the threshold. Hoku preferred Mexicans thought he knew little of their language.

"Answer."

"Small, Señora." Blood rushed to his face, heating his cheeks. Hoku spoke Spanish as well as any non-Mexican who worked for Vallejo, understanding the language better than he spoke it. He held his tongue when meeting with Mexicans—listening instead.

Luz turned to those waiting by the hornos. "Children, yoke fresh oxen, not two, all six. Put enough straw in the carreta for Father's comfort."

Except Teodoro, the gawkers ran as if pursued by wasps. He stood by the oven, his eye glowering under an upturned hat.

Luz strode into the adobe with the confidence of an aristocrat accustomed to men following her instructions. Hoku stayed out-side the room. The pressed-clay floor inside shined from splashed buckets of ox blood and sackcloth beatings. Floral stencils prettied the walls. A tallow-candle chandelier hung on a pulley over a thick redwood table. Next to a lacquered sea chest, a harp waited for a worthy visitor to entertain. To its right, a crucifix reigned over a kneeler, a rosary, a prayer book, and a clock.

Luz motioned with the ladle. "You fritter away my time. Come in." Quick steps toward a corner fireplace swept her skirt over im-maculate floors. "The children have packed fruit, blankets, and lanterns." She stopped and faced Hoku. "I expected so many more." Luz turned. "Eat the food while it is hot. We'll need your strength."

Enticements of stew heated with burned oak curled around Hoku's nose. His hunger and his wariness sharpened. No Mexican had ever invited him to dine with them. If soldiers caught him as-suming higher social privileges, they'd punish him.

The glow from the radiant fire cast an aurora outline of Luz's squared waist. "Come quickly." Her face softened. "Please. Eat first. Then we'll leave."

The abrupt courtesy troubled Hoku, an unwelcome breaking of precedent. Mexicans had never directed the word please at him. He studied her body language for hints of how much liberty he could assume in her presence.

Luz shouted instructions out the doorway over the clamor of exchanged corral animals. "Don't forget the food or goose down for Father. Francesca—"

She felt Hoku's eyes bore into her. "Is there a problem if we bring our bedding?" Her eyebrows arched. "We're not savages, you know. Don Guadalupe probably told you we were. We certainly are not. Had he said that? Savages? Tell me."

Hoku's biceps swiped his forehead. He dared not make idle talk within earshot of Mexicans, reserving his bold proclamations for when he walked alone. Edges of his hat rolled in his hand.

"Your silence says enough. Come in. Come. My husband rests in the other room." Luz cleared her throat, speaking with practiced formality. "This is the casa of Don Juan Chrisostomo Miranda. I am his wife, Maria Luz de Garcia Mesa Miranda. *Bienvenidos.* You are welcome here."

Her stance shifted, and she yelled over his shoulder, "*Tortillas. Andale!*" Luz pointed to the floor beside the table, "I told you to come in. Sit here." She plunged the ladle into one of two cauldrons suspended over the corner fireplace. "Is there anything else we need?"

Hoku shuffled in, tasting airborne seasonings on his lips. "No, Señora. Pikes. Lanterns. Grande carreta." He knew the smell wafting from the cauldron bubbles. His belly growled. He had expected stew flavored with peas, beans, peppers, and beef bones. *This isn't just beef aroma.* Averting his eyes, he tucked his hat under his shirt.

Luz had first seen similar woven reed hats on scurvy-ridden sailors seeking refuge from the Northern Pacific storms. Often in winter, vessels battered by the Manila Current appeared from fog banks in the Presidio lagoon, their lower decks filled with desperate men.

"Why do you not sit? Have soldiers whipped you for insolence, Don—well, what should I call you? Do you have a Christian name?"

"Hoku."

"Are you a savage, Don Hoku?"

A rounded face mirrored his surprise. "No. Hoku."

"We are not either. Don Guadalupe told you we were, though, didn't he?"

Hoku's eyebrows knitted. Pouting spread his platyrrhine features. "No, Señora." He feigned shame for his faulty Spanish. "Kanaka people. Far. Very far. Islands." He kept his head dropped and pointed his hand high toward the ceiling.

Luz drew a ladle of stew before letting the content plop back into the boil. She propped her hand on her hip. "Vallejo believes we are beneath him. He treats us that way today by making us wait." She grumbled into the pot. "He thinks he is *gente de razón*, and we're not."

Hoku nodded, starting to squat. Luz pivoted on her heels to face him. "Wait! Don't sit yet." The ladle slapped on the table. "I'll show you he's wrong."

An English prayer book lay unopened under the crucifix. She stepped across the room and returned with it open. A doomed Yankee sailor bequeathed her the inheritance at the Presidio. She leafed through pages held to her face.

"Do you read, Don Hoku?" Her eyes flitted from her proud possession to his silent, wide-eyed astonishment. "I do," she said. "You should be impressed. Loaves and fishes. See, I can read. Lamb of God. Why shouldn't I read? I'm gente de razón. Not savage. No different from Don Guadalupe."

Page after page flipped. "Holy Mary. God. Sacred heart—it's easy. Can you read that?"

Hoku's empty stomach twisted, his gut gnawing on itself. "Kanaka."

Luz moved the book closer. "I can. Baby Jesus. Amen."

Hoku had learned rudimentary English from a King James Bible at the Presbyterian School on the island of Maui. American missionaries pressed rote lessons on him in a stone church. He distinguished English words from Spanish words, and he comprehended a few sentences that pertained to Christian faith. Hoku recognized four words embossed in gold on the black leather cover: Book of Common Prayer. Luz had held the Anglican worship guide upside down while she called out random, religious bromides.

Hoku tendered a wan smile. "Kanaka," he repeated.

As she replaced the book in her hand with the ladle, Teodoro jangled into the room. His arm balanced a stack of tortillas from the hornos. Smoke filled behind him. Luz knocked on redwood. "Come closer. I present to you Don Hoku. Don Guadalupe sent Don Hoku to deliver your father to absolution."

Glints of fire reflected off an eagle head sword-handle hanging from Teodoro's narrow waist. He had not worn the weapon when Hoku first confronted him at the hornos. A kerchief then covered his forehead. No longer. Instead, a hideous, garnet-colored pucker winked from where his eye should have watched with its mate. On the other side of his bent nose, a large brown eye stared at Hoku with doubled hostility. Teodoro handed the tortillas to his mother.

"These are for you. Animals eat outside on the ground." He cut his eye at Hoku and strode toward the door, holding a leather scabbard to his leg.

Luz's glare followed him. "Stop! This home is my place. My place. Do you understand me?"

Teodoro turned back to face her. His frame painted an arrow shadow on the doorway. "I understood you," he shouted. "I also understood you to say the generalissimo would send us men."

"He's almost a man. Closer to a man than to a savage."

"Where are the soldiers? I expected soldiers, many soldiers. Generalissimo promised to dispatch his escort. Father will not be safe. What did you do to cause this?"

"Blame Don Guadalupe." Luz slapped tortillas on a six-sided plate, which depicted blue and white Chinese landscapes. Her words landed hard as the ceramic. "No! Oh, no, no, no. He told me, 'No savages. An honor guard. My best Kanaka drivers *and* an honor guard will walk at the side of my brother Juan.' So much talk. The man eats books and vomits platitudes. He had promised me, an escolta. I warned him not to send any filthy savages with his soldiers. The way he reacted, you would have sworn I had bitten his cheek.... No, Teodoro, your generalissimo was true to his word—he dispatched almost no one at all. No one, except this one boy."

"Squawk nonsense to your religious statue-dolls, not to me," said Teodoro. "Generalissimo must've arranged for soldiers to meet us on the trail. I came in here to protect you from this." He pointed to Hoku. "He's not a man. He's a mongrel. Mongrels belong outside with the animals."

Luz's voice tightened. "If you believe that, and if you assume you may wear Father's finest sword without his permission, then it's time for you to face the world as it is. Your hero, *el Jefe*, regards your mother as if she were a drunken soldier's concupiscence removed from African slaves. And he looks at you—you who bray he's beloved—he looks at you and your children as one or two irreversible generations from me."

Teodoro fidgeted with the scabbard buckle while Luz hoisted the cover on the other pot. She ladled burgoo of turtle, pumpkin, and corn over tortillas. The spoon round tap-tapped on the plate. She examined Hoku. "You're a man."

He stared at the offering transferred to the table. Steamy tendrils entangled him.

Luz said, "I insisted Don Guadalupe send me Kanakas with his men. You are broken and trained."

Hoku rocked from foot to foot. "Kanaka." His eyes stayed on the food. He patted his head, "Kanaka Hoku."

"Don't misunderstand me. My damaged son's concerns are justified." Her scrutiny narrowed. "Miwok, Pomo, or Digger, it doesn't matter. They stink and they lie. I should know. I have two who work for me. They're idlers. They're uncouth and they are liars. Liars. Just today, they lied and they thought I believed them. Lying of all things about spotting Mariposa prowling in the tule."

Hoku glanced up at the mention of the giant bear whose name had taken on mythological stature. The pueblo assumed vaqueros had killed the dreaded Mariposa after the last year's bull and bear fight. Soldiers never found its carcass. Since that chaotic day, the Indians had asserted many fantastic ghost-sightings.

"I don't want Vallejo to bring more trouble-making savages near my home." Luz cupped her elbows in her hands. "I have enough of them camped by the slough. If they didn't steal my horses, they'd rip the shirt off the chest of my dying husband. You're different."

She had once commented on the size of Hoku and the Pacific Islander men to Vallejo as he helped her off a mount at the Sonoma pueblo. The horse rumbled when he grasped Luz at her waist. Vallejo found ways to touch her as he lowered her body.

"Yes they're big," he whispered in her ear. "And strong warriors. Somewhat like your Zambos people."

Luz stiffened. Souls of proud Africans kidnapped to New Spain pulsed through her maternal bloodline. She pulled back and looked straight at Vallejo, waiting for her keen gaze to chill him. "Zambos? I should say hello. Perhaps, we're cousins."

He tugged his muttonchops. "Preposterous. How do you devise such ridiculous philosophies? I forbid you to talk with peons." In a confidential voice, Vallejo added, "Social interaction will confuse and upset them."

"Where's your exquisite breeding, Generalissimo? Gentlemen know it is polite to make introductions."

Vallejo's forehead reddened. "No. It's most improper. They are lower station. The Kanaka. Uh, than … your people."

"My people? Are you and I not fellow Californios?"

"First and last. What I meant Señora is…."

Vallejo's mouth twisted. He ran his fingers through his wavy hair, stopping with his arm bent. His shoulders flew back, and he laughed at the sky. "Jester! You pulled my hair." He blushed. "You did."

Luz fluttered her eyelashes. "We must laugh to stay young."

His olive hue returned. "You had me going. Your wit delights me. Nevertheless, so you understand, my dear, please know these Kanaka have no permanent station in our society. Take an old half-wit's advice. Do not approach them."

Californios had promised the recruited Kanakas their labor in Alta California would only last until they earned return passage. Vallejo paid them enough to cover their room and board, not enough for ship fare to the islands.

Luz recalled her conversation with Vallejo while she slid the dinner plate beyond the extended reach of Hoku. "Do you love our all-beneficent el Jefe?"

Hoku stopped shifting and peered at the plate.

"Hmm," Luz said. "Might you have once worked for Ortega?"

He shot a sidelong glance at Teodoro, who shuffled backward from the room.

Luz assessed the two men. "I see. Listen to what I am about to say to our guest, Teodoro." A hefty spoon, crafted of fine silver, clinked on the ceramic dish. "Here, my best spoon, and my best plate. You're a man. A man, not a savage, will accompany my husband's last mile. I wouldn't allow them near him before he enters heaven." She seized the dish from the table as Hoku grabbed for his meal. "You carry out a difficult task for me tonight doing work for me my son cannot. I cooked for you Kanaka food. Eat all you can. The road is long."

Luz again proffered the plate. "Honu," she said. Thick gravy slid to the lip.

Hoku's face froze in a grin. Wisps of spiced aromas teased his nostrils. He rolled his hat against his waist.

Mud turtle tastes nothing like sea turtle, he griped to himself. *But I'm famished.*

In pidgin Spanish, Hoku said aloud, "Thank you, Señora Miranda."

Muted sounds of children leaping off the carreta came through the mud-brick walls. Luz stared out the door. Her tongue shuddered under her lip. Hoku disclosed no comprehension of her anxiety. He acted as though he only cared how fast he consumed the meal, reaching out for the plate.

"Take it." She sighed. "There's no time for your daydreams."

A walnut-wide thumb dipped into hot sauce.

She thrust the ladle into his sternum. "Now sit. Eat your fill. Don't tarry."

He tucked his legs under him on the sticky floor. Calves, as large as her terra-cotta flue, bulged from his shortened pants. The wide sheathed knife strapped on his calf fascinated Luz. *Maybe he will be enough.*

Hoku attacked the tortillas. He had not eaten since morning. Despite its muddied terrapin flavor, he devoured the stew in gulps. As he ate, he noted signs of Luz's distress. Misaligned buttons gathered her dark dress to her bodice. Her hands quaked unless she throttled an object in her strong grip. A fine crocheted handkerchief, soiled with feces, bulged from under her cuff.

Hoku belched. He beamed at Luz. "More, Señora?"

"Quickly." She turned, casting a shadow from the fire.

A tapering moan swashed across the floor from a bedroom doorway. Doleful Jesus slouched on the wall crucifix between him and the room where Juan Miranda fought for his life. Smile deflated, Hoku bowed his head.

Luz's brushed her forehead, stomach, left and right shoulders. Meaty turtle stew filled more tortillas. She handed them to Hoku. "Baby Jesus will save Don Miranda once he's anointed at the mission." She eased the ladle on a hook. Idled fingertips trembled to her chin.

Hoku bit into the fresh tortilla. He had heard similar rattles from his elders as they died. His apprehension turned from the futile struggle in the bedroom to the weather crowding in from the ocean. Fog slowed carretas to a crawl, but death ran through the night in pursuit. Hoku had pledged to Vallejo to deliver Juan alive to the mission, or suffer the consequences.

Luz's gaze wandered toward the room where her husband lay. She shrank in front of Hoku. He understood the urgency to leave and wrapped the uneaten tortillas in the grape leaves saved under his shirt. Rising as a volcano from the sea, Hoku said in his native language, "May the gods protect us." The china plate dropped on the floor where it cracked. While putting on his hat, he added in Spanish, "Oxen team." He left the house.

Layers of fog draped the valley. The brace of cold wind sharpened Hoku's senses. Lingering animal skin fetor cut the hay sweetness. The stench might draw interest from nocturnal animals, in particular, bears. Uneasy oxen pairs sidestepped into each other. Hoku cursed Mexicans, fog, and his fate.

He laid the grape leaves that covered the burgoo tortillas on the ground. The voracious Indian girl ate while Hoku checked cinches. Satisfied with the secure bindings, he ran his hand over axles. Hoku yelled an order to the family members. "Torches!"

Returning inside, he addressed Luz in articulate Spanish. "With your kind permission, Señora, I suggest we leave now."

Luz gaped at him as if she misunderstood his well-enunciated words and did not recognize the manifestation of the person who delivered them. She couldn't make sense of how the syntax came from his mouth; though, she understood once they left the adobe,

Juan's departure would be forever. Juan and Luz would never again sleep under their roof as husband and wife. Her knees weakened, and she grasped the redwood table. If she squeezed its weighty slab, her strength might stop Earth's revolutions. With enough exertion, she could reverse the rush of time.

"Is all ready?"

"The hour is late, Señora."

Luz pushed off the table, slipping her lace handkerchief out from under her sleeve. She balled the cloth in one hand. Her other hand held her knee as she bent forward. "You will be gentle with my husband."

"Yes, Señora. Very, very gentle."

She straightened and stepped away toward the fire without looking at Hoku. "He's a good man."

"I understand, Señora. We must leave."

Luz lifted a pot lid. "I'll watch you."

Hoku's face registered concern. "It is late."

Head bowed, Luz closed her eyes. Entwined hands rose to her lips in prayer.

Gusts of fog rammed shrouds of smoke back down the chimney.

"Señora?"

Luz pushed the handkerchief into her sleeve. "Come with me. Señor Miranda is on the bed."

Her fingertips dipped in a clay cup nailed on a beam. She blessed herself with Holy Water before they crossed into the bedroom. Oil lamps rested unlit. Shades blocked light that might have penetrated the closed oak shutters. An impassive Infant Jesus of Prague stared at the four-poster bed. Dim illumination from a single votive candle lit its face and cast milky shadows of Luz's movement on the wall. The left palm of the crowned statue held up an orb, the other hand raised two fingers in a blessing. Its plump cheeks contrasted with the sallow head above the quilted blanket. Riffled contours outlined the flat shape of a body under the cover.

Luz had known no other man than Juan, father of her 14 children. She sniffled. "Do you hear him breathe?"

"He is, Señora."

She went to the statue and obstructed Hoku's sight with her back. Luz lifted the icon, tugging from its hollowed-out pedestal two parchments: one a hand-drawn property map, the other a government deed to their land grant.

Although an "X" applied to a piece of paper was her sole interaction with written language, she understood the importance of the scribble. The drawings she could have sketched herself. Rough borders and crude landmarks on the diseño defined their province. A cartographer had drawn simple renditions of familiar locations: her adobe and the valley; San Antonio creek; the slough; twin ponds; the mountain range; Vallejo's hacienda, and the road to San Rafael.

Luz slipped the documents under her sleeve while thinking of the young man she married in his prime. Juan could ride a stallion at full speed, pull to a thunderous stop, and turn in a space shorter than a horse-length. He could throw his lasso around the foot of any beast, or person, within reach of his lariat. Juan had stood tall in his stirrups with sinew braided from breaking wild animals, and men, to his will.

Luz detected Hoku's mounting apprehension. "Is he still breathing?"

"Yes, Señora. He's with us."

Juan's arm dangled over the side of the feathered mattress. A sheath of onionskin-textured flesh clung to his skeleton. Tea colored blotches stained his hand.

Hoku raised Juan's forearm onto the blanket, cradling his elbow and wrist. He feared his tissue-thin skin might rip, or his desiccated bones might snap.

Spent from the rising fluids gurgling in his lungs, Juan's awareness had darkened to a sole consciousness of strangulation without resistance. He passed in and out of coma. Although most body functions had deteriorated, the most primitive stem of his brain sensed lips when Luz kissed his forehead.

"Juan, my darling," she mouthed against his skin, "it is the hour."

Luz brushed her fingertips over his blackened eyelids, knowing they would never reopen until startled in death. Impressions of sunken eyeballs teetered along his cheekbones.

Hoku coughed into his fist. Luz smoothed the blanket, and she placed her palm on her brooch. "You may take him now."

Gathered in Hoku's arms, Juan's torso bent as if Hoku carried a rolled rug from the bedroom. They stepped into the night where the carreta lanterns flickered on the fog. The illuminated world narrowed to the dimension of a small stage. Teodoro waited. He tented the blanket for his father's bedding. A musket balanced on his thigh.

Luz approached him. "Where are the others? The family—"

"Get in second. Sit beside Father once I settle him."

"Young man, you listen. The family must stay together."

"The others will be together while they mind the rancho. I ordered them to stay here."

"*You* ordered? They're coming. Who are you?"

"I am Don Teodoro Miranda, family head now. That authority is my right. Father would have insisted. Ask the generalissimo when we get back in three days."

Teodoro assumed the legal responsibilities of the oldest male in the family hierarchy. No such imminent legal birthright existed. Mexican law held, unless overwritten by a family agreement, the wife inherited the house and the livestock. The law divided the land, the source of sustenance for man and animal, among her eleven surviving children. She expected the division to create eleven sources of conflict, eleven opportunities for Vallejo to foment the rancho breakup, and eleven openings for him to regain the land. Without land, her home and her cattle could not survive.

In the moment of reflection, Luz decided to wait until angels shepherded away her husband before she asserted her authority. She had positioned her son Mariano to lead the family. Until he returned from the geyser raids, Luz found appeasement more practical than confrontation with Teodoro.

She drew her shawl around her body. With the deeds hidden, Luz nudged Hoku's shoulder. He moved toward the carreta bed with her stepping close behind him.

Teodoro stopped Hoku, laying his gun atop the bedding. Tented blankets drooped. He tucked the quilt wrapping his father's arms and inhaled his still masculine scents. Nearer his body, he nestled and whispered, *"Vaya con Dios, mi Papa, mi Héroe."*

Luz fingered her brooch when Teodoro rested his ear on his father chest. He shuddered and rose to declare for the family to hear, "Father has passed the rancho to me." Teodoro tilted his head sideways, signaling to Hoku to go ahead.

He eased a step forward and laid Juan on goose-down bedding in straw. Luz crawled into the wagon without speaking.

"Boy!" Teodoro barked at Hoku. "We leave for Mission San Rafael de Arcángel *now.*"

Hoku motioned for the girl to join him at the lead. He jabbed the goad into the rump of an offended ox. Six castrated bulls strained yokes that linked the beasts and their passengers' journey. Leather thongs groaned. The carreta pitched. Its bed twisted. Green axles squealed in renewed torment.

Teodoro swung in a clumsy arc onto the wagon. He swayed facing his siblings. Hornos fire backlit their forms until the curtain of fog consumed them and the light from the adobe.

Fate moved the carreta travelers toward a stark world. Destiny waited for them there.

PIT

The wagon rocked southward, beating through *Camino de San Rafael's* impenetrable darkness. Netherworlds rumbled beneath the wagon wheels. Trembling outward, pinched lantern beams formed a tent that surrounded the carreta. The walls offered no protection. Obscure shadows swarmed outside their ephemeral barrier. Harsh, barking night herons skimmed over the tent top and darted through the light perimeter at sharp angles, zipping away with equal, hysterical abruptness. The air sifted in gray drifts as fine as diamond powder. Luz couldn't see the moon. Its presence slid by somewhere in the sky. The heavens neither rose above nor descended below her.

She strained to remember her happiest days when courting Juan. The taste of the first kiss he pressed on her at the *baile* came back to her. And she remembered how he carried her through the mazy steps of the *fandango*. They glided, as if no one else danced the floor. Juan called her his *novia* that night, and he astonished Luz with an immediate marriage proposal. Her cherished remembrances held for a moment, then slipped away, swallowed into the deep gut of fog.

A wet cough shook Juan and spattered Luz's prayer book. She tossed its spine against the wagon bed wall.

Damn Vallejo to Hades.

Her hands folded. She prayed aloud for protection from the evils concealed on the dark llano. "Virgin of Guadalupe most merciful, queen of virgins, by the power of God, cast into hell Satan's evil spirits who wander through the world seeking the ruin of souls. Amen."

She bawled Juan's name, uncertain whether her voice projected past the bell of her own thoughts.

Hoku turned, hearing Luz's cry. Teodoro's gun pointed at him. Hoku hid his smirk. *Glad you're awake, my broken-masted friend. Keep your father alive and keep your weapon at the ready. Eyes darker than your drunken gun barrel track us.*

Hoku listened to oxen lows and hoof falls for sounds of discomfort. He smelled for the faintest whiff of smoke that might warn of a failed axle. None manifested alarm, but tastes of saltier fog hinted the carreta advanced from the mossy forest, rolling closer to the bay.

Tallow soap slathered on the hubs at the start of the journey could have suppressed the planked-wheels shriek. He did not apply the remedy. The rock, bump, thump, and infernal, wagon whine offered a respite from the death rattle gurgling at the back of the carreta. The sound of Juan's choking had disturbed Hoku while he ate stew in the adobe; he wanted to hear no more.

Creeping anxieties wrestled with his dreams of the hot springs land. The Indian girl appeared in his muse. *She might be useful on my rancho. She is a pleasure for my eyes. Strong legs. Maybe I should keep her. First, I have to deliver Señor Miranda alive, or there'd be no reward, nothing more in my future. No girl. No hope, a life of broken promises.*

Juan's quiet interludes became longer than each that preceded it. The next guttural sound in the dark encouraged Hoku. It came as a robust snort—the strongest of the journey.

Señor Miranda has rallied. He still fights for his life.

From the steady pace that the oxen pressed on, Hoku estimated they'd arrive in San Rafael by sunrise with Juan alive. He relaxed his grip on the goad and smiled at the girl.

Her weight on my back wouldn't be burdensome. I should spell her from the trudge. She needs sleep. That dog Teodoro would not let her ride the carreta. We'll warm each other.

His welcoming hand extended toward her.

Crack! Wood broke—sharp and nearby.

The girl stopped in midstep. Her placid mien froze into earnest seriousness.

Hoku gauged the axles temper. They held intact. The break came not from the carreta. It came from the roadside above them.

He and the girl turned together at another snort, deeper than the last, not a human utterance—an animal's voice. Powerful lungs produced the sound through a snout.

Luz raised her head. She sat upright, intent to pinpoint the threat.

The Indian girl tugged on Hoku's shirt.

A tree limb snapped.

Hoku's eyes opened wide and furious. He yelled, "Make ready. Make ready." His tongue stuck out as if a brick weighed its tip. A heavy arm, thrust to the side, warded off the girl. He swung the goad. It landed on the head of the lead ox. The carreta locomotion jarred to an instant halt.

Teodoro hopped off the back. His eye squinted to better detect dark forms probing on the edge of the light. An ox bellowed. Two lows followed the others' deepening motif. A thin branch splintered—this time closer.

The animals quieted. Stillness weighed on them.

Luz laid her head across Juan's shoulder. She held him and prayed the next sound came not from her screams.

In the distance, high-pitched bugles of rutting cut the fog.

"It's an elk," shouted Teodoro. "Move on, you mouse. There's nothing here but an elk. I said to—"

Cracks of mashed acorns and branches drowned his words. An unseen monster, far more aggressive than a bull elk, hurtled at them.

Hoku aligned between the girl and the din, extending a nine-foot spear off the carreta to the rear. He stopped. Teodoro had taken care of himself. He rested his rifle barrel on his amputated arm, ready to fire. A mortal threat stalked in the darkness, fusing the travelers into a single, vulnerable body. Hoku tilted the metal-pointed pike to a defensive position.

Luz struggled not to weigh on Juan's shallow inhalations.

Teodoro scanned the gauzy periphery. He fought panic, turning his head from side to side, unable to judge distances with one eye.

The Cainamero girl shattered the silence. She screamed unintelligible threats at Hoku in her native language. Her meaning landed with sharp kicks at his legs. She scratched to pull from his clutch.

Hoku yelled back through her hysteria. "Stay. I want you to stay."

Above the tumult, Luz's quick ear caught another sound, neither snort nor grunt. Deep growls came from the hillside. The death harbinger emanated from a grizzly.

It had to be the bear's avenger, Mariposa.

Hoku and the girl stopped shouting. Barrages of panted breaths rolled behind the contoured edge of fog encircling the wagon. The air carried the oily scent of wet fur. Hoku drew his knife from its sheath. The girl had no weapon. He grabbed the other hefty pike, slapping the willow pole into her hands. Flutters descended Hoku's stomach. They rippled with the cloying upset of cream, and stiffened. He prepared to die for the girl.

Luz's imagined terrors multiplied in the night fog. Hunters had once protected her home and livestock from bears. Her family prospered from their decimation. Now the bears returned in ambush, she believed, guided by Mariposa.

They're here, grizzlies with a blood vendetta against those who slaughtered the bears of Alta California. They will eat my adobe and everything I love. This fulfills Juana's premonition.

The specter of an inevitable bear-confrontation plagued her life even before she had received Juana's warning. It began the evening she heard a calf's unusual bawling. Alarmed, she ran to the adobe doorway. Outside the corral, a gigantic, champagne colored grizzly lugged its prey by its neck over a fence. The pink-snouted bear, larger than any bear she had ever seen, more powerfully wrought than a merciful god had the audacity to create, carried a lanky-legged calf as if it weighed no more than a fingerling trout. The bear stared at her. While its strange coloration mesmerized Luz, its face transformed. She blinked and her visage looked back at her, taking on the round head shape of the bear. The hapless thrashes of the calf became a struggling Indian child. She recognized the child as the unearthed boy, the one who had writhed in the death-grip of the foraging bear. Again, she heard bloodcurdling wails from the boy as the bear ate him alive. Her knees buckled to the threshold. Waves of sobs wrenched her body. The bear, and their shared metamorphosis, huffed into the forest.

Luz never discussed the albino bear with anyone, except Juana. She explained to Luz that the transmutations meant the bear became their fellow Mexican conquerors, with Luz at its head. The calf, turned boy, embodied the vanquished natives. Luz and the bear now shared one identity—an inseparable fate—twin flames entwined in a cyclonic draft of destiny.

Over the years, dozens of curious grizzlies had observed the Miranda property while men built their adobe. Survival instincts steered them from the work site. They maintained a wary separation. The workers had no intention to coexist with the bears. They positioned carcasses over pits on the adobe border to lure bears in closer. Gunmen, covered with brush, hid crouched in the pits so when bears sniffed the bait, they shot from beneath them into their bellies.

Teams of horsemen did not wait for the bears to come to them. They went after them for exhilaration. Expert riders encircled any bear in the valley threatening human habitat—or not. They lassoed leather lariats around the flabbergasted bruin's paws and head. Trained horses then pulled the snared animal in opposite directions, as if rearing from the sight of a coiled snake. Either the bear ripped in uneven quarters, or its tongue strangled from its mouth in death.

The sport continued until hunters pushed the grizzly, which for thousands of years ruled the region unchallenged, into near-extinction. Mexicans justified their acts as a God-given right, the primacy of man. Eat or be eaten. Luz knew the settlers went further than necessary to protect their interests. They brought misery on other living creatures for selfish pleasure.

By 1845, hunters no longer killed bears for their rancho's security. They captured them to offer entertainment for staged bull and bear fights. As the animal's population dwindled, the spectacles' savagery grew. Mexicans paired bears in vicious death battles versus: feral bulls, dog packs, donkeys, and other combinations of damned beasts.

The victory of a surviving animal didn't merit the spectators' laurels. None left the pit alive. Their acclamation depended on the entertainment value of a ferocious mauling, either delivered or received. Mexicans pressed the Indians to bring them more bears. Included in the booty Vallejo reaped in his genocidal campaigns were regular supplies of live grizzlies. He demanded they deliver a pair for his bull and bear fights on every new moon. Fresh captures meant a fight must soon follow because confined wild-bears starved and grew weaker.

On the Mexican Day of Independence, tribes brought a special offering to appease their conquerors, three, not the usual two, grizzlies. The booty included a significant capture. A trio of cages six feet apart contained a seven-foot tall sow, her frisky male cub, and a twelve-hundred-pound albino male bear with pink-skinned paws. Proud to have captured a valued prize that had evaded the Anglo hunters, the Indians gave the massive bear the effeminate name of Mariposa. Vallejo might have perceived the sobriquet as an insult if he'd thought Indians had the intellect to concoct such provocations.

The pueblo held fights where the broadening slough met Tolay Lake. A long, wide pit straddled the landing. Its six-foot depth discouraged animals from fleeing. Strong wooden fences surrounded the pit. The arena staged a bizarre theatre of man's dominance over nature.

Vallejo sat with his guest, the English trapper, to enjoy the celebration. He threw his arm around his shoulders, pulling him nearer.

"See this pit? See the Independence Day pageantry? See the submissive beasts awaiting our call? The elements are all a unifying symbol. Something we share with our British friends. Now, you tell me what that is."

"To your point," said the trapper, "our reign over nature by men of reason."

"*Santiago!*" Vallejo shouted the old, Conquistador battle cry. "And over men impervious to reasoning, too. *Gente sin razón*. People without reason. That's what we call them. Observe how we have mastered the mighty bear. He was once wild like the Indios savage. Now both are under our heel."

Opposite a handful of penned tournament bulls, the bears seethed in the three tight cages.

"We've flushed animals from our domain into smaller and smaller spaces. Our vaqueros restrain them for entertainment and consumption. Or, when I speak of the Indios, I should be more careful and say *blessed conversion*."

The trapper laughed. "Savage like the fat beaver until they step into the jaws of my trap."

"We live in the era of Rational Man," said Vallejo. "Nature cannot escape our confines." He pointed to the bear hunters, their chinstraps cinched against set jaws. The tall men on caparisoned horses circled outside the ring. "See their reatas and their loaded guns? They keep them at the ready to kill cowards—any bear desperate enough to climb over the pit wall."

Vallejo touched his forehead and nodded at Luz who sat a row behind them. "Our Mexican grande dams sit close by us for protection. The men in their families prepare the bulls. We protect their women. Sit back. Drink. And enjoy how the bull breaks the will of the savage bear."

Luz attended the fight as an act of unity with her fellow citizens. During the bloody event, she pored over her shoes, slipping a loose gray rebozo around her head to block from her sight the spectacle of animal on animal violence.

With an approving smile, Vallejo lifted a finger. The flex of his digit ordered the afternoon bull and bear fights to begin. Confident voices rang out in happy agreement. The festivities began. An Afro-Mexican clown in red flannel drawers and a spangled shirt danced into the ring. Easy laughter rippled around the arena. The whimsical player acted as if he'd forgotten the reason he came into the pit. He gamboled away scratching his scalp but soon returned pulling the cub in its cage. Its sow mother, penned outside, viewed her cub. She bit sideways on her enclosure bars.

A rope tied a gray-haired jack donkey to a ten-foot tree trunk post. The donkey waited in the ring center, ears erect. Its nostrils dripped.

The clown opened the cage door and hauled its end. He shook the bars until the cub dropped out. The little bear bound from the pursuing clown. Agitated, the donkey warned the cub away, nipping at him when within range.

Men on the perimeter, fired by copious bumpers of aguardiente and mescal, cheered for the cub. The clown ran from the ring, rattling a cage behind him.

The young grizzly had no interest in bothering the ornery donkey. He left him nibbling on a tuft of green. The cub wandered to the fence near his anxious mother. He quaked on his haunches. Moist huffs answered his cries.

Drunken men jumped into the pit and lassoed its small hind paw. They yanked on the noose until the cub yelped in pain. The impatient men tied the other rope end to the center post, avoiding the territorial donkey. With an awkward dash, they made their escape and hopped back over barriers to the crowds' grateful applause.

The donkey approached the cub with its legs flexed, head lowered, and ears pinned back. It brayed a belch-sounding wheeze. The ball of bear fur rolled to the center post. Its mother swayed against the sides of its narrow cage. The crowd laughed harder with each nip from the donkey. Adolescent hooked claws enabled the cub to scramble to the top of the post.

The satisfied donkey pranced away, seeking a clump of grass it had been eating. Men leapt the barriers into the ring. Two strained on the rope until the cub tumbled to the ground. A third man whipped the preoccupied donkey with intoxicated vigor.

The enraged donkey moved toward the cub. Twice the animal whirled from the lash. It reared, and with a crack, kicked the ribs of the cub, bending its midsection. The cub struggled to its feet.

It raised its snout, hoping for maternal rescue. The donkey waited by its side, hind legs cocked. Once set, its sharp hooves hammered a mighty blow under the young chin. Head snapped backward, the cub collapsed on the clay arena. A fractured jaw rendered it lifeless.

Caballeros rushed the carcass to the *tassajara* to butcher, hang, and dry the thighs, a favorite treat of the generalissimo. Vallejo advised the trapper, "Berry-eating cubs are less palatable once they have eaten fish."

After caballeros removed the cub, they released the mother grizzly. She entered the ring smelling the ground where blood trickled from the ears of the dragged cub. The stunned bear rose to her seven-foot height, stretching her back knotted from confinement. She hopped a narrow circle, sniffing to identify scents of human, donkey and her offspring.

The crowd stood. They waited for high drama from a blood-thirsty revenge. Men extended a long-handled gaff hook from behind the wall to capture the donkey. They drew on the pole, hauling the challenger closer to the grizzly.

Steadied on four paws, the bear faced the approach in amazement. The donkey brayed a sour warning, as he had terrified the cub. She did not retreat. The adult raised her right paw and hit the donkey a blow that flattened its pinned ears. It sprawled as though granite had plummeted from a cliff onto its head. The heavy retribution broke its neck.

Fans howled passionate anathemas condemning Spain, represented by the prostrate donkey. Vivid-colored rebozos rippled from heads and shoulders in a wave around the ring. Vallejo and the trapper jumped to embrace the nearest women who encouraged them further with their giggles.

Luz remained seated.

Before the crowd settled, fast-moving caballeros anchored the sow by a twenty-foot chain attached to its hind paw. Scattered calls of "Toro!" converged into others until the galvanized mob chanted with one voice. Children clapped, skipping to the rhythmic, "Toro! Toro! Toro!" Vallejo shouted to the trapper, "This is what we've been waiting for. Now here comes the symbol of our masculinity."

A door on the pen rose, freeing an enormous dark-brown bull. Ominous horns spread four feet from the side of its rock-hard skull, curving up at the tips of its ears. The bull tromped forward, tail twitching high and proud.

Frantic for a place to hunker down, the bear clawed a hole.

The bull lowered its head, rocked its horns, and charged across the ring. It rushed in a dust-raising catapult at the bear and crashed into her leg. A dull white bone punctured a gash through her lower hindquarter.

Applause hailed the fine start made by the bull, while low opprobrium cast on the grizzly. Despite her wound, the bear acted uninterested in battle. Impatient, the bull roared deep and rammed the grizzly astride the post. It thumped with the sickening sound of an axe handle whacking a rotten pumpkin. The bear hobbled to the impression it dug. Incensed at the continued retreat, the bull rallied for a quick kill, jamming his horns into the side of the bear.

She turned, striking blows on the bull's nose. It wrestled him to the ground. They rolled over each other. The sow clamped her powerful jaws on a horn.

Frantic, the bull realized he battled for his life. He bucked and bent to free himself from his sudden danger. The bear slipped forward on its horns. With one mighty effort, the bull tossed the bear high into the air.

Excited spectators assumed the dazed grizzly feared another confrontation after crashing to the ground. The bull plunged its sharp horn at the bear. Before it completed the maneuver, the bear rolled.

Quicker than electricity, lethal paws slapped the bull on each side of its head. A wide, deadfall blow on its ribs knocked the breath from its body with a grunt. The bear seized the confounded bull by its nose, munching the tender snout with piercing-teeth.

Streams of its blood, and the labored bear's exhalations, burbled into the snout of the bull. It overwhelmed his desperate gasps for oxygen.

The grizzly shoved the upper jaw of its opponent downward. They rolled backward together. In another heartbeat, the bear sprang triumphant. The bull lay limp with its neck broken.

Stunned by the unexpected kill, the crowd sat silent. Before they renewed more fanatical chants of, "Toro!" horsemen dragged away the disgraced bull. Its last observation of life displayed cross-eyed befuddlement.

Men released a second bull into the ring to placate the crowd. The bull faced the exhausted bear while she licked blood on her leg. Although the bull appeared to be a larger, more formidable foe than its predecessor, it showed no outward aggressiveness. It capered back toward its pen. A caballero guided a whickering horse alongside the bull. Another caballero dropped a gate to close off its refuge. The bull rubbed along the horse. It knelt to scratch its snout on the ground. The outraged crowd hurled liquor-slurred scorn at the bull. They waved handkerchiefs draped on sticks behind the bear. Two men joined the caballeros. They spurred the shy animal with pike jabs.

In a bull and bear fight, the first minutes' advantages belong to the bull. Strength that lifts its gargantuan horns makes an attack by a bull indefensible by most foes. The musculature of a bull produces its principal vulnerability. When sapped from its heavy exertions, a bull thrusts out its tongue, panting. A combative bear, if able to survive the first blows, waits for that exhaustion and for the soft tissue to protrude from the mouth of the bull. When the bull convulses to catch its breath, the bear hooks the tongue with a horrible swipe. Then the bear continues shredding the ears and lower jaw of the bull until the mauled collapses, cries out, and bleeds to death.

The demure bull had no awareness of its mortal challenge. Trailed by caballeros, it stopped at center ring, switching its tail low and relaxed. It looked away, reasoning that by not eyeing the bear, its bovine cunning made its two-thousand-pound frame inconspicuous.

Unpersuaded, the bear dug in, excavating paws of soil into the air.

The bull had seen enough to convince him his subterfuge had failed. It bolted full-charge to the farthest boundary. Hoots from the crowd mocked the caballeros. They could not tolerate an insult to their prowess. The fleetest horseman thundered alongside the bull, snatching the base of its tail and hoisting its mass over its horns.

It tottered back on its feet. The bull wavered for a few seconds before caballeros goaded his pendulous groin. They pushed him toward the bear with a vehemence matching their sharp humiliation. From the ring barrier safety, the clown extended a pole above the bear, waving a red flag.

The crowds' taunts and the persistent jabs of pikes incited the bull into a state of confused madness. It lost its sense of self-preservation and it hollered an outraged cry. Blind anger propelled the bull across the arena into the bear.

It absorbed the blow. Scrambling to her haunches, she grappled her forepaws around the bull's head. She wrenched against resistance of its neck and chewed on its nose. Savage jerks shook the bull to a front-legged kneel. It could no longer retreat. The bear pressed the head into the ground to dislocate another vertebra. Clouds of dust rose from the squashed nostrils of the bull. Blood spewed from where its ear tore off, spattering into his eyes. Though the bull groaned with pain, it withstood the attack, determined not to budge until he'd gathered a reserve of strength.

He did.

With a swing of his neck, the bull pulled from the grasp. His horn slipped in the mouth of the sow. He raked his horn through the clenched bite with a rapid lateral movement. Broken teeth scattered in a horrid spray of blood. The bear staggered, her teeth strewn in dust among shiny clots of gore.

After garnering his last bit of strength, the bull hooked the bear inside her hindquarter. She shuddered. The bull spun her in the air. After she hit the ground, a final thrust lanced her bowels.

The bone weary bull lifted its head. Pink and purple entrails festooned its horns, adornments for a macabre circus. Its guileless stare defied the spectators to applaud their bloodbath staging. No longer able to stand, the bull collapsed to its knees. Crosshatched slashes flowed blood from its body. It panted heavy breaths and rolled to its side, cherishing relief from the maelstrom.

The crowd stamped and shook their seats to the wobbled foundations of the arena. Waves of men's hats set sail on the breeze grandiloquent oaths to the glorified rebellion. Hails to, "God and liberty!" consecrated the air, each pulse resounding louder than the cry before it. They demanded another bear—the greatest bear—and fresh blood flow to amuse the yet unsatisfied.

"Mariposa! Mariposa!" they shouted.

Caballeros removed the earlier carnage from the ring. Guitarists roamed the perimeter singing heartrending ballads in praise of Mexican women's chastity. The clown ran out. He planted an iron spike with streamers into the forehead of the dazed bull.

The arena cleared except for the wounded, one-eared bull. It stayed on its side, panting. Coagulated blood caked the streamers. They appeared as royal red plumes attached to a show horse bridle.

Vallejo nodded a signal. Commotion ebbed and rose to a manic level when the new cage entered. An undertow drew voices from the stadium and crashed their outcry back on the arena.

Vallejo's fingers patted his cheek. Opposite the ring from him, men brought in two more bulls. They stood excellent animals, one colored a dark aubergine, the second midnight-black, marbled with white. Caballeros tied their hind hooves to a post.

Volunteers leapt the barriers. They hauled in Mariposa's cage. The passive, bloodied bull did not realize his peril, or its imminence.

"Watch the ease with which we summon the wild to perform for our pleasure," said Vallejo to the trapper.

They shackled the prone bull to a chain fastened to the grizzly. Caballeros motioned their nervous readiness to open the cage. Vallejo clasped his hands over his head and gave the order to let loose the fury of Mariposa. Roars thundered from the crowd. The gate slid and a giant, ghostlike bear burst forth.

The startled bull labored to rock itself back onto its feet. Mariposa countered, fastening two-inch fangs to its side. He pressed on its flank and tore into its loins with astonishing malevolence.

The tortured bull struggled to his legs. It yelled. A fast chain allowed no chance of escape. Mariposa circled halfway around and seized his muzzle, ripping dreadful gashes the length of the snout.

The bull surrendered to its knees, blew out, and stiffened dead with part of its lower jaw in the grip of his ferocious antagonist.

Through the Sabbath Day witnesses' excited yells, a second Vallejo signal flew the ring faster than women blessed themselves. A band of caballeros jumped to the command and brought Mariposa to the ground. They tethered the two new bulls and their rawhide lines to the chain holding the bear.

The smaller bull, his coat as smooth as a brushed thoroughbred, surveyed his antagonist. He pawed dirt, preparing to pitch into the bear. More wary, the other bull looked around the arena and understood their danger.

The bear taunted the bantam. He braced his haunches in the depression dug by the sow before him. Outraged, the smaller bull bellowed and fired at the grizzly.

Mariposa absorbed sharp, rapid blows with deep growls, maneuvering into an embrace around the neck of the bull. Bulky muscle-mass above the shoulders of the bear, designed to drive its limbs and make the species powerful diggers, swelled. The grizzly squeezed behind the head of the bull until he threw it on his back. With catlike speed, he thrust his platter-sized paw into the mouth of the bull. Shoving, shoving, and shoving. Unformed moans pressed past Mariposa's forelimb. He raked backward, ripping out the tongue.

Before the stupefied bull bled to death, the other bull made a late charge, head tilted. The mighty bull caught the grizzly on its horn, raising it from the ground. He hurled his enemy 15 feet.

A chain link snapped.

Dumbfounded, the crowd tried to understand what had happened. Wild animals—their entertainment—roamed free. Bewilderment turned to screams when spectators realized that they, too, had become animal combatants in an unrestrained arena of the feral. Terrified shouts shred the air. Myths that held the pioneer society together: the myth of their shared birthrights, the myth of their omnipotence over nature, and the myth of their superiority to men of darker colors, broke apart with the failure of a forged chain link. Benign absolutes, faith in God and among one another, withered when confronted with unfettered, natural ferocity.

The crowds dispersed pell-mell toward the slough. Luz stayed. Mariposa, the albino bear, headed into the stands. She sat stolid—waiting. He closed. In a fleeting instant of mutual recognition, Luz knew the bear as it knew her.

He passed without stopping and sought the nearest barrier. Every step to the arena wall increased his speed. The mob's terror deepened as Mariposa vaulted the barricade. He sprinted into a crowd, knocking over a roan that challenged him.

The trapper yelled to Vallejo as they fled on foot. "We must outmaneuver the bear."

Soldiers and caballeros let fly a fusillade of lead from pistol and long gun. The bear bounded among the gunmen. Their errant shots jeopardized those opposite them.

Vallejo slowed to a walk. "No," he said to the trapper, who gasped for breath. He pointed at the Californios, revolvers drawn, the compatriots he commanded, and to whom he had pledged his life. "In all things, I only have to outsmart them."

Away went Mariposa to the slough faster than men could run. Horsemen chased. The bear splashed into the waterway, swimming its breadth into the tules. Sprays of gunshots trailed. He wormed into the maze of sloughs where horses couldn't tread and time held sway over men.

Mariposa disappeared.

Back in the cleared arena, the Mexican clown shot the last bull. No one remained to applaud.

BOOM!

The fog dome surrounding the carreta flashed a stab of light. A rifle blast reawakened Luz from her Bull-Bear Fight memories. Smoke from the gun swirled around her. Rumbles echoed from the hillside and rang in the guardians' ears, deafening them.

Teodoro darted to Hoku's station. Scents of burned powder rolled forward with him. Thin lips shaped excited words. "The bear! I got the bear."

Hoku disregarded Teodoro and swung his narrow pike to sweep away ripples of smoke. The girl squatted before him, her weapon angled out in a defensive position. Hoku checked on Juan and examined the condition of the oxen.

A muffled voice grew louder by him saying, "Go, you imbecile. Be after it."

Hoku squinted toward Teodoro. "Did you say something?"

He returned a glower. "You know how to speak Spanish well now, don't you? I said take your pike. Find the dead beast. It's at the rear, up the hill. I'll be behind you. Don't think about running away."

Hoku's lips folded into his mouth before he grabbed a lantern.

Teodoro unsheathed his sword, staring at Hoku. "Coward," he said.

Hoku inched off the road with his pike before him. A yellowed beam extended into the woods over the pole. He took cautious steps through low chaparral before marshalling a deep breath. A large lurking outline came into view. Hoku did not hesitate. He charged at the phantom, his full weight tilted against the pike shaft. The rush ended short of the target.

Teodoro hollered senseless threats from the rear at whatever he shot in the mist. He stopped when Hoku lifted the lantern and pike above his head. Teodoro edged to the side of Hoku, seizing the light. The root ball of an upturned tree wavered in its harsh illumination. A lead slug blistered its splattered bark. They found no animal, no fur, and no blood. The men stood silent. As the reverberations in their ears subsided, a tattoo of fog dripping from oak leaves rose from the forest floor.

"I wounded the beast—or I chased it off to die. No thanks to you." Teodoro passed the lantern. "Ortega warned me you Kanaka were half women."

A threatening swipe from his unpaired hand feinted at Hoku. Teodoro crossed himself. "God help you if Father doesn't get the sacraments. Follow me. You steal my time."

Hoku kicked at a mossy branch in the dirt. His tongue clamped within his teeth. It bled a reminder of his humiliation meted at the comfort of Ortega's emptied bladder.

At the carreta, Hoku gathered the girl close, placing the pikes within reach on the wagon bed. He assured himself a reckoning would come. One day, he, or his seed, would reap revenge on those who enslaved him on this land. For the present, he swore to find his way to coastal areas with the girl. If he commandeered an oil-barrel raft, they'd sail the gate to Yerba Buena, work onto a merchant ship, and escape to the Kanaka village on the Columbia River at Fort Vancouver.

An angry punta de buey thrust jolted the oxen. The travelers, no longer galvanized by common dangers, or goals, continued until they arrived in the territory of people who spoke *Hookooeko*. Juan would never leave the mission and Hoku would never return to the hacienda palace.

ASSISTENCIA

Luz's spirits ascended at first light along with the clamor of waterfowl rising from bay mudflats. Planked rafts, assembled on discarded oil barrels, bobbed in clusters at the shore edge. The change to lush variegated landscape from dried grasses meant the carreta arrived in the area of the San Rafael mission church. Luz prayed a friar waited there to administer redemption for Juan. The road they traveled uphill bisected the tidelands from stump-covered grounds. Vallejo's troops had ransacked the vineyards and hacked the orchards for grafting stock planted in Sonoma.

Near several mission outbuildings, two Indians emerged from a small patch of tobacco plants. One directed Hoku toward the derelict church. The other Indian ran to wake the mayordomo, Timothy Murphy.

Luz did not permit formal introductions to delay her. Before he tucked his shirt into his pants, she said to the stout Irishman, "I beg you. Send for the friar right away. My husband needs the Last Rites blessing."

Murphy breasted his hat. "I'm very sorry, Señora. Prudenico Santillan has traveled from the area. But you may take shelter in the church as guests of Señor Pico."

Pico had purchased the mission, built on Hookooeko land, from his brother the Governor who shared his African ancestry. He made the property available when he declared it, "Without an owner."

Murphy directed the Indians to attend to Juan. "We will provide you the comfort we can."

They carried him at a funereal pace to the church. Hookooeko women circled burned-sage around the concave edges of his abdomen, smudging his skeletal ribs. It did not last long. Juan died, eyes open, before the sunrise dissolved into the blue-milk sky of mid-morning. Luz's stamina drained with his final death rattle. She rued the futility of the overnight journey: a trip that might have hastened her husband's death, a trip to a place where no Juana Briones waited to console her, and a trip that ended without locating a holy man to absolve Juan of his sins. She peered unfocused while women-savages caressed and sang soft reassurances to her husband—the last blessing of his life. When they left, Luz folded Juan's arms under the quilt she had made for their wedding night. The hand-stitched blanket that had held the warmth of their passion now shrouded the flanks of their ashen union.

Luz waited in solitude for an hour before she permitted Teodoro to enter the room. She drifted away without saying a word to him.

Outside the church, Hoku and the girl cleared the carreta bed. Luz struggled to raise her voice. "Boy. Where's the food we brought?"

Hoku did not respond.

Luz rubbed her throbbing head. "Please, boy. Fetch me my figs. I feel weak."

"Stay with me." Hoku motioned to the girl.

"Boy! I said I'm hungry. I'm thirsty, too. Do you not hear?"

"You know my name."

"For the last time, bring me a little food and some water. I'm too weary for your insolence."

The girl edged from the carreta.

"Stop her," said Luz. "Is that why you delay? That mongrel stole my fruit."

Hoku shoved the girl's hip toward a tree line at the base of the hill behind the mission.

"Stop her right there, or I'll whip you."

The girl clutched Hoku's hand. Luz pointed at him. "You'll do as I tell you, or I'll report this to Generalissimo Vallejo."

Hoku shouted back, "I am not a boy, and we're not his cattle. Are you?"

A whimper strangled between her rope-tight lips. Her hands gripped their opposite elbows to stop from trembling. Luz patted up her chest until she clutched her wedding day brooch. She looked toward the church, hoping Teodoro might emerge with his sword and gun. No one moved near the building, except Indians tending to small patches of gardens. In his blubbering grief, her son did not detect his mother's cry of alarm. "Teodoro. Teodoro! The mongrels!"

She ripped the brooch from the rebozo and flung it at Hoku and the girl. It skidded in the dust before it reached them. The girl fled into the wooded hamlet followed by Hoku. Smoldering campfires, blunt tobacco-reefers, and Indian revenge provided concealment. They vanished in their thickening smokes.

Luz could not chase them. She wandered in the opposite direction until she spotted an isolated, hacked pear tree. Sitting on an overturned barrel, her shoulders heaved. She braced to sob until her heart emptied.

A low shadowy disturbance on hills beyond the mudflats caught her attention. An albino bear chased a swath of terrified elk. They poured together across narrow ridges and funneled a draw chute.

Luz sensed kinship with the wild tableau. In her exhaustion, she imagined that from heaven she and the animals appeared as one, an era flowing through an hourglass waist. Tears, laden with woes, ruptured her suppressed heartache. The magnificent bear, icon of the untamed West, faded from her sight, forever.

While Luz wept, men in other worlds adopted a dogma they called Manifest Destiny. It inspired a bellicose uprising from Alta California insurrectionists. They flattered themselves as *los Osos*, the bears. Economic hardship aligned other foreign men—rough and hungry for opportunity—to march her way. The emigrants stirred with no more awareness than Luz's understanding of what mysterious fate conducted them toward her homeland.

An American invasion followed the Osos' flag raising. Then a chance discovery brought a stampede of gold seekers to the Pacific Coast.

New invaders claimed Vallejo's conquests as their birthrights. Cloth of their ensigns, the Bear of the California Republic, then the Stars and Stripes of the United States, flew over Petaluma Valley. They renamed Frontera del Norte a republic, then a territory, and then Sonoma and Marin counties in the American state of California.

Among the immigrants, a young New Yorker, Thomas Bishop Valentine, came by ship from Eastchester to San Francisco. In 1850, he purchased the four leagues of Miranda Rancho property at a rigged probate auction.

Antonio Ortega learned of the sale. He slithered back from the shadows of a low-profile life he rebuilt in San Francisco. Standing before the non-Spanish speaking United States Land Commissioners, Ortega attested that Juan Miranda had defrauded him of his Rancho Arroyo de San Antonio grant. He neither sold it nor willfully gave it to Miranda. If the Court agreed, it would invalidate Valentine's title and default the property to Ortega.

In his new role as California State Senator, Vallejo, with his amigo Teodoro, testified in support of Ortega. They endorsed his claim in opposition to the Miranda family and Thomas Valentine. Experts paid by Valentine proved the diseño submitted in evidence by Ortega, the same map Vallejo and Teodoro swore to its authenticity, represented a sloppy forgery.

Legal battles to secure the Petaluma property raged for years. Arguments twice rose to the level of the United States Supreme Court.

During the ambiguous ownership, Valentine warned squatters to stay off his land. Despite his notices published in the local paper, occupiers established the City of Petaluma in 1858. Once more, newcomers, applying force and intimidation, seized the land.

In 1871, three years after Ortega's death, Congress resolved, *"For all time,"* the claim to Petaluma. They passed legislation for, *"The Relief of Thomas Valentine."*

Instead of evicting thousands of settlers, Valentine received an issue of United States land scrip equal to the number of acres in Rancho Arroyo de San Antonio. It allowed any scrip holder to claim their choice of federal land, with few restrictions.

Valentine Scrip absorbed within its cotton fibers the venality that formed the newly defined territory. Its essence created fortunes, it destroyed worlds, and it altered lives.

Ortega's rape of Francesca Miranda goaded the sins that created the scrip. They plodded into the future at the pace of an ox drawn carreta.

INCUBATOR
Spring of 1898

The day before Arthur Lloyd Dean left for Army basic training, he made light talk over an airtight waste drum at the Petaluma Incubator Factory.

His eager replacement snapped a stopwatch. "Time's up! That's it for test ostrich ninety-nine." He scratched a notation on a clipboard.

"And that'll be all for me, too." Dean reached inside a low shelf. "Let's see what we got." A tiny, gray beak expanded a partial crack on a large egg he withdrew. "Mark the big bird a heroic failure."

The apprentice opened the metal drum and dropped the fractured experiment among broken shells, yolks, and Leghorn chicks. With a deep thump from the side of his fist, he secured the lid.

Slow ticks from inside the covered barrel did not disturb them. If they waited long enough, the subdued cheeps, the gentle taps for air, the desperation that only mattered to one life, dwindled to a single weakened peck, then none. Dean called the drum the popcorn pan—once the last kernel exploded, they had completed the test run.

The taps might have been from seven thousand miles away, or from another time. The distraction did not matter. If the noise concerned Dean, he could have vented the lid to let in a gasp of air. Mercy came not under his job responsibilities. Lyman C. Byce paid him to build the best incubators in the world. Because he tended to his employer's business, Dean enjoyed the reward of long, easy interludes punctuated by moments of light labor.

He monitored thermostats, regulating their temperatures until each doomed test-brood finished its trial. Some eggs came from the incubator as hatched chicks, some came out as cooked eggs, and some came out as cooked chicks. No matter the result, he swept the test agents in the waste receptacle, an unremarkable, everyday routine.

Coal-lamp heated incubators established Petaluma as the most productive egg-processing region in the world. Small signals of despair from the drum metered the happy price of progress.

Dean's ice-blue eyes searched outside the factory windows. "I can't believe I'm getting my chance to get away from here to become a soldier."

"Lucky for you, the Spanish are waiting to oblige." The apprentice twirled his mustache end. "Come and try to fight me in your *leetle* sheeps, *gringo*."

"Hilarious, funny man. Tell your amigos I remember the Maine and I'll be there plenty soon with some *beeg* guns and some very *beeg* ships."

"The Spanish can shoot back, you know."

"Doesn't bother me. I'm ready to fight to the death for our God, for our nation, and to protect our town of Petaluma."

"Fighting for God and for nation? Sure, sure you are," said the apprentice, laughing. "But the attack in Cuba was a long way from Petaluma, and heaven is farther still. Why do you really want to go?"

"It's what a man does. Men have to believe in something big."

"From what your brother Leslie has told me, you could do your duty just as well by joining him in the Company C militia and stay in California. They say that's no different from fighting abroad."

"They lie."

"Leslie doesn't think so. Why don't you agree?"

"He is too young to remember when our Dad believed in a lie. They told him he could get rich by growing oranges in Southern California. He lost our family savings. We had to move north to Petaluma to find work after moving from Michigan to Los Angeles. Don't want that to happen to me. I will not ruin my life because I believed in somebody else's lie. I want to believe in something big. Something real. Something good. Like God, and America. This war is my chance to do that. I have to go to it. People will respect me the same way they respected my uncle who fought in the War to Preserve the Union. That was a big deal. It was good."

"Does he live in California?"

"My uncle died in battle."

Dean had worked his teenage years rising through the factory hierarchy. By twenty, he mastered the complex of overhead leather straps that wound from the boiler flywheel to the heavy equipment. He hole-punched a ruptured belt, aligned its ends, and laced the break faster than his peers retrieved the slapping strap.

Dean earned his engineer rank, in part, by surviving ever-treacherous machinery movements. If fledgling careers did not end with clipped fingers, the bearings' whine drove most young workers to resign, or to lose their senses.

With a sardonic smile, he explained to his replacement how he prepared to fight. "God put me in the middle of all that noise across the street to harden me for the battlefield."

By twenty-one, Dean had learned to draft and how to interpret a blueprint. Those skills provided the golden passport Byce required of him to move from the manufacturing plant to the safer, prototype assembly building. Hand drills, sheet metal cutters, and marked-up incubator plans covered his workbench-es. High windows lit the quiet room built over tall piers on the Petaluma Slough. From his airy bench, Dean gazed eastward over the water and across open grasslands to the foot of Sonoma Mountain.

The factory property had been an Indian village surrounded by ancient redwoods. Before the first American squatters had made camp there, it marked the Miranda Rancho northern edge.

"Now that you're leaving—" The apprentice raised an eyebrow to catch Dean's attention. "I said now that you're finally shipping out, all of a sudden, Pastor Jones doesn't approve of your guitar, does he? Says it's evil. Says a guitar could be the Devil's tool, even if it's church hymns you strum."

"*Hooey.* Where did that come from?" Though he tried to glower, his innate cheerfulness winked beneath his lush eyelashes. "I don't know why he'd say that. He's supported me after I told him I would leave the youth group." Dean's voice croaked with the embarrass-ing tenor of a younger man. "Just last week he prayed with me about my decision to join the Army. Told me he found the per-fect verse to carry with me, Philippians 4:13. I can do all things through Him who strengthens me."

"I'd bet old lady Hinshaw put him up to complaining," said the apprentice. "Money preaches from the tallest pulpit in church. That's why you'll never hear Pastor Jones criticize her organ music."

"Suppose not," said Dean. "Did Jones really tell you to tell me about that guitar humbug? Or are you feeling your oats to get me riled up? Maybe what you claim is an innocent coincidence, but Hinshaw heard me strumming, '*Savior Pilot Me*,' at the church yesterday."

The apprentice slapped the drum. "Sure he told me to pass it along. I don't spread gossip or make waves. It was his idea. Jones carries Hinshaw's water. It's as if God Almighty speaks to him through her donated Vocalion organ, instead of a burning bush."

Dean raised and shook his hands high. "Whoa, Nellie. When Hinshaw tottered into the sanctuary, I thought she'd turn me into a salt pillar. I looked like a dog passing a peach pit. That sanctimonious shrew took advantage of me to lecture that God wanted his hymns played on her Vocalion."

"Tight wads of money-rolls may be behind her words," said the apprentice. "But it's still hard cheese." He picked sawdust mites from his mustache. "What'd you expect her to say?"

"Nothing at all. The last thing I hoped to see was Hinshaw in the sanctuary. I didn't mind the scold so much, but I assumed I played—*and prayed*—alone. She surprised me." Dean tugged a curled hair on his forehead. "Well, her ire doesn't bother me now. I'll testify on my guitar from here to Manila and back. Coercion can't stop me. It's God's plan. If I sing His praises, He'll protect me from The Deep, the Spanish, and the old lady Hinshaw."

For Dean, the Spirit resided in the church. God's word manifested there for him in ways similar to how white light conquers the dark: invisible, yet ubiquitous. The stained-glass windows shone the splendor of God's revelations as light passed through their prisms, each transfiguring into a ribbon array that dazzled the pews. Each glass crystal held a prayer. Each colored ray that emerged through its refraction carried a promise to a brokenhearted supplicant. Dean identified his petition among the bluest of shades.

The apprentice closed his grip and bent his elbow, carving an imaginary knife downward into a vertical board before stroking slashes across his throat. "Can you imagine the hell to pay if old lady Hinshaw caught you defacing the church that night?" He whistled low. "She'd be shaking her black glove up at you while you squeezed your names from the steeple top down. I imagined you with your legs hugged around that pinnacle whittling like a woodpecker: Arthur Lloyd Dean and Henriette Elizabeth Rosenthal."

Dean resented the familiarity. "Pardon me if I say so, you cluck like a Leghorn. In twenty-four hours, you run this department.

Act like it. Here I told you a personal confidence, man to man, and before the morning is over you're blabbing about it. Wise up." He rolled the drum back and forth on its rim. "I etched only our initials, not our names. And not in that order. Ladies always come first. I suggest you quit your strut and learn about women, and life, my friend."

"Perhaps, so. Life's a mystery, and the fair maidens are more of a puzzle." He knitted his fingers, bracing to deliver a crushing rebuttal. "But I know enough about that Hinshaw-hag, who used to be a woman. If she ever discovers you vandalized her church steeple, I assure you she'll first tell your mother about your Jewess girlfriend, and then she'll tar and feather you straight out of town on a rail. You might have to stay forever fighting on that *Philadelphiaini*—or whatever it is that you call that Chinese island—with Dewey and his fleet. What say you?"

Dean disregarded his fancy for tittle-tattle. The secret was out. Church whisperers knew he spent time with a Jewish, San Francisco girl. She traveled to Petaluma with her salesman father. Dean's mother had heard the gossip, too. She warned him not to be reckless and not to betroth the Hebrew before he left the United States. He refused to share his mother's harsh sentiment with either the apprentice or Henriette, the woman he loved.

"I'll tell you what I say. I leave tomorrow to go to the Philippines, not to Philadelphia, not to China. With the Army, not with the Navy. And, it's a several-thousand island archipelago, not a single island. Oh and here's my last piece of advice, buster bright eyes, I'll return next year on Dewey's *sheeps* to reclaim my job here. I hope you'll act smarter by then. Thank you very much."

The apprentice's presumptuous cheek irritated Dean—and it concerned him. Fear of his mother's heartbreak and the hurt from her shun had weighed on him after the day he enlisted. He planned to mollify her objections to his girlfriend by coming back from the Philippines a war hero. Byce had assured him he'd keep a job open for him at the factory. Dean expected to return home to a wife, to a secure income, and with a veteran's esteem difficult for his mother to fault.

Outside of his workbench window, an egret shuffled a brilliant yellow foot in the water lapping on the banks. When Hinshaw had interrupted Dean at the church, the tributary had been the object of his thoughts. He was praying for safe passage beginning at the slough wharf, and then on through the war, until he returned home a hero. In his mind, the thirteen-miles of the Petaluma Slough unfurled a path connecting him to distant lands. Its waters had powers to convey him—to and from—past and future. A life transforming flux flowed in its channels.

Portions of a fantastic vision that recurred in his dreams had unfolded in reality. To secure the prophecy, he had climbed in the dark to the top of the church steeple with a knife. After he descended, he told Henriette of how he carved their initials. He explained he had to do it because of a dream he had that foretold their destiny.

"The dream starts where I set out alone on the slough in a Miwok tule reed boat."

"Like Baby Moses," suggested Henriette.

"Could be." Dean yielded to her altered vision. "As I drifted betwixt marshes, I stared back at Petaluma until the steeple on which I engraved our initials, my proclamation of love for you, dropped from sight. That's my promise I'll return to you—that's the essential part of the dream. I made it real. I made it big. And it's good. The posting of our names shows the world how much I believe in our love."

"Aww," she cooed.

He described how he glided farther into the uncharted slough, following wakes of flat-bottomed scow schooners headed to the insatiable city wharves with deliveries of gray stone, red board, and hay.

"At the end, the current spat me out and into the heave of San Pablo and San Francisco bays."

There the muddy slough collides with snowmelt from the Sacramento and San Joaquin Rivers and converges with ocean tides.

"Enormous forces pushed and pulled me. Powers greater than I have ever beheld drew me up to the glory of heaven and dragged me in surges down to an underworld near Alcatraz Island. I rode on water speckled with California gold dust and the blackest specks of her loam. I was of the stream, part of California's soul. The tide flushed me from The Gate and propelled me toward an exotic shore where I was to meet my destiny. ... My dream ends there."

For Dean, the world connected to the Petaluma slough, all of a piece that led him to the Philippines. He told Henriette he envisioned the journey as clearly as he saw Sonoma Mountain from his workbench.

To other Americans, the Philippines were a blank slate, an unknowable Oriental land seven thousand miles from California. The world published few English accounts on the Spanish archipelago. President McKinley had needed help to locate them on a map before he commanded young men to war there.

"Your brother tells me your mother has not taken this well," said the apprentice. "Leslie says she won't say good-bye to you. Maybe she's more worried you'll get engaged to a native girl."

"Leslie said that?"

"He did. But no good-byes from your mother?"

The barb hooked Dean's soft tissue. "No helloes—or good-byes. She won't speak to me, not since she scolded me the day after I enlisted. I hope she'll come down to visit me at the Presidio with Pitts' family."

"She will."

"I know I broke her heart, but to serve is a tradition I had to fulfill. Pass that on to my blabbing brother."

Dean volunteered for the war in part out of patriotism, and in part out of an ambition to find with something bigger than himself, but in no part out of political conviction. He assumed a soldier's life ran in his blood. God intended glory for him. His mother's grandfather fought in the Revolutionary War. And her brother from Michigan, his hero, died during the Civil War in Shenandoah Valley. His turn with immortality had come.

The apprentice reassured him, "At least your mother must be at peace knowing before McKinley declared war on Spain, he prayed on his knees in the White House. I read the story in the Courier. God told him to bring Christianity to the Catholic Philippines."

"He's the worst person to mention. Never say boo about McKinley with my parents. Father's a Bimetallist—free silver for him. He hates the industrialists' gold standard. And Mother disdains what she calls McKinley's phony mask of calm. She calls him a Gunpowder Christian. Says he has her brother's blood on his hands."

At the Battle of Cedar Creek, in Shenandoah Valley, then Captain McKinley helped turn a rout of Northern troops. His leadership won him popular acclaim and set him on his political rise to the presidency. Delia Dean supposed glory-seeking McKinley ordered her brother to his death. She never forgave him. Now President McKinley commanded her firstborn son into another treacherous battle.

"No matter to me who's president," said Dean. "I live the life the Lord meant for me. If God is for us who can be against us?"

"Anyway," said the apprentice, "you'll not be there long. To your good fortune, too, because, *just between us two chicken roasters*, I smoked out rumors your army buddy, big John Pitts, might have taken a shine to your baby girl Israelite. You had better race to get back to Petaluma from the war before he does."

Dean blinked three times. "Nah. We'll march home shoulder to shoulder." He stretched his arms behind his head and eyed a wall clock. "Anyone would take a shine to her."

John Pitts, a chicken rancher with sandy hair, sturdy shoulders, and narrow hips, had been friends with Dean since high school. He reinforced his scalawag's reputation the previous year when he and two unidentified companions overturned farmer Hogg's buckboard wagon. Pitts paid a twenty-dollar fine in local court for not identifying his accomplices. Thereafter, his cronies' practical jokes never again struck him as funny.

Pitts and Dean volunteered to join the Army. They wound up in different divisions. The notion that rakish Pitts could steal his girl stewed in Dean. Lustful torments, from remembering Henriette's ease the first day their bodies merged, crowded out his other contemplations. He confessed his anguish in prayers by the church stained-glass windows.

Dean's coworker shrugged. "She ain't bad for a 16-year-old. *Still*, some might venture that's a wee young sweetheart for a man of the world. No?"

"No. She's a full-developed woman."

The coworker unmasked his lechery. "How would you know?"

"Mind your tongue. Henriette's very mature, very smart for her age, and very, very opinionated. I doubt she would like you."

Dean picked up a ball-peen hammer. He struck it, tap-tap-tap, on a steel post while he hummed a spiritual. Plaintive strikes joined forlorn drum clicks. Together they radiated into the universe, indistinguishable pleas for mercy to an indifferent ear.

Dean stopped. He pointed the handle at the apprentice. "You could learn much from her. She insists Jews could migrate to the country ranches."

"That's a whopper." A froglike leer twisted into a frown. "My old man calls Jews radicals and anarchists. Can't stomach physical work. He says tell them to stay in their ghettos. Jews couldn't do as good a job on a ranch as Christians."

"Certainly not. That's what I told her," said Dean. "But it makes you think."

"Think?" said the coworker. "My old man doesn't think. He knows. He said Jews are better off in the city where they can stick to themselves."

"Up to the day I met Henriette, well, now I'm not so sure. She's a strong-headed lady. Says she wants to learn about chicken ranching. Sometimes I suspect it's to prove me wrong. I played along, promising to introduce her to a rancher. Pitts agreed to spend time with her before he left for the Philippines. That's all. That's the only reason he has had any contact with her. He's teaching her. I've told you more than you need to know—I trust her."

"You're speaking about a whole load of garbage reminds me I've got to get rid of this." The apprentice grabbed the waste drum. "Just my observation, but Pitts may have more on his mind than coal-oiling roosts and whitewashing nest boxes." He dragged the barrel toward a trap door above the slough. Metal rumbled across wood planks. "Peachy. You trust her. But do you trust him?"

"With my wife." Flush heated Dean's cheeks. "I meant life." He cringed, worried he betrayed a secret promise to Henriette.

The apprentice emptied the slop through the trapdoor. Discharge splattered as if he'd thrown a fistful of pebbles into a pond. He yelled, "Your last batch of popcorn, Short-timer."

When President McKinley declared war on Spain, Artie chose not to join the hometown militia with his brother Leslie. He sought the distinctive cavalry soldier's panache, enlisting in the regular Army.

Without telling his family, he set off to San Francisco on Steamer Petaluma and disembarked at the unfinished Ferry Building. Rushed construction workers slung temporary lights from its rafters. Dean elbowed through a rabble of Volunteers from Tennessee. His chest pounded from the sudden press of humanity. For the first time since after the Civil War, Americans from Northern and Southern states fought together on the same side. Red Cross greeters offered him apples and directed him to the Phelan Building where star-spangled awnings coaxed him to enlist inside the lobby.

A harried recruitment officer in an examination room crumpled Dean's excited smile. He said the cavalry had met its quota. The available slots were with the artillery. "Where are you from, farm boy?"

"Petaluma, sir."

"Do you want to go back home to Petaluma chicken ranches, or do you want to soldier?"

"Well, yes, sir, to be a *cavalry* soldier. The Lord built me to be one."

"Then disrobe—"

"But, sir."

"Son, I talk. You listen. Let's see how well the Lord built a Petaluma chicken pecker. Turn slowly, raising and lowering your arms until I order you to stop. No clucking."

The officer wrote on a pad:

June seven, 1898. This soldier has blue eyes, black hair, dark complexion, is five feet seven and three-quarter inches high. Indelible or permanent marks found on the person of recruit noted here: scar left chin, boil back of neck, scar from boil right elbow rear, and scar from boil back of second finger right hand.

"Stop!" He held out a form. "You're physically fit. Sign the enlistment papers. Next week, report for duty with Third Artillery."

"But, sir, as I said, I don't want to serve at home with coastal artillery. I want to ride with the cavalry."

"Glory. Is that what you think you want? No, son, you want to kill Spaniards. Get this straight. Third Artillery won't stay here lobbing practice rounds into an empty ocean. You'll go overseas to fight. Not with a cannon. We'll issue you a brand-new Springfield rifle to shoot into enemy dens. Not to gain glory. To kill Spanish. You'll love it."

Dean thought of his Union Army uncle in the Civil War, and he thought of his grandfather who fought along with George Washington.

The officer said, "I'll give you twenty-four hours to back out. If I don't see your yellow ass tomorrow, be at the Presidio in a week to report for duty. The Army will make you a man. You'll get your bellyful of *glory*, too."

Dean returned to Petaluma to weigh the United States Army opportunity against the chance to join his younger brother in the Company C militia. On the homebound train, he devoured Leslie's Weekly magazine. The cover portrait had a bugler playing "Reveille" under the American flag. Braided tassels dangled from his horn. A campaign hat shaded a far-off, westerly aspiration in the soldier's eyes. Beneath his elbow, words printed in bold type read, "*Your Country Calls You.*"

Dean fell asleep on the train. He dreamed he climbed the steeple. In his torment, he didn't know what to do once he reached the top.

The next week, he strutted to San Francisco and pledged his life to the United States Army. While he bivouacked at the Presidio, Henriette saw him daily. When he completed his practice drills, they took precious interludes from the Army.

One June Sunday, during Soldiers Day swimming races, the lovers picnicked in a Golden Gate Park dell near Sutro Baths. They exchanged modest jewelry and embraced on a bed of rhododendron blossoms.

Another afternoon, they sat on a seaside bluff. Artie played his guitar and sang ballads as the sun blazed in the West. He rested his instrument across his lap and pored long into Henriette's eyes before he spoke.

"I wrote down a very personal message for you."

She reached at him. "Let me see it."

"I'd rather not. I'm embarrassed about my penmanship. It's terrible. I prefer to read the words to you. There's a lot I've thought about us. This will help me get it out."

"I can't wait, Artie."

"Here goes. When I'm gone, would you please watch for me the sun set every day? Sunset at home will be noon the next day in the Philippines. Day and time won't matter to us. It's the same sun wherever we are, the only thing in this world we'll each see at the same time. So please, watch the sun and always remember times we spent together. Would you do that for me? Please. I will be doing it for you. The sun will make me feel closer to you, not so far away. I'll imagine I am looking at the sun with you. And I'll pray its beams carry my love back to warm you in California."

"Oh, my." Henriette giggled. "The sun? Pray to the sun? Of course, the sun." She pointed at the horizon. "Certainly not swear by the moon, Artie."

He crinkled the paper in his hand. "I knew I shouldn't've—"

Henriette wrest the note and clutched it to her breast. She pressed her eyes closed. "O! Romeo. My Romeo! Swear not by the moon, the inconstant moon, that monthly changes in her circled orb, lest that thy love prove likewise variable." Her face glowed with aroused mischief.

"Huh?" he said.

"You big cornball. Shakespeare. My father made me read it on the train. Romeo and Juliet. Just like Artie and Henriette, a classic love story." She laughed aloud, placing her fingertips on his cheeks. "Mercy. I do love you so."

Artie's mouth parted. Before he could apologize for his boyish manifesto, she kissed him. Soft lips pressed hard on his.

She pulled away, her eyes flicking back and forth, searching into the windows of his soul. "My love will follow you like the sun.

I promise to pray for you too, my darling. And I'll even visit your minister in Petaluma. He can pray with me."

While they relished the sunset from the bluff, the steamer Ohio sailed into the bay. A raked stack billowed thick black smoke over two reefed masts. The aged ship appeared from a fogbank as an intruder scrabbling up from the underworld. Artie identified the vessel as the first of the troop transports.

San Francisco Harbor, vast enough to hold the fleets of the world's navies, shrank before Henriette's eyes. The lyrical poetry she savored with Artie moments before vanished. Reality closed in on her. She couldn't know that specific ship would be the villain to carry off the love of her life. But the dread poisoned her heart. It shriveled into a painful, unspoken premonition.

Onshore breezes curved coal-exhaust forward above the vessel. Henriette remarked, "The smoke looks like the stinger on a scorpion."

"That's no insect," Artie boasted, astonished. "The Army chartered those transports for twenty-five thousand dollars per month—each! They are sending so many of us that we're going over in seven expeditions. Some of those ships are coming all the way from the Atlantic."

She murmured, "Hell is empty and all the devils are here."

"What? Shakespeare again?"

Henriette nodded. "I wish I could pay their invoices to send them back."

"Send back my future? Pshaw. Can't be done." Artie pointed his guitar at the sluggish ship, as if lining up a bead with a rifle.

Until this point in their training, the men had been a raucous bunch. With the harbingers' steady arrival through the gate, the soldiers assumed a gloomier demeanor. Sober mobilization of the war machine infected the city.

Weeks later, on the day Ohio left port, pandemonium reigned before the 4,900 men of the third expedition boarded their ships.

Led by fife and drum, they marched five miles over cobblestones from Lombard Gate to Van Ness Avenue to the Market Street long wharf. Henriette awaited for them there.

Overjoyed crowds streamed from side streets. Cheering drowned the clink of tin cups hanging from haversacks and the impassioned pleas of mothers begging officers to take care of their boys. Teenage girls stuck California poppies in shoulder-slung rifles. Women flirted for forget-me-nots and they tore brass buttons from their heroes' jackets, slipping the trifles into their décolletage.

At the wharves, children pressed oranges into soldiers' hands. A military band excited crowds into a fever playing, "John Brown's Body." Frenzied bystanders hurled flowers and tossed flags when the parade arrived. The patriotic mania rose to such a pitch one errant flag impaled an eye of a soldier.

Amid the commotion, Artie stood at attention waiting to board his ship. Flinty and unsmiling, he took in the massive steel hulk dimensions. The bay splashed odor of decomposition against the pier and its hull. Sweat pooled beneath Artie's haversack. He wondered how the tule reed raft of his dreams grew into the monstrosity before him. With twenty-days training completed, he readied to sail off undaunted, unexperienced, and unprepared to fight abroad.

A soldier who stood next to him kicked his boot. Artie shot a sidelong glance at him. He nodded to redirect his glower to the crowd. Henriette knocked about in the mob. She rose on her toes and fell flatfooted, struggling to catch his attention. Artie raised his hand to shoulder height and waved a restrained farewell. He mouthed the words, "The sun."

Once she realized he found her, Henriette jumped with the abandon of a terrier, throwing him rapid kisses and forcing her way to the rope barrier that divided troops from well-wishers.

An Army lieutenant barked, "Mark time. March!"

Soldiers stamped in rhythmic response, ready to obey an imminent command to stride forward. Artie yelled, "I'll be home soon." While Thomas Edison's new motion picture camera whirred atop spindled tripod legs, Artie stole a last glance at his heart's desire. He stepped in synchrony with the army.

Henriette's eyes widened. Tears washed her face. She held the shoulder of a stranger for balance and screamed a word impossible to hear in the uproar. Artie distinguished the plea from the shape of her rosebud lips. She cried, "Stay!"

Through a boil of handkerchief flutters, soldiers under brimmed hats bumped up the gangway. The steep line shortened. A lighted human-fuse sizzled onto a crowded deck. The explosive salute they ignited engulfed Artie, the glorious summer of 1898.

A week after Dean had shipped out, Henriette traveled alone to Petaluma to pray with Artie's minister. In the manse, next door to the church, Henriette's sudden, uncontrolled trembling belied the true purpose of her pilgrimage—she needed to confide in someone. Henriette carried a baby. She told the minister it might not be Artie's, but she prayed the baby was his. And Artie did not know anything about it.

She and the minister kept their secret for weeks until her draped clothing no longer concealed her thickening features. Her father banished his disgraced daughter from his San Francisco home. Afterward, she sought help from the minister she trusted. He communicated with a rabbi in the city who introduced Henriette to a widowed heiress. Mrs. Jennie Valentine, née Forbes, hired Henriette as her chambermaid.

Henriette sobbed to her new employer, "You would take me on, despite my expecting a baby?"

"Maybe I want you working for me *because* of the baby," said Jennie. "The rabbi knows I'm alone and getting old now. I grew up in a Baltimore orphanage and, you see dear, I had no family. It doesn't seem so long ago that I, too, was a young woman lost in the city. I remember how it feels."

The doyenne of San Francisco Society had lived unmarried most of her life. She moved to California to work as a schoolteacher. After a brief, childless union to an older Thomas Bishop Valentine, Jennie inherited his vast real-estate holdings, including Belvedere Island in the San Francisco Bay. Before her husband died in 1896, alcoholism-driven melancholia led him to gamble away some of his scrip. He lost enough of it in poker games with timber barons to catch Jennie's attention. She hid from him the certificates that remained to stem his losses.

After the birth of Henriette's baby boy, Jennie showered the fatherless family with love denied to her in her marriage with Valentine.

BUFFA
February 5th, 1899

Spain surrendered a few months after the US Navy sank her fleet in Cuba and the Philippines. The Manila Bay battle around Cavite lasted two hours. When the United States Senate ratified the peace treaty, California, more than anywhere else in the world, commemorated the legal end of the war. Pacific domination made America a global power and the Golden Gate a busy portal to empire, the richest empire ever known.

The morning of Petaluma's celebration, Henriette gathered a sweater around her torso slathered with insulating petroleum jelly. Jennie Valentine granted her the day off to travel from San Francisco to the North Bay. Twelve hours before the troop train arrived in Petaluma, Henriette trudged the Market Street Slot. She leaned against winds to the Ferry Building. Although the Army had not yet scheduled the voyage home for Artie, his brother Leslie and the Petaluma militia, headed back from their Fruitvale camp near Oakland.

If she had to wait for Artie's return, Henriette at least hoped to find refreshed memories of him in his sibling's resemblances and in his town where they courted.

A ferry brought her north, humping waves to the Tiburon Pier train station. The heated coach had not arrived on the track when the ferry disembarked its passengers. Icy tines pricked through her woolen outerwear while she waited outside shivering.

Before her pregnancy, Henriette had flown along the same depot platforms during school vacations when she accompanied her father on his sales trips to Petaluma and Santa Rosa. She had carried his valises to the train. He had noticed how she thrilled seeing men appreciate her youthful allure the way they ogled powdered women. To keep her mind off their distractions, he had her read Shakespeare aloud to him during their long journeys.

On one visit to Petaluma, as her father presented samples of imported dry goods to a merchant, a buffoon who smelled of sawdust and musk jabbed her back with a broomstick. Ringlets, which hung thick as grape clusters, bounced as she spun to confront him. Henriette's glare met an apologetic young man whose thin cameo features and sad blue eyes dissolved her vexation. His slack-jaw hinted he had never seen, let alone ever touched, a girl as lovely as Henriette. He introduced himself as, "Arthur Dean—Artie."

In the time it took Artie to sputter he purchased brooms at the mercantile for his boss, her softening gaze smite his ardor. He suggested to her father he call on Mr. Byce to present his wares.

They stopped at the factory the next day. Artie showed Henriette agricultural devices he expected would feed the poor and hungry of the world. "It's the right thing to do. So many people have nothing, while we have so much. I just wish we could get these out the door and onto the lowboys faster for delivery. But my job is to make sure they work before we ship them. Still and all, it gives me a good feeling."

"Are you religious?"

Well, kind of. I play guitar for the youth group in church. My minister preaches us that the Bible says, 'Inasmuch as ye have done it unto one of the least of these my brethren, ye have done it unto me.'"

"*Tikkun Olam,*" Henriette said, smiling.

"I don't know what that mean, but it sure sounds pretty coming from your mouth." He handed her a fresh-hatched chick. "I hope it's my future."

And she fell in love.

While Henriette waited at Tiburon, that memory warmed her from long before this winter morning. Frigid air blasting off the bay leaked through the weave in her clothes. As she bent her torso from the chill, the baby rolled on her inflamed bladder. Henriette clutched her stomach. Her arms undergirded the strain until an engine hissed into the station.

Though the winter sunrise cast a melancholy light, the morning aurora comforted her. Wherever her Artie took in the brighter side of his tropical sun, he lived in their tomorrow.

Henriette negotiated high steps to the coach. A middle-aged man on the aisle stood, allowing her to wedge into his row.

"Please sit here."

She touched her heart in gratitude and aligned her weight in front of the seat.

The man peered at her back and removed his derby. "When's the blessed event?"

Henriette frowned at her midsection. "I guess I don't hide it well, do I?"

"No. Oh dear me, no. I suppose not." He snapped taut the waist of his vest. "Honestly? No. Not at all."

"I must look like a reefed mainsail." She managed a weary laugh and sighed. "End of March, possibly early April. I feared my baby might have arrived before the train."

Henriette lowered onto the seat. "It feels grand to sit."

The man's face drew together around taught lips, unbent at the corners. "My wife would never travel when with child."

"I wouldn't recommend it," Henriette replied with a tired smile. The wooden seatback pushed on her spine. She gazed out the window, hoping they soon moved so steam heat flowed to the coaches from the locomotive. The train started. Clashes of steel blocked the man's reply. Henriette turned. "What was that?"

He removed his hat and condemned her with a level stare, "I said, Madam, it's not the Christian way to behave."

"Oh. It clearly isn't the smartest thing I've ever done."

"What church—" Another jolt rocked him half a step. He held the seatback corner for balance until the train rattled to a steady beat. "I say, are you a Baptist?"

She slanted perplexed. "I'm not Christian."

"Didn't think so." Spikes of hair stood in clumps, as if stalagmites had crystalized under his hat on a rock-hard head.

Henriette gathered her wraps. "Perhaps I should move."

"Keep the seat, young woman."

She rasped, drawing on the last reservoirs of her strength. "I'm sorry."

"Why aren't you confined?"

Henriette struggled to rise. "It was the first coach."

"Your husband should be ashamed."

Henriette stopped and squinted hard at the man. Sunlight poured through dirty windows behind him. "Of me?" Her hip joints ached and her legs weighed heavy with fatigue.

"Of himself." His voice rose. "Even a Jew should know better."

The life within Henriette twisted, reminding her of the acute pressure on her lower abdomen.

"A decent husband should have forbidden you to leave his home in your vulgar condition."

Her calf muscles cramped into a knot. "Ow," she moaned.

"Perhaps, I am unfair to the baby's father. Yes? Maybe you're not in a connubial relationship and I spoke out of turn."

Aches caused her to turn from the man, shifting her weight back on the seat. Swollen hands stretched and clutched under her knees. Henriette lifted her left leg. She took a breath and lifted her right, extending her feet to where the man had sat on the bench. Her dress slipped. The exposure uncovered strong legs beneath gray cotton stockings.

"I was sitting there," he said.

Henriette leaned forward and labored to untie her laces. She pulled off a high-ankle shoe. Its solid heel turned toward the faultfinder. "The day my *husband* marches up Market Street with Admiral Dewey, I'll be sure he thanks you for your kindly intended advice. Your name is—Mr.?"

"You people should wander back to where you belong."

"I asked your name, sir."

He jammed his derby on with a pop. "Jesus killers aren't welcome here. Turn around and go to the city. Stay there." The man stormed up the aisle toward the exit, his hat tipped to the side, expecting other passengers to applaud him.

Seen through the salted lenses of tears, the bigot's figure pooled into an inky blur and trickled into the next coach.

Despite her tribulations, the journey remained worthwhile. Petaluma embodied the best location for Henriette to celebrate the end of the Spanish American War. Reminders of Artie's spirit and love lingered in the town. The Senate had ratified the Treaty of Paris that day, marking the legal cessation of hostilities between the United States and Spain. Everyone in America assumed fighting had ended. Peace reigned.

Henriette trusted Artie would soon return, meet the infant shifting in her womb, and they'd become a family. She envisioned their names penned in fine script on Presbyterian Church marriage documents. Artie had promised he spoke to his minister about his marriage proposal. The minister counseled him that if he married an Israelite it did not concern him, or the church. Artie never knew the secret Henriette later confessed to the same minister: she carried a baby before he went overseas.

During the later hours she waited at Petaluma Depot, a waning Wolf Moon sailed with Jupiter and Venus over Sonoma Mountain. Beyond dazzled hayfields, frozen solid as iron, smudge pots blazed holes in the frosted air. A stranger might mistake them for vagabond encampments climbing the orchard slopes.

Red rockets, whizzing from a distant landing, caught her attention. Slow rumbles of a train braking for the bridge electrified the throng that had gathered while she mused. From atop Clay Hill, the Civil War cannon "Dog of War" answered the rocket's signal with an emphatic boom from its brass barrel. Church bells pealed jubilant hosannas.

At exactly seven o'clock, the town band struck up patriotic airs. Factory steam-whistles shrieked the cry of scalded dragons. Henriette's arms muffled her swollen abdomen. A flag-adorned locomotive thundered into the depot, parting a dense wall of sound. Soldiers stood on the engine and waived from passenger car windows as they shouted responses to the spirited welcome.

Henriette flinched as a bright blast from a gunpowder mound spun an anvil skyward in a fountain of yellow flame. The revelry thumped sharp and uncomfortable on her breast. Above the din, full-throated huzzahs welcomed the soldiers.

Men disembarked after the trill of an officer's whistle dismissed them. The heroes' precise march met the crowd surge. They blunted against a raucous mass of milling revelers, military indistinguishable from civilian.

Henriette rose from a waiting room bench and embraced Leslie. She kissed him, imagining she held his older sibling. "Welcome home soldier."

He picked her up and swung her around a tight circle. "Henriette. What a smooch." Leslie returned kisses on her cheeks salty with exuberant tears. "Whoa! You really have grown." He placed her feet on the ground and covered his mouth. His campaign hat rolled, exposing his forehead arched in bewilderment. "I meant grown up."

Henriette giggled. "I should cuff you, but I'm too happy."

He poked an enormous protrusion pressing under her coat and staggered backward. His haversack squashed into revelers jostling behind him. Leslie pointed at her midsection. "Are you?"

Henriette cried anew, nodding her head in affirmation.

"My brother never told me."

"He doesn't know. I didn't want Artie to have to worry about another thing, or feel trapped." Her hand trembled as it pressed in her rumpled coat. "Maybe he'll hate me. Don't I look awful? —I am awful."

"Oh, no! I forbid you to say that." Leslie hugged her again. "Artie will be in heaven."

Henriette burrowed her head into his shoulder strap. She sobbed. "I hope so."

Crowds streamed from the train station as he stroked Henriette's hair. "Be happy tonight. The new daddy will be home with us soon."

She smiled and wiped her sniffles away with the back of her glove. Buttermilk glow from gas lamps illuminated her face. "Well, at least the damn war has ended." She rubbernecked over his shoulder at the mob. Hats, packs, and torches eddied toward downtown. "The world is gay everywhere. Isn't it? Peace is gay!"

"Yes it is."

"My Artie will be home soon."

"Yes. There's no reason to cry." Leslie smiled. "Look at all the stars."

"They're so lovely," said Henriette. "Perfect and lovely. But wait. I have more news to share. And I should have told you it first. This is all so embarrassing—backward and all that. However, if I don't tell you, I might burst."

"Fill me in quick. Then we can go celebrate."

Henriette blurted, "Before he shipped out, Artie asked me to marry him!"

"And for me to stand as his best man." Leslie laughed and hugged her. "I knew *that* much. You'll be my kid sister."

"You must make it our secret. Promise you will. I'm scared of your mother's disapproval."

"Keep your distance until Artie squares things up." Leslie scrutinized the crowd of heads. "But don't worry about it tonight. She won't be here. Pop's chilblains are acting up."

"And she doesn't know?"

"Not a hint." He scratched his ear. "Still, it'll be easier to visit when Artie returns."

She drew from her purse a cardboard-framed photograph taken in Manila. The image showed Artie in a corporal's ceremonial, white uniform, girdled in military buckles, straps, and leggins. As he had warned Henriette, he felt uncomfortable baring his emotions in his illegible longhand writing. She relied on John Pitts for insights into Artie's exotic new world. Letters flew back and forth between her and his high school chum.

"I received this in the post this week after I sent him a ten-page letter and an asphidity belly band to keep those jungle diseases away. No note, the photograph is all I got. It's a heavenly miracle that Artie sent even this much. But that's sour grapes. He's coming home soon. Oh, isn't he divine?"

Leslie slid his arm under hers. "Later, little sister." He patted her hand. "There's a party for me on Main Street. We don't want to miss a moment."

Henriette glanced at her treasure before returning it to the purse.

Leslie shouldered a path for them through a sea of merrymakers. Wooden crate bonfires roared at each intersection, lifting hung bunting from buildings in graceful streamers of stars and stripes. Rascals wove through hailstorms of sparks while mobs jigged to snap-flashes of fireworks and beating drums.

Men carried tall torches strapped with slender hoses. They blew clouds of lycopodium through the tubes into the flames. The ignited powder flared brilliant red fireballs. Parisians often triggered similar flamethrowers at their Grand Opera House, pumping lightning jets over a darkened stage. On this night, the hellish illumination bathed not an enthralled Parisian audience and their troupe, but giddy Petaluma players, unwitting actors in an opera buffa of their own.

At that hour in Manila, on February 5, 1899, across the International Dateline, the day the Spanish American War ended, Corporal Dean jumped to a commander's whistle. He rose in a skirmish line, marching quick time up a sweltering slope toward a bamboo thicket. Widening strides moved refreshing breezes through his unbuttoned shirt. He stole glances at the sun. A camouflaged trench, resembling a bear hunter's pit in Alta California, appeared at his feet. Black powder grime on his chest offset a glint from a silver cross necklace. Henriette had given him the jewelry at Sutro Baths. It fixed a bright target.

A shot!

Spiraling lead whistled from a Mauser barrel to his exposed torso. A 7mm bullet pierced him with the precision of a slender dowel, knocking him back with the heft of a mill-sized sack of chicken feed. He blinked in disbelief. Above and to the right of the cross, a dark-red hole with a tiny flap of skin tucked into a neat dimple. Around the wound smoked a puckered weal. It appeared as if someone flipped a white coal on his breast.

Nervous giggles preceded the tang of blood flooding his mouth. Artie's lips breathed, "Henrie—"

Another shot!

It bore into his cheek with savage velocity. The back of his head hit his spine between his shoulder blades. Bloody saliva arced high.

Artie lurched, stepping low and forward, as though he sought to congratulate the shooters. His outstretched hand danced an odd, spastic flutter.

Arthur Lloyd Dean collapsed facing Filipino gunners he believed he had liberated.

While his lifeblood puddled on steamy foreign soil, far away in the frigid, pastoral valley of his home, crimson revelry flushed on the cheeks of Henriette.

Word of Artie's death arrived three days later. The news crashed on Petaluma. A rose-covered cottage on Fair Street went dark. Mournful church bells tolled, and the incubator company extinguished its boilers. Inside the quiet factory, Leslie burrowed his head in his arms. He and the apprentice who replaced Artie, wept at the workstation above the slough. Several hours passed before Leslie could bear to go home to face his mother.

The Petaluma Daily Courier's headline read: *FELL AT MANILA*.

A series of sub headlines and doleful reports relayed the news.

Arthur Dean of Petaluma, One of the Heroes Who Died Fighting for Old Glory.

Fell before the savage onslaught of the Filipinos.

The news has cast a gloom over the city. The parents were prostrated by the news, and the mother who was continually worried over the safety of her boy, can scarcely be made to realize her son's death.

Young Dean was a quiet, unassuming young man, a regular attendant at the Presbyterian Church and was esteemed by all who knew him.

The blow comes unusually severe as the war fighting was supposed to have been all over, and our boys on foreign shores, safe from danger.

A terse military report listed Corporal Dean's effects for the Army archives.

Late a Corporal who died in action near Manila PI on the five day of February, 1899 by reason of gunshot through the heart, and was buried at Battery Knoll Cemetery, Manila PI.

Inventory: watch, brown canvas coat, leather purse, nightcap, Specie $1.50, Spanish Phrase Book, Guitarra Method in Spanish Book, White Helmet, Campaign Hat, Guitar.

All sold at auction.

A captain volunteered a personal, handwritten epitaph into the file.

Remarks Service, Honest, and Faithful.

Americans had assumed the fight concluded in victory—a mission accomplished—but the worst Pacific war savagery had just begun.

Henriette endured her grief in solitude at Valentine's Baldwin Hotel penthouse in San Francisco. On the Atlantic coast, President McKinley nibbled sweet pastries as he read casualty lists in the morning paper.

The steady arrival of letters from Pitts to Henriette stopped soon after Artie's death. She received the last message in April.

VALENTINES DAY
February 14th, 1900

One year and nine days after America descended into the madness of the Philippine-American War, Kevin Corcoran ran from the San Francisco Presidio YMCA vestibule. He headed to the cemetery to report a military funeral for his newspaper. Soldiers waiting by caissons restrained spooked horses as he raced by their teams. A lone woman yards away from the building followed him. They settled a discreet distance from the cemetery's open graves and from each other. She breasted the sun without acknowledging Corcoran's presence.

Fingering a tweed brim, he set his cap on a defiant angle across his brow and recorded his observations. He had noticed the woman avoided the Petaluma crowd that gathered at the YMCA for the funeral. She had kept masked behind an expensive mantilla and turned from the Dean family. Corcoran wondered if the nose of death and rotting salt marsh seeped under the veils of rich women who concealed their pain from the world.

The azure winter sky, ankle-high wild strawberries stretching from the bluestone rubble wall, thousands of saplings sprouting from sand hills, a glistening bay, and the heaven-kissed, emerald headlands encompassed a cruel backdrop for a solitary lady in mourning clothes, he wrote.

Northeast of the cemetery, a fleet of exhausted transports swung at anchor. Before them, docked at the Black Point pier, Ohio off-loaded coffins disinterred from Manila cemeteries. The Army had painted its hull aspirin-white. Two summers before, the former oil-drum dark steamer had slipped in a fog bank carrying Corporal Dean away to the Philippines.

Corcoran had last seen the brutish ship in June 1898. The *hoom-hoom-hoom* of propellers wedged its prow through a flotilla of saluting watercraft. On board, 1,033 adventurous men crammed deck and rigging.

Harried Mare Island workers, trained to build gunships, had converted Ohio from a commercial workhorse to a primitive troop carrier. The ill-designed retrofit and the incompetent loading of the holds left commodities needed for passage buried under tons of cargo. Sixty crestfallen men listed on the manifest did not fit on board and had to stay at Camp Merritt.

Farther offshore, Hancock rocked with bodies of 462 dead soldiers. In a few days, Indiana would dock, carrying 200 more in its hold. Soldiers stacked off-loaded caskets by the hundreds on the wharf. On every train they departed, freighted east. More dead arrived to replace vacated spots along the Black Point cove. If a poor family could not afford to bring their loved one home, the Army buried him in a clustered, daily service witnessed by strangers.

One corporal and eight privates had escorted Artie's body to the YMCA by Lombard Gate. A twenty-four-hour honor guard of blue clad, white-gloved sentinels posted around the building.

Corcoran scribbled: *The Army has converted the YMCA, which once exemplified a high church of youthful vitality, into a morgue for dead young men.*

After he jotted his notes, he flipped the pad from his right hand to the left and tipped his hat. The standoffish woman provided a story opportunity. She might be a source of filler material. Charming glints sparkled in his eye and he smiled. "Good day to you, ma'am. Kevin Corcoran. I'm a reporter from the Petaluma Courier."

Henriette gazed beyond him and did not answer.

With his cap held over his heart, he said, "Sorry, ma'am. I can't hear you from under your shroud."

The veil rose. "Henriette Rosenthal." Something shifted under her shawl, high on her shoulder.

He glanced at the ground. Beads of fine sand slithered low over the soil. White grains piled into snowy windrows outlining the empty, dug graves. "Hope I didn't disturb you, ma'am. I was afraid I might have to jump into one of those ditches to get your attention."

"A cemetery is not the place for shenanigans, Mr. Corcoran. Even an Irisher should respect that."

He glared back and mocked her in a quiet, caricatured brogue. "Deary me. You be knowing I'm as American as you are, missus. Do you work here?"

She paled and paused before answering. A painful expression narrowed her face into a wedge. Her cheekbones rose to where a gemstone-tear weighed on her lashes. "I hate this place."

"Very well, then."

Soft baby cooing came from under Henriette's fluttering wrap.

"Och." He slapped his forehead. "I didn't realize. Bad manners weren't called for, ma'am." He stepped backward, wishing he might stumble into a grave and have the earth swallow him.

Henriette dismissed his apology, concentrating instead on a bundle of folded papers that stabbed her skin. An epistolary of the war years, every letter from Pitts, and Artie's sunset vow penned in unsteady hand, pinched between her blouse and her heart. A letter from the top of the stack, the longest letter she carried, read:

My Dearest Henriette,

By the time you get this letter, you will already have heard our best friend Artie was killed in battle. No words of mine could make you, or me, feel better. But please know he died like a hero, brave and fighting for God and America.

I'll write as much as I can before we pack up. I'm part of a big expedition that's heading from San Pedro Macati up the Pasig River to a town called Santa Cruz. I wish you could see our splendid forces. There are the river gunboats, Laguna de Bay, Napindan, and Oeste, together with six steam launches for towing the troop's 15 cascos coming with me.

If this letter has to end all of a sudden like, it's because a postal carrier is leaving soon and I have to make sure you get something from me. I tried to write this twice but my hand trembled too much.

The night the shooting that killed Artie began, we thought we couldn't lose and the whole mess would be over before we had our beans for lunch. Yet, here it is almost April and I head upriver to give another spanking to the enemy.

We found out soon after we arrived, these niggers lived no better than ours did. The Kansas boys call them Indians. Chinese say the Filipinos are too small to be men, but they're too big to be monkeys. Knowing the people who were our little brown brothers murdered Artie makes his death even more awful for me.

The night the fighting started, Artie and I enjoyed a fine circus. We had to leave in a hurry when bullets ripped up the canvas tent. Citywide firefights broke out and Artie died before the next evening.

No one slept the dark night it began. We were on guard for arson, or cut water pipes. We couldn't wait until sunrise so we could attack. I helped Artie's unit roll their two cannons up in the dark to support the assault ordered on La Loma Church.

The morning light showed the American lines marked by red flags to help the naval ships separate friend and foe. They were barely off shore. Dewey's boys zeroed in on the enemy.

Imagine what a start it would be to have the US Navy fleet glaring at you before breakfast? That must have been a crowing, Petaluma cock's morning eye-opener for them!

Our guns boomed the scariest thunder you ever heard, tearing the air with such fiendish howls my head ached. Barrel-bodied devils flew through the sky. You could only be made out over the guns if you shouted. Those beautiful, giant steel ships sat abreast the beach, crisscross to the enemy lines manned with savages carrying bows and arrows. Gunners almost had to tilt their barrels down because they were so close. They laid into them good, blasting cannon shells and canister POINT BLANK into the closest trenches.

What pieces the big shells left behind, the rattle of the quick-firing Maxims took care of. They sounded like the rapid click of hay machines on a hot Petaluma day. And it felt plenty hot and steamy. We didn't care. We fought during the heat just the same. This shocked the natives who learned from the lazy Spanish how to fight. Or, I should say, not fight. They were told soldiers rested during the day. Ha! We woke them from their siestas with well-aimed rifle volleys. Their random return shots went wild. They are the most wretched shots. All of us chased them, and they fled like crickets before a fire.

But I guess some savage got lucky with Artie.

You should know Ernest H. Ward volunteered to retrieve his body while he risked his own life.

Artie told me, if anything happened, he wanted you to have his guitar. I hate to tell you this. They auctioned it before I could get it for you.

The handwriting flow quickened.

It looks like it's time to pack and line up. Just one last thought. Some things happen for a reason. When I come back home, I have a big question I want to ask you. Until then, be kind to my chickens.
John

A bell pealed by the parade ground. Henriette flinched. Her eyes cast toward the Civil War chapel.

"A sad day ma'am—sad for all of us. For whom do you await?"

"A soldier. A friend who used to write to me from the Philippines. He stopped writing when his heart was broken. We lost a dear friend in battle. I expect he's come home with his Honor Guard."

"Very likely. There's quite a crowd headed our way."

"Have you seen John Pitts among them? Do you know him? He's also from Petaluma."

"Pitts?" Corcoran's voice lowered. "The first caisson is for a Minnesota boy—"

"Pitts wouldn't be in *his* Honor Guard."

"However … the next two are our Petaluma boys."

"Boys?" said Henriette, shaking her head. "You must have meant boy. Two Minnesotans and one Petaluma boy. You misspoke."

"Beg your pardon, again, ma'am. The second caisson is Corporal Dean's."

"That's where he should be marching."

"And the third caisson is for Private Pitts."

Neither of them breathed until Henriette moaned. Corcoran put his hand out to catch her, fearing she would fall to the side. "Private Pitts died last April at the Battle of Santa Cruz. It's been in all the newspapers, ma'am."

She buried her face in her shawl, sobbing. "I haven't touched one of your damn newspapers after Artie's name …."

"Yes." Corcoran removed his hat. "Mighty sorry, ma'am. Life goes by before we know what it is."

At the chapel, a deacon pulled a rope and inverted the church bell into its stays. The ringing stopped. Whir and pound of drums from the Presidio Band shattered the short and foreboding silence. A military funeral dirge began. Corcoran turned and walked to the knoll above the gravesite. He spat on loamy soil and ground the sputum with his shoe. After he scratched his ear tip with a lead pencil, he opened a pad to add notes to those he wrote at the YMCA.

Henriette positioned herself by a tree. Scores of unfilled graves gaped at her, a ghoulish nest of open-beaked chicks impatient for grubs. For the rest of her life, white marble conflated with plangent music sickened her.

A detail of infantrymen, paced to woeful horns, filed through iron gates. The ground resonated with the rumble of heavy wheels and the tramp of feet. Marchers followed the post chaplain, head bowed in prayer on a mule-drawn ambulance. Three flag-draped caissons ridden by artillerymen, a mounted corporal in charge of each piece, followed. Six military pallbearers marched beside the caskets. Mourners in carriages and on foot, idle soldiers, and curious spectators swarmed in the gate.

Gloomy events unfolded. The next day the newspaper ran Corcoran's story derived from his jottings:

Every flag in Petaluma at half-staff Wednesday.

The Pitts family went down on first train, and Dean family on 8:30 train.

Wagonloads of wreaths, bouquets, and set pieces sent to San Francisco by townsfolk.

Rumors an anonymous woman church member donated funds for a memorial window at First Pres.

Funeral scheduled at two o'clock—best light.

First casket lowered into earth bears the name Arthur L. Dean, Corporal. Another follows. John W. Pitts, Private, placed beside his old chum. A third follows, and the name is Earl W. Osterhout, First Nebraska Volunteers.

The Rifle Squad wheels to a sharp command of their officer. Three loud volleys ring out and echo from vale to vale. It occurs so often now mockingbirds do not cease their warbling.

Dull clods of soil clattered on the caskets. Corcoran peered from his pad. He recognized Leslie Dean in his Petaluma Militia uniform. Leslie held his mother to prevent her collapse. He averted his anguish from his brother's graveside ceremony and looked toward a tree. Corcoran followed his line of sight to where their eyes met on Henriette. She had retreated farther from the gathered mourners and hid behind another Cypress. Her sodden mantilla cupped into her mouth and clung to her face. Each man shrunk at the bent figure cradling a child with one hand and holding up a crinkled piece of paper with the other.

Artie's handwritten declaration of love stretched toward the sun.

Corcoran added a conclusion lengthwise on his pad: *An angel has graced my life.*

Years later, the young mother married Burton Feldman, a respected Jewish attorney. He adopted her out-of-wedlock son and gave him his religious faith and his last name, calling him Arthur Dean Feldman.

While on her deathbed, Jennie Valentine gave newly married Henriette the scrip she had stolen from her deceased husband, Thomas Valentine. She warned Henriette to keep the secret inheritance as her sole property, and not to let anyone learn she had it, nor share it with Burton Feldman.

"Stash the scrip so the wealth stays in your son's bloodline. Don't trust your husband. You are my family. Conceal it where no one will look to find it."

Illusions of coincidences, many and large, had cloaked the lives of Artie and Henriette. When their fates intersected with the destiny of an ambitious young woman, a Pandora's Box of Valentine Scrip opened.

SCRIP
1920s

Ida Jewell Cason's father arbitraged prices of winter wheat bushels. He bought the bargain and sold the dear between the Kansas City Board of Trade and the Pacific Futures Exchange. With his profitable investments, he parlayed million-dollar gains into sailing vessels, a manor home south of San Francisco, and a reclusive widower's life on his estate with his only child, a cosseted daughter.

After he died, Ida revamped her bluenose persona. She adopted flapper fashions of knee-high hemlines, deep-red lipsticks drawn in Cupid's bows, and Dutch-bobbed hair slicked over her ears. Conspicuous glamour suited her tastes. She threw away years of tutored refinement and turned a spotlight on herself, opening her mansion doors to the world. The striking, the fashionable, and the scandalous of San Francisco floated in on clouds of aspirated colognes. Spontaneous coteries slipped away to bedrooms for guiltless couplings—and groupings. With tittering laughs, they described their carefree unions as, "*Barney-muggings.*" The Roaring Twenties encouraged shameless lusts, and Cason Mansion offered boundless opportunities to fulfill them.

Arthur Dean Feldman, son of Henriette Rosenthal-Feldman, followed his stepfather Burton Feldman into his successful law practice. Young, handsome, and raised in the tony Pacific Heights of San Francisco, he made Ida Cason's list of orgy invitees. Early in his career, he had earned an excellent reputation as a California real-property attorney. Although a devout member of his conservative temple, he enjoyed a reputed weakness for WASP women. Their temptations shimmied in abundance at Ida's parties.

Whispers that Feldman had mysterious, real-estate charms meant little to Ida. He presented to her a standoffish, arrogant face; though, if seen in diffused light, an alluring softness in his blue eyes made him a worthy sexual partner. She enjoyed that gauzy side of him under her silk bedsheet covers.

Over time, Ida bored with her domestic amusements and entanglements. She yearned for ventures beyond the cypresses bordering her property. While tossing aside magazines on a coffee table, she saw a Time report that ownerships of private islands had become a popular vanity for East Coast affluent.

East Coast? Why not Westerners? Ida sulked to herself. *If dour Easterners can play on their own islets, then I can, too.*

For Ida, desires lived not as insipid fantasies born and discarded with flips of glossy magazine pages. Ida thrived on the impulse of her passions. For with her father's fortune, she inherited his audacity to take risks—a trait not condoned in women of society.

She telephoned Arthur Dean Feldman and explained her new itch. "I want an island."

"Whose?"

"My own. You're a real-estate expert. Do you know of any available?"

"Maybe. Where are you interested? Maine? Florida?"

"*Lawd*, no. The East Coast is so yesterday."

"Washington?"

"Mexico, probably. They have no use for all their little islands."

111

"I suspect the Mexicans have already accounted for them. And a gringa would not be a particularly welcome neighbor."

"Just watch me. I'll find a great spot down there. When I do, I want you to handle the *blah-blah* work required."

"You mean the title."

"I mean for you to get paid to help me and not to lecture me."

"Call me when you plant your flag."

In 1925, Ida set sail alone in her yawl, San Salvador, through the Golden Gate to the impoverished nation of Mexico. She intended to cajole government officials to part with one of their insignificant Pacific island possessions. The long cruise hugged the coast and sheltered in California ports. Fair winds and following seas propelled her onward.

Eager to get south of the border, she dropped her sails at an overnight destination, Avalon Bay on the large Channel Island of Santa Catalina.

A moored fisherman helped her find wind-protected anchorage. She wound her lines, covered the canvas, and secured her vessel. Once she stowed the equipment, Ida two-finger whistled the tuna fisherman to come aboard San Salvador. She shouted through her megaphone an offer to share a drink as a gesture of her appreciation. He saluted and hurried over to meet her.

Gripping a cleat to relieve a chronic hip pain, he eased into her boat. Maritime odors of diesel fuel and dried fish guts thickened the surrounding air. Sun-bleached hair and whiskers resembling artichoke fibers swirled around his leathered neckline.

"This here cripplin' is from me standing on a steel deck too long."

"Land sakes—" Ida caught herself and giggled. "*Sea* Sakes? Why, bless your heart, you're an authentic seaman."

Gray-green eyes, faded as old glass net floats hung on a barroom wall, widened. "Authentic? Hmm." He rumbled deep in his chest. "Is that a two-dollar word you slick San Franciscans use for ugly?"

A pang of embarrassment surprised Ida. His unvarnished presentation beguiled her. Stammering, she said, "I'm not that brazen. I meant *weathered*."

A smile split his face flaked with dried skin. "Keep reeling in those fancy descriptions till you get to calling me a chum bucket. Then you can gaff me. No need for courtesies, captain, it's your boat." He crinkled a wink at her. "I'm likable enough, but don't be fretting, young lady. I don't kiss on the first date."

Ida's face relaxed with a knowing grin. "Pity," she whispered in flirtatious confidence, "In San Francisco, I've got a reputation for never stopping at a kiss."

"Whoa. Ho! What sea mermaid have I hauled in here?"

An eyebrow sloped over her eye. "Ida. One of a kind."

"Sweet as apple cider," he sang. "Indeed, you are. Indeed, you are." He puckered his lips and hummed while tugging on his nose. "Hmm, hmm, hmm. Well, dear—*lady*." He snapped a salute. "Let me be a lesson to you. Don't spend your life on the sea. This miserable face is what happens to you when you waste your youth staring into water brighter than you are."

She set a coquettish pout. "Than I am?"

"No, no. That's not what I meant." He cackled and slapped his knee. "But you already crossed me. You stole my wind. See, the ocean has made me stupid. Don't ever marry a fisherman."

His gusto lifted Ida's spirits. "Noted." She punched her fists on her hips and leaned to his face. "May I try to at least drink like one?"

"Drink?" Her feminine gaze lured him. "Like a fisherman?"

"Yes, drink. Like the saltiest of old salts. San Salvador's ballast is half-filled with hooch."

"Ho. Hoo! Sure. I'll show you how to drink as if you've got a wooden leg. Set 'em up."

They drank amber rum and fresh squeezed juice from grapefruits stowed for her journey. She told him of her quest for an island. And he told her tales of the Pacific, the ultimate frontier of the mighty West. He described how monstrous waves pushed from the Gulf of Alaska, rose on the shallow banks near the Channel Islands, and tossed defiant thunder back at the sky. He spoke of when Manila galleons, filled with priceless booty from Eastern Asia, sheltered from Pacific storms on Santa Catalina. Stories jigged from the grand sweep of history to the petty behavior of celebrities, spinning yarns of scandalous Hollywood visits to the islands. The monologue ended with absurd local myths. Before he completed his final tattle, they had committed the last grapefruit rind to a solemn burial in the deep. The remaining rum, which swirled in the bottle base, they gulped straight.

The fisherman rolled his head in one direction, then back in the other. "Are you drunk?"

"Pissed. Boiled as an owl."

"Me, too, even *pissed-er-ed-er*." He waived his hand. "Don't let that gull you. I've got a mind like a leaky copper bottom."

They shared a chuckle.

"Don't go and spring a leak now. We have more rum." The last of it sloshed into his cup and onto the deck. "Tell me more about treasure ships. Tell me tales of pirates long ago."

A dark pall descended over his face. "All right. I'll tell you of pirates. But real pirates, and not from long ago. Marauders are here today."

"Oh, scary."

"Heed me. What I'm about to say is true."

"Aye, aye, Blackbeard." The empty bottle flipped over her shoulder into the water. "Or should I say, Whitebeard? La-di-da."

"Pirates are bad luck."

"*Ish kabibble*! I don't believe in pirates and I don't believe in luck."

"That's makes for dangerous sailing." The fisherman's puffed eyelids narrowed, staying on the bottle until its bobbing neck slipped under waves. "Don't doubt me. Not all pirates are on the water. And without some luck, none of us could leave shore. You may have more luck than most and not even enjoy it."

Ida inched forward to understand the sailor's thick enunciations. Her head tilted to the side, deflecting breeze in her ears. She shouted over slapping rigging, "Make it short. I sober up fast."

The fisherman caught the tide of his thoughts. He told her of a legend that a guano-covered islet in San Pedro Channel, between the mainland and Santa Catalina, belonged to no sovereign nation. "The pirates would love to take it. But it's just there."

"Darling, everything, and everyone, is owned by somebody."

He coughed. "It's a sleeper."

"A what?"

"A sleeper. A piece of land that belongs to the government, but the Washington bureaucrats don't recognize it's there."

"They don't know an island's there?"

"No they don't. No government does. What's more, it should be open to homestead." He crunched from his pocket a greasy receipt for ice and fuel oil. "Here, I'll show you its location." He sketched on its back and slipped the crumbled paper between Ida's knee and elbow. "A gift from me to you, an authentic treasure map from an authentic seaman. Don't let the pirates get it."

"My, my, Captain Hook. This map is indeed a great gift. What's in it for you?"

He removed his hat and scratched his scalp. "I don't want the bastard pirates to have it."

Ida teed her chin on her cupped hand like a golf ball. "Who may those big bad pirates be?"

"Pirate Wrigley and his mates. All these robber barons think they're entitled to their own land and any on their borders."

"Oh, fiddle-faddle! Mr. Wrigley's a fine man of high station. He owns every piece of land that breaks water here. You're tattling that scuttlebutt because of those nasty whispers he's funding the Chicago KKK—"

He cut her off. "Doesn't matter to me."

"Nor me," said Ida.

"What does matter is, hell, his kind has looted almost every acre of California from the people."

"Little people don't need an island. And I'm sure Mr. Wrigley would be more than content if he just owned Santa Catalina," she said. "It's big enough for him"

"Uh-uh. A pirate can't be satisfied. Wrigley and his pals would take more land but they don't think there's any left. Well, they're off beam. They have a snootful of education that's beyond their brains. This here island is hidden right under their pointy, green eye-shaded noses."

Ida pulled the man's thick palm into hers. "You're a dear. And you're sure generous for a first date. But let's be honest, this tale is grog talking."

He withdrew his hand. "Young lady, I covet nobody's property or no nothin'. I just want to make sure pirates don't get it. I ain't planning to live forever. The few years left for me I'll spend on the water. There's one way to come into this world—"

"Yup. We all make the same entrance."

"But I'm choosin' how the hell I go out. Before then, I don't want no part of spending my life in bait-trap courts fighting with lawyers of rich men. Your sails are better reefed for those heavy seas than are mine. Besides, I like you."

His somber tone surprised Ida, hastening her sobriety. "I'll keep this treasure map framed in my cabin to remind me of our intimate night together." She flattened the paper on her thigh. "You, Captain, are the real treasure."

Ida couldn't recall ever being alone with a man and enjoying his company as much without having a carnal thrill. His tall stories recompensed for the rum, and his absurd legend provided her thorough entertainment.

He left the yawl, and Ida studied the map. The small island he identified on the crude chart as White Rock Island rose near busy Fishermans Cove. Everyone assumed chewing-gum magnate, William Wrigley, Jr., owned the island and the outcroppings around it as part of his private domain. A businessman who paid close attention to detail, Wrigley belonged in the pantheon of astute corporate titans. He purchased Santa Catalina Island because it ranked as one of the most valuable pieces of property in the world.

How ludicrous, she thought. *The well-meaning old sailor, undoubtedly, is misguided. Wrigley must hold title to White Rock Island. Surely, he did.*

Her inquisitive nature trumped her skepticism. She inspected the island that evening despite her rum-addled condition. Ida coaxed her small outboard motor to circle it twice.

Under the floodlights of San Salvador, cobalt waters reflected a marine paradise. She drew in salty-sweet night breeze. Birds, which resembled military couriers carrying urgent dispatches, shot from the island. Castle pennants of plankton glowed and sparkled beneath the waves. Porpoises spun from the inky ocean surface, bursting from one fluid paradise into another.

Despite the natural glory surrounding its shoreline, not much on the island captivated Ida. The topography comprised two barren acres of guano chalked tableland covered with stunted malva rosa and prickly pear. A beetle-browed cliff bulged at one end and the terrain sloped to a natural pool. Ida couldn't find a cove to set anchor.

With the moonrise over the silver flanks of neighboring Santa Catalina, she considered the intangibles. She might own an enigmatic island in America—not Mexico—a property that oozed with the snob value of Wrigley as its neighbor. It titillated her imagination. As the sea pulsed, Ida's blood pumped with a timeless meter begun at creation. It was her heartbeat. She wouldn't let any man take it away.

Back at her mooring, Ida collapsed in her bunk. She thought it senseless not to make inquiries about the property's availability. With that whimsy, Ida surrendered to the fatigue of a day filled with sails, grog, and schemes. Bouquet of salt and sea, blending with the mild pitch of her boat, soothed her in to a deep sleep.

By next morning, Ida's fancy to own White Rock Island became resolute. She abandoned her cruise to Mexico and beat back to San Francisco where she petitioned attorney Arthur Dean Feldman. They arranged for a private meeting in the financial center of the city, this time for business. Concealed in a curtained-entrance booth, they talked while dining on broiled Pacific sand dabs. When a tuxedo-jacketed, Slavic waiter stepped away after delivering their second round of cocktails, Ida told Feldman, "I'm going to absolve you of the first rule of Cason Mansion. Do you remember it?"

"Rule number one. We never discuss our lovers."

"You're damn right. Nevertheless, if you disclosed our little tryst, I would no longer care a whit. However, if you agree to research the title of my island, you must swear to maintain absolute secrecy of our business intimacies."

"Not to worry," he said. "Haven't I always kept our secrets? You should not be concerned."

"This is bigger."

"Why?"

"If anyone learned of my inquiries, I would face retribution from one of the wealthiest men in the world."

"Who?"

"None other than William Wrigley, Jr."

"You're kidding me."

"I'm as serious as this deboned fish. The island I want is part of the Channel Islands. It's right near Santa Catalina. If he were to discover he didn't own it, Wrigley would use his political clout to snatch the island from me."

"He must own it. And if he didn't, that battle could bruise you."

"Not just me, he'll ruin anyone who tries to assist me. Can you handle that?"

"I can't guarantee anything," Feldman said. "It won't be easy to confirm the property title without drawing attention. You're playing against big boys. Mr. Wrigley is well connected and tough."

"I didn't retain you for easy," said Ida. "I've offered you a significant amount of money for a reason. There are a great deal more billable hours behind that if you can do the job."

"Done."

"The billing clock has started. Tell me how you will earn your pay."

Feldman removed a cocktail napkin from under her glass. He laid it on his napkin. "First, I'll overlay the modern plat on the appropriate diseño."

"Plats? Diseños?" She ripped a piece of sourdough from her bread plate. "You've lost me already."

"Plats. You've heard about them. United States property maps. Maybe you're not conversant with diseños. They're hand-drawn Mexican maps of Californios ranchos. If the diseño-napkin corners line up with the modern-plat napkin property lines, then you have a confirmed title. The legwork will be to compile a list of cleared-title Mexican land grants. Last, I'll review Mexican property claimed under the Treaty of Hidalgo's articles."

Ida snapped a celery stalk from her bloody mary. "What is it you just said?"

"I said I'll learn if Wrigley—or anyone—owns your island."

"Do it. But keep it quiet."

A month later, Feldman completed his work. White Rock did not belong to Wrigley, and the island belonged to neither the State of California, nor the United States. And, it did not belong to the last possible titleholder, Mexico. White Rock belonged to no one. There could be no dispute. The island was on no government plat.

"It's terra nullius!"

Feldman's astonishment reverberated in the anteroom outside of his closed office door, surprising his secretary even more than himself. She rushed in knowing his nature disinclined him to air excitement.

"Are you all right?"

"Yes. Yes," he replied, unable to suppress a grin. "Get me Miss Cason on the telephone right away. Ha-ha! Terra nullius."

"Yes, sir."

The secretary scurried from the room. She found the unfamiliar Latin term in the law dictionary. Terra nullius meant, "*Land belonging to no one.*"

Gleeful, Feldman advised Ida, "The Department of Interior cannot dispute the land is unclaimed."

"Does that mean?"

"It does. Go get your island."

Elated by the report, Ida made her assertion public, hoping to make her father's spirit, and the fisherman, proud of her. She hounded the General Land Office in San Francisco to accept her claim to White Rock. Clerks there rebuffed her as if she were a crackpot. Cartographers had not recorded the island on their plats.

Feldman counseled her, "Go over their heads. Skip the regional office and travel straight to Washington. Tell them it's there. Claim the property. Show them you are a sane person and assert you are making a legal request."

In Washington that summer, Ida tramped through the wardrobe-wilting city until she found the General Land Office at the

Department of the Interior. Her high-heeled shoes drummed an impatient beat the length of its marble hallway. She stopped beside a frosted glass door.

On the interior side, a government official unwrapped waxed paper from his lunch. Shadows on the glass caught his attention. The dappled forms adjusted a jacket hem before the door flew open. A stylish woman in trimmed hat and smart tailored suit, carrying a brown leather briefcase, stepped inside the office. She shut the door with an assertive click.

"Was I to knock?"

"Come back when you have an appointment." He unfolded a cloth napkin. "We are on our lunch hour now."

"Good Lord, I've searched for you all morning. Is there someone else I can speak with about my matter? You said we."

Fat fingers unbuttoned his collar. "We work alone and we eat at this hour." A mouth puckered in his fleshy face. Mottled cheeks squeezed his lips open. "You need an appointment."

"I've traveled all the way from San Francisco. I'll wait over there, on your bench, until you're finished. We can talk while you eat."

His forehead had grown around his pince-nez the way a tree absorbs rope banded around its trunk. The official picked up a paring knife and carved into a yellow onion in his left hand. As he fed slices into his face, he nodded without enthusiasm. "I know who you are." He pointed the knife at the ceiling. "You must be that Cason lady."

"Yes. I am Ida Cason. How did you identify me?"

"Our register in San Francisco warned us you were headed our way. Your reputation preceded you."

"How rude," she snapped.

He held up the roughhewn onion surface to Ida's face, a signal for her not to talk. The exertion of eating darkened his white shirt at the armpits and at the dome of his belly. "Before you say anything else…."

The official reviewed in detail what the San Francisco Register had told him: there was no plat of her claim. It encouraged silliness to speculate on the notion.

"Boats travel between San Pedro and Santa Catalina Island daily. It's preposterous, dare we say, rude, to assume no one knew of its existence."

"Nonsense. Anyone can see it. That's not what I'm saying. Nobody owns it. That's the difference. That's why I claim it. Don't you understand?"

He radiated pleasure seeing her face flushed. "It did not appear on our oldest Western District maps."

"How could it exist on your silly maps before you have surveyed it?"

"We are very busy, and very, very hungry." He loosened a necktie. It extended no farther than his breast pocket, as if he had knotted the fabric to draw attention to his protruding gut. "If an island breached surface where you thought it lies, the United States would have claimed that island. No claim means there's no island. No survey is on file. No zoning, no taxes, no plats. No island. End of story. Are we through? We would like to eat our lunch."

Having come near to rescue the island from geographic oblivion, a pompous clerk would not deter Ida. "I'll write you a check. Name your price."

"Madam, whether an underwater volcano erupted off the coast of Los Angeles forming an island, or the land splashed into the ocean like a meteor from the sky, it still wouldn't be for sale, no matter how large a check you wrote. The United States government doesn't sell public domain willy-nilly. In addition, from the imaginative description you provided my Western colleagues, your island holds no timber, no grazing, and has no homesteading potential. Even if it existed, it wouldn't meet the basic United States criteria to put it up for sale."

"White Rock is there by God and I want it. I'll pay for it. Right now. While I'm here. Today. Come over here." Her briefcase snapped open. "I've brought my bank and brokerage statements. Look for yourself. I can cover any amount you say."

Shuffling to the counter, his empty pant pockets gaped like bad mussels. Onion bits sprayed from his mouth. "The General Land Office preserves American land for everyone's benefit, not just for the rich."

"Just take the money. That's how deals are done."

"We don't *deal*." Thick fingers strummed on the counter. "Perhaps your husband should know if it existed, there are two ways he could own this new Atlantis—"

"White Rock Island." Hardened, icy stares separated them, as if they extended jousting poles. "Put that stinking onion down."

"Yes." The official's cadence slowed. "As you say, White Rock Island. The law stipulates your husband first must go to the property, enter it, make a habitable home on it, live on the land for three years, and thus your husband might gain title to the island under Homestead Law. You should start there."

"These details aren't helpful. For obvious reasons, sir, I don't care to possess the island if I have to live on it for three years or three days. I'm happy, however, to imagine you staked to its ground so your liver could be pecked by my seabirds."

"No doubt, you would." He licked the onion face. "The other way to acquire unsurveyed property would have been to exchange two acres worth of Valentine Scrip for the title."

"Two acres worth of what?"

"You told San Francisco that's the size of your fantasy island."

"It's my estimate."

"Then you would need certificates for two acres."

"You called it something different."

"No matter. That scrip doesn't exist anymore. Pity."

"What doesn't?"

"I said scrip. Now, kindly dismiss your humble civil servant whom you've elevated with your allusion to the Greek god Prometheus. Our liver has a mere forty-five minutes of lunch hour left for nourishment."

"Scrip?" Her voice swung to a sudden, innocent lilt. "Hold on."

"Sorry, it's time to take our modest lunch break." He turned. "But do enjoy our fire."

Ida smiled, appearing painfully charmed. "No, please. I must have misunderstood you. This humid, swamp heat has me lightheaded. Scrip something? What's all that?"

The official removed his glasses, rubbing them in circles on his belly. "Land scrip. Scrip is scrip. But Valentine Scrip is special. I should say *was*. It allowed the scrip holder to claim unoccupied, unappropriated, nonmineral land, whether surveyed or not."

Ida leaned toward him pouting. "Yes. Yes. But your San Francisco office didn't mention this thing."

"They probably don't—" A narrow knife lighted over his mouth, an ineffectual baffle to deflect a belch. He picked at his teeth. "They probably don't know of Valentine Scrip."

"You just said it again," blurted Ida. "I've never heard of such a Valentine's Day document."

"Naturally, you haven't. You're a modern woman. Nevertheless, it's inconsequential. I haven't seen any Valentine Scrip in years."

"Valentine?"

He returned to his desk, nibbling crumbs picked off his short tie. "Come back after you've gotten an appointment. Perhaps, by then, Mr. Wrigley will have heard your funny little story. And perhaps, he would appreciate a call from us. Then we wouldn't have to concern ourselves about this matter anymore."

As he sat, Ida added two goals to her plan to obtain the island: collect a California bushel of the papers, whatever "scrip" was, and to return to this office, without an appointment, and shove the wad of paper into that haughty bureaucrat's throat.

⛏ ⛏

Back in San Francisco, Ida met again with Feldman. She told him of the confrontation in Washington DC. "I haven't been able to sleep. I have this nightmare of Wrigley paying that toady clerk a bag of golden onions for telling him about the island."

"It could happen," agreed Feldman.

"If it hasn't already. You've never heard of this Valentine Scrip?"

"No."

"Then I've lost. There's no way I could camp on that rock for three years."

"Those are the General Land Office rules. If you want to homestead, you must farm, graze, or forest the land. But it's moot if they cannot even agree the island exists."

"What else can I do? This is insanity." She cried. "You have to help me."

"We've given it our best shot. I'm sorry."

"I can't get rid of the image in my head of Wrigley hammering a stake with the words, My White Rock Island. Though, he would spell 'rock' with three Ks."

"KKK?" said Feldman.

"Why not? That dreadful man bought off those scurrilous rumors of his Chicago KKK connections."

"I've never heard that."

"Oh yes, the anti-Klan newspaper *Tolerance* found a KKK membership form with his signature on it. He denied it like a grifter."

"The *Tolerance* wrote that? Do you believe him, or do you believe the paper?"

"Wrigley doesn't pass the smell test. He bailed out the man who established the Chicago KKK when he bought his baseball club. My Jewish friends won't buy Wrigley's gum. They chew Beemans."

"I have no objection to candy," Feldman said. "But my family holds no quarter for bigots."

"To be fair, maybe I shouldn't gossip. I can't swear whether it's true. I do know he's a pirate. Not all pirates are on the water, you know."

"It's very, very unlikely I could find some Halloween Scrip."

"Valentine."

"Let me try. I might have a friend of a friend who could raise some. But don't get your hopes up."

Ida agreed that if he unearthed the scrip, no more than the quantity she needed to win White Rock, she could never ask questions seeking where he found it, or never tell anyone from whom she got it—*never*. His quick insistence that she reciprocate his confidentiality pleased and intrigued her.

To Ida's amazement, within a few weeks, he delighted her with the precious scrip.

"Where did this come from?"

"You don't need to know. Besides, you agreed not to inquire."

Feldman himself didn't know from where it originated. Only his mother had that information. When Jennie Valentine died in San Francisco, her estate attorney hadn't listed her holdings of Valentine Scrip among her assets. During her last days, Jennie had passed the scrip and a note of advice in secret to Feldman's young mother, Henriette. His mother decided that her son did not need to know the source. He just knew that his mother possessed them and hid them at the Presidio.

"Darling," Ida cooed, "I've seen you under sheets. You are of the Hebrew persuasion. You have a big reason to be proud." She winked at him. "Jaspar! Really big. Let's not put up false barriers.

You can tell me. Does this have something to do with a secret Zionist society?"

"I seduced it from someone who loved me."

"You sheik! For services rendered?" Salacious laughs rounded her lipstick-reddened lips. "Pity me. Pity me. I know I should know better. Cason Mansion rule number one: talking about lovers is off limits."

"And so it shall remain."

"Oh, pooh. All right, but I'm curious who she is."

When newly married Henriette had acquired the scrip certificates at Jennie Valentine's deathbed, she accepted them believing Artie directed the gift to her from heaven. When he graduated from law school, Henriette entrusted her son with the knowledge she hid valuable Valentine Scrip documents somewhere in the Presidio.

"Why there?" Arthur Feldman admonished her. "Mother, that's rather eccentric."

"My choice of a vault is not without reason," she said. "It could offer you a life lesson: *Where your heart lies, so shall your treasure.*"

That was all the information the shrewd lawyer ever needed. The most sacred spot in his mother's world was the San Francisco National Cemetery in the Presidio. There was no advantage to him if she knew he knew.

After Arthur Feldman outlined Ida Cason's real estate predicament to his mother, he added, "Remember the story you told me of the bigot that accosted you on the train? I may not have been born, but I was there with you. You very much felt me rolling around in you. Remember? That's what you told me. That hateful man bothered me, too. This is our chance to get back at his kind. Wrigley is KKK. He's no better than the thug on the train—he's just a richer bigot. It takes a wealthier woman, like you, and a bigger shoe heel, like your Valentine Scrip, to strike back at him."

Henriette agreed. She'd sacrifice a small number of scrip to thwart a powerful anti-Semite. The intervention aligned with their moral obligations.

"And it's for this one-time—only," promised her son.

A week later, she provided Arthur Feldman with the scrip he needed.

"Where *exactly* was this hidden?" he asked, hoping for further insight into the secret vault location.

"You'll know when you are ready to know. Receive your good fortune with humility and share it in the Hebrew spirit of *Tikkun Olam*. Use it to heal the world. In time, as you grow to understand its proper role in our lives, you will know its whereabouts."

With the equivalent of two acres of scrip in hand from Feldman, Ida Cason bolted back to Washington. This time she brought her attorney, Feldman, a land surveyor, and her fiancé, Edward Chesebrough, Jr.

Her surveyor presented legal proof of the existence of the island to the clerk, saying, "You have no grounds to object. Everything's in order." And her attorney remitted the Valentine currency for irrefutable possession of White Rock Island.

The bulging-faced official surrendered a patent to the property, holding out the forfeited papers to Ida. She nodded for him to hand them to Feldman, whose arm extended with a new gold cufflink.

Ida fluffed a laced handkerchief to her nose, hiding her smile. She reached into her purse for a long-marinated revenge. "Here. I brought you refreshments from San Francisco." Rows of bracelets soft-jingled as a package of Wrigley's spearmint chewing gum dropped on the counter. Ida shook her head and said through the perfumed cloth, "The onion."

Turning, she swept from the office, heals clicking the marble on the foot-worn hall.

Ida Cason did not believe in luck. She believed in her innate intellectual superiority, applying it to learn arbitrage from her father, the commodity speculator. As he had once swapped bushels of wheat among Midwest grain elevators and West Coast ports, his daughter made the shrewd trade of two unexceptional Petaluma acres for two unique Channel Island acres.

Feldman learned a lesson from Ida: when matched with mistitled properties, Valentine Scrip had fantastic powers to gain wealth and to overwhelm the strongest opposition.

The more he thought of the unmatched power of the scrip he presumed his mother kept hidden in the cemetery, the more he rationalized he could remove, without asking, other certificates for the good of Judaism. He would share his new prosperity with his temple. Opportunities might be lost before he explained his righteous plans to his mother.

Unlike Ida, whose island property dropped into her lap, Feldman dug through land records from the Seattle tidelands to the Florida Keys. He mined two real-estate gems with defective titles in his home state of California. One property he expected to be easy pickings. The second claim required an inventive application of Valentine Scrip by a cunning lawyer. He envisioned making a fortune on both subterfuges.

In the summer of 1941, he struck for the first property. Arthur Dean Feldman contested title to fifty acres of prime mud flat properties on the City of Long Beach harbor. It bristled with oil wells and piers. Surveyors had not accounted for shifting sediment, and they incorrectly platted the tidal land. Their error invalidated the deed, leaving it vulnerable to easy seizure by Valentine Scrip—or extortion.

San Francisco's Chinese power brokers, the financial backers for his portfolio of conventional real-estate investments, aided him.

To their misfortune, before they had time to present the scrip and win a favorable court ruling, their destinies collided with World War II. They had targeted a location with an essential source of the United States energy supply as a war commenced.

Press reports alerted Henriette to her son's intended breach of trust. Newspapers said he pledged to swap rare Valentine Scrip to secure the title to the Southern California property. Before Arthur Dean Feldman could steal Henriette's scrip from the Presidio Cemetery hiding place, she called on a young, cemetery worker. He had been kind to her over the years when she visited the grave. His name was Ramon De la Cruz. They chatted each February at Dean's graveside. He had shared with her that he moved from the Philippines before the war. The hard worker lived a lonely life in San Francisco without family. Reminded of her younger self, she took him into her heart, as someone had done for her in her youth. When her son betrayed her and she had nowhere else to turn, she disclosed her greatest secret. Ramon agreed to remove and convey the scrip to a Petaluma church for Henriette. Her long-time friend, the minister, hid the Valentine Scrip and complied with Henriette's written request carried by Ramon.

Henriette's furious response to her son's chicanery compelled him to revise his plans. He decided to delay his second land grab until her death.

Fate had other designs. Star-crossed, Feldman predeceased his mother. His scheme, which included stealing the scrip he thought remained hidden at the cemetery, lay dormant, secured in an office safe until found by his heir and executor of his estate, Griff Feldman.

Quirks of fortune played out in their lineage. Instead of the father's plan outlining a roadmap to a treasure, the directions led Arthur Dean Feldman's child, Henriette's grandson, Griff, to the edge of the Golden Gate Bridge.

CUSE
1970s

Winkle. No—BEAR—Winkle! Bear? What the hell's a Bear Winkle? Would any of our Pocahontas-whipped, Indian-appeasing administrators hazard a guess? ... I didn't think so, but I'll tell you, pilgrim. It's not a name. Hell, no. It's an affliction.

So began a disjointed, college newspaper column by a drunken journalist, Mick Mallory.

The object of his tirade, Bear Winkle, disagreed. He liked his name, liked it very much. And he liked his first name more than his last name. His mother gave it to him. Winkle assumed the name passed through his maternal family because he never knew his father's name. Neither did his mother. And he had no recollection of his mother. She poisoned herself with alcohol two years after his birth, leaving him without a legal guardian.

Trickles of his mother's Miwok and Cainamero bloodlines obliged his affiliated tribe members to share responsibility for his upbringing. Tribal law did not allow adoptions by non-Indians. Assimilation cloaked another form of white man inflicted genocide.

The tribe passed the orphan among themselves. Winkle slept as a transient on kitchen floors until each pitiless host shooed him into another temporary shelter. The pattern repeated throughout his loveless childhood.

Winkle grew into a heavy, muscular teen's frame, animated with a dangerous, easy-to-provoke temper. Wary tribe members avoided the sullen boy who strutted around the rancheria shirtless and angry. His bare chest exposed raised scars, crosshatched from self-mutilation.

When he became a tribal adult on his 17th birthday, Winkle exercised his right to speak to the Miwok Petaluma Rancheria Council. The council granted him two minutes. At the bottom of a circle of white plastic lawn chairs inside a school trailer, he took shallow breaths and lisped, "I've come to share a prophecy."

"Hurry it up," said the chairman.

"Coyote spoke to me. I'm destined to be chief of the rancheria." He expected an immediate response. Hearing none, he hesitated and said, "That's it. That's the prophecy."

Amused councilmen whispered ridicule between one another. They exchanged knowing winks and grins before the chairman delivered a scold. "Your wood is dry and burns quickly. Your roots are shallow and you cut your trunk with deep scars. Someone who cannot grow himself straight cannot grow a tribe. You're unfit ever to be a chief."

Winkle twisted the plastic chair arms toward his lap. His lips flexed. "Who are you to decide? Old white ears don't hear the words of the Coyote."

"Watch how you speak, boy," the chairman said. "We are the Miwok voice."

A long-bladed knife, passed at his birth from the generations preceding his grandmother, chafed under Winkle's pant leg. The grandmother had received it as a girl from a forgotten Kanaka ancestor. Winkle had once slashed with the swift weapon, removing the ear of a molester.

"Miwok? There are no more true Miwok on the rancheria."

A toothless councilman yammered, "You chatter like a snared squirrel."

Winkle jumped up with a startled expression—as if he discovered he sat in a nest of rats. "I spit on your Anglo-Injun asses."

"Get out of here," a one-eared council member roared, "or I'll shoot you."

Winkle picked up the chair and beat it against a whiteboard. "You're drunk on white man's spirits. You crave his white sugar. White flour. White everything. Where is your Indian hunger?"

Storming to the exit, he yelled from the doorway. "Whoever wants a real chief follow me." He paused, surprised. "No one?"

"Go," the council shouted together. A bottle of cola smashed above Winkle's head.

"Just wait. One day, you'll all follow me."

Winkle ran away from the rancheria that evening, hitchhiking to San Francisco where his heroes, Indian activists who had occupied Alcatraz years before, lived in the Castro district. He found their residence on Church Street. Hopi and Apache tribe members invited him to live with them. They fed him sheep they roasted on their apartment floor, offering occasional peyote buttons during special prayer ceremonies.

Night after night, leaned against their sooty walls, or rested on horsehair blankets prickling his neck, he listened as they educated him on the aggressions of the White Man and the Indian resistance movement. The benefactors taught him his key lessons, "Indians are the rightful caretakers of the lands occupied by the invaders, and Alcatraz Island embodies the political epicenter for Indian land battles. One day an omnipotent chief will come from the East to destroy our enemies. Our first goal is the reoccupation of our symbolic home in the middle of San Francisco Bay. When we take back what is ours, it will set off tremors that'll shake white America."

Winkle's adolescent prophecy, that he'd lead his rancheria, solidified under the influence of the militants' creed and the hallucinogenic effects of peyote. The dream became an article of faith. Coyote guided his destiny. Every Indian nation would unite under him. He envisioned that on Alcatraz beat the heart of a reconstituted Indian empire.

In 1895, the Northern California island dungeon held nineteen Southwestern Hopi who dared to challenge the United States with their audacious proclamation: *This land is our land. These children are our children. You may not take them from us.* From where Hopis had cried for their children stolen to reeducation camps and mourned their land despoiled by speculators, Winkle heard their spirits' call for an Indian capital to defy the world.

Winkle spent his days camped in the aisles of the Civic Center Public Library stacks, mastering high school curricula to earn a General Education Development certificate. After applying to colleges, the Native American Studies Department of Syracuse University accepted him into their program.

Before he departed for New York, Winkle made a pilgrimage to a windswept strand in the shadow of the Golden Gate Bridge. There an ancient Yelamu village had thrived until the 18th century. He scooped bay water in his hands, flinging droplets into the air to bless the birds and the fish. On bent knee, he troweled fistfuls of sand, squeezing the granules to honor villagers that time had ground to dust. The grains slithered from his grip, mixing with wind, water, and earth, as had his ancestors' spirits. He vowed to the Coyote creator god, one of many Indian gods with powers stronger than the White Man's dead god, to return Alcatraz Island to the Indian people.

⇥⇤

The drunken college journalist, who wrote the criticism of Winkle's name, endured an insecure childhood. Mallory had shared an unheated dormer-attic with four younger brothers. He feigned sleep every night while he monitored bumbled entrances of a monster into his house. Fantasies had no place in his youth. Fiction had to wait for news stories he would write as an adult. His young life measured real bumps in the night: a monster's shouted threats, the house-shuddering blows of an elbow through unpainted drywall, and the heart-tearing sound of jagged rips of cheap linoleum floor hurled onto midnight snow.

If heavy footsteps rumbled across a tiled line into his mother's second-floor bedroom, he did not have to absorb hurt for his younger siblings. Someone else would take the beating. On one side of the floor's lined demarcation lay safety, on the other side peril.

He envisioned how the monster rustled sheets and shook bedside lamps with every blow. He knew in advance, where bruises appeared on his mom's neck in the morning. He felt the violence, the blows from left and right hands, plastic hairbrushes, glow-in-the-dark rosary holders, and wooden hangers. Without being in the room, he visualized her assault in detail while never understanding why it had to happen.

Bear Winkle and Mick Mallory attended Syracuse University simultaneously. Winkle led the Central New York Native American Student Society and Mallory edited the student daily. During those years, Native Americans objected to the school mascot, an absurd, mythical Indian called the Saltine Warrior.

Winkle went to Mallory's office to demand the newspaper support the Native American Student Society campaign to replace the farce. Before he sat, Mallory spoke, mouth curled into a cool approximation of a smile.

"Man, we know what you're here for. It ain't gonna happen. Dead Indian grievances, blah, blah, blah. This is the nineteen seventies, not eighteen seventies. Why don't you and your crazy-ass band of Indians suck it up and let it slide? Our grandfathers settled our treaties honorably. Give peace a chance."

Feet on an armless oak chair howled. Winkle dragged it to Mallory's desk. The chair disappeared, eclipsed by his wide shoulders. He tried to conceal his sibilant lisp. "May I sit and discuss this?"

"What's there to talk about?" Mallory pulled back thick hair into a ponytail. His muffin-shaped head sprouted sideburns covering his cheeks.

Imposing hands opened and closed at Winkle's sides. "Thank you for—"

"Indian wars are over. We won. Bury the hatchet, Geronimo."

Winkle swallowed. "Okay. I guess you talk faster than I do. I'll speak more quickly."

"*Pleath.*"

Winkle drew smile under his teeth. His mouth popped releasing the suction. "I came here to discuss the Saltine mascot. Would you really rather take our time to tell me our war is over? All right then, as a courtesy, I'll respond to that statement. Yes and no. It's a fact, Euroman stole land. Yes stole, not won. And you're naive. The war is not over. The battles go on."

"Who did what?"

"I said Euroman. He took what wasn't his from the Indian. The battle ended before we knew an invasion sailed to our land. But it was a battle, not the—"

"Whoa, whoa big fella. Back up. What's with this Euroman garbage? I expected a windbag like you to come in here all high-horsed. But give me a *friggin'* break. Euroman? Do you mean Americans, big guy?"

"I mean what I say. I speak about European invaders. Real Americans seek justice—"

"Oh! Justice. Is that what you're here for today? I think you've gotten enough. How many calories are there in justice?"

"What are you talking about?"

"You must get plenty of justice because you look amply fed."

"Make some sense."

"Do United States of America food stamps mean anything to you? Does that make sense? Dollars and cents, perhaps? How's that for American justice? There's nothing European about that free food you eat. Let me guess. Syracuse put you in on a charity ticket, slipped you in the back door with a wink and a GED."

"And?"

"Bet you've never been inside the bursar's office to pay a dime for your education. Wish I had suffered from so much injustice. Cry me a welfare river."

Winkle leaned forward, massaging his calf. "Hear me out. You're Irish, aren't you? Native Americans are no different."

"Hardly."

"You pledge revenge on your oppressors," said Winkle. "So do we. You sing your father's songs about revolt once a year in a pub—Indians resist daily."

"Look, dude, I write today's newspaper. Loud and cheap. Not yesterday's news. What's relevant today goes between the margins of my column. Anything outside of those lines is unimportant. The past is over."

"Wrong again," Winkle said. "The past never dies. It waits patiently. It continues. But okay, let's deal with what you can make right today."

Mallory stifled a yawn. "Hold your fire. I get it. You say Euroman, but you must mean urologist."

Winkle rolled his shoulders. "You asked, what's there to talk about. If you insist that we start there, then okay, let's discuss who is an authentic American and who is a Euroman. It's the Indians' birthright to take care of this land."

"Says who?" Mallory grabbed a small foam-rubber basketball off his desk, snapping his wrists. The ball arched off a wall. "Euripides?"

"Along with genocide against my people, Euroman developed a perverse sense of entitlement over the land."

"You have some nerve to come in here and complain about entitlements." Mallory held his arms over his head, hands bent forward. "From what I remember learning at a *real* high school, we fought over all this long ago. America won. Throughout the history of Western civilizations, winners have destroyed losers. No conqueror ever felt guilty enough to give the vanquished free food stamps and casinos. They wiped them out. All of them. What makes you losers think you are entitled to different treatment?"

"My point. We're not *gone*. We're still here. We fight on. You haven't won yet."

"Eh, not really. Read the newspapers. It's over. Too bad we had to kill all those Indians to persuade you that you're lucky to be American."

Winkle flattened his palms on the desk. "The school mascot is a cigar store caricature of an Indian warrior. At a minimum, our student newspaper should back our peaceful actions to get rid of it. Can you please agree to support at least that?"

Mallory angled back in his chair, placing his feet on the desk. Worn sneaker soles touched Winkle. "Let me get this straight. Your guys disrupt my basketball games at Manley Field House. Right or wrong?"

"Right."

"Where do you come off occupying my center court?"

"The movement is not about basketball and it is not about me, it's about my people."

"I get that nonsense. But I love basketball. Keep your problems outside of its lines. Inside the lines is where we play. If you ruin my games, that *is* about me. You ruin my cheerful disposition—stay off my floor."

"Your Saltine mascot entertainment is my insult."

Mallory bent back his fingers, one after the other. "Uh-huh. And you're mad at this Euro-dude. He ain't me, chief. If you want to whine about how crappy it is being a Tonto in a Lone Ranger world, go ahead. Knock yourself out. I don't care. You stay within the lines of your reservation. I'll stay in the lines of mine. I happen to like the Saltine Warrior. Be proud of it. Stop freaking out all over this school in protest."

Winkle rose. Flesh between his lip and nose mounded as if soft bread padded his gum. "It's a white man's fantasy."

Mallory swung his legs off the desk. He stood toe to toe with Winkle, looking up into his chin. Scents of tobacco and cannabis clung to Mallory's breath. He raised his hand. "Thumbs-up for the Saltine redskin."

Winkle's eyes scoured his freckled face. He turned to leave and stopped. "You're a bigger asshole than they said you were."

A satisfied smile broke Mallory's lips. "Oh, my. I'm an *athhole*. Custer's my martyr, *thilly* boy."

Winkle pivoted back toward his antagonist to see Mallory kiss the air. His mallet-sized hands hammered on the desk.

"Hey!" Mallory shouted.

A powerful, piston-stroke thrust from Winkle's shoulder, blasting across the desktop. Papers and a bobble-head Indian crashed onto the floor.

Mallory picked up a ceramic figurine, balancing the chipped doll on the center of his desktop.

Winkle positioned the chair feet in the precise spot where they set when he arrived. "The fight hasn't ended." He turned and left the office.

From then on, Mallory referred to Bear Winkle in print as, "*Chief Boo-Boo.*" Public animosity smoldered until the school replaced the stylized savage mascot with an emasculated citrus.

The day of the administration's decision, a Great Lakes blizzard blanketed the deserted streets. Mallory sat at his typewriter, tangling sentences. Spent long-necked bottles of Labatt's Blue littered his desk, battlefield casualties of a lost war. Mallory emptied a half dozen while he wrote his bleary-eyed outrage over the conspiracy to murder the Saltine Warrior. By the time the last beer spilled on his shirt, he had completed the crazed editorial. Printers put the text to bed for the next day's paper, setting his words in type for the university to see.

If Mallory had limited his description of Winkle to the pejoratives of, *an affliction,* or *insufferable interloper,* or even *Rainbow Indian,* Winkle might have forgiven and forgotten his words. Instead, Mallory's mindless essay excoriated him, substituting asinine vituperation for reason. The final phrase sealed his fate and their relationship. Mallory disparaged Winkle as: *An off-the-reservation member of the California Bear Fag Rebellion.*

Winkle resented those sentiments for a lifetime.

Before the next evening, Mallory's printed rants, exacerbated with his refusal to apologize, compelled the university administration to fire him as editor of the school-funded newspaper. Defrocked and spurned on campus, no one came to his defense.

Late that night, Mallory wandered university streets amid lumpy lines of plow-thrown snowbanks. He tramped away from the din of Friday night parties, a pariah isolated in a hellish snow globe of his own creation.

By midnight, he waited alone on a dark street corner for the next off-campus bus to pass. Snowflakes danced in suspension under a low sky and floated up again, plump and weightless after flirting with the ground. On the horizon, through a snowy veil, a weather beacon atop the MONY office building glowed. The tower flashed a signal that the temperature had dropped to near zero. Another Arctic storm approached.

Mallory lifted an unbuttoned denim welding-jacket around his face.

Occasional, frosted automobiles plowed out of the dark, kicking up broken cakes of hard-packed snow. Behind the glare of headlights, wheel studs chomped into the ice until the whir passed, sound faded, and the car taillights blinked out.

Their departures left him lonelier.

Boots crunched snow crust on a lawn. Mallory turned. A bus approach recaptured his attention. He stamped on the ice, adjusting gloves around his wrists.

Mallory turned from the slow-moving headlights. Bent over, he moved sideways into the street. Iced panels lumbered inches past his face. A rear bumper brushed his shoulder, and his palms snapped up into a claw. He dropped into a crouch, clasping the bus. Joints straining, a mad brute pulled him.

Soles of Mallory's sneakers read the streets the way a blind man's fingers comprehended Braille. They recounted stories of his snow country youth bumper hopping, a crosstown odyssey called *skitching*. Squatting into a malodorous exhaust cloud to clutch frozen chrome with wet, woolen gloves, and to have a motor vehicle drag him over a snow-covered road, left him then, and now, blissful.

An upright skitch behind a fuel tanker ranked the highest conquest. Neck bracing cries of, "Oil truck!" aroused a stir whalers knew when they heard, "Thar she blows!" With the alarm from the neighborhood lookout, a stampede of boys in metal-buckled boots jingled headlong toward a chin-high rear bumper. Gangs draped over the horizontal beam. Packed snow-zigs flew past their sides.

Mallory preferred, as in most endeavors, to go it alone, catching sedans at stop signs. Irate drivers burst from their doors to pursue him. They never reached Mallory. As long as they stayed outside of a Mallory-imagined line, drivers fell into a hapless farce, slipping around their idled vehicles. They couldn't hurt him.

Boy's gleaming eyes circled Mallory's performances, as would timber wolves haunt a deathwatch perimeter. In the end, the exhausted pursuers capitulated, hurling meaningless threats over their car roofs. Outclassed and winded, the drivers flopped back into their automobiles, rewarding Mallory with hand waving, fishtail glides past whoops of street corner cronies.

His propensity to instigate turmoil set the pattern for Mallory's life: creating a ruckus for others' entertainment drew the admiration of a crowd. If he stayed on his side of an imagined line, even if the demarcation constituted a line of newspaper prose, he stayed safe.

On the night of Mallory's banishment from the college newspaper, melancholia walked him back into frozen streets, wandering between lines of snowbanks where he felt safest. When he caught the city bus tail, lurches and shifts excited his mood. His jacket billowed to life with the élan of a cavalryman's cape.

Under the gear-grind, heavy boot steps caught his attention. A dark blur raced over the snowbank. Its hefty shape tackled Mallory, enveloping his torso.

The side of his head slammed onto the road. Mallory's ears sang from the thud of his skull cracking ice.

High taillights coasted away, his empty gloves gripped to the bus bumper.

Mallory reacted as if he'd fallen out of bed, reaching up into darkness for support. He grasped a man's padded shoulder and rose to a knee. The man stood and kicked Mallory in the chest.

Mallory's cheek hit the road surface. Mental calculations reeled. He floundered to understand what had happened, asking, "Why are you—"

A kick to his side arched his back to the silhouette of a Halloween cat. He went limp. Another kick flung him off his hands and knees. His ears rung from the clapping of his teeth. The force rolled him into a snowbank.

Hands pressed on Mallory's ponytail and mashed his face into sharp ice crystals.

He couldn't breathe. His brain starved for oxygen. Heavy, incomprehensible gibberish, and the hammer of his heart, beat a death march in his ears. Snow filled his nostrils, pressing into his mouth. Suffocation. Mallory panicked. Tried to shout. It came out as a bleat, dull and distant. Blackness slid in from the periphery. He saw death. Adrenalin induced madness made him frantic.

The assailant lifted him by his hair.

Mallory gasped, arms windmilling, seeking a chance for mercy or violent retribution. They found neither.

Gloves twisted Mallory's jaw, wrenching his view up into a ski mask. Small pillows of liquored breath surged through the woolen knit.

He clawed to find an ear and bit sleeve padding. Before he staggered back on his feet, the man kicked him again.

Bolts of nausea seared from his groin to his abdomen. He spit bile, doubled over, and retched. His nose flowed blood.

A hammerstone-sized fist glanced over Mallory. The man spun, slipping on ice from wild momentum.

Mallory sensed a last opportunity to survive. Wobbling to his feet, his head held no thoughts, only pain. He pulled his jacket inside out over his sleeves, wrapping the coat around the man's neck to stop his fall. His weight strangled the man.

Mallory circled him, striking furious uppercuts into his blinded opponent's face.

The man struggled to tear the garment from his head. Heavy boots kicked at Mallory and missed.

Unable to select a vulnerable target, Mallory saw contours of a skull and a padded body. He yelled a primal roar and swung fists at the mass.

The man crab-stepped and staggered, leaning his bulk over Mallory's lanky frame. Another sharp blow glanced across the man's neck. He gurgled.

A lull.

The coat lifted, exposing the man's jaw. Mallory leaped. His full weight, concentrated behind his fist, crashed into lips. Something cracked against Mallory's knuckle. A frightful wail pierced his ears.

He couldn't lift either arm to hit the man again. A gash seeped on his index finger. His hand could not close, the digits swelled to twice their size.

Blood burbled from where breath jetted from the mask. He threw Mallory's jacket off his shoulders. It landed on red-spattered snow and road salt.

In one motion, the man drew a wide-bladed knife from an ankle sheath, roaring the furor of a wounded animal. A glint rocketed toward Mallory's head. Dizzy, he tilted back, holding up an unjacketed arm.

The blade tore through his shirtsleeve, carving a channel that zigzagged across his forearm.

A painless tug preceded a fuzzy sensation of heat, spreading from elbow to wrist. Mallory screamed at the sight of sterile bone and tendon. Blood spurted with his rapid heartbeat.

A whir of studs turned the corner, accelerating into the roadbed. Headlights dazzled the bent combatants. The assailant ran, moaning into the darkness.

Mallory ignored the car, fearing if he glimpsed up, he'd pass out. He packed snow into the wound and wrapped his coat around it. Spasms twitched his arm. He held it high, staggering a few steps toward the campus emergency room.

The automobile skidded alongside. Chevrons rolled into his view. And he fainted.

When he regained consciousness, a doctor sutured his arm. Not knowing how much time had passed, Mallory muttered his first concern. "Did you see what I wrote?" He expected the doctor, and the whole world, to have had read his editorial.

A surgical mask hid her wordless reaction. She asked Mallory for answers.

Mallory lied, saying the cut happened at a dormitory urinal. "I suppose I fell down drunk."

He parried the doctor's inquiries. "Could've been to a floor party. Yeah. No. I was pissing. That's right. I stumbled to my side while I shook icicles off my mistletoe. Put out my arm to break the fall and went through a glass window.

"No, I can't remember the dorm name. Nope, can't recall who partied with me either. Was I with someone?"

Outrageous excuses flew with such conviction, the exhausted physician believed him, or declined to invest her time to consider otherwise.

He might have beguiled the doctor, but Mallory refused to delude himself. Timeless primeval tribal battles once fought using sticks and stones on hard plains and on spongey peat resumed in Syracuse with a modern sophistication. Mallory again monitored nighttime footsteps to identify his attacker. This time the hallway stretched as long as his life and as wide as the continent.

By senior year, Mallory published an independent student magazine. For its inaugural cover story, he wrote an exposé on how the United States Indian Termination Policy blighted the nearby Iroquois reservation. The publicity ignited a political firestorm that led to a congressional investigation.

Central New York's Native American Tribal Council mailed Mallory a peace pipe as a token of their appreciation. A leather strap tied a note from Bear Winkle invited him to attend their next meeting. They offered to adopt him as an honored member of the proud Iroquois Nation.

Mallory accepted the invitation but confused the council by responding he assumed the gathering not to be a *BYOF* affair.

Winkle opened the powwow with an apology to the council for the honoree's cryptic reply. He leveled his chagrin at Mallory, who sat smiling cross-legged in the circle. Winkle informed the elders the initialism BYOF meant, "Bring Your Own Firewater."

And what do you know? Mallory thought. *The council members laughed. Everyone but Winkle laughed.*

They inducted Mallory, smudging burned sage across his chest and giving him the Indian name, Morning Smoke Signal. Chiefs further honored him with a hand-carved, hickory lacrosse stick, welcoming him as a brother. Once anointed, Mallory jumped up, waving the stick, war whooping, and clogging an Irish reel.

He pulled Winkle aside, sage ash running his ribs black with sweat. "Let's bury the hatchet."

Winkle agreed, and they became wary acquaintances. Mallory sought to hold his enemy close until he had proof of who stabbed him. And Winkle hoped he might have the opportunity to stab him again.

Winkle graduated and returned home. He joined the San Francisco police department.

A Boston newspaper hired Mallory as a sports reporter. His terrors followed. In the haunt of his adult nightmares, his mother's ghostly cries from downstairs, "Pete. Please Pete, no. Don't!" stole his slumbering hours. Sleep deprivation became an ally that allowed him to gather news other journalists missed. An editor chided the fledgling, "You nap as if you're snoozing next to a firehouse pole."

Mallory's sports beat brought him to San Francisco. There he visited Winkle, insisting he had an interest in his cop stories. Winkle suffered the pretense of Mallory's scrutiny until fate introduced him to a pair of wealthy white men, Griff Feldman and Edward Chesebrough III. They offered Winkle fulfillment of his cherished prophecy and distance from Mallory.

Their destinies flowed toward the Presidio National Cemetery, where buried sins and secrets of historical California awaited their rediscovery.

BELVEDERE

Edward Chesebrough III knew why Griff Feldman had invited him to his North Beach law office in 2007. He wanted a favor.

There's always a favor, he thought. *Could I publish another editorial railing against environmental activists and supporting his real-estate projects?*

Feldman, as had his father before him, represented the Cason-Chesebrough family's publishing interests in real-estate matters. He had drawn up the contract when Chesebrough liquidated his mother's Cason estate.

The strenuous climb up three flights of a marble staircase to Feldman's office provoked Chesebrough to swear it'd be the last time he ascended the stairs. He seized the glove-worn banister for support, bristling with the knowledge Feldman stretched two steps at a bound. His conservative suit, double-breasted with a wide tie concealed his waistline bulge. But the heated flush on his face revealed the strain on Chesebrough's frame. Each step elevated his blood pressure and sour-churned his disposition.

He panted into the top floor office complaining. "It's easier to hoof up California Street from Montgomery to the P-U Club than it is to climb your spiral stairs."

"Hello, Edward." Feldman waited for Chesebrough's breath to moderate. "Are you okay now?"

A cable car bell clinked from the rails below the open window. Chesebrough grunted. "I'm here."

The drape and hand of Feldman's suit complemented his athletic stature. He aligned his bowtie edges. "I'll get right to the point."

"Before you make your point, mix me a drink. Scotch and soda, no ice. Cold water on the side."

"Not yet. Time for that later. First, I want to share a secret in strictest confidence."

Chesebrough frowned. "You won't offer me a damn scotch?"

Feldman hooked his thumbs into his vest. "My point is, Edward. I have a grand opportunity that warrants your serious attention. Father gave me an ingenious project and—"

"Hold on there." Chesebrough winked over his spectacles, silencing Feldman. He raised an eyebrow. "Your old man has been gone a long time."

"The project has been saved in his vault, and its success requires Valentine Scrip. May I continue?"

"I climbed all the way up here because I thought you wanted to talk about something substantial. Do you need money?"

"I have money. And anyway, money can't buy this deal. That's why it requires Valentine Scrip and would benefit from your participation."

"You asked for my serious attention and you bring up a lark." Chesebrough coughed into the back of his hand. "You and I both know, finding, no less using, Valentine Scrip is a lark. My family hasn't forgotten what happened to your father in Long Beach. Hurry and pour us *both* a scotch, would you please?"

Chesebrough referred to when Arthur Dean Feldman had failed to contest the City of Long Beach's title to properties on their harbor.

"World War II exploded on Father."

"No. Playing fast and loose with Valentine Scrip blew him and his partners up. I don't need that kind of spectacle," Chesebrough said. "Luckily, my mother avoided your father's limelight on that one. We almost lost everything."

"Father made a mistake in his timing. Bad luck was his fate. His application for the title was a legitimate claim. That error won't happen again with this new project in his vault."

"Why are we wasting our breath? Valentine Scrip is no more," said Chesebrough. "I heard his Long Beach gambit was all a bluff. Extortion. He had no scrip. Even back then."

"Don't be presumptuous."

"If this plan had legs, and if your father had scrip, he would have acted on it while he was alive."

"Father waited until he thought the time was right." Feldman dabbed his lip with his pocket square. "His plan, now mine, is far more audacious than the Long Beach scheme. And its time has arrived."

"Sure. Sure." Chesebrough rocked his empty hand, as if he held a cocktail glass. "He didn't execute this second project, or any other project, because of the drubbing his partners suffered in Long Beach. It was dying then and it's dead now."

"Time heals many wounds. Key elements of the plan are more viable today than they were when Father drew them up. Do you want in, or are you out?"

"You not only refuse to offer me a drink, you haven't had the courtesy to share with me where the target property is located."

"The plan will make those who participate very, very rich."

"I'm already rich. Where is it?"

"I'm talking dynasty money. Execution will be easier if your various resources are behind me. Don't forget my father was there for your mother in her hour of need." Feldman toed a wastebasket containing an empty antacid bottle.

"What's my buy-in?" said Chesebrough, lacing his fingers across his chest.

"First, tell me whether you're in or out."

"That's how you expect me to decide? In or out? I require more information than that. Where's this El Dorado you hope to claim?"

"All right, I'll tell you."

"Well, where is it?"

"Alcatraz."

"Alcatraz?" Chesebrough launched from his chair. "Bullshit! Big stinking bullshit." He squeezed his temples with the heels of his hands, unsure whether to laugh or to run.

The allure of Alcatraz Island, with its views of San Francisco Bay and Golden Gate Bridge, offered indisputable enticements. No other public land in America matched its cachet. The notion the federal government might release its ownership flirted with lunacy—or an act of war.

Feldman pushed back from his desk, glaring through Chesebrough. "If that's your sentiment, then we didn't have this meeting."

"Don't mock me, Griff. Give me something to hold on to, something rational. Did you discover the Alcatraz land title is invalid?"

"It's as solid as the rock itself."

Chesebrough looked at him as if he had seen a unicorn horn grow from his forehead. "What in hell's bloody bells? You're not well, Griffo."

Feldman pulled his bowtie knot tight in the center. "Take a serious stare to the right at Alcatraz when you cross the bridge tonight. Think about how far your family has come and think about the legacy you will leave to the future. The heart of San Francisco could be yours. Or you could throw away this opportunity for the pleasure of landing a few asinine insults on me. But I'm a bigger man than you are. The project's come a long way. This is the moment I invite you in. It's a favor my family owes your family."

As he spoke, Chesebrough gave Feldman the "gentleman's stare." Feldman had endured silent scolds before at the exclusive club to which he and Chesebrough belonged. To receive a stare meant, *"You're not a worthy man. You're not your father. You inherited your prosperity. And, worst of all, exceeding the other indignities, your enjoyment of wealth can't be sustained. Anything you propose is the desperate grasp of a doomed man."*

The stare marked you as a disease-carrying host. It warned other members away. You might contract the pox of failure in its presence.

Feldman had shunted condemnations at the club. He fortified himself knowing if he brokered a spectacular transaction, one greater than the acquisitions completed by his father, success would establish him as a bona fide San Francisco icon.

Chesebrough eyed the antacid in the wastebasket. "Sorry for being blunt. I've heard in the cigar lounge whispers about club arrears."

"Don't fret about my finances," said Feldman. "I'm set. The Dragon Head is behind this."

"Tongs in Chinatown? Even after Long Beach?"

"Money moved offshore from San Francisco decades ago," said Feldman. "My relocated financiers, though farther away, command limitless influence in Washington."

"China?" said Chesebrough, leaning forward. Feldman did not answer. Chesebrough eased onto his chair, as though he sat on a deflating beach ball. "You're serious. Aren't you?"

Feldman said, "Are Chesebroughs still trusted friends of the Feldman family?"

"By tradition." Chesebrough's high cheek muscles slackened into his jowls. He mumbled in baritone, "Speak. I'll listen."

"I remind you we're meeting in confidence." Feldman sat back. "Chinese communists in Macau. They know I have access to a few thousand acres worth of Valentine Scrip—"

"Thousands!" Chesebrough interrupted. "You hold scrip certificates for thousands of acres. Why didn't you tell me?"

"You didn't need to know." He handed him a torn certificate from a folder on his desk. "Father left this scrap of Valentine Scrip from the time your mother bought that sea stack off Santa Catalina."

"White Rock Island."

"There's a piece missing from the corner. Father couldn't take the chance the Department of the Interior might reject the damaged certificate. He had to present the exact amount required. So he retained this one. I'm sure the match is with the rest of the cache."

"Let's see them."

"You can't."

"Why not?"

"Grandmother Rosenthal threatened to expunge Father from her trust if she ever again suspected he had intentions to take her scrip. Although he knew how to find them, he waited until she died before he pursued his plan.... I don't know precisely where they are."

"You don't?"

"No, but Ramon knows how to recover the scrip. I don't."

"Who's *Ramon?*"

"Don't know that either."

Chesebrough held up his hand. "You've never met this, Ramon?"

"Father had. There's a phone number in his safe and a note from him saying ask for Ramon. A Crocker Bank trust pays an annual retainer to his PO Box. Ramon cashed all the checks. It won't be hard to find him."

"This scrap is all you've ever seen of the scrip?"

"There are strong reasons to conclude the rest are secured at the Presidio cemetery."

Chesebrough struck his fist into his palm. "You're dragging me down your rabbit hole." He wheezed a laugh. "A *cemetery?* What's wanting with your father's vault, or a safe-deposit box at Crocker, for crying out loud?"

Feldman eyed his desk. "That's a reasonable question for which I lack an adequate answer."

"You said Presidio Cemetery?"

"I did."

"Wait a minute, that's just looney enough for it to be brilliant. We misjudged your old man, Griffo. Arguello Trust protects the cemetery. I mean, the trust runs the Presidio. Your family's turf. I get it. It's secured. The army built secret bunkers there to survive a nuclear attack—stronger than any vault. And nothing goes on there without your family's knowledge. Maybe this scheme isn't so harebrained."

"I'm confident I can access it."

"Your father must have locked the documents in a nuke-proof bunker like Building 1648." Chesebrough referred to a top-secret, Cold War site, which housed army controls for nuclear-tipped, Nike missiles.

"Or something like that," said Feldman. "What matters is recovering the documents is crucial to Father's plan. Without Valentine Scrip, no one could execute this transaction."

"They're hidden in plain sight."

"My grandmother might have influenced their unorthodox location."

"Okay. You got a plan, a phone number, a scrip remnant, and a contact for more. Is that a fair summary?"

"That's all I can reveal to you without a commitment to absolute confidentiality."

"What if you're wrong? If this is another disaster, what am I risking?"

"If this isn't a viable plan, your role will never get off the ground. No one will hear of it and you'll be invisible. The loss won't cost you anything but pride. However, if this works—"

"If it works, I get Alcatraz."

"Exactly."

Chesebrough smiled as he inspected the piece of scrip.

"I need your commitment," said Feldman.

"Then I'm a go. Now it's your turn to answer what I had asked you earlier. What's my buy-in?"

Feldman described the witch's brew of legal, historical, and financial ingredients constituting the plan. "Chicago thinks they own a substantial property that should be titled to the United States government."

"In San Francisco?"

"No. It's the property of the former Fort Dearborn Military Reservation. Forty acres at the mouth of the Chicago River, the city's posh business center."

"I don't get it. You lost me, again."

"Stay with me. Here's the kicker. Father discovered a dirty little secret. The land never rightfully belonged to Chicago."

"How could that be?"

"In 1839—"

"1839! Oh, brother."

"—In 1839, the Secretary of War sold the abandoned military fort to Chicago."

"Ancient history, but it sounds kosher."

"It's *treif*." Feldman rubbed his chin, smiling. "Two material problems with that sale. First, the Secretary of War didn't possess authority to sell United States public domain properties. Second, the War Department marked on the face of the plat, *Public Land Forever to Remain Vacant of Buildings.*"

"So what? They wrote the contract on the map," said Chesebrough. "It's still a *bona fide* contract. He sold. They bought. It's in writing. End of story."

"Not end of story. That plat is the only source of the title the city has ever had to the property. Informal transfers aren't how real estate is transacted."

Chesebrough stretched in his chair and put his arms behind his neck. He blew a low whistle. "No one but your father knew about this?"

Feldman stifled a laugh pressing to burst through his smile. "City officials knew well about the flaw. A century ago, the Chicago City Law Department discreetly, and repeatedly, advised not to erect buildings on the property. But greased politicians developed deaf ears while the city and the railroad interests encroached on the grounds of the fort, making a fortune."

"Chicago politics." Chesebrough shook his head. "Damn, you've got to love those guys."

"The title is defective to a fare-thee-well," Feldman said. "If we establish the flaw in court, it reverts to the United States. Then the property immediately becomes eligible for Valentine Scrip to claim. We present the paper and, *Voila!* The breast of Chicago is ours."

"Not the body part I imagined. But thank you very much."

"You're welcome," cried Feldman.

"What does this have to do with Alcatraz?"

"I'll tell you …."

Days before Feldman showed the plan to Chesebrough he disclosed by telephone the details to his Chinese backers in Macau.

They reminded him their historical real-estate interest centered on Old Gold Mountain, in particular, San Francisco properties. "Chicago has nothing to do with our interests."

"Agreed. It's a red herring. We don't want Chicago. Our plan is to take Alcatraz. The title on Alcatraz is beyond reproach. However, we'll propose a generous swap."

Feldman made sure Macau centered their attention on his next revelation. "You'll need to exert your influence on United States politicians. Cooperation of senators at the very highest level would be required to pass this through the American system. Please realize beforehand this will be a public and a contentious acquisition."

A measured voice on the phone said, "United States Senators acting as cat-paws for speculators is undignified." A lighter struck, followed by a huff and an extended exhalation. "Their cost is high. Your father shamed us once. We suffered a regrettable loss of face because of him. Why should we trust his son?"

During the 1941 Long Beach fiasco, wartime legislators had accused Arthur Dean Feldman's Chinese American backers of anti-Americanism, threatening charges of treason. *"Were they Japanese sympathizers looking to sabotage the energy supply?"*

Years after the debacle receded from the public memory, Arthur Dean Feldman's Gold Mountain partners had warned him, "Your Valentine Scrip holds bad joss. Be rid of it."

Griff Feldman answered the distant voice on the phone. "You should trust his son because I have the plan and the scrip to succeed. Give me your attention and I will share with you the details."

After that confidence-building conversation with Macau, Feldman called Chesebrough to his third-floor office to share his proposal.

"Do the Chinese know how outrageous it is for what I ask?"

Chesebrough twisted his eyebrow end, as if he wound a conductor's watch. "They understand better than you do. But do you understand what they seek?"

Feldman rubbed his thumb and forefinger together. "Even the communist Chinese want the same thing we do, a windfall."

Chesebrough picked up a gold-speckled piece of quartz on Feldman's desk. The stone cooled his hands. "The communists have enough capital, they want high ground. What better place to observe the West than from a 14-story high island in the harbor of the most technologically strategic city in America? For decades, Russians have observed everything we do from Cow Hollow. Antennas bristle from their consulate roof. But they've had the FBI parked across the street jamming them."

"Observe?" Feldman plucked the quartz from Chesebrough's grasp. He eased the Black Hills deep-mine extraction back on his desk. "That sounds as though you mean espionage talk. I don't condone that. Accusations of treason sank the Long Beach deal."

"They want to look over the horizon. It's business," said Chesebrough, "business intelligence. Besides, we have no knowledge whether that's their intention."

Feldman opened and closed the clasp on a gold cufflink. It lay on cotton in a Shreve & Company box on his desk. "First things first," he said. "None of this plan will make sense unless we win absolute discretion to develop the island. It's essential. Macau doesn't want the FBI in their backyard. My plan calls for a sovereign nation to hold title. A sovereign nation won't need to comply with United States regulations. That caveat is my idea, not Father's detail. A project like your Indian reclamations will give us cover. We need a tribal partner. You can provide that, can't you?"

"Eureka!" Chesebrough snapped his fingers. "I didn't think for a second you invited me into this for the price of an editorial. I get it now. A sovereign, hands-off Indian nation seated in San

Francisco Bay—like the 1969 Indian occupation. What a brilliant deflection. This makes sense."

"Can I rely on you to help make that happen?"

"You bought yourself a boy. I own this." Chesebrough chopped his hand. "I'll secure you an Indian nation faster than I can climb your stairs."

Chesebrough called a San Francisco Police Department detective later in the day. The detective headed a Petaluma rancheria Miwok tribe. Chesebrough had funded his application for federal tribal status, expecting repayment with a bonanza of casino advertising revenue directed to his media companies. He first heard of him when the recruit served as the sole Native American in the police. The soft-spoken officer with cable car shoulders had a firebrand's reputation in college. He carried the discordant name of Bear Winkle. Chesebrough wanted Winkle to work for him. He passed along anonymous crime tips for him to make arrests. His Press-Republican then trumpeted the busts. Favorable publicity resulted in the new officer's steady promotion.

One day, the newspaper invited Winkle and other Bay Area Native Americans to voice their concerns at an editorial board meeting. At the forum, he argued Alcatraz Island epitomized legitimate Pan-Indian claims. "The American Indian Movement should have held Alcatraz. The sacred land is our charge. We are its rightful caretakers. I'd take it back for good if I had the opportunity."

Winkle's radical passion planted an idea in Chesebrough's mind that developed while he listened to Feldman's proposal.

He left Feldman and called Winkle. "Do you enjoy relations with any Chicago area tribes?"

"Potawatomi," he responded. "We're brothers."

"If you can agree," Chesebrough said, "I have a plan to return Alcatraz to the Indian, but you must win me Potawatomi cooperation."

After hearing the Alcatraz plan outlined, Winkle said, "If the Indian holds sovereignty for the silent partners, majority control of the casino, and unrestricted access to and from the island, then I'm your warrior."

⚔

Weeks had passed since Winkle agreed to the plan to retake Alcatraz. He had not yet delivered the Potawatomi allies cooperation. The delay prompted Feldman to demand Chesebrough get together with him. They met at Chesebrough's Belvedere home after he refused to scale Feldman's office stairs.

The brown-shingled mansion commanded a lot on the southwest tip of Belvedere Island, terracing to the San Francisco Bay. From sunrise to sunset, Mediterranean light passed through its Palladian windows. When the late afternoon sun stretched away and descended off the coast, the view encompassed a gilded enchantment radiating on a panorama that included Alcatraz Island.

Feldman waited near an archway, tapping his toe off a grand staircase riser. His crisp bowtie flowered from a buttoned collar. In front of him, a wall-sized Flemish tapestry dominated the great room. A frenetic Shih Tzu scattered Thai silk pillows across its crème carpet. It snarled at Feldman as it shook the cushions. The dog's underbite jutted with tiny teeth defying Feldman to step from the foyer. He ignored the annoying threat until a canine hair lighted on his blazer lapel.

Flicking the mote off his chest, Feldman yelled, "Bah!"

The dog lurched and tumbled backward over itself.

"Griff!" bounced back off the open beamed ceiling, as if a bark had come from the animal. Edward Chesebrough turned the corner, wearing sweatpants, brown tasseled loafers, and no socks. An unzipped jacket exposed a martini-olive sized nob protruding from his navel.

"Welcome, counselor." He rubbed a white terry cloth towel over his lumpy nose. "Pardon my late and ignoble entrance. Had to get in my blasted cardios."

160

Feldman stroked his trimmed beard, glancing at the flab rolled above Chesebrough's waistband. "Good evening, Edward. Glad to see you're getting fit. You concerned me when you said you couldn't make it up my stairs."

Chesebrough smelled of soap and scotch. "I merely needed to carve a little time out for the gym."

"Then you should wake up earlier. I get my exercise in at dawn swimming the bay."

"You were made for the water. Watch this. You wouldn't know, but this is what marriage will do to you. My wife made me fatter than a butcher's dog." Chesebrough pressed his stomach sides, pinching a larded cleavage resembling a fat mouth. "Woof! Woof!"

"Brilliant."

Chesebrough laughed, swatting at Feldman's taut midsection. He flung the towel at the dog. It seized and shook the cloth with a terry-muffled snarl.

"How'd our rock look from a seal-eye view?"

Feldman raised his eyebrows, nodding at the kitchen where someone prepared food. "We should sit by the fire." A redwood mantelpiece carved with depictions of extinct California wildlife centered the wall opposite the tapestry. "You'd be warmer there."

Chesebrough pouted. "I'm fine. Let's go out on the deck. Scotch?"

"Bourbon. Neat."

Past a laddered library, Chesebrough sidestepped into his kitchen, sliding a silver tray of deli meats, breads, and cheeses off a limestone counter. "*Hasta mañana*, Francesca," he called out moments before a garage door closed.

Behind the mansion, cut crystal decanters of brown and clear liquors waited for them on a zinc side table. Chesebrough poured. Beyond meticulous gardens, designed to attract the admiration of passing pleasure crafts, a waterside boatlift impaled the bay.

"From here, we can keep our eye on the prize. Isn't that sucker beautiful?" said Chesebrough.

Feldman scrutinized Alcatraz. "The Chesebrough and Feldman families weathered many intimate and contentious business dealings as a team. Agreed?"

"Sure have. All the way back to White Rock Island." Chesebrough pointed his glass at Alcatraz. "And this one will be a hell of a humdinger."

"I'm worried the outsiders' delay could destroy our families." Feldman downed a draft of the whiskey. "My friends are ready to abandon ship."

"They won't go anywhere. Stop worrying." Chesebrough emptied his glass and discarded a lemon twist in the thick lawn. "It's time for the *Chinks* to get to work." He pulled back the corners of his eyes. *"Chop-chop."*

Feldman shot him a withering sneer. "My good friends did their part. Will you bring the Indians?"

Chesebrough rolled a slice of pistachio mortadella around a slender wedge of schloss cheese. With his other hand, he clawed a silver bowl of foie gras. "Winkle is in." He sucked the mound of meat from his fingers. "Relax."

"I'm not talking about Winkle." Feldman rammed a breadstick into his chaise longue. "What about his contacts in Chicago? That's what matters."

Chesebrough spoke while chewing. "I'm on top of it. I phoned him when you were harassing my dog. Winkle's people are good to go. You'd better get moving before he changes his mind."

"You're sure he can bring the others along?"

"Yes."

"Good," Feldman said. "We'll file the legal claims for the Potawatomi Nation against the City of Chicago."

"That's what I call moving, counselor."

"Just get the notice into the *Chicago Tribune* classifieds," said Feldman. "Run the ad for five weeks. Less attention called to it the better."

"Nobody reads that gobbledygook."

Feldman reached over and pushed Chesebrough's forearm away from his mouth. "This is not the time to be sloppy."

"Hey! Easy does it, boss. I'm in touch with people at the Trib. They'll slip the notice in the second run tomorrow. Don't worry."

Feldman scratched the short hairs on his cheek. "I worry about everything. The day after the briefs are filed our Indian band—"

"Hold it," said Chesebrough. "Say Pan-Indian or Potawatomi Nation members. This guy Winkle doesn't have a fast fuse. He has no fuse. None. Show the *Redskin* respect, some class." His mouth opened round to repeat and emphasize syllables, "Po-Ta-Wa-To-Mi."

Feldman blanched at the sight of masticated cheese and meat. "Suddenly, you're enlightened."

"I don't give a crow's foot about political correctness," said Chesebrough. "It's business."

"Indeed. As I said, the Potawatomi need to post on the streets of Chicago the notice I gave you. You remembered it, didn't you?"

"Winkle took care of it." Chesebrough poured himself another scotch. "He sent them a copy on his tom-tom."

"This review may amuse you. Nonetheless, the law requires these steps," said Feldman. "Put your drink down and pay attention."

Chesebrough's head lowered. Deep puckers separated his eyebrows; his voice became a mechanical monotone. "They have to file an affidavit that states they did so. Then they can hold their press conference." He sipped his scotch.

"Correct."

Chesebrough cocked his head, smiled, and popped his finger from inside his cheek. "Winkle told me he wished to be there to post the flyers on the hilts of Potawatomi arrows." He pulled back on an imaginary archer-bow.

Feldman's shoulders relaxed. Others could now do the heavy lifting. The plan was working. His confidence soared. "By the time

I retrieve the scrip from the cemetery, Macau will have larded Swiss bank accounts of key senators."

"Toadies," said Chesebrough.

"Regardless, their expensive support for the Potawatomi declaration will be paid beforehand, and paid in full—irrevocably. We're past the point of reconsidering."

Orange sunset reflected from hundreds of Pacific Heights mansion windows across the bay. Feldman imagined the blaze on each grand home as fiery tongues adding luster to the owners' wealth. Chesebrough saw a hail of Potawatomi fire-arrows striking their marks.

"Far be it from me to brag, but I'm eager to update you on another thorny matter."

"How's that, counselor?" Chesebrough's attention swung back from his musings when he heard Feldman's serious tone.

"Remember that nettle where we had to secure a right-of-way at Crissy Field before the word leaked?" said Feldman.

"Uh-huh. If we don't get easements, I can't imagine how else we can run water and electricity out to the rock. Make any headway?"

"Done. I rolled the Arguello Trust Board. Before those dunderheads realize what they've agreed to, the strip of beachhead property will cede to the Indians."

"Beautiful. How'd you crack that nut?"

Feldman boasted in cultured French, "*C'etait un facile pour moi.* I touted the proposal as reparation to restore an aboriginal village."

"Hot diggity damn," said Chesebrough, in a faulty French mimicry.

"Easy as swimming." Feldman giggled. He stood on his chair. A splashing pool lane from his childhood boarding school extended to him. "Step up!" His voice echoed in the cool air. He adjusted imagined goggle straps behind his ears. "Take your mark!" His arm rose to its fullest, and his trigger digit bent. "The gun!"

Feldman hopped back on the patio deck, exuberant as a child. "And we are off. We've taken the plunge."

Chesebrough mimicked the cry with a lusty laugh. "Taken the plunge! Over the falls—into the brink. Did someone say drink? Don't mind if I do."

He poured another dram of single malt for himself, holding aloft the decanter of bourbon. "I can run that Presidio Landing story in the afternoon edition." Chesebrough swirled the bottle, waiting to pour.

"Downplay the Indian reference before you do," Feldman said.

"Got it covered. The Press-Republican will call our beachhead a Discovery Center."

"Three fingers then, Mr. Hearst."

Feldman flopped into his chair. He held his glass to the side with the insouciance of an emperor. Bourbon splashed over the lip. The fluid settled. Feldman squinted through the tumbler cut prisms at the blurred sunset. He raised his drink toward the water. "To our fathers."

Chesebrough kept his glass pressed to his mouth. He tipped a rolled rye and cheese snack.

After Feldman left the Belvedere estate, the moonrise bewitched a galaxy of navigation lights from the bay. Chesebrough sucked a caraway seed from his tooth and stirred ice with his pinky. Admiring his backyard constellations, he hummed a boozy paean of self-satisfaction. *Chicago politicians understood there was no upside for them if they risked a court case over Fort Dearborn, especially if the Feds paid their extortion.* He drafted in his head an editorial headline he intended to write to promote the casino: *A Proposition with a New Preposition, Escape to Alcatraz.*

Chesebrough fell asleep, confident in his presumptions.

⊷⊶

Days later, a Potawatomi spokesman stood on a Chicago street corner with a scrum of reporters. A scalplock and a porcupine roach holding an eagle feather crowned his fresh shaved head. The

Indian read a statement reclaiming Fort Dearborn in the name of the Pan-Indian Movement.

"We have Valentine Scrip to secure the deed. We will put our claim before the Great White Father's courts."

"Valentines? What?" A mystified reporter jeered, "Ya' don't bring valentines to court."

Another beat writer, wearing a stained Chicago Bears jacket, cried, "What are you smoking in your peace pipe? The city is broke."

The spokesman ignored the gibes. "Though we're confident we'll win our case, we stand ready to offer a deal. A compromise that is fairer to Chicago than the federal government has been to the Indian. The Pan-Indian Movement will give the land back to the city in exchange for other stolen Indian property."

A sardonic voice called out, "I don't have a clue about what you're talking about, chief. However, assuming you do, why don't you take old Wrigley Field, instead? The Cubs don't know how to use it."

"No," said the spokesman. "The city should not bear the burden alone. We will give back Fort Dearborn to Chicago if the federal government cedes Alcatraz Island back to its rightful Indian owners."

"In California?"

"Our offer is more just than the white man's treaties. Alcatraz is a smaller property than Fort Dearborn and it's not occupied."

The day of the Chicago declaration, Macau transferred untraceable gold bars into several politicians' Zurich bank accounts, and Feldman called the mysterious Ramon's phone number to arrange a rendezvous in the Presidio.

The final die had been set for midnight.

EL PRESIDIO

Griff Feldman removed gold cufflinks from his sleeves. Though his father had not bequeathed them to him, or to anyone, he claimed the jewelry as a rightful inheritance. How smart, how ebullient, his father had appeared with the clasps bracketing his business attire. They gleamed with a triumphant aura that arched over him, wrist to wrist. The amulets held no such incantations for the younger Feldman. Their weight diminished his stature.

Feldman rolled the trinkets in his palm, as if he assessed cold dice, before slipping them into his tuxedo pocket. Folding the jacket along its center seam, he draped the garment on a rail over rashes of paint flakes. A prayer shawl had once received the same care and reverence he now tended to his fine-stitched wardrobe. Tradition commended the heirloom to him the day he came of age at 13, decades after his father received the same honor. He assumed his father misplaced the tallit over the years until he uncovered it in the safe under the cufflinks and assorted blaze of his family's history.

Starched French cuffs doubled over Feldman's hands protecting his fingertips from the cold wind. He swayed forward out on a pitted girder. White and green fairies frolicked on his patent leather shoes, prancing from below when navigation lights slid into view.

A petition of salvation fortified him. He last chanted the prayer when he wore the tallit. "May all the people of Israel be forgiven, including all the strangers who live in their midst, for all the people are in fault." The Torah's plea repeated into the wind three times. With each exhortation, Feldman drew in lungfuls of stinging salt air.

Fast automobiles approached from behind him. Tires whistled derisive and sharp. A concerned look over his shoulder found yellow and red lights flashing among rows of guardrails. He shuffled farther on the shortening escarpment. On the lip of the beam, he leaned at the waist. A head tilt beheld twenty-two stories of open air between him and the cement-hard water. His knees weakened with a jerk, bobbing his weight forward. He gasped at his loss of balance. Sharper barbs rasped his lungs.

The mad part of his brain wondered—*what would it be like?*

Updrafts *pop-pop-popped* his ears and buffeted him from the edge.

A Western Gull hovered through a shaft of light to his left. The red dot on its yellow bill distracted Feldman until the bird tilted a wing, wheeled, and plummeted away. Rising gusts it rode to the sea braced Feldman on the girder. The columns of wind ripped through the harp of steel cables, howling low and portentous under the whine of tires.

Feldman waited for the gusts to cease. They did—sooner than expected. He upstretched his arms. A pleasant sensation of rising, of floating weightlessness, snapped him from the bonds of Earth.

Free!

His feet stabbed into the night and he fell from the Golden Gate Bridge.

The Pacific Ocean flew up toward him at ninety miles per hour. Docile waves, which he had sliced during swims from Aquatic Park to Alcatraz, became vulgar drool from a capacious mouth, something audacious that intended to consume him.

Ankles scissored apart. Wild, pinwheeling legs and arms fought for control. Kaleidoscopic orange bridges whirred past his desperate search for the horizon. Gangs of fists pummeled him from impossible directions.

Whipping accelerated. Jet blasts dilated Feldman's lips. They wedged open his jaws and rammed his panicked screams back into his throat.

Then it was over.

A breathless stillness hung in the air. Nothing moved on Earth. Nothing moved in time. Motion had stopped altogether for an instant—for an eternity.

Feldman completed footsteps others had begun on the Petaluma Valley floor. Strangers tread on the land more than one hundred and fifty years earlier, and then his body slammed into the water at the gate. His life, similar to the steel span from which he had leapt, bridged past and future—a transition—an end on neither side.

While Feldman slipped from the bridge, a cacophony of buckets and long-handled tools rattled up the Presidio cemetery hill. The wheeze of sagging springs silenced the din when a pickup truck stopped. A petite woman, under a perspiration-stained hat, exited. She held open the heavy truck door and glared over the hood at Mick Mallory, sleeping on top of the car in front of her.

His pinched face stiffened in the headlight illumination. It reflected a yellowed confectionery, the color of week-old sheet cake. A corduroy jacket he wore splayed unbuttoned, exposing a blue, crewneck sweatshirt. Two faded lines imprinted across the shirt read, "*Montauk*," and "*The End*."

The woman eased shut the truck door. Before the latch clicked, she thought, *crematory*.

Turning to the graves, sifted morning light exposed to her scores of monuments. Shapes, indistinct and spectral, formed in the distance. Nearby, snails slimed pewter tapes on white marble.

A man stepped toward the woman from netted shadows. His hulk swelled, as would the physique of someone who lifted bricks and stones for a living. Black footprints crisscrossed wet grass where he walked. Cigarettes and small pieces of broken monument littered his path.

The woman slipped off her gloves steadying her hands. Her voice modulated to the tone of a church usher. "My name is Juana De la Cruz. You may call me Jack."

The darkness of his hair and eyes, the bridge of his nose, his melded, exotic features, suggested he carried dominant Pacific Islander bloodlines. A high-pitched response surprised her.

"You're the gravedigger? That was fast. I expected a guy, and not so soon."

"Cemetery technician," she said, posturing with a prideful, uplifted chin. "Second generation." Each rounded vowel sounded savored, giving as irresistible a pleasure to her mouth as they did to the listener's ear. "I am here."

"Technician it is." An asymmetrical grin exposed a gold-capped front tooth. "San Francisco Police Detective Bear Winkle—first generation." His right fist lay across his heart. "I'm the sorry SOB who called your boss for help."

Winkle extended his hand. Its ochre skin tone resembled dried rubber cement she had sliced on archived burial records. De la Cruz craned her neck to better view his face. Centrifuge-molded features pulled up toward his brow and stretched away from his ears. The rest of him, a mocha-ebony amalgamation of oversized body parts, coupled with his peculiar name, offered her no sure clues of his race.

Winkle's physical anomalies did not matter. Her own taxonomy classified everyone she met. De la Cruz developed the system in her youth, shadowing her father in the graveyard. Similar to the way a good bartender matched a drink and a dismal story to a patron before they settled onto a stool, her method defined her world. She categorized each acquaintance by where they fit within a cemetery.

Some people she regarded as nobodies, destined for Potter's Field, or laid into common, low-profile graves after they threw away an existence indistinguishable from the ever-dead person next to them. The scandalous she imagined as double buried atop their lover, or lovers. Big shots filled their presence in mausoleums, or in columbarium vessels displayed in prominent alcoves. Then there were the rare memorials, the ones that towered over the rest. They had rich tales written on them. Winkle fit that category. She classified him as a centograph of a man. Life had cold-chiseled a complex story into him in a language she could not understand.

Several yards away, an immaculate Lexus coiled inside the perimeter wall. Twenty feet from the black sedan slouched Mallory's green Volkswagen Karmann Ghia. It appeared as if metal-eating insects devoured sections of its rusted frame. Behind it rested the pickup truck. Its exhaust pipe pinged in the chilly bayside air.

Before Mallory had driven his car from Manhattan to San Francisco, he replaced its crushed, driver-side door with a salvaged one of robin-egg blue. His body, as dented as the automobile, arched across its low contour hood.

De la Cruz turned toward Mallory. Her hand, knotting her gloves, pointed in his direction. "Detective, why is he sleeping here?"

The question had Mallory's full attention before Winkle took notice. Whether awake or asleep, Mallory spied whatever stirred around him. A third eye, only known to him, peered from worried folds on his forehead. The shameless eye never rested, never blinked, nor ever cast away in embarrassment.

He listened with equal vigilance. His boyish-cupped ears funneled sounds with the acuity of a bat ear trumpet. They monitored the low thrums of the night, the strained vibrations of lies, and the faintest clacks of metallic tooled devices.

Unalterable spirits had moved Mallory, Feldman, Winkle, and De la Cruz together. The journeys they walked, they had to walk. All that went before them: the lives of the Mirandas and the Vallejos, the journey of Hoku and the Indian girl, the discovery of gold, a war in the Philippines, sacrificed chicks, all they had done, everything fortune had done unto them, the accumulation of those disparate occurrences, and more, bound their lives with those of the others. Destiny set their fate when Feldman didn't retrieve the Valentine Scrip from the Presidio that evening.

While Mallory weighed De la Cruz and Winkle, the night easternmost reach lightened to a pearl-gray canopy. Stardust debris retreated from the changed hues. They etched fine meteor arcs into the dark, western void.

To the east, spears of sunlight burst through a burned seam in the sky. One golden javelin flashed beneath a leaded dome of fog rising from the bay. It slipped over the ruby lights of embarcadero tugboats snoring against their hawsers. The rod of energy zipped toward the peninsula coast, threading between blue gum, pine, and twisted cypress. Speeding past the walls of the old, Spanish fort, *El Presidio Real de San Francisco*, the light splashed upon a low-set gravestone. A supernal touch illuminated words etched in white marbled relief, "WAR WITH SPAIN."

Torrents of light sprayed in every direction. Where they met the bridge towers, narrow shadows wavered over the face of the Marin headlands.

On the spindrift comb of the retiring night sea, wine-dark fires marked flare paths leading to distant Asian shores, and the unknown. In their speckled wake, the disjointed body of Griff Feldman folded and tumbled under the waves. Ebb tide surges flushed his shoeless carcass, and the fate of the scrip, toward surf-fishing lines stretched from the boulder shore of Battery Cranston.

NOTHING IS DEAD

Juana De la Cruz worked war dead. She knew fallen soldiers had no need for company, neither during day nor during overnight hours. Nothing weighed their conscience from past lives. If troubles followed them to the grave, the press of heels above their remains could not assuage the regrets. They existed on another plane, in another dimension, than did those who mourned for them. Soldiers killed on a battlefield feared no fictional terrors that spooked the living. They had confronted real hell, passing through its tart miasma to become one with horrors the living dare not imagine.

Visitors offered no consolation to De la Cruz's dead. They were of no use to them—or her. Mourners and tourists who trampled on her graves during daytime were a nuisance; trespassers, who dared violate visiting hours at night, intolerable. De la Cruz's eyes focused from Mallory to Winkle, the men whose very presence defiled her cemetery.

"Detective ... Bull ... Winkle. Correct?"

He flashed a disarming grin. "You got the detective and the Winkle parts right, Jack. But, it's Bear. Just Bear not Bull. Bear Winkle. SFPD."

De la Cruz placed her palms on her chin. Her lower jaw rocked side to side. "What happened here, detective? What did you and that guy do to my cemetery? My graves look like someone set up a circus tent on them."

"Wish you could tell me. I'm the cleanup crew. Evidently, this mess resulted from a minor trespass by a wacko. They let him go before I arrived. I noticed nothing missing. Do you?"

A pained smile pulled the corners of her lips. Fiery words crowded to erupt from her mouth. "Respect." She turned toward her truck and cursed under her breath. "You can go now."

Winkle flourished a pen from an inside breast pocket, clicking it several times. The impatient gesture carried to Mallory's ear. "A couple of easy questions first, then I'm gone."

"I want you both gone."

"So do I. We're on the same side." He extracted a notepad from his outer coat and angled the pen to paper. "Tell me about what happened last night. Any tiny, little detail at all. Help me fill in the blank spaces for my report."

Twisted lips screwed her visage. "I got here after you."

"Perhaps, you heard whispers, or noticed an object out of place on the way in." He waited to gauge her response, surprised by the pushback he had received.

Winkle worked best in the jellied hours that slithered through midnight and dawn. In that familiar milieu, he interrogated people along city sidewalks with cynical aloofness. His hustle didn't bite in the cemetery. De la Cruz's lips didn't snake dance for him with the nervous chatter of a street denizen. She scrutinized him, standing with her arms folded and hips squared, measuring the man, as if he were the subject.

"I saw and heard nothing. So, you should go now. And take that guy with you," she said. "Whoever he is."

Until a few hours before he arrived at the cemetery, Winkle had confidence Griff Feldman would get the Valentine Scrip to him. His responsibility, as laid out by Chesebrough, then called for Winkle to deliver the papers to Chicago. The plan went sideways. He couldn't afford to have De la Cruz delay him further.

"That guy," he said, pointing his pen at the vehicles. "The half-alive mug over there, who only looks as dead as everyone here except you and me, is a second-rate reporter from the Press-Republican. Mallory. Mick Mallory."

She appraised him with the expression of a shopper sniffing bad fish. "Nothing is dead in the Presidio Cemetery, Detective." Clipped pronunciations emphasized the vowels in each syllable. "Don't you understand that? Nothing."

Winkle flipped his notepad under his chin and nodded. *You're playing me, sister,* he thought, kicking the heel of his thick-soled shoes. "There must be something special about this section." His stance widened a few inches. "Tell me what makes these graves different from all the others? What's here that'd motivate anyone to go out of their way to mess them up?"

"All the sections are pretty much the same."

"That's what I really need to comprehend. Something made these guys stand out. Who specifically are these guys?"

"—Heroes." De la Cruz turned away, staring into the distance. At the foot of the cemetery hill, wedged between a cast-iron fence and the bay, lanes of headlights streamed off the bridge. Commuter traffic sluiced out of Pacific darkness into San Francisco violet. "Your companion is a guy. These soldiers are heroes, not guys. And now they have been dishonored."

"Sorry." Winkle lowered his voice timbre, wanting to avoid further interruptions.

False notes of his apology rumbled with the soft growl of a threat. Her eyes canted toward the security of her truck cabin. The haven appeared farther away when a knife handle bulged from under his pant cuff.

Winkle said, "I already noticed the men in this section died in the Spanish American War. Are they the only ones the Spanish killed? What else can you tell me about them?"

"They're soldiers. Nothing more than it looks like."

"I don't make a connection with last night," said Winkle.

"Wouldn't expect you to. And I don't care whether you did. You don't belong here and there's nothing here that can help you." Her hand passed across her mouth. "Just go. That's all there is. It's not my fault if you don't want to accept what's in front of you."

Winkle smiled a lopsided grin.

Be cool man, he thought to himself. *The stress of Feldman not getting the scrip and the fatigue from this lousy day is overwhelming my patience. I can't allow that to happen. Not now. But to be standing on Indian lands while that cemetery mole talks at me as though I don't belong here.... If she had been a man, I'd have picked her up and body-slammed her to the turf.*

"I see what's in front of me—Jack." He cracked off the "K" in her name, as if breaking a small bone with his teeth while he smiled. "Have you considered I might see things here you don't, Jack."

De la Cruz wished she had a heavy rake in her hands to pull through the thick grass. It might relax her. And she could use it to defend herself. "I doubt it. My family and I have worked here for a long time."

"Really? Your family has been here a long time?"

"We have."

Winkle loosened his shirt collar. "Well then, you've seen where the Spanish dumped my ancestors outside their fort walls." He did not pause for her answer. "Or over there, after all your years of looking and knowing everything about this place, you must have visited Petlenuc. It's there. See it?"

"Wait, what? That's Crissy Field."

"It's the Indian village called Petlenuc. Right there by the shore. Can you make it out now? Can you hear children laughing? I can. They are my family. They have been here a long time, too. Look hard."

De la Cruz shook her head. Whitecaps offshore breathed chilled morning air on the bay. "It's just a cold beach."

"You're the one who can't see what's in front of you—Jack. A creek connects Petlenuc to the Chutchui village near Mission Dolores. It's under concrete. But it's alive. It flows. Like blood. Like time. I sense it. You don't. I smell fires from earthen ovens. I sense more than three thousand years of Indian land. Three thousand years of Indian life. Children. Birth. Cry songs. Dance celebrations. All that is very clear to me. Yet you don't see it. It hasn't died. Not for three thousand years. How long has America claimed this land? Less than two hundred years. Betcha that feels like a long time for you, huh? Compare that blip to more than three thousand years of Indian culture thriving here. You can't imagine that much time, nor understand its enduring significance. Can you?"

"You may talk a lot, and have a vivid imagination, but you're still talking about Crissy Field."

"It will always be Petlenuc. This area is sacred Indian land. Native Americans are its caretakers. Not the Spanish. Not the Mexicans and not the United States—nor its cemetery technicians."

Thick underhum of traffic and the shiver of gum tree branches filled the sudden silence.

"You've lost me. I must have missed something. If you have questions I can answer, let's hear them. Otherwise, you're abusing my time.... Please go back to where you belong."

Winkle pulled a strand of hair stuck to the corner of his mouth. "Sorry." His eyes softened to a warmer brown. "I'm my worst enemy.

I run off at the mouth when I'm worked up and tired. It must be in my blood. And, frankly, I'm exhausted. Sometimes I forget I'm not talking to me."

"Well...." De la Cruz tugged on her hat brim. "Hmm."

"Please," said Winkle, "just tell me what you can about this section of men and I'll shut up."

"*Okaaaay*. Wow. Anyway, I can tell you most of these men left America to—"

A loud metallic waffle from the Karmann Ghia halted De la Cruz as Mallory stretched his legs. Winkle directed her attention back to his interest. "You were saying?"

"Um, I was saying the older graves are for men who fought in the Philippine-American War. It wasn't as you presumed, the Spanish American War."

"I've never heard of a Philippine-American War. You're right. I'm guilty as hell for presuming. You'd think I'd know better. I hate it when people presume I'm not Native American. I'm guilty of presuming, too. That's bad. For example, when I first laid eyes on you, I mistook you for Japanese American until you gave me your name."

De la Cruz bent to pick cigarette stubs and candy wrappers off the grass. She smirked. "I'm glad my mother never heard you say that. I'm definitely not Japanese." Cellophane litter crushed in her hands. "Mother won't even let her children buy a Japanese car, like your Lexus. It's forbidden."

Winkle stepped away to the gravestones.

"Let's walk downhill," said De la Cruz. "There are more historical monuments than these to inspect. Maybe you'll have questions about those."

As Winkle passed the row of grave markers, he wrote each name and date of death in neat black ink on his pad. "Wait up."

She shouted back, "If you walk this way, I can tell you more."

"Why can't you buy a Japanese car?" He called out. "I'm listening. Turn around and talk in this direction."

"Family history. The Japanese killed Lola, and wounded my mother, on February 5th, 1945."

"Who?" Winkle lifted his pen. "Are you for real about that date?" He came back toward her at the middle of a row of gravestones, beckoning with his hand. "Come over here. That's terrible. I want to hear more. But this guy in that beat-up grave died on the same day."

"No, that hero didn't." De la Cruz turned from where he pointed.

"Yes, he did. Please. I promise not to bark. Look for yourself. Is there a connection with him and your family? Tell me about this guy—this hero."

She took a few unhurried steps toward Winkle. He waited by a dark gravestone cut at acute angles, not formed like the other rounded monuments. "He's just an anonymous hero."

"But here's another odd thing, the stone color is off," said Winkle. "What should I be seeing here?"

The gravestone to which he pointed presented a gray face unlike the white slabs in the row. Grave carvers etched most 19th-century, military markers on single white stones. Inlaid within shields were grave plot numbers, initials of first and middle names, and last names. That might be the only recollection of a tragic existence passed on to posterity. Sometimes, the government included: the home state, place of death, war, or the particular victorious, and only victorious, battle that claimed the life. More often, with proportion and placement declaring it the most significant identification, bold letters, USA, anchored the shields' bottoms.

Winkle stared at the only one not carved from a single piece, but stacked three sections high. On the lowest, polished slab, the size of a large wedding-dress box, balanced a second beveled stone with the words, "*Our Dear Boy.*" At the top stood a rectangular pillar etched with a depiction of a heaven gate swung open and "*HERALD*" written across the gate's six planks.

Below the image the dedication read:
ARTHUR L. DEAN.
KILLED IN ACTION NEAR MANILA,
FEB 5, 1899.
AGED 23 YEARS.

"Same month and day as my family's tragedy, yes, only a half century earlier," she said with derision. "And shot by Filipinos. Not Spanish. And, certainly, not killed by Japanese. The war with Spain, the war with which you're familiar, had ended by then. I learned that useless trivia from Tatay, my father. I guess that's something real and right in front of us I can see, and that you can't. That makes us even."

She tried to step aside. Winkle stopped her. "You said your mother and Lola. Who's Lola?"

"Tagalog. Like Tatay." De la Cruz's expression hardened. "Lola means grandmother." She walked down the hill.

"Wait up. I want to hear more about your father and family." Winkle shouted after her. "Japanese shot your grandmother and your mother?"

"Not shot. Hacked. Cut—sword cuts. They killed Lola. Did worse to others. Mother's scar won't let her forget."

"Sliced by Japanese soldiers? As a child?" Winkle shuddered. "It must have been an Imperial Army long blade. My God." Stringed sinew in his cheeks twitched with his quickened heart. He imagined how exciting the smooth and pebbly textures would feel if he hard-rubbed his thumb over her scar tissue, its warm softness belying the chaos that created the wound.

By the wall, Mallory squirmed knowing Griff Feldman, the reason he waffled on a metal hood, had left the cemetery. He had escaped his surveillance while Mallory endured De la Cruz's family stories.

Police had done their job filing a report: an alleged trespasser, Griffin Feldman of San Francisco, desecrated the national cemetery grounds after midnight. Responding officers caught him in the act, restrained him, and then released him.

No one disputed the *who, what, when* and *where* of the police blotter.

For Mallory, he hadn't recorded the important story. He felt it drifting out of reach. The opportunity to seize its essence moved farther away each minute. Mallory needed the indispensable *why*, before it was too late.

The back of his head rocked on the unyielding windshield. A notebook gilded with the words, "*Love Siobhan,*" slipped from his lap to the hood. He lurched for it. The stretch dislocated his car keys. They jangled from his jacket pocket. Mallory pinned the leather-cover under his wrist. His keys slid over the fender slope and onto the ground.

The commotion reminded Winkle that if not for Mallory's attendance, he'd have finished and left. *I need a clue to where else Feldman might have been looking for the scrip before Mallory comes over here. This gal's uncomfortable, and her family seems too connected to this area of the cemetery for it to be a coincidence.*

He waited for a deep foghorn blast from the bridge to end. "I'm sorry for dwelling on your family's loss. Let me change the subject. What does scrip mean to you?"

De la Cruz dropped her glove. "Scripts?" She fumbled the glove she held and bent to pick up the other. "Like movies? TV shows?— I don't know. Means nothing."

"S-C-R-I-P. Scrip. Nothing at all? You're sure?" His hand swung at the headstones. "What about Feldmans? Any Feldmans near that Dean guy?"

She whispered, "Feldmans? Do I remember any buried soldiers named Feldman?"

"Yeah." Winkle assessed the sincerity in her face. "Near here."

"No. Not Feldman. A Jewish name? There weren't many Jews in California then, less so in the Army. But I may be wrong. Let's go down to the visitor's center. We can check. The dead are listed there."

Winkle noted the way she intended on moving him away from that grave. He calculated the time of day in Chicago. If he didn't gain the scrip soon, the delay would unravel the plan to take Alcatraz.

"Tatay, your father—"

"Ramon or Mr. De la Cruz. Only his family calls him Tatay."

"You said you were second generation … uh."

"Cemetery technician."

"He maintained the grounds here before you?"

"Yes."

"Does he recall anything unusual about these graves?"

"No."

"You sure? Nothing?"

"He knew lots about a lot of things about this cemetery—lots." Her eyes glistened. "Unfortunately, Tatay died a while ago flying back from Manila."

"Oh." Winkle stopped writing in his notepad.

"You would have been better off talking to him. He saw things that even I can't see. His soul was bigger than mine." A droplet tickled the end of De la Cruz's nose. "Tatay believed in silly Filipino mysticism. My priest calls it Folk Catholicism. Tatay learned it when he grew up with it in the Philippines."

"You must have thought he was a special guy."

"Yeah. He observed things most people missed. I'll give you an example. On the Island of Corregidor in the Philippines, shoreline pebbles have red spots. He said blood of dead soldiers colored them. He really meant it. And here in the cemetery, one of many details he noticed about these headstones was they leaned."

"Leaned?"

"He said they leaned like stretched fingers, yearning for a more peaceful resting place over there, on the island." She pointed beyond the stones, which covered the groomed crest to the bay.

"Alcatraz?" snapped Winkle. "What did he tell you about Alcatraz?"

"Not Alcatraz. Angel Island." A white pennant of fog streamed off the island crown, northwest of Alcatraz. "Tatay perceived beauty no one else could understand."

Winkle plucked his lower lip. "I wonder whether he could have picked out the beautiful words, *Free Indian Land* from here. They're powerful and mystical, too. The words are on the Alcatraz water tower from sixty-nine."

"I don't know much about Alcatraz. Neither did Tatay." A bead of moisture disappeared from her nose in a sniff. "For each of us, the cemetery begins and ends everything important."

Winkle scratched his thumbnail across his wrist bottom in the nervous cadence of: *locate Feldman, find the scrip, and get it to Chicago.*

"And there was nothing he thought special about this section of graves?"

"Nope."

While De la Cruz deflected Winkle's questions, Mallory juggled his recollections about the night events. Lyrical story elements flourished around him: anxious faces; a dramatic cemetery, with its rich catalogue of young lives destroyed in battle; the smell of bay and ocean, and the sudden cloud breaks that unveiled etches of meteor tails. All that sensuous, emoting *crap*. All that drama. All that had once mortared his story lines together set nothing in place to explain the vandalism. No matter how often he reviewed the details, or rearranged their order, a coherent story didn't pull together. It lacked the *why*.

Mallory refocused on the overnight moments Feldman had sat on the damp sod in black tie, clawing at grass where he rocked. Mud slathered his gold sapphire ring.

Figuring this out is like trying to sweep back this San Francisco fog with a broom. Why did Feldman come here?

When they searched the grounds that night, the cops had leaned a redwood post behind a police car near Mallory. On the whitewashed side, faded letters "H-E-R-A-L-D," indistinguishable carvings if not for the slant of a headlight beam, raised an edge on the weathered surface. The word intrigued him. Catholic education fixed "herald" in his parochial school-formed brain. He couldn't dismiss its religious connotation: *something extraordinary is imminent.*

A rosary decade of black veiled nuns had encouraged him to delve his awareness deeper than the physical world, embrace the realm of spirits. Sisters said his Irish-Catholic heritage imbued him with a special grace that connected him to the dead. The underworld hovered in his presence, a prayer away.

Maybe in Feldman's presence, too, he thought. Feldman had rocked on the ground blabbing *non-sequiturs* on scripts, tradition, and Alcatraz—no different from a haunted soul rambling from a park bench.

After police flashlights swept the graveyard that night, a gloved clap signaled an end to the inspection. "We're done." The commander pointed to the turf. "These old folks deserve some sleep."

Sleep. That notion became Mallory's resolve. Feign sleep. Don't leave until he found the story. Dwell among the dead as the Sisters had taught him. Listen for spirits.

Back East, Mallory had almost permanently joined the dead when he crushed his skull against his car ceiling. Before the crash, captivating narratives flooded from his imagination with tales that chronicled the contemporary lives of New Yorkers.

The night his decline began, he skidded and flipped on the Westside Highway. They cut his broken body out from the turned over door wreckage. Firefighters swept the shattered glass. They sopped up the dirty oil mixed with blood. The car and Mallory mended.

Mallory wished they had designated his celebrated passion to write stories, "Dead on Arrival." If they had drawn a sheet over his body and desires, instead of jolting his heart back from death, it would have been merciful. Their rescue left him alone, devoid of inspiration, and lost in a dank cemetery the breadth of a continent from his former glory.

Mallory had blundered to the Presidio cemetery because of his terror he might fall asleep in his apartment. When he slept, disembodied wails from the car accident clawed his conscience. The reminders triggered panic attacks. Mallory awoke choking, as if a peach pit wedged in his windpipe. When he recovered from the psychological traumas, he came back less alive and in more pain.

To avoid the nightly assaults, Mallory left his apartment. He drove in the San Francisco dark, following the route for the 49 Mile Drive. The tourist circuit signs returned him to his apartment by daybreak if he lost his way. During this night's excursion along the city edge, Mallory observed a diffused glow in the Presidio graveyard. Intrigued, he flitted from Doyle Drive into an invisible web, set between him and the light.

Hours had passed since he arrived at the cemetery. The rising bay aromas, the new visitor in the truck, and the quickened traffic buzz stirred his senses. His lungs craved nicotine. A hungry, reflexive twitch of his diaphragm drew in the bite of eucalyptus oils. He coughed hard. His head rose and slammed onto the windshield. Mallory's hand danced across his chest, slipping from his jacket a bent cigarette smoked to near its end. He sat up on the hood and peered with an unfocused gaze at the couple staring back at him.

His jawline pulsed. *Be where you are.*

Mallory kneaded the curved stub within his lips. He struck a match, drawing a cloud of smoke into his lungs. When the short butt whitened to ash, he launched its nub. It smoldered a high arc and landed at De la Cruz's feet.

She looked up at him.

Mallory swung his arms over his head. His torso flowed over the fender until his duck boots steadied on the perimeter road. "Whoosh!" he croaked, rocking backward along the green body to the blue door. His slouch braced against its metal frame. Rivulets of dew trembled to the bottom of the side window. They pooled inside his belt. The gathered hem of his jacket dampened, chilling his kidneys.

That night he had entered the graveyard for the first time, and for the first time he saw the plots up close. He had observed the graves in hurried glances when he drove by the ancient fence. On this closer inspection, he thought each grave appeared concave, dimpled by final inhalations that the dying hoped never to release.

Mallory had seen violent deaths in his work. Gore did not bother him. But the military graves deceptive symmetry, placid as white swans mirrored on a flat pond, unnerved him. The diabolical, antiseptic sameness of the plots obscured the chaotic savagery that required their construction. Whatever macabre horrors entombed in the buried, fungus-lined boxes, he assumed fed the sweet tang of mowed grass. It turned his stomach.

His chin pressed on his neck. The curve of his thumb wiped his mouth, rubbing a scowl from his lips.

"A triumph of geometry obscuring barbarism." He proclaimed it loud, so the others took notice.

That night, such horrid contemplations made Mallory reluctant to leave the road. When cops gathered farther along the row of graves, he declined an invitation to join those who smoked cigarettes. He inched nearer to where Feldman clawed at the grass.

A scrap of engraved paper flapped on the ground. It blew from a copper box next to the damaged tombstone. At first, he thought the shard might be a torn dollar bill, until he noticed its blank underside.

He picked the remnant off the turf. Print rose on fine stock. Mallory edged to the box from where it came, careful not to cross over grave tops. The exterior verdigris contrasted with its bright-orange interior. When he leaned over the empty container, Feldman gave him a wild-eyed smile.

Someone called. Mallory slipped the folded scrap into his pocket.

A leather-headed police sergeant grasped his unease. "Hey Mallory! What are you doing, puking your Guinness? Let's jump on a grave together."

The sergeant spread her elbows and laced her fingers behind her close-cropped hair, thrusting her pelvis in exaggerated swings. A heavy utility belt jingled with each pump. Other cops howled.

Jump? Mallory shuddered at the thought he might plunge through a grave cap. He even feared to walk across a grave—no less jump on one—especially at night. Pressing weight might eruct putrid gas sealed under the sod, or a flesh-shredded hand might reach up and cinch a tattered, gray clasp on his ankle. He had laughed off his trepidations among his drinking-buddies. In his secluded moments of dark candor, he thought his nightmares possible.

Morning light helped allay his anxieties. Mallory sauntered from the car, striding past De la Cruz to Winkle. Raised, punch-scarred eyebrows gave him an expression of astonished amusement, as if he shared a jest with those who met him, regardless of his disposition, or theirs.

"Bear, baby! Hey, Boo-boo. Wanna steal some picnic baskets?" He threw his arms around Winkle and embraced him, patting his back.

"It's about time you got up, Mr. Mick Mallory," said Winkle.

Mallory pulled his jacket across his sweatshirt, sniffing the air. His ears opened wider to the San Francisco clamor building on the cemetery perimeter. A chorus of songbirds enjoined in an a cappella, pushing against the awakened rumble.

Winkle read most faces. He had to—his safety depended on identifying friend or foe. Nevertheless, he never interpreted Mallory's face well, less so since Mallory had his disfiguring car-accident. Winkle couldn't decipher his mien, or anticipate his responses. Scattershot comments darted from his mouth without forethought or hesitation.

"Say, brave brother from another squaw mother, where can a reporter get a *friggin'* bagel around this joint? I'm famished."

"You're not in New York any longer."

"Tell me about it." Mallory drew in a sour breath. "Take a whiff of these California eucalyptus trees. *Pee-yew!* Smells like cat urine. I hate the smell of cat boxes."

Winkle sighed. "We're overstaying our welcome. Before we book out, I have to ask you a few questions."

"There are a few things I'd like to ask you, too. First of all, when did you get here? Second of all, make this first of all, do you have a cigarette?" Mallory fingered his lips.

"Late. You were asleep." Winkle handed him a hard box of American Spirit cigarettes. "Take what I've got. Save them for later. No smoking on cemetery grounds."

"Is that a joke? No smoking here? In a cemetery? What are these Californians worried about, secondhand decomposition? Cops smoked last night like one of your Indian sweathouses. Who cares?"

An admonishment choked in De la Cruz's throat. She gazed up at the canopy of trees. Bayonet-leaves flickered from blue-ash to olive.

"Let me ask you a few questions," Mallory said to Winkle.

"Later. For now, you tell me about the suspect."

"Suspect of what?"

Winkle's cheeks filled with the breath of a trumpeter. He blew hard. "What's your take on him?"

"Oh, you mean the dirty guy? Not much. Looked like a big bag of dog droppings in a good tuxedo."

"What did he say?"

"I didn't hear him say anything I remember, other than his name."

"And what was that?"

"Freestone? That sounded like it. I'm almost sure about that. Before I forget, thank your blue-suit guys for the offer to sleep here last night. What a great idea. Didn't think the Feds allowed it."

Winkle shot a glance at De la Cruz who held still while she studied the side of Mallory's head. Bark twirled from trees onto her overalls.

"Let me introduce you to the *man* in charge around here," said Winkle. "Miss Juana De la Cruz." An awkward grin twisted Winkle's face. "She runs this place. From what little information she's offered me, I think she might have been born here."

Mallory turned from him toward De la Cruz. "Top of the mornin' to you, too, Chief. Mick Mallory." He scratched a match and pressed its flame to a cigarette. "You were here last night? Didn't notice you either. Watch what you say to this cop. He doesn't mess around. I know him. He's an old friend. Right, Boo? He once tossed a junkie through a plate-glass storefront. Then arrested him for breaking and entering." Mallory extended the package toward her. "Here, boss, take one."

"I'm not the boss, sir. I'm just a cemetery technician, the one who picks up your trash. I don't need your cigarettes, or your opinions. And to answer your question, I arrived here a short while ago."

"Thanks. You do a great job. I've always said Mexicans make the best gardeners."

"Cemetery technician. I'm not Mexican."

"De la Cruz? Sounds Mexican. Or *Rican?* Wait. Don't tell me. I'm good with names. No! No, no, no. I'm damn sure of what you are. Of course. You, Madam, are a dead ringer for Japanese."

De la Cruz drew back, as if he had poked a stick into her stomach.

Mallory grinned. "*Ohayou*, Lady Gardener."

Her eyelashes fluttered. "Any decent minded person wouldn't consider smoking or dropping his litter on the resting place of American heroes."

"Hey. I'm sorry, De la Cruz-san." He bowed in mock subjugation.

She pursed her lips, sucking words back up through an imagined cocktail straw. Her tongue clucked off her palate. "Montauk. The End."

"Say what?" Mallory responded.

"What's your sweatshirt mean?"

"What? Oh, this old thing?" Mallory craned at his chest. "It means I'm cold."

She smiled at him, as though she had a mouth full of dental cotton.

"Got this in Montauk." He nodded back. "A town at the end of Long Island. East Coast. That's why the shirt says that, 'The End.' I went there once with my wife."

De la Cruz's arms folded across her bosom. Mallory noted her hands, small and manicured, an odd pair of hands for a gravedigger.

"Wife?" She leveled a smirk at his ring-less left hand holding the cigarette. "You? You're married?"

"Since 1980. Long time ago. I looked like a drop-dead gorgeous hunk of a lovemaking machine then. Surprised?"

"Charmed."

Mallory tapped his cigarette. "Because you asked about the shirt, I'll tell you. Bought it when I dropped out of sight after writing a series of top-fold columns about Ron Spelotti. You've heard who he is, right? New York mob boss."

"Nope. Never heard of him."

Mallory raised an eyebrow. "Wink, tell 'er. This is the real deal." Winkle gestured he agreed.

"Well, my wife she was a worrier, always afraid this Spelotti gangster guy was *gonna* kill me. Hell. I didn't care."

He swung a buffoonish uppercut at Winkle. "Anyway. You'll love this, Wink. We went to this isolated Long Island beach resort to get away. Way out on the East End. We strolled along the shore real early in the morning so no one might recognize us. Rained like a son of a bitch the night before. God, you should've seen the beach. One of those full moon tides flooded the shore. Horseshoe crabs humping in salt water covered the parking lots. No one was around, except some surf fishermen.

"Oh, excuse me. Did it again. Forgot we're in California. You'd call them fisher-persons.

"All along the beach were hundreds of these dead blowfish, and thousands of see-through jellyfish. Everywhere. Storm pushed them in. Looked like a truck dumped a load of those *whatchamacallits*?"

Mallory cupped his chest. "Silicone breast implants. All over the place. Know what I mean? Anyway." He freed an adolescent giggle. "Anyway, wouldn't you know it, but who comes power walking down the beach? Like he's Neptune slipping from the sea mist, sporting a thigh-high hotel robe. Ron 'The Swan' Spelotti. Spelotti! I swear to God, Boo. I froze. But I'll be damned. I don't think he saw me. Strutted right past us. The robe fit him like one of those peekaboo wraps chicks wear in a massage parlor."

Mallory put his hand to his mouth, whispering sideways to Winkle, "The hem barely covered his junk."

He turned back to De la Cruz. "Anyway, he missed me. I guess he thought I was a goddamn puffed-up fish with my mouth wide open."

"Your poor wife," De la Cruz said. "You're really married? And you use the word *chick* in her presence?"

"Very really.... I should've said I was. She's dead now. Gonzo."

De la Cruz's eyes widened.

Mallory sucked a drag of his cigarette. A nervous laugh brought on spasms of coughs. He wheezed, hugging his sides. "Ouch. I know what you're thinking. Her death had nothing to do with Spelotti. That's why I wear this shirt. It makes me bulletproof."

She winced, searching into his pupils.

"A freak killed—a freak." Mallory closed his eyes. "A freak accident killed her."

He counted deep, slow breaths, one through nine, again one through nine, and again. A therapist had advised him to tally his inhalations and exhalations. He promised the mantra brought succor. Mallory fired the therapist. With the money he saved, he bought gin.

Winkle shouted, "Mick! Mick. Are you okay?" Mallory woke unaware of how much time had passed while in his mantra trance.

Glazed eyes drifted toward Winkle. "Yeah. I'm fine. Why?"

Winkle patted his head. "You're not with the program."

"I was just daydreaming. But I got work to do now."

"I can talk with you on the way out. We want to keep this among us. That means no reporting. You're here as my friend. Right?"

"Sure," Mallory said. "I've never had a friend like you."

"If you're a reporter, you're a trespasser. A *jailed* trespasser. We don't want that. No stories. And, by the way, you left your car lights on."

Mallory had kept his lights on to better see the grounds. The command from Winkle not to write his story concerned him, not the inconvenience of a dead battery.

"Well, they're off now," interjected De la Cruz. "I'll give you a jump from the truck if you need it."

"Push start would be quicker. I'll pop the clutch." Mallory nodded at Winkle. "Gotta talk later today, Bear."

"I said no reporting."

"Copy that. But before I get your quotes, I've got a question for Jacko."

"Name's Juana, not Jacko."

"That's what I said. Anyway, how come the headstones are not all the same? Most graves seem alike. Why's that one there dark marble? An officer?"

She shrugged. "Officers are interred in the circle over there. We'll never know why this grave is different. Burial site details—including their size—are a strict privacy issue. You would have to have access to the archives. It's a violation of federal law even for me to see those files. This is the only national cemetery where they allowed custom headstones."

"That's it? Who cares? Did you take a gander at that fancy one, Wink? That marble has more warmth than you do. Boring!"

Mallory stopped to cough. His chest burned from raising his voice. "Okay this has been lovely. I'm *outta* here. So Jacko, would you give me a push?"

Her eyelids clenched. "Don't tempt me, Mr. Mallory."

He laid a glance of approval on her. Lavender fringe from a satin bra peeked from under her jumpsuit lapel. He associated the intimate wear with small ankles and painted toenails. "Are you sure you're not from New York?"

"The clown knows better," said Winkle to De la Cruz. "Please give me your phone number in case I have any follow-up questions."

She repeated it to him and walked with Mallory to the vehicles. Winkle stayed, writing names into his notepad.

At the car, De la Cruz brushed Mallory's arm. His elbow recoiled to his ribs. "Wait," she said. "There's more you should know about that dark headstone. That guy here last night, we know his name wasn't *Freestone*. The name might be Feldman, right?"

"Oh."

"Well, my good Filipino father—not Japanese." Her condemning eyes leveled at him. "He worked here before me. Told me stories about how that guy's grandmother visited that grave each year in February. Not in the spring. Never during summer holidays when most visitors pay their respects. February, rain or shine. California's seaside weather can be brutal for anybody in winter, even worse for the elderly. She came to the cemetery in a chauffeured limo. The driver and Father took plywood from the trunk, putting the boards on the grass to that headstone. Tatay suggested it. That lady first placed a flower and a stone on the grave to the right of Dean's. Then she visited the Dean grave. Father acted kind to that lady. And she was good to him."

"This is important because?"

"In the early days he laid the boards so she could walk across the grass. Later, toward the end of her life, Tatay pushed her over them in her wheelchair. Father said she carried what sounded to me to be a shortened fencepost. I've no idea whether that's what it was. When she was too weak to carry it, she rested the post across the wheelchair arms. It must have held great value."

"Maybe she carried a pogo stick," Mallory said. "You seem to know everything else about her. Not a bad soliloquy for an innocent who claimed to Winkle she never knew the name Feldman."

"You overheard that?"

"I'm a good listener."

"Did you remember seeing Mr. Feldman with it—something shaped like an old, antique post?"

"Yeah, but I don't care about stuff in the past. Tell me about last night. Tell me about the name on that headstone. Dean, not Feldman."

"I'm surprised you're not aware of them. Feldmans are prominent San Franciscans. West Coast Kennedys. Have been for generations. They funded the Arguello Trust that runs the Presidio. "

"I would've known them if they had lived in Flatbush, but they didn't. Tell me about the security lapse. Do patrol cars—"

"The Feldman grandmother's maiden name was Rosenthal."

"Enough! Histories don't concern me, especially family histories." Mallory covered his ears. "If you insist on continuing your genealogy lecture, wake me after your begats finish with Cain and Abel."

Her tone changed to that of a best friend confiding over a kitchen table. "Father told me this Feldman family lore as if they were royalty and very important to the graveyard. If they affected the graveyard, they were important to him, as they now are to me, too."

"Sweet, but I make my living telling stories. Sorry to break this news to you, kid. Stories, especially father's stories, aren't always true." Mallory crossed his lips. "Tell me this. That Dean name. That's not Jewish. Is it?"

She touched his cheek with her fingertips. "Are you pulling my leg?"

"Forget about it, bring me to the present." Mallory stroked his face where she touched him. "I've got to go meet somebody. Tell me something that relates to last night."

"Someone moved that headstone. They didn't just beat it up. The epoxy on the foundation is broken."

"What gives? Why do you dump all this on me, and not Detective Winkle?"

"I don't like his attitude and I don't like outsiders who think they belong here nosing around my graves. Call it Filipino mysticism." Her low whisper carried urgency. "The question you should ask yourself is why didn't Winkle tell me?"

Mallory's throat tightened. "Here's the deal. Cops reassembled that stone last night. I saw it. They put the urn back."

"Urn?"

"Yeah. Said this was a big mix-up. A misunderstanding among gentleman. Feldman acted drunk. Bumbled into the cemetery. Then into the headstone. Like the guy who gets up in the middle of the night to go to the bathroom and awakens in his neighbor's house peeing on the living-room carpet. In New York, we would say that's the whole megillah."

"Was he drunk?"

"He wasn't drunk. I was drunk. End of story. Now you tell me something. Who's in the grave next to that one?"

An upturned hand stopped him. "You're sure what you saw was a post, and you saw an urn? Shaped like a box? Opened?"

"Closed. Who's in the other grave?"

"Pitts. The name is John Pitts." She pressed. "They put it back?"

"What? Yeah. Put it back." A bitter expression hid the truth. He had not seen them replace the post in the urn. It wound up in Winkle's trunk.

"Anyway, what's the story with this stiff, Dean? Where'd he come from?"

"Tatay said Petaluma."

"Peta—what? Where?"

"Petaluma."

"What's a Petaluma?" Winkle's predatory eyes glowered their way. Mallory's voice trailed. "Winkle thinks we're talking about him. Play along with me."

"Play what? Speak up."

"Ah, hell, get over yourself," Mallory shouted loud enough for Winkle to notice.

"Why are you yelling at me?" De la Cruz shivered her head. "So was Pitts. Dean *and* Pitts. Both from Petaluma."

"It's just a goddamn cigarette." Mallory bawled with more force through his coughs. "Get over it, Jacko."

"What are you saying?"

"How about that push, so I can exit this compost factory?" His ribs ached from the exertion.

"Wait, there's more." Her eyes swept side to side, not toward Winkle.

"Better hurry," Mallory whispered. "He's inching closer."

She smirked and faced the automobiles, arms flexed at her sides, fists clenched. "It's none of his business. Listen up. I vowed to my father long ago I'd never discuss this. I haven't. Never. Not with anyone. Not even with my mother, and I live with her."

"Bet you will with me though, a broken-down scummy New York reporter you've just met and don't like." Mallory sighed. "*C'mon.*"

She pondered her father's lessons. *How can I be so familiar, so trusting, with this despicable stranger?*

"I can't believe I'm about to tell you this, either." De la Cruz nodded. "But there are times that are meant to be. So don't mess with my head. Answer me straight-up."

"Go ahead then." Mallory snapped an ash from his cigarette. "All right already. Go ahead." His lungs throbbed. He delivered a stream of cooling smoke into his chest and elevated his chin.

She bore deep into his shifting eyes. "Are you a good man?"

Mallory spun on his heels. A smoke cataract burst from his nose. "What the? Am I a good man? Hell, no," he exclaimed. "Jesus Christ. That's obvious enough."

"I need a serious answer. Please, don't turn away." De la Cruz wheeled his shoulders toward her. "Stop it. Look me in the eyes."

He flinched. Extraordinary strength from her small hands pinched his arms. He laid his palms on her. A voice-twitch betrayed his doubt. "I'm not messing with you. I don't understand what you mean, Juana."

"Just tell me." Her softened speech calmed him. "Are you a good man? I'm listening."

"Don't know. Maybe. I don't know whether I even try. I don't know." Mallory breathed in the morning air and blew out. "Once. I once hoped I could. I once was...."

Winkle edged closer to the automobiles, still beyond range of their sotto voices.

"Okay," De la Cruz said. "Listen. This is the thing. Father confided to me there might have been a treasure buried here."

Mallory compressed his lips to suppress a laugh. "In a dead man's chest?"

"If the jackals got word of it, they'd tear this place up. Do you notice the bronze sculptures?"

"Where? I don't see any bronze."

"Right. You don't see them because the jackals took them. If there's anything worth stealing, they'll come back. Keep everyone away from those graves, especially that nosy cop. Those heroes buried there went to the Philippines to help my people. They've earned their peace, and my family's respect. Father said it's our responsibility to protect them. We owe them that much."

Mallory's eyebrows puckered. "You said they were killed by Filipino guns. Those are your folks who killed them."

"American soldiers trusted their leaders' lies. They thought they fought to do right for the Filipinos. It was a lie. The truth killed them—not guns."

"And beauty killed King Kong. Okay. Rest assured your story is safe with me. Nevertheless, I'm exhausted. I've got to get sleep."

She threw her hands to her sides. "You've been sleeping."

"Real sleep." He tore from his notebook one of its few clean sheets of paper. "Here. Write your phone number for me, too."

De la Cruz wrote, and he shoved the crumpled paper in his pocket. Mallory turned toward his car. The window reflected Winkle's hand cupped to his ear.

You sure as hell won't shut me up after all these years, Bear.

Mallory roared loud enough for his voice to cross the bay. "Who the hell knows? Push till it hurts Sweetheart." He added to De la Cruz in a croaky whisper, "Can I meet you here this evening? We'll figure out a time. "

"Do you believe me?"

"Not sure whether I do, but I'll meet you back here. I guess we're both slaves to the occult of Irish intuition and Filipino mysticism. I'll call you."

Mallory dropped into his car, ignoring the familiar mess of soiled coffee cups and thick newspapers layered across the floorboards. He rolled open the window, knocked an ash from his cigarette, and toggled the stick shift before grabbing for the keys he'd left in his jacket pocket. A heavy pounding on his car roof made him jump.

Winkle dangled the keychain outside the window.

"What the hell are you doing with those?" Mallory said.

"We need to talk."

"No, you need to give me my goddamn keys."

"I will. First you listen."

"Get the—"

Winkle growled, "You're lucky your ass isn't in jail right now. I'm protecting you."

"From what?"

"Yourself! Keep your voice down. This matter is between us, Morning Smoke Signal. You should be under arrest for trespass. Still can be. I'm your friend. Your brother. Go home. Nothing happened."

"Indian boy, you must have been smoking *shrooms*."

Winkle reached into the car. He slapped the keys on the dashboard. Withdrawing his hand, he punched Mallory's windpipe with his fist edge. "*Nothing* happened."

The blow triggered a chain of asthmatic wheezes. Breaths had required an increased effort from Mallory. After the trauma to his windpipe, he choked, as if he inhaled clouds of steam—the hot pain indistinguishable from suffocation.

Winkled stepped back from the car and nodded to De la Cruz. She snugged her truck, against Mallory's bumper. Vomit discharged out his window.

GULLED

De la Cruz nudged the Karmann Ghia to a roll. Powerless treads ground the loose gravel. Mallory shifted the car from neutral to second and engaged the clutch. The engine bucked. A cough from the tailpipe started him forward. He raised his middle finger and flicked a cigarette stub toward the Lexus. While the high smolder curved to where it landed, Mallory raced out the gate propelled along his own arc of destiny.

At the bridge parking lot, he stopped to phone his editor.

"Rich. Mick." Bitter tar rasped his inflamed larynx. "Good morning." Mallory cleared his throat. "Listen to me. What's a Petaluma?"

His head reeled. *What must I learn first?*

"That's right, Rich, all night. Danced all night. Who wouldn't sound exhausted? ... Sorry. I couldn't call in to you. ... A town?"

Foghorn blasts shuddered the parking lot. They obliterated the voice on the phone.

"—How far?"

A Golden Gate Transit bus rumbled past. It headed south to the Financial District. Through its smoked glass, shadow-shaped commuters jumbled in the glare of laptop computers. Slack-jawed riders buttressed against the windows, others leaned against one another.

"Can't make you out. Speak up," he shouted. "What? … But what does?"

Mallory waited.

"What does it mean? C'mon I'm freezing here." He pulled out his pad. "What else? Uh-huh. … Why is he in this early? … And he wants me. Me? You sure? Then put him on. … No. No way. I'm working a lede from last night. … Give me Chesebrough, would you?"

Mallory's Adam's apple ached from Winkle's jab.

"—Yeah that'll be the day you do me a favor." He raked his fingers through his hair. Jagged lightning bolts pulsed from his scalp. "How nearby?" Mallory stopped fidgeting. "I heard you, already."

From Russian Hill west, he scoped the city hills. "Society guy. Pacific Heights. Okay, I'm looking in that direction now. … Uh-huh. Jumped." He snapped back, "Well, that's where I am. … Who?"

Mallory covered the phone, holding it the length of his arm. He bent over and mouthed an inaudible, *"Fuuuuck!"*

Another foghorn blast rattled the plaza. The receiver pressed over his ear. Traffic din absorbed the voice.

"Couldn't hear you again. Give it to me. Spell it. F—just say it. … I got you fine. F. … Go ahead I said. E-L-D-M-A-N."

Mallory wrote the name while he thought: *What a self-centered, rich prick. There goes my story.*

"Possibly a sidebar," he stuttered. "If I can. I'll call you back. First, pass me Chesebrough. …Okay, Rich, I'll wait."

Mallory folded the notepad into his pocket and tore a match to strike for his next cigarette. The matchbook cover concealed a foil packet of pills. He bounced his knuckle on his front tooth. *This is not going to be good.*

An oil tanker glided high and light under the bridge. It rode from the Port of Richmond headed to Valdez for a new load of Alaska North Slope crude. Tall, rusty flanks slipped by the gate. Mallory noted that when ships passed the bridge, the span changed. It looked different, similar to the way the fabric of Christo's environmental art, or a Broadway set panel rolled across a stage, transformed the ordinary. Lateral movement of great ships transitioned time and place. For the observer, the fixed bridge streamed like a flag while the hundred-thousand tons of ship momentum held still.

The setting struck Mallory in a way that befitted his style of writing. He wrote dramas, juxtaposing the mundane with the absurd. Embellishments inflated his stories until they were about-to-burst balloons of tales. He rubbed them over his scalp with such vigor their headlines crackled with the fury of downed power lines. Each word sparked with the intention to tingle reader's fine hairs.

At his peak, New Yorkers hailed Mallory's kindred pugnacity. For his services, competing newspaper owners offered him princely bonuses, and spigot-keys to their ink barrels. He splashed every drop of their spirits to sustain his public feuds. His columns spread a thick schmear of blue-collar cynicism on the hard crust of urban existence. Mallory stung the political, the powerful, and the privileged with equal venom in his published opinions. Manhattan's high-society lions snarled at his insolence. He pushed back from the front page, demolishing adversaries with the whine, and unyielding pressure, of a city garbage truck compactor blade.

His singular reward came from overhearing New Yorkers raise his name in a question. He imagined the question echoing throughout the five boroughs. High above shovel-scraped avenues, they asked the question. With eyebrows raised over tortoise shell glasses, they asked the question. Burrowed in damask-rose paneled breakfast nooks, they asked the question. On Wall Street, at precinct houses, in gritty Off-Track-Betting parlors, and in coffee shops where foreign-sounding men decanted bitter perseverance into faux-Greek cups, they shouted the question. It mattered little to Mallory whether he enraged, confused, or amused the inquisitors. He received thorough satisfaction knowing his name sparked New York's day-priming *hoo-hah*, "Did you read what Mallory wrote?"

For years, he floated unfettered on ethers of celebrity. One night, his world crashed with heart-stopping suddenness. Elite detractors jumped on the opportunity to sneer, "The Irish Icarus got what he deserved."

Injuries he sustained dulled his wit. Unable to attack his nemeses, or to defend his opinions, the accumulated vengeance of powerful New Yorkers befell him. A pox of litigations and retractions blistered his columns. Friends rumored corrupt cops set him up for retribution. Readership declined. Mallory lost his swagger. The bosses swiped back their ink barrel keys—and they fired him.

In California, an important daily offered him a trial job. Mallory saw the opportunity as his last chance to write one more big story. If in San Francisco he again heard, "The Question," he would return to New York and reclaim his life on top of Sinatra's heap.

Mallory disengaged the phone call on the Golden Gate Bridge to his San Francisco office, surprised he still had his job. He squinted at what he scribbled across the matchbook, *Lou Rash. Petaluma source.*

He conned the name from Edward Chesebrough III, his boss, the publisher of the family-owned San Francisco Press-Republican. Mallory didn't bother to ask Chesebrough whether he called Lou Rash a friend. Chesebrough, similar to Mallory's relationships, had no friends.

The day Chesebrough hired him he warned Mallory he'd keep him on a short-leash, choke collar. "Mallory, I'm not wowed by your resume. We understand you don't know diddly squat and you're a lawsuit magnet, but you acquit yourself well."

Chesebrough had a condition of his employment. He had to swear never to ask him for anything again. On day one, he allowed Mallory ninety days to regain his New York mojo, ninety not ninety-one. After that, the experiment he called his, "Old Rat Running a Maze," ended without appeal.

"Find the cheese," he said. The clock had begun its wind down eighty-eight days earlier. Chesebrough extended no reprieves for rats.

He had just instructed Mallory on the phone, "I have a special assignment for you. Write a story on the tragic drowning of Mr. Griffin Feldman that occurred while he fished."

"Fishing? The desk told me the Coast Guard found him wearing a tuxedo shirt. I saw him—"

"You're not listening, are you? Keep it short. Be sensitive to the family's heartache. They're prominent people."

"But last night—"

"Pay attention to what I'm saying. Not last night, today."

"But—"

"Don't bring up last night, Mallory. The first call I got this morning at home woke my Shih Tzu. Goddammit. And what sent my baby, Pio Pico, into frenzy? I'll tell you what. A person called to inform me you were drunk. Your concentration drifted again. It affected your judgment. Didn't it, Mallory?"

"Who called you? Are you up to speed on what happened?"

"It's not relevant because nothing happened. Nothing else."

"Seems everyone thinks a lot of nothing happens around here."

"Shut up and listen, Mallory. I'm doing you a favor. A big favor. You want to work here don't you?"

"Accidental drowning."

"Now you're concentrating. A sad misfortune. A few inches of copy. Short and sweet. Innocuous and humane. No drama."

"Got it."

"What else do you have to work on?"

Mallory's first thoughts collided with the protests of his conflicted notions. He delayed a response until a commuter bus, painted to resemble an egg carton with the words *East Petaluma 76* on its marquee, passed him. "What's a Petaluma?"

"Is that a question?"

"No, that's my story."

"Did you actually say that's your story? Mallory—"

"Yeah that's my story. If your reporter, who is concentrating really hard, wants to know the answer, others would probably find Petaluma of interest."

"That standard of journalism is not the Pulitzer-quality material we expected from you."

"I'm sniffing for moved cheese, boss. I could use a little help here."

"Okay," said Chesebrough. "Give me concise and professional copy on the drowning. Then call on one of my former reporters. Lou Rash works up there. Write this.…"

Jotted beneath Rash's name, home address and phone number, Mallory scrawled, "*Small daily. North SF. 101 to Petaluma.*"

"Make sure you inform Rash you might visit. Call first," said Chesebrough, "and get me the accident story."

"—and make it humane. I'm on it."

Mallory bent matches back from the inside cover. He removed a single pill among those wrapped in foil. Two more pills and three empty indentations lined up beside them. Mallory had others. He swallowed the pill, closed his eyes, and wheezed, "Sunshine Superman."

The medication took effect, and he called the phone number for 254 Gate 6 Road, Sausalito. A woman answered, "Rash here."

Mallory exhaled. "My name is Mick, Mick Mallory, reporter for the Press-Republican. I'm seeking Lou Rash."

"Do I know you?" the wary voice responded in his ear.

"Your husband might. We worked for the same guy."

"Guy? And—"

"Oh, dude. Sorry," Mallory said. "I was given his name by my boss."

"His name? What boss?"

Mallory held the phone away and stared at it after the woman added, *"Dude."* He spoke with greater caution. "Publisher boss. Yeah, Chesebrough at the Press-Republican."

"Eddie?"

"The third. Right on. That's him. Or should I say that's he? I don't know. Anyway, I was saying—Eddie? Oh, *Jeezus*! I'm tired. Spent my night visiting a Frisco cemetery. I need a nap."

"It's not Frisco, and I'm Louise Rash."

"Sorry. I'm from the city. New York. Anyway, I'd like to meet Rash about a story. Wait. You're a chick."

"A woman." She sighed. "Hold on a second and take a breath." Rash placed the phone on a needlepoint pattern of vintage printing presses stretched for a frame. Next to the fabric, lay a dish of sticky bread crusts and melon rinds. She picked up the plate and plodded outside the room through a sliding door onto her houseboat deck.

Unorthodox arks, tied to docks or anchored offshore, surrounded the residence. From the nearby freeway, where sundown hookers loitered at the exit, the bright-painted, angled houseboats appeared mashed together, a pile-up of broken hard candies.

Rash leaned on a railing, fixated on the morning's horizon. The sun slipped low over the abalone-colored bay, gilding the white undersides of gulls. They raced toward her deck from where she cast breakfast remnants on flat water.

While married, Rash had lived a few miles from her houseboat in a Belvedere mansion overlooking the bay. On a boozy night after her divorce, she hurled her wedding band from the houseboat in the same direction as she had thrown the food scraps. She expected the ring to skim the bay until it crashed on the peninsula rocks—a dramatic remonstration to her failed relationship. Neither her wedding band nor her vengeance ever reached the beach. There were no gay, aerodynamic skips of retribution. The ring sank in the high tide where thrown, *"Ploop!"* without a ripple roiling the water or her revenge.

Rash slanted back across the tilted floor to the phone, away from the high-pitched melee. "Are you still there?" she said, hoping he wasn't.

"That's some racket. Couldn't tell from that background noise whether someone made violent love to you, or you strangled a bird."

"What's your name again?"

"Mud. No. Only kidding. *Only* kidding. Not Mud." His voice softened. "It's Mick Mallory. Please call me Mick."

Rash cupped the phone on her thigh. The receiver swung to her cheek.

"Try me again after you take a nap. If I confirm Chesebrough gave you my name, I suppose I must meet you later. I'm leaving for work now."

"I won't be sleeping. What I meant is I wanted to catch my breath … some typing to do. See what I'm sayin'? I can come right over if that's better for you. I could use your help on an angle I'm working."

"Look Mick, I don't have time for a retread from Chesebrough. Perhaps this idea of meeting isn't so smart."

"Just give me a chance."

"I'll call Chesebrough. If you check out, we'll get together. Understood?"

"No. Please, Lou. Don't bother with Chesebrough. Time is not on my side."

"Awfully sorry to say this, but you sound like a guy on a bender."

"You're a reporter. I'm a reporter who needs you to trust me. Extend me a professional courtesy. You feel what I mean?" said Mallory.

"What's this story that's so important to you and has wholly ruined my glorious sunrise?"

"I need background on a local soldier named Arthur Lloyd Dean."

"Dean?"

"Lived in Petaluma and he died in the Philippines in—"

"Eighteen ninety-nine. Buried at the Presidio cemetery."

"Eighteen ninety-nine and he—yes. Eighteen ninety-nine. How the hell?"

Rash waited. "I've read about him."

"Then I must come over right away, okay?"

"Not okay. You're one of those pushy, hard-drinking New York reporter types, aren't you? I can tell."

"Politely persistent, but sincere and sober."

"Meet me after two o'clock at the Argus-Panoptes office in Petaluma. I'll talk with you then about Dean."

"Argus-Panoptes? That's the name of your paper? Petaluma isn't an odd enough name to place on your banner?"

"The paper is named for a Greek giant with one hundred eyes."

"I knew that."

"Sure you did, wise guy. See you at two o'clock."

Mallory appraised his third eye. It dimmed in its significance to the creature's one hundred. "Thank you," he said.

"Hope I can respond later today that you're welcome."

"And hey, Lou, I sometimes say stupid stuff I think is funny. Sorry. I can't control myself. It's as if I have some goofball form of Tourette's."

"That *shtick* might amuse in New York City. Not here. I don't have time for nonsense. And for heaven's sake, knock off the polite persistence. It's neither. It's just plain irritating."

"*Ixnay* the charm bombs."

"Eddie Chesebrough gave you my name?"

"Said you're the one I need to talk with about Arthur Lloyd Dean."

"Eddie knows about Arthur Lloyd Dean. Weird."

"Maybe he said I need to talk with you about Petaluma. Something like that."

"I'll see you later, for Eddie. You'd better be sober."

"Dry as a bar towel."

Mallory's gums bled. The call couldn't have ended soon enough. Fire ate at his bones the way a lightning-struck tree burned from the inside out. The same affliction that whacked him once a week now hit daily. It hurt.

He returned the phone to his jacket and perused his torso. The sweatshirt looked no more soiled than yesterday, not much different from how his attire appeared on any other day. Yet his ribs ached, as if a demonic sea monster had wrapped itself around him. The invisible creature refused to let go. Mallory thought it more credible if giant tentacles twisted his body than to see nothing there except his disheveled clothes.

His spine and rib cage stretched against the constriction. He spit tacky saliva. The spittle caught on his mustache corner.

His hand slipped under his collar and brushed a heavy silver chain. He hooked the necklace from under his shirt. A wedding band, hammered from a monstrous force, dangled from the chain. Fingering its golden crinkles, sharp contours retold the last violent moments of a gentle life.

"Oh, Babe," he whispered and closed his eyes. "How far from Petaluma are you and heaven, Siobhan?"

While Mallory had made phone calls from the bridge plaza, Winkle went from the cemetery to the strand of the razed Petlenuc village. A quick sweep of the beach satisfied him no one lurked within listening distance. Winkle tossed sand into the breeze where he prayed the day he left for college. He splashed water into the skies and asked cunning Coyote, the trickster who taught life's lessons, to guide him. He rubbed his forehead and lowered his hands.

Winkle called the duty sergeant going off his shift at the police communications center. "Tony, this is Bear. I'm at the Presidio. Did park police call in the cemetery 10-14 last night? ... Cell phone? Not the park service? ... Do me a solid and give me the number."

Winkle wrote the information in his pad.

"No. What recovery? Don't see it. ... Who?"

He hung up and called Chesebrough. "Bad news," said Winkle. "We've got a problem. Police arrested Feldman for trespassing at the Presidio cemetery. The news gets worse. Feldman's dead."

Chesebrough paused. "I'm aware of it." A police commander had called him twice, once with the arrest news, then later to update him on the suicide. "My reporters will take care of the story."

"You should have called me. How could you have known all this and not called me?"

"I felt too fragile. What's more intriguing is why you were at the cemetery. How could *you* have been there and not have called me?"

"Who told you I was there?" Winkle's voice rose. "It was police business and no longer matters. What's all-important is to find the scrip. Where did Feldman hide it?"

"I don't have an inkling. Do you?"

"The scrip was in the cemetery, wasn't it?" said Winkle. "That's why you sent your reporter to trail Feldman."

"Hold on there. From where did all that come from? I have more to lose from this disaster than you do. The editorial I wrote supporting the rezoning for your Crissy Field Landing is on the street."

"Then call off your dog. He asks too many questions."

"I had no one follow Feldman. What's this reporter's name?"

"Mick Mallory," said Winkle. "I'm familiar with him. He has a reputation for stirring up trouble."

"Mallory. You needn't tell me about Mallory. Leave him to me. I'll kick him like he's a toilet handle in a bus station. Now, for god's sake, go find that scrip."

"I'm counting on you to back me up," said Winkle.

"Don't worry. Mallory is on a trip to nowhere. I'll keep him busy at the Argus-Panoptes newspaper office up in Petaluma."

"What's he doing in Petaluma? That's my town."

"Nothing important. He's in my sights." Chesebrough thought to himself: *I have each of you in my sights.*

Winkle held the same sentiment. He disconnected and dialed a number handwritten on the back of a business card. Feldman had slipped him the card with the phone number after their first meeting. Winkle could never tell anyone of the number, not Chesebrough, not anyone.

"Call the number in an emergency," Feldman had said to Winkle. "An emergency is if anybody kidnaps, arrests, or kills me."

With two out of three criteria fulfilled, Winkle determined he had ample justification to make the call. The country code routed to Asia, the East. It reinforced Winkle's hope the recipient might be the Great Spirit Chief coming to restore the Indian to glory.

A distant voice answered. "Speak to me."

Winkle shuddered. *How might the demigod respond?*

"Feldman is dead."

"Did he get the scrip?"

"Not that I know."

The phone disengaged.

Once more, Winkle had to survive on his own. If he located the scrip that day, time remained for the Potawatomi to complete their claim to the Chicago property. Winkle no longer required guidance from Chesebrough. He needed the scrip. Without proof of custody of the scrip by the end of the day, Macau's paid political muscle atrophied. Their loss of face—and gold—endangered his life.

Winkle longed to draw a razor edge across his chest. A straight red line of Indian blood would cleanse away the white man's duplicitous pus. Orgasmic relief from self-mutilation had to wait. Fulfillment of prophecy lay in immediate jeopardy. *Chesebrough and that gravedigger lied about what they knew. Or they conspired against me with help from Mallory.*

The trio had positioned themselves on dangerous ground that separated Winkle's ambition from the Valentine Scrip.

TRAVELERS

Mallory's apartment perched 1,000 feet up the eastern slope of Twin Peaks, San Francisco's geographic center. Its wall-to-wall, floor-to-ceiling windows took in the length of Market Street, "The Slot," to the Ferry Building. At night, if he bunkered in the apartment, Mallory stared down at a dismal lattice of fog-sodden streets. The Muni's electric trolleys crisscrossed the grid. When their contacts slipped from their wet overhead-wires, brilliant incandescence arced through the murk. Mallory distracted himself imagining that the white bursts came from magnesium bombs dropped from black helicopters. The dark absurdity shattered his gloom. In daytime, the apartment window cityscapes of golds, salmons, and turquoises held no compensating cheer. Mallory prized the vista for only one reason; in the direction where the sunrise aligned over the East Bay hills, Manhattan awaited his return.

After a feverish late morning typing a draft, he showered. Mallory dressed in the same soiled clothes he had been wearing the previous night. A leather covered notebook and his loose-leaf draft of the story lay on a dining table. They preserved observations of Griff Feldman at the cemetery and the conversations overheard between Winkle and De la Cruz.

He stuffed the notebook in his pocket and he shoved the typed sheets in his car glove compartment.

By noon, Mallory approached the conceit of San Francisco's past, the gaudy shock of international-orange rouge smeared across an old lady's cheek. At the bridge midspan, the sun checked the advance of fog. A silver lace rose over the city. Distorted cable shadows leapt through the retreating mist to the waters lapping the headlands.

Sea air pounded his car. The ocean smells carried scented-memories of shoreline walks and his last days with Siobhan.

Do I want to see the pictures of her when they brought her into the hospital? Pictures of her? A doctor asked me that. A doctor!

Mallory seized the car window handle and cranked it shut. He ejected a Paul Simon tape from his obsolete console, kissing the cassette with the side of his mouth. Its nicotine-stained replacement crashed into the deck.

On the north end of the bridge, the road skirted hills of Marin County.

What time was it Back East? He wondered. *Three hours earlier? Or was it later? Where would Siobhan have been now? Would she be on the Long Island Railroad, her gaze fixed on the Manhattan skyline approach?*

During his happiest days with Siobhan, nothing gave him more joy than her easy amusement. Her laugh chimed sweeter than church bells on Easter Sunday morning.

To tease a giggle from her, Mallory exaggerated a one-eyed squint and growled, "I love you more than a pirate loves gold—Arrgh!"

With his flirt, her milk-white hands flew to his sideburns and held his head steady. She'd tickle kisses on his forehead and murmur, "Goofball."

Siobhan lacked guile. The exquisite details she found in commonplace occurrences, such as the morning plumes rising along the city's horizon delighted Mallory.

One early winter, her eyes reflected in their commuter train window. Mallory pretended to read a trifolded newspaper while he transfixed on her profile haloed in gold.

Outside the train, steam billowed in corkscrews from power plants squatted along the East River. Behind the generators, atop pinched skyscrapers, higher steam spread from serrated rooflines in gossamer wisps. The morning prayers of an awakening city floated to heaven. Siobhan's aspirations joined them, blooming lacy as willows on the frosted glass. She traced a sideways figure-eight infinity symbol on the moist window.

A moment passed. She whispered, "I bet New York glowed enchanting like this when our parents were young. And even before their birth."

"Check out what the Yankees did. Another hot stove trade. Never changes. Players come and players go."

"Sad. Isn't it?" said Siobhan.

"What?"

"The passing. We never knew those lovely people."

"It's the Yankees."

"Or is it beautiful?" She turned toward him, as if waking from a dream. "I hope we're remembered. Tell me, just this once, isn't it all so beautiful?"

Mallory snapped a new fold. A polished fingertip pulled his newspaper crease. Siobhan peered over its top. Her eyes glistened.

"Why don't you ever tell me it's beautiful? I feel connected to those people who lived here generations ago. Don't you see great beauty in those ties? Don't you, at all?"

"No."

The sun-mottled river melded with her profile. "Not even a teeny-weeny, little bit?"

His eyes drilled into the newspaper. "Steinbrenner's a dope."

Siobhan bent the corner of his reading farther from his sight. "Oh, Mick, it's all so beautiful." She turned back to the window, guiltless as a kitten. "I wish you knew it was beautiful."

Rose scented perfume lingered on Mallory's paper. "Very pretty," he grumbled.

The train approached the line's end. Palisades of beam-ribbed buildings slid fast up the track, rushing closer and closer.

"Boom-boom. Boom-boom."

Steel wheels pounded the rails. A shrill horn whistled and side doors buckled. They descended. The train went dark. An ear-popping bang and roar filled the coach. They hurtled deep into the river tunnel blackness.

White, red, and green lights streaked across the windows, flashes from a subterranean meteor shower.

The train surged. "Boom-boom. Boom-boom."

Standing passengers swayed together in the dim light, graceful as ice-skaters on a moonlit canal.

Mallory beheld Siobhan's enchantment in her window. She sailed outside of the car and gazed back, an ethereal voyager beckoning him to follow. Her wan smile drifted. Soft strobes flickered on her cheeks.

"Please, Honey, tell me our lives will never change."

"They won't," he insisted.

"Boom-boom. Boom-boom."

She could not hear his response. And with heart-aching suddenness, there appeared a bright sky of California blue, into which Siobhan vanished.

CLARK KENT

The Karmann Ghia had arrived at the southern rim of Petaluma Valley. Marine clouds, snagged overnight on high ridges, tattered themselves on live oaks in their struggle to return to the sea. Green road signs changed from US Route 101 to the Redwood Highway. Mallory had no recollection of the forty-mile drive between there and the Golden Gate.

His arm, spread atop the steering wheel, supported his chin. A cigarette stub ground against his teeth. He approached a thin bridge descending over the Petaluma Slough. Beneath it to his right, a tugboat prodded oyster shell filled barges toward the town. To the left, platinum-sided grain elevators reflected the midafternoon sunlight at the water's terminus.

Mallory sat up straight and shoved a Stevie Wonder cassette into the dashboard to blast away melancholia. As the music began, he rolled down the window and macaw-bopped to a funky beat. Warm breezes curled in the cabin. They reeked of manure fertilizer sprayed on pastures upwind of town. Three hurried wrist pumps returned the window to its closed position.

"Wow, Petaluma," he shouted, impersonating Stevie Wonder. "Just like I pictured it. Skyscrapers and *everythang!*"

Turning from a boulevard onto an office block, a cracked stucco building, with a freight train track behind it, matched the street address in his notes. A tilted wooden sign mounted on a flagpole pointed to the back of the parking lot. It read, *Argus-Panoptes, Eyes of an Empire.*

Yellow newspaper racks guarded an unornamented glass door entrance. Inside, an elderly receptionist inserted advertising supplements into a pile of newspapers. A pink Lego bracelet, matching her lipstick color, clacked a steady rhythm as the plastic hit the desk. She did not look up. Cosmetic flamboyance masked the ravages of her life with the subtlety of a gambling parlor facade. An eyebrow, shaped as if with the blunt end of a mortician's pencil, quivered.

Mallory waved a wide circle in the air.

The woman craned her head, acknowledging the visitor standing in front of her. "Paper or ad?" The words pelted like pitched beanbags.

"Meeting." A delighted smirk warped his lips. *If potholes talked, they'd sound like you.*

"I asked paper or ad?"

"And I said meeting."

Reading glasses dropped on their chain. A necklace holding a Byzantine cross and a bottle opener straightened. She rose in her chair. "Do you want to subscribe to the paper, son? Or are you here to place an ad?"

"Neither. I have an appointment at this esteemed periodical with Lou."

"You mean Editor-in-chief Rash." Fingernails, painted with white checks and black polka dots, drummed an impatient tattoo on the desk. "Name?"

"Not paper. Not ad. It's Mick Mallory, and I'm from the Press-Republican, published in the Golden City by the Bay."

The receptionist's grin exposed a dark gap where an eyetooth once dangled. Her sudden, assumed familiarity surprised Mallory. "Ha!" she laughed, building to a slow caw utterance, as if a crow approached and flew overhead. "Ha. Haa. Haaa!"

Mallory sighed to register impatience. His lips drew into his mouth. "Did I say something humorous, ma'am?"

"Nah, kid. I'm too old to think bullshit like yours is funny. You're as lame as a one-legged pigeon."

"Have we been introduced before?"

"I heard all about you earlier today. Ain't nothing like what I expected." Her hand trembled from laughter. A ruler pointed toward a woman across the office. "Editor-in-Chief Rash is over there."

Mallory spotted Rash leaning over a backlit desk. She manipulated galleys of newsprint strips into a dummy page layout. He had not seen that method of typesetting used since college.

The receptionist croaked, "Hey folks! He's here. Mr. Clark Kent has landed without his cape."

Mallory did not wait for her permission to leave the lobby. He sashayed away, throwing an exaggerated kiss over his shoulder. In a nonchalant hail, he called out, "Here's lookin' at you, kid."

The repartee volleyed back with a come-hither wink and a lewd pout from glossed, withered lips. Mallory shivered.

Rash beamed up from the page layout. Auburn hair, pinned behind ears adorned with tiny earrings, fell to her collar. A fine brooch of pearls and gold hyacinth clung to the curve of her breast. Her eyes opened wide. Mallory strode into the room, head swinging side to side, as if he were a baton-pumping drum major.

Rash came toward him with a warm smile that disquieted her associates.

"Mr. Mallory. You're early."

"Hey, Lou. Lookin' good, kid. Must be Pioneer Day around here. Is that why you're laying out your paper the old-fashioned way?"

Clatter from a half-dozen keyboards fell silent. Rash arched a quizzical eyebrow. Her back straightened under a tight, olive-green knit sweater. She dropped her tone to a perfunctory business pitch. "In my house, I prefer Editor-in-Chief Rash. Please come with me, Mr. Mallory."

Long legs swished beneath her wool skirt pleats. Fragrance of lilac talcum powder trailed her steps. She escorted him from the pressroom to a corner office hung with a Venetian blind. An archaic Linotype printing machine, as tall as the ceiling, and as wide as a wall, dominated the room overlooking the dung-colored parking lot. Rash rattled a metal magazine bolted on the behemoth and lifted out a few brass type matrices.

"William Randolph Hearst had this relic in San Francisco."

"What might that relic be, Editor-in-Chief Rash? Your vain title? Your layout process? Or could it be your receptionist?"

"Cute. The Linotype printer. And now that we're alone, please call me Lou. As you've observed, our operation is spare and professional. Maybe a few years behind the times. But so what? It's tight. I'm the boss. And I'm proud of the staff."

Mallory pointed to the Linotype. "I'm sure you're at least not using that old mastodon."

"Not recently, but I could if I had sufficient motivation to fire it up. Ran wires and bumped out a wall to squeeze it in here. It's as loud as lawn furniture thrown in a wood chipper—but it still works"

A desk, a phone, two metal chairs, and a sunken-in leather couch crammed into the space not swallowed by the Linotype. Mallory toed a crack in a dark-green floor tile. "It pulls the room together."

"I get my opulence fixes elsewhere. This Linotype is more important to me."

"One would hope," he said.

"The last hot lead slugs it composed were the words to my father's *obit*. Dad worked in our business, too. He was a classic, old-school newspaperman. Had integrity. The tired, old Linotype had nothing to say after it compiled his sad farewell."

She tapped brass pieces of type together. "I think Dad haunts its workings. Who knows? Someday he might have something to report again. I'll keep it around."

"Those machines were from the days when journalism sounded authentic," Mallory said. "The press burned hot, roared loud, and acted you-can-kiss-my-ass outrageous. Not correct and cool. Not like that pantomime of a press room outside the door."

She shrugged before glancing at the Linotype. "I admit it. Sometimes, I miss the clatter of this big boy. Click. Click. Clink! Tap—*clunk!*"

Rash laughed at her deep mimic of the clunk sound. She slapped the thick metal side of the printer for emphasis. "And it sure rocked and rolled. When I visited New York City as a kid, Dad showed me a dozen of these in simultaneous operation. I fell in love."

Mallory twirled his palm under his nose. "They had a pleasant electric smell, like summer air after a lightning storm. Imprints of millions of their tiny leaden slugs formicating on broadsheets that covered the city."

"*Formicating? Broadsheets?* Good lord. Is that an attempt to talk dirty, Mr. Mallory, or do you write like you talk?"

"Usually better," he said.

"One would hope." She giggled, as might a wisecracking teenager who had surprised herself. "Sorry, that was awful of me."

Rash withdrew from a small refrigerator an ice water garnished with a cucumber wafer lanced on a twisted bamboo. "Welcome to Petaluma." She handed him the frosted glass. "Now, Mr. Mallory, may we talk as if we're not dueling columnists?"

"Mick. Let's get this straight up front. My name is Mick, inside and outside of this office." He sniffed his sleeve. Mallory turned his head to cough. He flushed.

Rash flipped open a can of diet cola. She read its label the way a sommelier selected Bordeaux until she gained Mallory's attention. "I'm hard to surprise." Her eyes moved from the can. "I looked you up after I called Chesebrough—"

Mallory cleared his throat to interrupt. He sniffed the glass. "Gin?"

"Water. Best thing for a man who's as dry as a bar towel." Rash smiled and sipped her cola. "You, sir, came as advertised, an unrepentant wit. I have to ease into that."

"Mick."

"From all accounts, you were an outstanding writer."

The bamboo skewer massaged under his gum to relieve an unreachable ache. "What do you mean *were?*"

"Don't be coy. You won a Pulitzer Prize. That's terrific. I had no idea."

"I got lucky."

"Moreover, you graduated from Newhouse School at Syracuse. Well, guess what? We were neighbors." She held up a fist. "Cornell. We've come a long way since we were Central New York kids in college."

Mallory stifled a belch into his elbow flex. "Farther than you could imagine."

Rash cocked her eyebrow. "Then again, perhaps not." She placed the soft drink on the desk. "Downtown Petaluma has a vibe like Upstate New York along the Erie Canal. The turn of the century buildings and the old stained-glass windows here will amaze you. Scads of darling antiques stores line the boulevard. We have lots to see."

Mallory tossed the bamboo skewer and cucumber toward a metal wastebasket and missed. "Sorry, kid. I'm not much into buying dead people's stuff. What I want is your background on Arthur Lloyd Dean. I must get back to the city."

"Oh, pooh. You'll thrill at these blocks of historical landmarks. Petaluma once hailed as the world's egg capital. We still have an annual Butter and Eggs Day parade."

"How exciting." Mallory brushed his arms. "You're giving me chills."

"Okay, have it your way. But you might find this poky, little town intriguing. Petaluma can surprise you." Rash winked. "You'll see."

She plowed scattered papers cluttering her desk into a drawer, leaving one long strip of newspaper. Rash turned a corner of the clipping. "This editorial is for you. First, tell me something. What's it like? I mean, how does it feel to win a gold-prize Pulitzer?"

"It's a crystal trophy, and it sucks. What do you think?"

"I think it would be rapture. If I might be so bold, seeing you said on the phone we should trust each other, one *guy* reporter to another, professional courtesy and all, well, if you wrote Pulitzer prize quality copy, for heaven's sake, in Manhattan no less—"

"Is there a question in your bloviating?"

"Excuse me? … You caught me off-guard, again. Fire a flare to warn me the next time you're about to say something obnoxious. Okay?"

"Your question?"

"My question is, sir, why are you here in Petaluma? What the hell happened to you?"

"Come again?"

"Oh, stop. You know what I mean. Once, you were Jimmy Breslin's heir apparent. Now, here you are in Petaluma, former egg capital of the world. That's hard to fathom. Used to be there. Now you're here. Spill it."

Mallory set his glass on the desk, pushing the water away with the back of three middle fingers. Rash lifted her drink and strummed the metal tab on the can.

"Let's move this along," said Mallory. "The sooner I can leave this guano-smelling chickentown the better. There's work to finish in Frisco."

"*San-Fran-cis-co.* The city. I know. That's what Chesebrough said."

"Did he? I didn't think a buttoned-up guy like Chesebrough would be so liberal with his comments about his business, and mine."

"You read him right. He's chatty with me, though. We have a history."

"Oh?"

"Eddie was my husband."

Mallory recoiled. "That guy?"

"He remarried. I'm okay with it now. It meant I had to move across the way from our Belvedere mansion. That's all."

"Belvedere is high rent. You must either get paid well here to afford to live there, or you reamed him for alimony."

"Wish it were so. No, you're mistaken on both counts. He had an ironclad prenup. Trust me, I checked. When I said I live near him, I exaggerated a little. I live on a small houseboat across Richardson Bay from his mansion. That's why you heard gulls when you telephoned me. My home rises and falls on tidal mud. From my deck, I can see Eddie's place up on the bluff."

"Houseboat? Brutal. Your home could sink if your toilet overflowed."

"I'll ignore that. As for Eddie—eh! He's still my ally, a powerful person to know in this business. We do each other favors. *Professional* favors."

Railroad flatcars waddled behind the building. They hauled redwood to the city of Vallejo. Rash paused while steel wheels shrieked from the train.

She inspected her cuticles after the rumble subsided. "Why were you so desperate to meet me about Dean?"

"I wasn't desperate at all. And you can go ahead and tell Chesebrough. It may surprise him. Your *ex* treats me like a loser."

"Just tell *me* what happened to make you come all the way up here."

"Last night opened a window of opportunity to write a great story. This morning it became an exit for my lede to self-defenestrate."

Rash laughed. "What does all that verbosity mean?"

"Don't know yet."

"That's what happens when you're overtired. Eddie said you stayed at the Presidio Cemetery last night." She crossed her heart. "That's all he told me. Said to ask you about the cemetery, so I could brief you with what's relevant about Dean and Petaluma. I ask, so I can help you. What curious lede did you find in San Francisco that made you scurry here?"

Wrinkles above Mallory's eyes deepened. He spoke in a measured pace. "Nothing made me want to come here except that I'd never been to Petaluma. The sights here topped my slop-bucket list. Nice place."

An ice cube fingered from his glass cracked between his teeth. He crunched on the frozen rubble until his palm pressed his jaw.

"Okay, then. That looks painful." Rash pushed the newspaper clipping toward him. "We can chat later. Right now, critique this. It's an editorial I wrote last week. Tell me what you think."

His fingers spread atop the paper, rotating the page so the text faced Rash. Mallory took in her rich, hyacinth brooch. "Did you know your blouse is the color of your eyes?"

Rash scowled at the staff staring back through her open doorway. She shut the door and dropped the blind. A low newsroom hum resumed.

"What was your excuse for the uncouth things you say? Tourette's, right? Your remark was another of those. Wasn't it? You utter the most inappropriate remarks, Mr. Mallory."

"Mick. Do I?" He sauntered to the wall and bent back the blinds slats. A stuffed Leghorn chicken stood on a desk wearing an oversized gold medal. "What about Dean?"

"Dean's coming. Assignment number one is for you to read this editorial. My house. My rules. It'll take but a moment of your time." Rash pushed the paper. "After that, tonight I'll show you other relevant files."

"What's this?"

"You've got to trust me."

"Lou, c'mon. I don't care about your community. More important, I don't have until tonight."

"Eddie instructed me to take care of you. Remember? If you want Dean, I'll get you Dean. Trust me." She pulled her blouse at the waist. "Can you abide by that?"

Mallory collapsed onto the printer's chair attached to the Linotype. Creases intersected his face the way storm waves mount one another on a turbulent sea.

"Let's be friends." Her voice softened. "Do you want to tell me why you're not still a writer in New York?"

"No."

"If you do, then go ahead. I'll listen."

"I said no."

Mallory wanted to say yes in the most desperate way. He wanted to tell her he felt broke, more now than ever. Not broke from lack of finances, he received royalty checks each quarter from his books and ghostwritten movie scripts. He suffered the worst type of broke, in arrears for squandered opportunity and talent.

Although Rash shared with him the same trade as a journalist, Mallory thought she could never understand how much he loved his craft. He had elevated journalism to an urban art, creating illusions he wrote to the individual readers. New Yorkers supposed he scribbled them personal dispatches from behind gilded lines, where the city power elite schemed—and schmoes were not welcome to trespass. He ciphered reassurances to the common man. "Hey, Bud. We nailed it right. We're being screwed. Their scams can't con us." Mallory imagined his readers balancing paper coffee cup ridges on their lower lips and responding, "Yeah, baby. *Effin A.* Stick it to 'em."

Esteemed journalists called his trade, "news reporting." Mallory knew better, he described journalism as, "nonfiction fantasy," an ongoing drama rich in heroes and villains.

He ached to tell Rash he ran and ran and ran, but couldn't get away from what chased him. When he spoke to old acquaintances, they engaged him with blank expressions—shocked by the man he became after the accident. Their faces resembled swiveling binocular stands you pay a quarter to use on a boardwalk, eyes staring wide, glassy, almost human, but cold, steely and impenetrable.

Even those who knew him not well knew he was not well. Since he had the accident, ideas sometimes started in his head clear and sharp, then thickened and stuck to his cheeks. When that happened, words fell from his mouth malformed, directionless, and no longer rifled with his celebrated wit.

Would she care that's why I don't talk so much unless I've dropped meds into my gullet? So what if now and then I need boosters? They're just other murderers in the crowded race to kill me. If I can't talk, then I can't develop my ledes. Without ledes, I won't ever make it back to New York. Spill my guts to this wannabe? … Right.

He refused to acknowledge to her, or anybody, even to himself, death closed in on him. That admission would force him to let go of the future, of the hope for a change of fortune, his last possible salvation. Instead, avoiding the pit limited him to live in the unbearable present. He wanted to tell Rash. He wanted to tell *anybody* his fears, though he dared not let the words out. If he released them, despair could turn and kill him.

Rash said, "Married?"

"Separated. You're not my kind."

"Ha … ha. No, I'm very much not your kind. But your message has been received. I won't ask any additional personal questions."

"Her name's Siobhan."

"Oh, but—Oh! Siobhan. A beautiful name."

"It was."

"Separated. Yech." Rash twisted her mouth corner into a frown. "Welcome to my club. Better days are ahead. Here. This background is a taste of what's coming." She held the copy in her hand. "It won't take you a minute to read this editorial. Call it an appetizer." Her jaw jutted in an absurd stereotype of a patrician. "A worthy fillip to sustain you, *Sir Pulitzer.* The main course is on the way."

"Name's Mick. Don't play the comedian for my sake. Levity is beneath you."

Rash measured deep into his eyes. "Women can tell jokes, too." She pinched his cheek between her thumb and forefinger, giving his flesh a sharp twist. Before Mallory finished howling, she shoved the clipping into his chest. "Poor baby Mickey. Just read it. Be right back."

She strode into the lobby more surprised by her sass than Mallory.

His cheek reddened where her sting and seductive perfume tingled upon his senses. "Fetch me some decent gin," he shouted. The office reverberated with the last word, *gin!*

Echoes of, "*tonic,*" came back, and a distant door clicked closed.

Mallory's eyes riffled across the paragraphs forced upon him. *"Son of a … She knows all about this guy."*

He thumbed out his fourth, or fifth, pill of the day from a foil packet and tossed it in his mouth. Mallory took notes while he read Rash's editorial.

What if They Gave a War and Nobody Remembered?

"A people's memory is history, and as a man without a memory, so a people without a history cannot grow wiser, better." Yiddish poet, Isaac Leibush Peretz.

Our editorial is more than one hundred years overdue. Unfortunately, the issues we raise are as relevant to our community today as they were at the turn of the twentieth century. We write concerning our war dead and their honored remembrance. Specifically, we remind our readers of a young Petaluman who went off to war, died for our country in the prime of his life, and then we forgot him. Corporal Arthur Lloyd Dean was the first Sonoma County soldier killed in battle overseas. He would not be our last.

The fortuitous recovery of First Presbyterian Church's stained-glass windows from a henhouse reacquainted us with this man. Dean was a member of the congregation.

The year of Dean's death was 1899. Petaluma was a small town with a population of 8,000. Our community sacrificed a dreadful toll for a war so befouled with politics historians still quarrel over its very name.

The conflict was the Philippine-American War, a beastly, three-year muddle that followed the glorified Spanish American War.

Whether fate rendered our soldiers deaths in obscure skirmishes one-hundred years ago, or on famous modern battlefields, time and place should not concern those who stayed safe at home. What matters is they died in our name—far from Petaluma. That is important. It is as relevant today as it was in past times. What we should remember is their ultimate sacrifice.

Should Petaluma soldiers, who may give their lives today, expect the same shameful indifference generations hence?

For a town without a permanent war memorial, the most forthright answer is "Yes."

Even at Arlington National Cemetery, no specific memorial for the Philippine-American war dead has been erected. The reason lies in a one versus two, or three, conflicts issue. The government for many years classed the Spanish American War, the Philippine-American War, and the Boxer Rebellion together as one conflict. Government records of these men, including government gravestones, will read, "Spanish American War," though the Spanish had nothing to do with their deaths. Monuments erected to Spanish War Vets cover all three.

Dead generals, high on their bronze pedestals, and presidents painted in somber oils, have earned their places of honor. Fallen citizen-soldiers deserve even more veneration. We, the grateful, should chisel their names into Sierra gold and granite mined from the heart of Mother Earth, the same sacred crucible from which God forged our common-man heroes.

The Argus-Panoptes urges the city council to build a memorial for all our war dead. We must never forget our Arthur Lloyd Deans. Until then, we look forward to seeing the First Presbyterian stained-glass memorial windows when the church displays them again.

-30-

SUSTENANCE

Rash returned carrying a water-stained storage box. "Stop," Mallory said. "Who wrote this about Dean?"

"Guilty."

"Damn." He fingered the editorial corners. "Now you've got my attention."

"I'm glad it got your attention, but I had hoped you liked it. Maybe even say, I wrote well."

"Okay. It's not terrible."

"I'll take that as a compliment—I guess." Rash released the box handles with the flourish of a magician. Heavy papers smacked on the desk.

Mallory reeled back. "Do I smell cats? I *do* smell cats. I hate cats."

"What your large and gnarly proboscis detects is twenty-four karat gold. This file is a memoir from more than a century past."

"Our war hero Dean wrote this memoir?"

"No," Rash said. "Pennypacker did. He's the local paper founder. Pennypacker wrote this before Dean's birth."

"Then it doesn't interest me."

"It should."

"Well, it doesn't. What I'm interested in is being gone by now. Tell me where you found your background on Dean."

"First, you have to see this." She sat and rocked open the box lid, removing a sheaf of papers entitled, Audubon's California Elephant.

"This was in the basement of a deceased employee. He kept it safe all these years. What's fascinating is there are references to John Woodhouse Audubon, the second son of legendary John James Audubon. There are numerous connections here with Audubon's California Elephant."

Mallory plucked the thick file edges. "I've heard of the bird guy, never Pennywhacker." He pinched the cover sheet and lifted it to better view the title. "But it doesn't matter because I don't care about Audubon, his elephants, or his birds. Was he a circus performer?"

"Not Pennywhacker—J. J. Pennypacker. Joseph Judson Pennypacker, from Pennsylvania. A member of a famous family. Governors, heroic Generals, Medal of Honor winners, Underground Railroad safe house providers, and on and on." Rash's lips arched into a tight smile. "And I said, Audubon's Elephant. *Elephant* is a Forty-niner expression. It has to do with the enormous struggles Argonauts faced to reach the goldfields."

Mallory wiped his chest. He grabbed a pack of cigarettes and punched its bottom against the heel of his hand. "This is too much. What happened to you didn't have time for a guy described as a— what was it? Oh yes, a retread. Fine. I'm a retread shredded all over the highway from here to Frisco. Get rid of me by telling me about Dean. I have to return to the city." His face curdled.

Rash hummed while withdrawing more files. She stacked neat rows on the desk, ignoring his agitation.

"*Hello?*" he said. "I'm not talking to the Linotype machine. Did you hear me?"

"With perfect fidelity. Hang in there. Eddie ordered me to provide you with everything I had on Petaluma. Those were my instructions. This will give you plenty of background to write. They're interesting connections between here and New York that fill the box. I'm certain you'll love it. You'll see."

"Not a chance in hell."

"I'll make it easy for you. Consider this. Audubon came to California from New York. Just as you and I had emigrated from the Empire State. Pennypacker traveled with Audubon's gold seekers called the *California Company*, financed by wealthy New Yorkers. One, who at least started from New York with them, Thomas Bishop Valentine—the guy who owned this property along the slough all the way down to the Marin border—he came from New York. Other New Yorkers, who arrived by various routes, also made big names for themselves in Petaluma. Denman. Mecham. And what do you know? Now the biggest blowhard yet to hail from Gotham, Mick Mallory, has also wandered from New York into little old Petaluma."

Mallory sucked an erect cigarette, essaying its unlit yield through his lips. "Give me a break."

"Seriously. Isn't that strange?" Rash said. "There's weird cosmic juju going on here. Why else would there be so many connections between this literal backwater and Manhattan?"

"All roads lead to New York," mumbled over the bad-tasting tobacco that dangled from his mouth.

"Don't be a pain. That must intrigue you. Such coincidences have to make you wonder about fate."

"Damnation, not fate. And I'm not interested." He looked up. "What time is it?" A wall clock gave the answer. "Hell—almost five. Civics lesson's over, professor. Talk about Dean now."

Rash's ankles crossed and uncrossed. "Audubon is far more provocative. Are you sure you want background about this local kid, Dean, instead of the great John Woodhouse Audubon?"

"Dean. Dean. Or Dean. Take your pick of any of those three subjects to discuss."

Rash stroked her chin. Slow sighs escaped her lips. "We won't talk about Audubon. Or fate. But you may regret your decision."

"Try me. I'm Irish. I've a black belt in regret."

"All right, but it comes back around to this box. It's your vein to the motherlode."

"Wait, a minute! Just wait a minute here. I'm in a hurry. I need the lowdown on Dean. Stat."

Rash waved the editorial. "This and this box will get you closer to Dean. That's all I'm saying. If that's not close enough, I have an additional special source. That's the deal. From what Eddie has told me, you're here to write a story on Petaluma. Eddie would be very unhappy if I let him know you deceived him.... Don't worry, Mick. I'll write the story on Petaluma to appease Eddie. For your part, I want your professional opinion on where the storyline runs in that box. I need a solid story. Eddie will publish it, but I want something that will gain bicoastal recognition. I think it's here to be found. You can help me. Easy peasy. Do we have a deal?"

Mallory's hands ran up the sides of his face and hair. His sleeve drew back. A welt jagged across his forearm. "If I flip through this memoir, you will then point me to more sources on Dean?"

"Consider it the cherry on the cake." Rash cast the editorial toward him. "The other lede will open a window into his world. First, you must help me. Then I'll get you to Mr. Dean in a Petaluma minute."

Mallory tapped the top of his wrist. "Clocks run backward in this town."

Fingers knit, Rash stood in front of his chair. "Find what's interesting. I'll do the heavy lifting, write the story on Petaluma, and credit you by including both our bylines."

"Mallory doesn't appear on a byline with anyone else."

"Make an exception. You need the copy. There won't be a newspaper left for you to write for if you cross Eddie."

"Your story's about Petaluma, and only Petaluma? And you'll convince Eddie that's what I worked on when I came up here. Check?"

"I do the legwork. I do the research. I keep Eddie happy. *You* only have to share your professional judgement and name on the byline."

If he forfeited her cooperation, Mallory had squandered a precious day he couldn't get back. "I blow through this, and we're out of here. If I play friendly, you bring me to your other source of information on Dean?"

"That's all I ask. If I wrote with Mick Mallory, it would give me the creds to put me on a metro paper. That means my name's there on our story—top billing." Rash crossed her chest and held up her right hand. "We're not friends, just collaborators."

"Can the melodrama. Let me see what you've got."

She pushed the box toward him. "This is complicated but fascinating stuff."

"You must have waited a long time to corner someone who might listen to you."

"Hush. The story centers in Alta California in 1845. First, I'll tell you where Pennypacker falls in the arc. I pick up his life near Valley Forge, Pennsylvania. That's where John James Audubon, the father of Woodhouse, ice-skated on the river as a kid …."

Mallory lit the cigarette twitching from the middle of his mouth. He squeezed the match out with his fingers.

She'll never write this.

Head tilted back, he inhaled smoke and leaned forward. Mallory picked up the water glass, tapping a pencil on its side. "Gin?"

"My God! That's right. Look at the hour. Go ahead and begin to read. I'll return with sustenance. It will save you time. When I return we can chitchat."

Mallory stared at the box. A lodestone anchored his neck to the desk. He grumbled, "Sustenance."

LAST CALL

Fog had thickened by the time Rash returned to the office building. The newspaper employees had left. Her BMW and the Volkswagen remained the only cars parked after dusk.

The aroma of warm sandwiches distracted Mallory's attention from the stacked papers. He looked up and saw Rash had entered the room. A one-gallon brown growler weighed her arm straight at her side. The other hand scrunched a bag containing three paninis, nested red cups, and roasted peanuts.

"I relented and brought you some fresh beer. This is heavy."

"Didn't I tell you gin?"

"Count your blessings you got this much." Rash placed the parcels near him. "There's a beer garden up the street."

A flick of his wrist swatted away a peanut tossed at him. "This is it?"

"Expecting a seven course meal?" She poured a cup.

He tilted the beer to his lips until it emptied. Popping the cup back on the desk, he poured a quick refill. "No, funny girl. I mean aside from whatever trivia I might scrape from this memoir, your saccharine-sweet editorial's the entire body of the Dean-guy information." A late fist throttled a burp. "An altar boy goes to war and dies a hometown hero. Blah, blah, blah. I don't buy it. That narrative doesn't come close to explaining the menstrual cramping around this kid's grave."

"Dig in the file. That box is how the bigger story begins," said Rash. "Pennypacker's memoir backfills in the editorial. More or less. Yeah." She peeled foil from a grill-scored sandwich and handed it to him. "Dig, dine and discuss. I'm interested to get your take on last night."

"I dug.... Lady, this man's papers are so difficult to read you need to hold them close to your face and inhale the dried pee of his cat before you can make it out." Mallory took a gulp of beer and ripped a hunk off the panini.

"Gosh, for a tough New Yorker guy, you're so, well, so pissy."

He bit on the bread, blanching. Pain seared his molar. "For Christ's sake, you're not funny. Stop embarrassing us both. This box is a load of hooey."

"Hooey? Another brilliant word," said Rash. "Keep working. Or remember, no cherry. I have one more source to share." Dressing ran down her middle finger. "Oh, I'm curious, did you come alone?"

"Geez, Louise. I've already warned you I'm too old for you."

Rash laughed in an enthusiastic agreement that Mallory did not perceive as flattery. Her breasts angled into their most opulent profile as she hoisted the heavy brown bottle with both hands. "You didn't come alone. Why didn't you tell me? Your friend should come on in. Walked to the beer garden with me. At least *he* wanted to hear about stained-glass windows and about Petaluma history— thought they were intriguing."

Mallory's brow contracted and fell.

"Remind me of his name," she said. "What is it? Tell me. A clever name for a big guy. A real big guy. The guy's a giant. He said he'd wait for you in the parking lot. Filled me in all about you. Quite the character, you are. Go ahead. Invite your friend to come and dine with us."

Hard edges cracked in Mallory's voice. "I don't have any friends. Who was it?"

"Aw, poor baby. Eat worms." Rash rubbed her eyes and faux wept, "Boo-hoo. Boo! Wait. That's his name. Boo. Your friend said you once called him Boo-Boo. Cute."

"Here, you eat," she said crossing to the Linotype. "I'll show you how this big boy works. Boo-Boo might think it's cool, too. He should come in here."

She flipped a switch. A barrage of clattering metal overwhelmed the first hum of surging electricity. Rash banged the keyboard. Lead ingots melted in a pot, sizzling to a molten consistency. Steel rods prodded brass molds to form words. The room rattled to a deafening din, obliterating any chances for Malory to ask more questions.

He rubbed his thumb against his index finger's knuckle and glared through the outside window. A large man in a trench coat darted from the BMW to around a corner.

Rash concentrated on the complex machine operations and overlooked seeing Mallory race from the room. He ran down the hall and burst from the building. The short sprint, and the sudden cold air, strained his breaths. Stench from ruminants, alive and dead, permeated the air and filled his mouth. Fog droplets mixed with spit swirled in front of him when he snarled into the night, "I saw you!" He saw nothing. No traffic passed on the street.

Mallory leaned into the void—listening. Lanyards slow-pinged against the metal flagpole. Barren cows bawled from a slaughter-house. A hushed voice from behind him stiffened his neck.

"Mick, it's me."

Winkle stepped into a mottled street lamp circle with the casualness of one who often appeared from shadows. Mallory lurched, flailing wild swings and deflected blows. Winkle muscled Mallory's jacket over his face. Muted threats came from under twisted corduroy. "Should have kicked your red nuts in the cemetery."

"Cool it, man." Winkle laughed. "We need to talk. Cool it."

"Let me go, you goddam freak. What are you doing here? You—"

"Nothing." He shook Mallory's shoulders. "I'm not here. You're not with me. We're both ghosts. I'm heading out to my rancheria where I'm chief."

Mallory couldn't wrench from his grasp. He dropped to one knee. Heavy panting came from under his jacket.

"Stop struggling. You'll hurt yourself," said Winkle. "Just listen. Chesebrough asked me to bring a message to you."

Mallory willed his legs to stand, but couldn't muster the strength to lock his knees in place. He wrestled into Winkle's coat placket. "How do you know Chesebrough? Who told him I was drunk last night? Bet *you* did."

Winkle removed the cloak. "Relax." He pinned Mallory's arms to his side. "It's Bear Winkle. Your brother." Winkle freed one arm, slapped him, and seized his arm again. "Stop fighting, brother Morning Smoke Signal."

Mallory grunted, wriggling against Winkle's hold.

"I don't like Chesebrough either but this is the deal, Morning Smoke Signal—"

"Blow me."

Winkle slapped him a vicious shot. "Chesebrough plans to fire you. Said you were supposed to write about that fisherman who drowned last night."

Mallory's ear swelled elephantine; its center numbed and pulsed hot at the tip.

"That was no fisherman. You know who jumped."

"No I don't. You tell me."

"Suck my—"

The recoil of Winkle's hand raised to slap him sounded as if a small bird buzzed his tender ear. Mallory flinched. Winkle withheld the strike and brushed his crumpled collar, releasing him.

Mallory refocused as he opened his eyes, one at a time. His face confounded Winkle as it had since their college days. He had an enigmatic look of a winking dog. Winkle often wondered whether Mallory intended to sniff his ass, or go for his throat.

"We're Indian brothers." Winkle poked Mallory's chest. "One people. Ohlone from California, Iroquois from New York, Potawatomi from Chicago, and that includes my adopted brother from Ireland. Wherever we came from—one people. Don't forget."

"Chicago?" Mallory grunted.

"One people. Hold that thought. That's what counts. If it's good for our people, it's good for you. If thieves stole from us, they ripped you off, too." Winkle shook him. "We're one. Right?"

The incongruous mention of Chicago and stolen property softened Mallory's expression.

"Okay, good," said Winkle. "Take a breath. Nice and easy. Ponder it for a moment. Collect your thoughts. When you're settled, tell me what you uncovered about last night. Anything at all, Morning Smoke Signal."

Mallory's lips trembled.

Unsure whether he struggled to breathe, Winkle leaned closer to check. He concentrated on his mouth to where he could count the sores on his lips. They quivered and puckered. He moved closer still—near enough to smell his breath.

Mallory spat into his eyes.

Winkle's face flared a wicked aggression. "It's over with you!" He twisted Mallory's wrist behind his back, turning him. Bones wrenched from connective tissues. Their crunch felt good in his grasp. The agonizing contortion on the arm increased. Winkle drove his other hand between Mallory's legs, clutching his scrotum. His body stiffened.

"This is what you're going to do." Heavy breaths panted in Mallory's ear. "Don't write about last night, or what you might have thought you heard. Leave. Don't get near my people's property and me. And don't tell Chesebrough's slut anything. That means nothing."

Cries whimpered from Mallory until Winkle released his hold and spun him to his face. "Go back to where you belong."

Mallory gasped an anguished breath. Merciless fingers hooked his sore trachea. He wheezed. His eyes widened. They confronted the sulfurous glare of dark pupils, despising him and every European generation that preceded him.

Winkle released his clench.

"God, oh, God help me7," tumbled from Mallory. "Hold on, Wink. ... Bear." He groaned an incomplete petition. "What? Feldman ... Doing?"

"Tell Chesebrough and his whore not to play me."

Mallory's lungs filled. "Bear." A weak palm patted Winkle's chest. "Somebody's got to tell your side."

Winkle cried a barbarous howl and lifted Mallory. He smashed his body off the building.

A distant thud and a sizzling flash stunned Mallory. He fell forward from an indentation where his back had molded the stucco wall.

Winkle dissolved into the night saying, "I should have cut your tongue out in Syracuse."

Someone clutched Mallory's triceps and helped him off the pavement. He turned to strike toward the arm.

"You're okay," a feminine voice reassured. Hazy forms became Rash. She daubed sticky blood thickened under his collar. "I couldn't hear you. I'll call the police."

"Don't. They've been here already." Mallory pulled away.

"What?"

"Boo—" A sharp cough whipped his head. "Your friend Boo-Boo. He's a cop. He's worried I know your plans."

"*My* plans?" Rash sat him on her BMW.

"That's why he did this to me. It's not safe to go to a hospital."

"This is crazy. I don't know him—I don't even know you. How would I know he's a cop? Besides, I don't have any plans."

A shaft of light glinted at an odd angle from her car fender. The front tire rested on its rim. A tear appeared as if a large knife had punctured its sidewall. Rash peered around the dark parking lot obscured by streetlight glare. Her stomach contracted. "Let's go inside." Grasping Mallory's arm, she directed him to her office where he clanged onto the Linotype stool. Pong of blood and molten metal fumes from the rumbling machine nauseated his innards.

Rash pressed a wet hand towel over Mallory's wound while toggling a switch behind his back. The room fell silent.

Pushing away the cloth, he slipped a small rectangle of folded aluminum foil from his breast pocket and he held the stiff packet corners on its axis. "I've got to have this story and I don't understand why I must fight all Northern California to get it." He clipped the square, giving the pouch a rapid spin. "You need to tell me what's going on. First Feldman goes dumb, won't open up to me, or to anyone else now, evidently."

"Feldman joined you there last night? Griffin Feldman? Griff? Eddie never told me that."

"No? Did he ever tell you why Feldman whined about Alcatraz and a script? Is he producing a movie?"

"Don't be ridiculous." She sat behind her desk. "Feldman was there?"

"Okay then, tell me why your Chesebrough pal is busting my balls. Why did he send me on your wild goose chase? And Winkle. The guy who beat me up is Detective Bear Winkle, not Boo-Boo.

You knew that, too. Didn't you? Then you can tell me why Winkle was *hyper* about scripts and Alcatraz, too. He brought it up with the gal at the cemetery."

"Why in heaven's name was Feldman there?"

"Another good question, Lois Lane. Why, indeed. I just had the snot knocked out of me. Now I bet you're also about to take your best shot."

"Drivel talk."

"Is it?" The foil square rattled. Mallory peeled apart its seams. "Winkle told me you still bed Chesebrough." Two blue pills rolled into his palm. He held them out, as if he presented his essence to Rash.

"Put those damn pills away. You eat them like they're Pez. Come on. Let's get you to the hospital."

Mallory clenched the pills and shook them thinking, *Their toxicity should have killed me by now.* "I blame you for this," he said aloud. "You set me up."

"Just stop. I won't allow you to get under my skin. I've never met this guy Winkle Boo-Boo, and Eddie told me zilch about last night."

"Winkle seems familiar with you and your boyfriend Eddie intimately enough. How could you not have bumped into Winkle in your reporting? He's the big Indian chief around here."

"What nonsense. " Rash laughed. "Now he's not a detective?"

"You know he's both."

"I don't know Winkle, and he does not know me. No big chiefs live near Petaluma."

"He told me he was."

"Yes, there's a rancheria. It's a ghetto trailer park, hardly a shining city on a hill—or a place you'd admit leading. And Eddie isn't my boyfriend. You can lash out to hurt me, but vehemence won't solve your problem. There's history here in Petaluma you should learn."

"History has nothing to do with me. Not one lousy event that happened a hundred years ago—especially in Petaluma—affects Mick Mallory today. Got it? Today's all I care about. Why did this Feldman dude throw conniptions on a grave today? Today. This world."

Mallory's mouth gaped. The pair of pills clicked against his palate. He struggled to swallow. "Ever since Siobhan. Well. This is it."

A catch in his voice surprised them. Although the drugs invigorated Mallory's thoughts, muted pain lingered in his weakened body. He had expected his flesh to rally. *Where's Sunshine Superman? I need you now, baby.* His eyes trained beyond the room, past the parking lot.

"Siobhan?" said Rash. "She walked out on you?"

Mallory glanced from the window. "I didn't expect it."

"Okay." Rash rubbed her neck the way a mother kneaded the back of a newborn. "Look, I swear I've never met Winkle until this evening. He must've known me through Eddie. That's the truth. I once worked my way up to a top-level job at Eddie's newspaper. I worked hard. Our breakup splashed a cold reminder I worked *for* him. Not *with* him. We had—He has a palatial home on Belvedere. He lives there now with his current philanthropist girlfriend. Younger. New ones are always younger. Yes, if you have the bad manners to ask, I will tell you. I've been with him since then."

"In the biblical sense?"

"You figure it out. And oh, in the interest of full disclosure, I owe him this job. Is that enough of this world for you? Have you had enough of today yet?"

Mallory's shoulders hunched. "Not if there's more."

"There is. Eddie called me after you ran outside the office. You must make him nervous."

Mallory raised his head. "How do you come to that revelation?"

"For one thing, he yelled at me to turn off the Linotype."

"So what? It's loud."

"He never yells."

"People yell at me all the time. He couldn't hear you over that mechanical racket."

"Maybe he heard more than me talking. I wouldn't do it."

Her eyes met Mallory's gaze. "Then the creep threatened me. He shouted at me not to talk with you when you came back inside."

"Big deal. I get threatened, too, by the best in the business."

"This morning, Eddie says to pump you for information while slow-walking your research about Petaluma. He wanted me to keep you busy here. Now, all of a sudden, he orders me to cut you off."

"All that smelly boxed stuff of yours?" said Mallory.

"None of it will lead you to Dean. I stalled. Sorry, Mick. I don't give a hang about your laurels, and less so for your all-consuming present. I played along because Eddie reminded me I owe him. Yes, I fluttered my eyelashes and acted interested in your answers. Honestly, though, I'm not interested. Not at all. I debased myself, and I debased you, for him."

"For what do you owe him?"

"Everything. Luxuries I enjoyed in Belvedere. My introduction to San Francisco society. For turning a shy Jewish girl from North Shore Long Island into—"

Mallory slapped his hands together. "Well, knock me over with a Bloomingdale's bag. Another sad story of *goy* meets girl."

"Stop it. It's not funny. I lost many nice things. Part of me died the night Eddie left me."

Mallory stood. He bent forward, holding his knees. A roseate flush bloomed on his cheeks. "Go back to *Lawn Guyland*. I don't have time for your pity party."

"You know what?" Rash wrinkled her nose at him. "You're a pathetic bigot. Don't take cover behind your Tourette's excuse. You're stoned, and you're ugly."

"Ugly, yes. Stoned? No. I'm in too much pain to enjoy a high." He smiled. "No, no. It's not that. I'm just an asshole."

"I would never say that."

"You should." Mallory straightened and shuffled to the couch arm. He played with upholstery piping. "It's a shame you have the hots for this guy, but screw Mr. Cheesehead. I'm good with words and I'm sure O-W-E is not synonymous with O-W-N."

"You don't understand. I want my old life back," said Rash.

"Maybe, I do. Maybe, I understand exactly what you mean."

"You don't. My life here in this little town is dreadful. I miss the city. I liked being known. I used to dine at the Metropolitan Club with senators. Now I go to the Rooster Run Rotary breakfast buffet where we start each meeting with a rousing cry of cock-a-doodle-do—I have to leave here. I have to do something significant. Eddie has the power and position to get me out."

Mallory picked up a newspaper thick with advertising supplements. A reporter had dropped it on the couch before he left. "Are you kidding? How long do you think it will be before you're the one he has stuffing these?"

He flung the paper. Wide sheets rustled harsh as the wings of panicked birds entangled in a fine net. Color advertisement supplements fanned across the room and landed on the Linotype, draping its steel elevators and rails.

"If Eddie owns you, he'll never let you out of here."

Rash scoffed. "You rage like a maniac."

"Good! I don't rage enough. When do you rage, Lou? Tell me. When do you ever rage?"

Her lips quavered. "I don't."

"How about yelling? Do you ever yell?"

"No."

"You said your Eddie never yelled either. You two must have acted out your marital quarrels in mime."

"I've learned how to express myself like an adult."

"Then yell dammit! Go ahead. Show me you're real. Yell as loud as you can. Let them know it's you on Long Island. Try it. It's your right. Rage like a maniac. If you're angry with Chesebrough, let it fly. Better yet, here, I'll make it easy for you." Mallory poked her shoulder. "Come at me. Bring it."

"Don't touch me! I don't need your permission to rage. I rage when I'm alone—not in public. I rage every night on my houseboat. Of course, I do. Don't you think I pine for the luxuries I've lost? You think I've been waiting for you to come along so I'd have an incentive to rage? Get over yourself. At least I don't yearn for Chesebrough. Sure, his toys frolic in my dreams: his wealth, his status, his multigenerational roots in San Francisco society, all that lovely prestige, they grace my dreams. Never Chesebrough—the scum haunts my nightmares." Her hands balled into fisted outrage.

"You speak so reserved, so civilized, but look at your hands." Mallory pushed her arm. "Look at them. Whom do you want to coldcock? Me?"

Dull aches stabbed her temples. Rash stared at her whitened knuckles, easing her fingers open.

His thumb tip stuck her shoulder. "Huh? Huh?"

She crossed her arms and turned. Her mouth trembled, as if she tried to speak with her lower lip.

"Release your inner bitch," yelled Mallory.

"Damn you." Rash turned her back. Heartache overwhelmed emotional ramparts that had protected her from indignities. She slipped a tissue from her desk and dabbed makeup smeared on her cheeks. Her chin twitched. "If I play along, there's at least a chance he'll restore my fairytale life. Otherwise, I have no recourse but accepting this life. And I hate it." Her attention wandered across the office's spare décor.

Mallory's hands steadied along the desk edge. A sheen rose from his pores carrying odors of cigarettes, beer, and red onions. "Revenge works even better than rage."

Rash pushed her chair back from him. He leaned farther in her direction. She retreated.

"Does Chesebrough want the story written about whatever Feldman went after in the cemetery? … No more games. Yes or No?"

"It's not a zero-one answer."

"It is, if you want revenge. Or do you want to settle as his cheap, second-choice lay? Go ahead and ask your receptionist. She'll tell you even that won't last long. You can't have it both ways. What's it gonna be, Lou? Does Chesebrough want the story in the paper, or not?"

"No! No, he doesn't. Eddie had me stall you. Save your breath for once. Don't ask me why. I don't have a clue about what Feldman was doing last night, and I don't know why Eddie doesn't want it reported."

"Then I must write about it," he said. "We can investigate together. You can help me smash him and his high-society circle-jerk. Now that's revenge."

"You can't. Publicity would be too big an embarrassment for Eddie. Besides, he may have worked on a development with Feldman. I have no reason to hurt Griff."

"Hold on." Mallory's eyes shifted to the side. "Chesebrough worked with Griff Feldman?"

"I've said too much."

"Did he?"

"Yes. With an Indian, too, possibly from an Eastern tribe. Their little plot has nothing to do with anything around here in Petaluma. I'm sure it doesn't. It couldn't."

"That must be why Winkle showed up at the cemetery. Feldman and Chesebrough work through Winkle. He's the Indian. When Winkle castrated me outside, he warned me to stay away from Chesebrough."

"Are you sure?"

"Absolutely. Castration is one of those things you know when you feel it—yeah, I'm sure. But what has any of this to do with the cemetery? Or Petaluma?"

"Nonsense," said Rash. "No more than 15 minutes ago, I got off the phone with Eddie. I relayed my whole conversation with Winkle. Eddie didn't indicate any awareness of him."

"Why did Winkle say you were Chesebrough's slut? Who would have told him that?"

"Your happy pills are babbling. Winkle never said such trash."

"His words, not mine. Let me give you some advice."

"Great!" Rash stood and flopped on the couch. She threw her hands over her shoulders. "Just what I need, more advice from you."

"Would you like to kick the bastard where it would hurt?"

She pressed her palms against her ears. "I'm listening to the gibberish of an unstable person."

Heavy perspiration circled Mallory's bloodied collar. Sweat dripped on his chest and forehead. He swiped his sleeve up his chin and over his face to see the wall clock.

"If you want any chance to leave here and to get back to the city highlife, work with me to write this story. Today's story. Not that litter box of Petaluma piss-history. Here's your opportunity for a real attention-grabbing feature article with your name under my byline. I've never volunteered that to anyone. Revenge *and* status, you can have them with my byline."

The more Rash agreed with Mallory, and she *thoroughly* agreed with him, the greater her disdain for him intensified. If they implicated Chesebrough in a cover-up, the scandal could destroy his media empire. But if she struck at the emperor and missed, she stabbed a dagger in her career.

Mallory paused for a breath. Open faced, devoid of guile, he eyed Rash. His voice thickened from congestion building in his lungs. "You should have told me to vamoose from here this morning. You didn't and you still haven't. Why not?"

"Don't you get it? I pretended to like you. My pretense distracted you. The plan worked." She rose and paced around the room.

"Now we've got a new plan," Mallory said. "You thought you did me a favor, gave me a cheap feather-dance tease, a show to titillate a lonely guy who's had his heart ripped out. Congratulations, Gypsy Rose Lee. It hurt more than you understand. You can stop spinning your tassels. No more games. You gave me your full disclosure, and I sincerely appreciated that. Now here is mine. I think we're in the same outhouse without a roll." He sat arms spread, ugly as a vulture drying its wings. A forearm scar peeked from under his cuff, its color a morbid gray. "Take a good look. I am the great and powerful Mick Mallory. Not very pretty, am I?" He slumped forward, and fell to a kneeling position. "I'm lost."

"Get a grip," said Rash.

He prayed, as if administering his own last rites with deathbed repentances. "Bless me Father, for I have sinned. It's been thirty years since my last confession—"

"I said knock it off."

Mallory smiled at Rash before a sour frown drew in his face. "I trusted fate meant for me to write one more story, one excellent story. That goal kept me alive."

Rash browsed out the door uninterested. "Are we whining?"

"You don't have to act cruel any longer. My inner demons have you licked. I fancied I once deserved to live a special life, too. Now I realize I've gotten by like everyone else. No better. Probably worse. That's who I am. I suck."

"Hold on. You're the New York cynic. Remember? You're the one who said fate was baloney. Now you say fate predestined you to write one more story. A great story. In Petaluma, of all places. What a bunch of self-centered rationalization." She loomed over him. "Say, Mick, while you're down there on your knees, ask your father-confessor whether he performs exorcisms. Let me know, because my head's about to rotate."

Terrified, Mallory waited for her to continue; she might burst out laughing.

"Stand up, you fool," she said.

He struggled to raise one knee. Failing, Mallory placed it back on the linoleum. With his hands propped on the floor, his head slouched below his shoulders.

Rash rustled the paper bag she'd brought from the brewery, withdrawing a peanut. She broke the shell. Its snap lingered in the air.

He stared at her. Pain contorted his face into a burl. "Perhaps, you *should* take me to a hospital."

Rash faced the Linotype. She pondered her journalist father's life. Flung pages slipped from the machinery, revealing its complex of steel components. The inner voice of a younger woman addressed her father.

I'm nobody's whore, Daddy.

After a small cry, she shouted as loud as she could. "Damn!"

From his low vantage, Mallory saw her shoe stamp on the tiled floor in front of the Linotype. "Damn!" she yelled. Her vehemence increased. "Damn! Damn! Damn!" Worn leather soles slapped on each exclamation. She pulled off sheets draped on the machine. The papers tore on sprockets.

Rash spun toward Mallory. "Is that rage loud enough for you?" Her face pulsed with heat. She gathered the papers into a crumpled ball and heaved the mass. Its violent impact toppled the trashcan. "You said new plan? Well here it is. It's my plan. Not your plan. We're going to a church." She pointed at him. "And I told you to stand."

She lifted her desk phone from its cradle. "This call is for me, not you. I need that byline."

A tired frown weighed on Mallory.

"My name comes first," said Rash, dialing. She announced into the phone, "Pops, I'm coming to see you now."

Mallory raised himself, feet numb, and his balance unsteady. "Forget it. I'll drive myself home."

"Hold on." Rash glared at him. She snarled, "Sit. Sit down—right this instant. Right now. Give me your keys."

"I'm not going to a church. They condemned me. This soul is beyond absolution." He pressed his elbows to crawl onto the couch.

"Give me your keys," said Rash. "I won't ask again."

Mallory settled in to the cushions. "Catholics wear on me."

Rash rolled her eyes. She said back into the phone, "I'm sorry. You can work a little longer. I need you. I want to see those items now. Yes, *now*. Well tell them they must go. You have a previous appointment. You can fit a meeting for me. Fifteen minutes. Bye."

"I told you Catholics wear on me."

Rash pounded the phone on the desk, strangling the handset in her grasp. Her head bowed. A small vein on her temple throbbed. She twisted her neck toward Mallory, groaned, and pointed the phone at his head. Her eyes enlarged. She roared, "It's a *Presbyterian* church."

Mallory held a weak smile. The possibility he might go to any church rekindled long-extinguished memories of his Catholic youth. His religious nostalgia sparked anew when he saw at the cemetery the wooden post carved with the word, "HERALD."

Mallory had dreaded the nuns at his parochial school from an early age. They demanded he and his first-grade classmates leave space on their folded bench seats for their guardian angels. The sisters warned them that, even after school, the guardian angels watched them. Legions of shadow jumping, winged monitors—resembling Emerald Forest monkeys—followed him home. Mallory believed in guardian angels as much as he believed in nuns.

He remembered Sunday visits to the church sanctuary. The setting, enchanting and forbidding, fascinated him with its sensuous abundance: pungent odors of burned incense, jelly-apple glows from rows of red glass candles, dead firemen's-badges under glistening chalices, altar bells that chimed like ice-cream trucks, and the incomprehensible Latin liturgy, which bent his ears.

His mother had taught Mallory that when an altar boy rang the crossed brocade of sanctus bells, a supernatural blessing occurred behind the altar curtain framing the priest. The tortured body of Jesus descended there from heaven. It changed into flat bread. His catechism obligated Mallory to cannibalize the Lord, or face excommunication.

A venerated monsignor had lectured to his all-boy First Communion class. He taught them the proper etiquette for receiving the unleavened wafer. His deep voice intoned over the pre-penitents' twitter, "*Never* let your teeth touch the Holy Eucharist."

Serious faces riveted to the monsignor's attention.

Delighted with their response, he rested on his vermilion throne arm, cupping his hand to his ear. "You wouldn't want to condemn your soul to purgatory for violating the Lord. Would you?"

The confused schoolboys dared not quarrel with the monsignor, even if his brogue enunciation sounded as though he said the forbidden word *teats*, and not teeth.

Crumpled on the Argus-Panoptes couch, Mallory reflected on how there must exist somewhere another curtain like the one his mother had drawn his attention to in church; the one behind the altar the priest faced during the Latin Mass of his youth. He imagined a finer drape hung in the holiest of holy places, a golden-threaded weave that barred his soul from the *sanctum sanctorum*. Siobhan waited for him behind that curtain until he earned his way back to her. The day they reunited, clouds of frankincense would billow from swinging chandeliers of thuribles, polished sanctus bells and sun-blistered carillons of the world's churches would chime together, and he and Siobhan—purified—would merge as one. They'd transfigure into something more joyful than they experienced in this world, something singular, and something eternal. He'd see her face shine again.

Mallory's concentration wavered. He struggled to sit up straight on the couch. His head tottered as a helium balloon held in the hand of a child. He worried he wouldn't have energy to rewrite the draft he completed that morning into a more polished copy.

But at least he had a draft in his glove compartment—a sensationalized, dramatic Mallory draft. The story, "As is," had earned his byline, even if he had to share it. The first tortured sentence held the hook:

Griffin Feldman, heir to a West Coast dynasty, vandalized a military cemetery in Baghdad by the Bay before he took a post-midnight plunge off the Golden Gate Bridge.

Whatever nefarious ties Mallory might uncover among Feldman, Chesebrough, and Indian tribes could only make the story more scandalous. Even if Rash ginned up no more details for him, national editors and scriptwriters would drool to get their hands on the material he planned to put together. That draft in his car punched his ticket back to Siobhan. Albeit imperfect, the composition held what mattered to him now.

The newspaper office grew darker. Rash turned off the lights room by room.

A limp hand rose to hail an imagined bartender, "Last call, Buddy?"

Rash didn't hear what he said. Mallory hoped someone would.

THROUGH A GLASS DARKLY

Mallory couldn't remember the short ride from the Argus-Panoptes office, or recall why he woke in his passenger seat in an unfamiliar town. When his eyes opened, an unfocused outline of a church formed in his windshield. Its bulging steeple soared from white cinderblock walls. In the misty grayness enveloping the roofline, he perceived the looming edifice had a colossal washing machine agitator crowning its heights.

He muttered his confusion. "Where are we? And what are we doing at Our Lady of Maytag?"

"It's First Presbyterian Church of Petaluma," said Rash. "We're here to meet Minister Haggard, and to see some stained-glass windows. Most importantly, we're here for me to get my story."

"Huh?" Mallory feared his drugs' toxicity had warped him into a sardonic insanity, where he embodied a barroom joke punch line. The irony was, for him, too rich to leave unspoken.

"Did I ever tell you the one about the Jew who took the Catholic to a Presbyterian church?"

"Save your wit for someone else who cares." She slugged him with an open hand. "What you *should* have told me about was your hole in the floorboard." Rash pointed to where road salt had corroded a cavity, the shape of France, on the driver-side footwell.

"Why are you complaining? I covered the space with a newspaper."

"The paper sucked out on Western Avenue. I could've lost my foot."

"Life's a vale of tears. Ain't it?"

"Get out."

"Gladly. I can't let you waste any more of my time."

The church in front of them had replaced a traditional house of worship, built when Petaluma rose as a prosperous frontier town in 1885. The old tapered spire once projected bedrock Yankee values, counterpointing the squat, mudbrick iglesias of the Californios. A translucent bracelet of stained-glass memorials, backlit by gaslight fixtures, had graced its white clapboard walls. Affluent member names adorned the windows they funded, except for one. The honored individual merited the added respect to have his death recorded in the leather bound Book of Minutes. A dip-pen entry in the ledger archived: *February 5, 1899, Arthur Lloyd Dean, Killed at the Battle of Manila.*

By 1963, a misaligned joint on a potbellied stove vent had dried and degraded the old church beams. The damage obliged a city inspector to condemn the building. The congregation replaced it with a new house of worship at another Petaluma location. Its contemporary design prohibited reinstallation of the memorial windows. The elders stored the stained glass on the ranch of a member until they could agree on a respectful means to dispose of them.

The night before the old church demolition, a painter who maintained its exterior, diagrammed a plan on a beer-dampened bar. He schemed with an antiques dealer friend to saw off the steeple top before a wrecking ball destroyed it. The painter swore that God's sword sliced, "HERALD," into the redwood pinnacle. Each time he had ascended the peaked roof with fresh whitewash, he deepened the letters with his knife to preserve the testament.

Before sunrise, the barroom-conspirators carried off a three-foot length of spire in a duffle bag. They secured the relic in the garage of the antiques dealer's home, where he lived with an alcoholic brother. A few months later, the inebriated brother stuck a lighted candle in a Styrofoam mannequin head and burned down the house. The painter and the dealer assumed their good works had incinerated in the conflagration. They did not know that days before the fire, a limousine driver traced the steeple to the dealer. The brother had swapped the artifact for a showy Cadillac ride to a neighborhood saloon, a bottomless mug of ale, and an attentive ear from his inquisitive new beer-buddy. The chauffer drove back to his employer in San Francisco with the steeple and church gossip elicited from the brother.

Mallory followed Rash across the parking lot, scattering a flock of chickens. "What's with the birds?"

"Egg capital—one follows the other. Keep walking."

Threads of smoke unwound from a cottage stovepipe. A dim sign over the front entrance welcomed visitors to the First Presbyterian Church Office. They entered after their knocks went unanswered.

"Hello, Pops?"

Mallory winced as dry heat curled over him from the opened door.

"He should be in here," said Rash.

Five stained-glass windows angled from floor to ceiling upon the walls of the tiny room. They crowded the aisles and left little space to navigate around file cabinets, desks, and folded metal chairs.

Rash again called out, "Pops?"

A toilet flushed and a deep greeting came from behind a door in the far corner. "At the baptismal font, folks. Be right there."

"Is that him?" said Mallory.

"The minister is trying to sound amusing."

"Not the man. The stink. Is that smell from him, or are those mud-smeared windows covered in chicken crap?"

"Hush," said Rash. "This is a church. And *you* should talk."

"It's not a church. It's a church *office*. Why does everywhere in this town reek like a barnyard?"

The bathroom door swung open. A twanged-voice cried over the splash of running water. "Petaluma only reeks on the hottest days of the year, when you keep your windows open. Our dairymen say that's the odor of money. No need to be contrite, they say. Yep, that's all it is, the smell of money—*their stinking money.*"

Out stepped Jay Haggard. In his youth, he cut a dramatic pro-file, a fair-skinned Indian prizefighter from the hill country of Texas. They had called him the *Apache Popper.* His marquee *nom de guerre* puffed up his speedy jab and his fractional Indian bloodline. The calling to ministry, in time, grew bigger than the anger in his fists. He headed to California, and he matured from the rebellious ring-name into the affectionate persona of *Pops,* beloved by church members and the community. The accumulated weight of bearing others' burdens hunched his tall shoulders. Rash had written a feature story highlighting how Haggard fed indigents who arrived at his doorstep at wee hours of the night. Often, town passersby saw his works as the lone figure who offered free graveside services at Potter's Field.

A strong Texan voice declared, "Jay Haggard." He crab walked among the furnishings to greet them. A window frame splinter caught on his sweater. Unconcerned, he tugged and released the snag.

"Don't say a word! Don't say a word." Haggard pushed back his sleeves. Self-tattooed petroglyph arrows inked his forearms red.

"What an honor. Lou informed me this morning she might bring a Pulitzer Prize writer from Manhattan to visit us in old Petaluma. I confess that revelation made this country boy nervous. Hope you don't mind, but I put out calls to my religious friends in New York. And what did they tell me? They told me Brother Mick Mallory is a bold defender of the little guy."

"Hi."

"Hi? Hallelujah! Brother Mick, we're on the same side. Welcome to First Presbyterian Church." He smiled. "I mean Church *office*—ha, ha! I slipped your counterpunch."

His clothing revealed he had priorities other than his appearance. Paunch established a permanent claim beneath the minister's blue wool cardigan. Holding Mallory's hand in his wet palm, his puffed eyes stayed on his face. "You must have had a long day, brother. You've got the pallor of a ballerina."

"I don't like strangers calling me brother, Father."

"Minister. I'm not a priest, never loved God enough to become a celibate." His smile widened. A horse-chin whisker stretched across his jaw line. "Everyone's my brother, but my friends—and that's everyone who knows me is my friend—calls me Pops."

"Before people get to know me, they call me Mick."

"You caught me with a hook." Haggard bobbed from side to side. "Okay Mick. Your round."

"In case you didn't guess already," said Rash, "Pops was once a boxer."

"But God's still my corner cutman. And I need him. I'm a bleeder."

"Don't pay him any attention. Pops wouldn't hurt a fly, but he still talks like he's a fighter. They called him the Apache Popper."

"Almost a full Indian. Almost a champ." He turned from Mallory to Rash, smiling. "I'm *almost* somebody."

"Well, I'd love to talk about your boxing, but you know why we came here. And Mick doesn't have much time."

261

"Okay, ref, I'll return to my corner. So Brother Mick, there they are—"

"Mick."

"Mick. Those are the windows I told Lou about and she made famous, sight unseen. Aren't they beauts?"

Rash held her hands cupped over her nose. A nasal-toned response quacked from their sides. "They're in sad condition."

"Sad is better than not at all," said Haggard. "The 1906 Earthquake smashed most of the stained glass north and south of here. It skipped underneath us. Spared our library's stained-glass dome—the largest in Northern California. There's a spirit in old colored glass. Even still, it's a blessing the old congregation didn't ground the church glass into rainbow dust and pour it into the new church foundation. That's what some churches have done. And if good Rancher McDowell hadn't reminded us he stored the windows on his property for half a century, his henhouse might have collapsed on them."

Decades of chicken guano encrusted the panels. Soft lead came, holding the glass in place, sagged. A few plates had broken after they fell from their frames. Their beetle-bored wood, chipped with layers of seagreen paint, needed fumigation.

"Our elders Steve, Ted, and Mike rolled the stone from McDowell's chicken coop crypt this afternoon. They're just a few of the many good disciples in this congregation. They trucked the resurrected windows over here."

Haggard, who had a solitary appreciation of his own witticisms, chuckled. "Chicken coop crypt. Resurrected." He wiped an eye. Tiny flecks of dandruff dusted his sweater when he laughed.

He tilted one window from the wall. Bold colors, sublime and opalescent, emerged through the grime. An artist had brushed the name Arthur Lloyd Dean on the base.

"That's the window you wrote about," Mallory said to Rash.

Haggard pulled down his sweater sleeves. He rubbed a threadbare forearm over a muddied plate. "Through the glass darkly, then face to face. That's what old Paul said. That's when you find glory." He inspected the defects. "With some elbow grease, water and a rag, they'll be fine. Secure the leading and we have done the Lord's work. We should have them all displayed on the chancel ready for the main event."

Haggard turned to Mallory. "You should visit us for Christmas worship. I promise you we'll get the money-aroma of chicken poop off before then."

"Church? You picked the wrong guy." Mallory smirked. "Not my circus. Not my monkeys."

"Ha! Ha!" laughed Haggard. "You sure have a stained-glass way of communicating, brother—colorful."

"I don't have a beef with you, but I'm not a holy roller. Words are my god."

"Close enough for me," said Haggard. "*The* Word is my God. What do you say to me introducing you at our next worship for a blessing? We all could use a little more grace. Will you step into the ring?"

"Attending church doesn't make you holy."

"Hell no," said Haggard. He hitched his pants in the back. "If you face life on its own terms, you walk with the living God already. Who needs a church?"

Haggard nodded at Rash. "Or a temple, to tell you what road you're on?"

"Bingo," said Mallory. "Pun intended."

"Good jab. That's the way I see it, too. That's the way it is. It is, indeed." Haggard's voice rose as if he addressed a congregation. "You don't need some namby-pamby, minister church-guy who's never gotten punched in the face to tell you what life's all about—"

"It's late," said Rash.

Mallory spoke up as if from a sudden daze. His words came out one slow word at a time, struggling to speak them in order. "Is this a sermon you prepared for me?"

Rash interjected, "Mick's not well. He's getting tired."

"I didn't want to come." Mallory's tongue adhered to the roof of his mouth. "Got to get back to Frisco."

"He's in a hurry to return to San Francisco."

"Okay," said Haggard. "Here comes the knockout. Wait for it."

"Quickly." Mallory's ears buzzed. He braced his hand on a desk and bent at the waist.

Rash tapped her fingernails across a window frame. "We really must go."

"You're like a church, Mister Pulitzer Prize winner. That's what I wanted to say."

A faraway, boyish grin ruffled Mallory's cheeks. "No one ever accused me of that."

"Think about it. Your stories meld hundreds of various life experiences. Readers trust that if they turn to your page, they will find truth and perspective. A good church does that, too. Both remind us we are not alone. What has been will be. There's nothing new under the sun—our work is timeless."

Mallory looked at him glum-faced. "Fine."

"See? Your calling is similar to a church's, isn't it? Your stories, and the books in the Bible, brought us together tonight." Haggard pressed his palms over his head. "You're a church without the pointy hat."

Irresistible nausea gyred Mallory's gut. He pointed to the window set back along the wall. "The Dean window."

"That's right. Yes. The one you're interested in seeing," said Haggard, "Nice colors. These windows are like fragile crystal vaults holding keys to our past and hints to our destiny."

Weariness grew over Mallory, as if someone tightened a blanket around his head. "Keys? What about Dean?"

"That's why we wanted to see you on such short notice," said Rash. "We need to research Dean. Mick's on a deadline."

"You should know you aren't the only ones interested in Dean," said Haggard. "Your editorial in the Argus caused quite a stir. A friend of yours, a large police officer, visited here earlier, inquiring about the same window. The palooka moved like a heavyweight."

"What did he tell you?" said Rash.

"He told me he learned about the windows from you. And, oh—heck, I must have forgotten, he said for me not to speak to you, too. That's what he told me. He said not to speak to the *big-mouth* reporter from the city. As a man of the cloth, I solemnly swore not to breathe a word."

"Sick ... I ..." Mallory's pupils swirled. His eyes rolled up into his head. A spot of foam bubbled at his nostril corner. Mind and body twisted in opposite directions. The room contracted around him. He pirouetted as a human auger, banging into a desk, before collapsing on the floor. Fingers fumbled into his lips to expel an obstruction not there. He tasted metal. Dirty nickels and dimes filled his cheeks, inching into his throat, unreachable.

And he sweated. Got colder. Chills. Flames shot from his skin as forks when he shook. He couldn't run, yet he hit a wall. Might be a floor, or a ceiling. He spoke in tongues, and four-and-twenty blackbirds flapped from his lungs. They swirled into shape-changing, fluid murmurations. He tingled with electricity, struggling to stay alive. Spasms shuddered over his body.

Dark. Dark.

Dark—

Blink! Blink—

Light!

Blink—

Blink—

Light!

SUFFICIENT UNTO THE DAY

"Mick, are you still with us?" Haggard slapped his cheek. "Mick, come back, brother. Mick."

Mallory's eyes opened wide. "Oh. Man. Ow—ouch!" He supported himself on an elbow. "God, my head hurts."

Rash clutched his arm. "We got you. You're safe. Mick. Do you hear me? Mick, you had a seizure."

His bloody gash oozed fresh blood after he hit a metal desk. "I'm okay."

Concern strained Rash's face. "I'm calling 911."

"No, I said I'm okay. How long was I out?"

"Took an eight count." Haggard examined the back of his head. "May need a stitch."

"Long enough." Rash stroked her hands and touched her fingertips to his chin. "I mean too long. That looked horrible. We're definitely going to the hospital."

"No. These have happened before. I can't afford to delay. Tell me how much time have I wasted?"

"The story can wait." She seized his wrists. "Don't fight me."

"Heed the man," said Haggard, tapping his chest. "It's his fight. Let him judge for himself."

Rash nibbled her lower lip.

"I'm running out of strength." Tears prickled Mallory's eyes. "Can't let that happen until I get my story."

"If there's a story it's *our* story," said Rash. "Two bylines. It's important to me, too. But it's not as important as your life."

"You'll never understand, but yes, it is."

Mallory grabbed the foil wrapper in his pocket and tore two pills from it. They moved from his open palm to his mouth so fast he slapped his nose. He gulped and patted the foil side. Residual powder from a crushed pill formed a faint line. He glanced at Rash and snorted. Within minutes, the megadose hammered bones behind his ears with a sudden crash. Pushed by a wave of unnatural energy, Mallory talked more—and loud.

"Remember I told you I separated from Siobhan? Remember, Lou? Well, I lied."

He faced Haggard. "That's right. A damnable deceit. She's dead. My wife, Siobhan. I tried to find her the day. The day. You know. That day I never saw her again."

Mallory stiffened, as if he had bolted a gyroscope to his head. He couldn't lean, or bend his neck. Grunts rumbled from his chest top.

"I could hardly see that day. Dust in my eyes.… Blood clogged my ears. I moved toward soft screams—must have been her. Had to be. But there were no screams, never were." His mouth warped into a pained smile. "Only sirens. Screaming. They were. The world. Everything. Screamed. All everything the same. All making the same screaming sound."

Rash hovered near him. "Don't talk."

Heels of his hands pressed into his eyes, blocking the unwelcome compassion. Pain seeped over his cheeks. "This young doctor from the morgue came into my room." Mallory wiped his lapel across his face. "'Would I prefer to see a digital colored-photograph of how she looked when they brought her in?' instead of … instead of … you know. Seeing a corpse."

Haggard squeezed his arm. "You're coming around, brother."

He tilted away. Misty thoughts reassembled. "The doctor emphasized the word *digital* as if technology promised a cool, new way to deal with grief. 'It'd be easier on me to see her this way.' That's what he said, easier. His words had no context in my reality. No words did."

Raised cheeks rimmed tears into a large droplet running to Mallory's chin. Across the room, stained-glass Easter lilies diverted his attention. He itched.

"Then, the doctor, the doctor, he talked nervous. Really fast, as if overwhelmed with other priorities—or, maybe, he was on drugs, like me."

Rash looked at the ceiling, bewildered. "The night you drove, you were high?"

A sour smile creased Mallory's lips.

Haggard rubbed his shoulders. "We're still listening."

"So the doctor, he said it would be less painful. Less painful? He actually said that to my face. Before I could answer, he flips out a photo of my Siobhan from a yellow folder. Whap! And I sat there pushing my knuckles into my mouth, wailing for all the world like one of those god-awful, muted sirens."

Haggard hooked Mallory from under his arms.

"I got it," said Mallory. He struggled to stand while straining to see over his shoulder. "Long time ago, anyway. Right? I thought your God meant for me to follow Siobhan with the crud He pumped into my lungs. My Docs estimated I'd be around a maximum of five years. I'm in my sixth.

"The second I learned I had an old man's cancer I gave up drinking—for life. That pledge lasted for twelve hours. Maybe three. It's not the life I expected. They had me take eight. Ten? I don't remember. Lots of tablets, capsules. Inhalers. Every morning. The doctors' *cure* puffed me up like a knish. I had a short zap of chemo. One month was all I could take of that crap. Even my balls hurt."

"Okay, enough. Let's try to rest," Rash said.

Mallory bent his head toward his shoulder. "I'm sorry for the French, Padre, but your mouth. My mouth. Tongue. Split like a snake's. Couldn't taste the difference between a honey sandwich and an uncooked fish.

"One day the doctors counseled me, 'The therapy hadn't worked … No point in fighting me about it anymore.' Fighting me? They said, fighting *me*—not the cancer. 'There was nothing more they could do for me.' That sentence goes around and around in my mind."

Mallory's shoulders rose toward his ears. "Worst is at night in bed. I try not to do that. Instead, I drive asleep around the city."

"Drive asleep," said Rash. "Are you totally—"

His lips whitened. "If I lie there alone in my apartment, I cuff my head and think I'm trapped in a cemetery. And I imagine how it is to suffocate underground with heavy dirt on my chest. My arms can't move. Down there, no one can hear me shout. I can't say good-bye—or I'm sorry. And it's forever. I get the willies. Other times, I'll look at fog from my apartment late at night and think I'm in a nightmare in which I remember I'm dying. I try to wake— to shake it off my mind. The problem is I am awake.

"My brain swirls thinking of things I've done. Bad things. People I've hurt in the past. Not that I meant to hurt them. But I didn't try not to, either. It's a feeling of madness, jumbled thoughts. Decades of memories—good bad—all at once.

"If I doze, I wake gagging and think I'm dying. Then I realize I've waked from a nightmare. But I really am dying and Siobhan's already, well, Siobhan is…." He struggled to exhale. "Siobhan is—"

"You've said all that needs to be said." Rash pressed her eyelids with the crook of her thumbs.

"Not yet I haven't. While I'm still alive, I need a few words with Siobhan to say good-bye. That's all. My words can change everything. They always have."

Haggard coughed into his fist. "Words are a poor way to pray."

"I never pray. I write," said Mallory. "That'll be enough."

"So you say, brother. I'll get you water."

Mallory blubbered, "Mick, goddammit." He pulled his collar up to wipe his eyes. "If I write a great story, the way I used to write, I can get back to Siobhan. That's why I wear the same clothes. Drive the same crap car she and I rode together. Do everything I can to make my world the way it used to be. I know—it's fucked—but I want to get as close to that feeling of her as I can."

"Then go write fairytales." The minister rose with an athletic abruptness that startled Mallory. "But trust me when I tell you, brother, inventing myths about the past to lessen the guilt of who you are today doesn't work—at least not for long."

The sharp edge to his voice lifted Rash's eyebrows. "That's not kind."

"What was, *was*," said Haggard.

Mallory pressed his mouth into his sleeve and glared over his forearm.

"No matter what you write or do, it won't bring Siobhan back." Haggard paused before he hurried into the bathroom.

"Even if you knew what you were talking about," blurted Mallory, "your shit-covered windows aren't helping me."

Haggard returned with a ceramic mug and paper towels. "The Dean window might help you find peace. Be with it for a while, but don't use your words." He pressed a wad against Mallory's wound. "Here, this will stop the bleeding."

"The window tells me Dean is dead. I knew that. He was dead yesterday. Still dead today. He'll be dead tomorrow." Mallory gulped half the water. "I want to know why a mob of anxious people poked around his grave last night. Ask Rash. She knows

I must run back to the city to discover what spooked them. The story isn't here. Someone buried it there. I don't have a minute to lose."

Haggard held the bloodied towels aloft. "Mr. Griffin Feldman was in attendance at the Presidio?"

Unpinned hair fell on Rash's face. "You knew that, too?"

Before Haggard answered, Mallory said, "Wait. How did you know Feldman?"

"Of him," said Haggard. "Gossip spreads like wildfire over a backyard fence."

A rooster crowed on the church lawn.

"There's a lot of interest in that clown." Mallory craned his head.

"It's stunning how your pettiness invigorates you," said Rash. "For your information, the Feldman family law practice is among the most influential real estate groups in California."

"You and Feldman are friends?" said Haggard.

"I dated him before I met Chesebrough."

Not wanting to withstand the pain of laughing, Mallory gave a wry turn of his head. "Eddie had more to offer you."

"It was none of your business." Rash shrugged and pinned fallen hair behind her ears. "I knew the Feldmans well. I'm proud of them. Their family financed the Zionist Benevolent Free Loan Society in San Francisco."

"Good Jews," said Haggard. "Lived in the spirit of *Tikkun Olam*."

"How do you know so much about them and this *tiki* stuff?" Mallory shook his head. "I can't even spell it. And what's the big deal with this loan thing."

Rash said, "Fortunately, not everyone's like you. In the 1920s, the Benevolent Society funded Eastern European Jews from *shtetls* to emigrate to Petaluma ranches. They came here instead of going to Palestine, or to Soviet Russia."

"That's a big deal?"

"It was a big deal in Petaluma—and around the world. Their vision held significant political risk." Haggard gazed out the window. "The experiment made for a very big deal. Even Golda Meir visited the Petaluma ranches in the 1930s. Landed bosses don't like it when people get self-sufficient."

"That's right," said Rash. "Especially when those people are Jewish-immigrant communists."

Mallory slowly wagged his left elbow. "Must've raised left-wing chickens."

She flipped a dismissive wave.

"Do your magic windows tell you why *Adopt-a-Babushka* chose Petaluma?" He struggled to test his balance, avoiding her scowl as he wobbled.

"Oh, you'll see," said Haggard. "There's more to learn from those windows than you may want to believe. Your kind friend here inspired me to dig into church archives about Brother Dean. I found a journal that might throw light on why there was a caterwaul in the city last night."

"No! No. Both of you, enough. Mick has to see a doctor. We don't have time to keep going into this."

Blotches of red spread across Mallory's face. "Yes, we do. If it will help me get to the story, and to my Siobhan, we do."

She held up her cell phone the way a startled hiker might aim bear spray. "I will call for an ambulance."

A muscle below Haggard's lower lip pulsed. "Leave him be, Louise Rash." His second flash of anger pinched Rash's face back by the ears. Haggard rumbled hoarse. "Just leave him be."

"Lou, I'm not going anywhere else in Petaluma," said Mallory.

A car decelerated as it passed outside the office. Haggard snapped fists to his chin. Rash grimaced and stepped back. "Are you intending to hit somebody?"

His hands opened outward, as might a tired boxer, off-balance and woozy. "I was considering how some men need a fight to stay alive. It's a reflex. Forgive me." An unfurled handkerchief from his pocket swabbed grime from a crown and anchor stained glass. "Like that cock crowing outside, some men don't back from a fight they believe is right. They can't." He blew his nose into the darkened cloth, balling it into his palm. "That's not my sermon. That's Mick." Haggard twisted his cauliflower ear. Redness encircled his eyebrows, their pigments draining from the follicles. "I made a mistake and ran from a fight once. But not our dear friend here. He's exchanged haymakers with Goliaths. Leave it for the rest of us to run. Not Mick. He nailed his towel to his corner post. No one is throwing it in the ring on him. Don't try to do it."

Rash eyed Mallory. "What's with you people?"

"Come with me, both of you," said Haggard. He held Mallory, who scrutinized him as if for the first time.

Haggard escorted them past a stained-glass lyre, near the bathroom. They crowded into his office. Smells of burned candlewicks, oak kindling, and stale curried meals adhered to the walls. A small Christian cross, entangled in an Indian-crafted dreamcatcher web, hung behind a standup desk.

Haggard said, "Grab the stepladder near the bathroom. And bring a chair for Mick, would you?"

"I'm hot," Mallory complained, yawning. "Turn that stove down."

"Hades portal. An antique from the old church. Burns like the Day of Judgment, don't it?"

"I only know it's hot." Mallory sat on the chair when Rash carried it in from the outer room. Unshaded, double-hung windows allowed him to view outside the room. Pitch darkness hid where Rash had parked his car in the fog. He placed his feet up on a tea chest holding a potted coconut palm. A sun-faded photograph of Asian children peeked from a wall behind its trunk.

"After Lou comes back in, you'll see this Dean fellow mentioned in a former minister's diary. There's evidence he had secrets."

"Dean or the minister?" said Mallory.

"Yes—both."

Rash brought the ladder. "Don't you want to sit?"

"No, I want you to stand." Haggard peered up at a ceiling door. Two flimsy floor lamps reflected a yellow light around its frame. Shadows formed wedges from a molding on the attic hatch where he pointed. "Would you mind if I asked you to reach up into there and bring down a basket for me?"

"*Okaaaay.*" Rash pulled her hair back and climbed the ladder. "If you think it's warm down there, you should feel the heat up here."

Haggard enjoyed the sight of Rash's legs stretched on the rungs.

"Let's hurry it up," Mallory said, eyes closed. "I'm going to rest my eyes, but only for a minute. Don't worry. I'm fine. Wake me if I fall asleep."

Rash pushed open the enclosure, shaking her head. Sharp ammonia odors accosted her nostrils. She wiped her nose and blinked down at Haggard.

"Mothballs. We throw a cupful in the rafters to repel vermin. We get roof rats."

"Does it work?"

"Can't swear that it does."

Rash groped in the unlit space, probing cardboard box sides and cool ceramic faces of religious icons. Gossamer materials brushed the back of her hand. "This is creepy and disgusting."

Haggard shouted up, "Be careful what you grab. No one has stirred those items for decades. There might be nests."

Their muffled exchange came to Mallory as if he listened from under the shelter of his childhood pillow. His concentration scattered.

Chesebrough orders me to report Feldman likes rock fishing in a bespoken tuxedo suit. What's more, he lets me think I pulled one over on him when I split to this quintessential dead-end on his nickel. What a sucker I assumed he was. All the while, I'm the fool. He's set me up to puke my guts to his ex. Maybe I'm losing it, but nothing will stop me from getting this story filed.

It's for you, Siobhan, the best story of my life. Love you more than gold—

Haggard watched Mallory nod forward, mumbling a piratical. "Arrgh."

Rash glanced downward and shrugged. She looked back up into the eaves, tugging at a wicker container crammed amidst rafters. The ladder squeaked, swaying from her exertion. "I can't see a darn thing, but think I've found it," she yelled into the crawl space.

Haggard shouted over the wicker straining against her pull. "That old basket better not break."

She leaned, bending at the hips. "What's in here, anyway?"

"If you've grabbed the right basket, it contains papers the demolition crew found in the old church. A former minister had hidden them near a broken stovepipe vent. It's very, very dry."

"Here goes." Rash concentrated her weight and gave a vigorous yank on a handle. "One more pull—"

The contents in the lopsided container shifted. Through the hatch flipped a white-wicker, baby casket. Rash squealed, her voice trilling into the whistle register. The casket flopped upside down into her arms. "Oh! Oh, my God. Oh, my God. Take it away. Take it away."

"That's it. Hold it carefully." Haggard reached up the ladder. "It's at least one hundred years old. You wouldn't want anything to fall from it." He laid the casket on his standup desk.

Rash hopped off the steps, missing Haggard's rueful grin. From the casket, he removed a satchel covered in brown butcher paper tied with string. Haggard slipped a knot and opened the package. The wrapper held letters, newspaper clippings, and a minister's diary from the time before they built the new church.

"Sorry for having a little fun at your expense. I stuck that casket basket out of the way yesterday after I skimmed through its contents. I already have a good idea what's in here. We'll respect the diarist's privacy. I'll be the only one to read it. There's plenty on Dean. After we sort through this pile, I'll read to you from the diary some Dean references I noticed. I pray you two can find a morsel here to have made your visit worthwhile."

Haggard set the stiff leather diary aside, handing Rash newspaper clippings and documents.

Deepening furrows twitched on Mallory's forehead. He asked from his slumber, "Who clicked a pen?"

"Nobody," said Rash. "Go back to sleep. You need to rest."

Haggard lifted a bundle of cracked-edge papers from the file, sliding an envelope from the bottom. He tapped its folds across his palm. "This is the last letter from Dean's friend Pitts to Dean's girlfriend. I prefer you read it in silence. It's difficult to stomach."

Rash hesitated before taking the multipage letter. She flashed at Mallory, whose eyes remained closed while he repeated, "Pitts."

"This correspondence is sad, isn't it?"

"Regretfully, it's sad in many ways. Mainly, it's about Dean's death."

Rash swallowed to moisten her throat. She read to herself the letter Pitts hurried on a Philippine riverbank, where he described the hateful day Dean had died. Midway through her perusal, Rash laid the obscene correspondence facedown. "I can't finish this. It is terribly bigoted." She eased against the desk and brooded over the evil sentiment she had given new life. "Times then sure differed from today. Didn't they?"

"The Bible says what hath been, it is that which shall be," said Haggard. "You should finish the letter."

Rash picked up the papers again, as if she held infectious hospital linens. She trembled her hands before she burrowed her attention back into the Pitt's wartime observations. She finished and folded the letter, wincing. "That's rough."

"War makes sinners of us all," said Haggard. "But the powerless pay the penance for our sins."

Mallory stretched his arms and leaned backward, bellowing a loud yawn. His chin plopped on his chest and he snored.

"Another county heard from," said Rash.

"The minister's diary gives the story added texture." Haggard held up the leather book. "It would be a violation of my ministerial pledge if I let you read this, but I can give you a sense of its contents."

"Understood."

"What happened is that after Dean had shipped out, his girlfriend confided to the minister she carried a baby. He kept their secret until her father disowned her. The minister then communicated with a rabbi friend in San Francisco, who introduced her to an heiress. She hired her as a personal assistant."

"Sounds like a soap opera," Rash said. "Hire her with a baby? I doubt that story."

"More likely, *because* of the baby. Years later, the young mother married an attorney of her faith. Her husband adopted her out-of-wedlock son, Arthur."

"Is that why her letters are here? I guess if she brought keepsakes *and* her son from her first lover into her marriage, it would've been awkward for a newlywed." Rash lifted the letters and laid them down. "But she couldn't bear to destroy the letters, either. She saved them where she trusted they'd be in the minister's safekeeping. I can understand that."

"Evidently, that was the case. And he recorded their ministerial conversations into his diary. Later in her life, when a new remorse weighed on the woman's mind, she entrusted that burden to him, too."

"This is the Henriette whom Pitts wrote to after Dean's death?"

"Before and after. Henriette Elizabeth Rosenthal—a heartbroken young lady."

Mallory spoke from his sleep in the closed-eyed pace of a toddler. "Feldman's grandmother.... Gravedigger told me."

Rash examined Mallory. "Is he right about that?"

"He is. Henriette Rosenthal married Burton Feldman. Henriette's grandson if Griffin Feldman."

Mallory let out a long, low groan and stretched his legs. "Let the past die, Rabbi." He wheezed, falling back into a stupor.

Haggard studied Rash with a puzzled expression. "We've come to the part that has me bewildered."

"It must have been painful for her to share her darkest secrets with clergy of a religion not her own," said Rash.

"As you will see. Rosenthal's declarations may answer your question about why there rose such a tempest last night." He opened the heavy bound book to a page earmarked with a scrap from a Sunday bulletin.

Timbers in the office outer walls creaked as if offset by a minor seismic tremor. Rash and Haggard, inured to life in an earthquake-prone region, didn't notice the rumble. Mallory's stomach clenched.

"The San Francisco society woman who hired pregnant Rosenthal was Mrs. Jennie Valentine," Haggard said. "It doesn't say how, but her deceased husband Thomas made a fortune speculating on Petaluma real estate. He had valuable bonds. The minister wrote the word scrip here in the notes. S-C-R-I-P. Must be an archaic word that meant *bonds*. Debt instruments. Special bonds. I've never seen one. But I imagine if we saw this scrip paper we'd know what we looked at, because they must be engraved and they must look official, right?"

"I guess," said Rash. "What about them?"

The words *scrip* and *script* clanged around Mallory's consciousness while Haggard spoke.

"It turns out the rich, and not-so-nice, husband might have had a drinking problem. He gambled away some of the so-called scrip to timber barons. Here's the uppercut. Henriette Rosenthal informed the minister that Mrs. Valentine hid the rest of her husband's certificates before he lost them all at a poker table."

"You're describing Valentine Scrip," said Rash. "You never heard of Thomas Bishop Valentine? Congress exchanged scrip with him for his Petaluma land grant—the old, conquered Mexican lands."

"You mean stolen Indian lands," said Haggard.

"Spain's land. Grizzly bear's land. Whoever's land. What difference does it make?" said Rash. "They weren't bonds. The scrip was worth more than gold, or Petaluma real estate. Far more. It had some esoteric clause that made them rare. Mr. Valentine developed Israel Kashow's Island into Belvedere with the wealth he derived from the scrip."

"But they looked like bonds and were a legal authorization for taking the Miwok's homeland—the land right here under our feet?"

"I don't know how they looked. They were worth a bunch, though. More than Belvedere if you could imagine that."

"Do you think it might work in reverse?" said Haggard.

"What do you mean work in reverse?"

"Could Native Americans exchange the paper to get their Petaluma land back?"

"No way," said Rash. "Petaluma is under private ownership. Scrip holders could only claim defective land deeds that should legally convert to the federal government, or they could buy government properties normally forbidden for sale. That would not include Petaluma. Nevertheless, that encompasses most of the West. Men die in pursuit of the power a currency like that creates. Others kill for it. Its value would be priceless."

Haggard closed the ladder with a loud clack. "Value and price are not the same."

"Not a close call for me," said Rash. "Think about it. A Petaluma acre swapped for a Belvedere acre. Quite amazing. It all must have been redeemed years ago."

"What makes you so sure?" said Haggard.

"It would have to have been. If someone had that *carte blanche* today, who knows what distinctive properties they could buy with it?"

Haggard tapped the dreamcatcher and cross hung in the window. They swayed. "I'm sure the Indians would have good ideas of what to do with it. They'd buy what the white men stole from them. Petaluma might be an appropriate beginning."

Mallory mumbled in his sleep. "They'd turn your steeple into a tepee."

Rash ignored him. "Indians can't even afford good schools. Valentine Scrip would be out of their reach. Besides, this is all fantasy. It doesn't exist any longer."

Haggard said. "The minister's notes say around the time Jennie Valentine died, she gave Henriette the scrip she had stolen from her husband, Thomas." Soft breezes dropped from the open ceiling hatch onto Haggard. "When Henriette Rosenthal accepted it, she considered the scrip her property, not her husband's."

"That sounds nutty. Why would she do that?"

"It was her legal right." Haggard closed the diary, placing it back in the casket. "More important to her, the wealth stayed in Dean's Petaluma bloodline—not comingled with her husband's family money."

The room became quiet, except for stove cracklings and Mallory's labored breaths. Haggard fixated on Rash's eyes until he had her attention. "Henriette placed the scrip in a metal box hidden in a graveside monument she had built for her lover, Arthur Lloyd Dean."

"There's scrip in the Presidio?" Rash gulped. "Feldman has scrip in the Presidio? My goodness, no wonder he was there. Then Eddie knows too."

Claps, louder than treetop thunder, pealed in Mallory's ears. He heard footfalls outside the one-story building before anyone else. Mallory bolted from the chair, as if he had been startled awake in a tenement fire. "It's Winkle!"

A boar-like commotion thrashed from the church shrubbery. Rash leaped before Mallory to the sill. Haggard missed a grab at his arm and chased him to the window.

Brake lights splashed the church's white, cinder block walls blood red. A car's engine raced and headlights flared a scimitar over the blacktop. The automobile swerved, roaring from the parking lot with its horn blaring a warning not to follow.

"I've got to drive back to Frisco," Mallory wheezed. "That cemetery woman knows more about this. Winkle realizes it, too."

Rash said, "You can't chase him to the city. He has already beaten the hell out of you to shut you up once."

"Twice."

"This time he'll kill you."

"He'll kill my story."

"Our story."

"Maybe Winkle will kill your Eddie-boy, too."

Rash's cheeks drained from sanguine to ashen.

Haggard ran to the anteroom. He squeezed past desks and stained-glass windows, throwing open the front door. A startled rooster, perched on the steps, crowed.

"The car has headed toward the freeway." Haggard pivoted to the ruckus approaching from behind him. He spun as if he nailed his toe to the floor. "If you hurry, you have a puncher's chance to catch him. You might get lucky."

Mallory pushed Rash aside. "C'mon, c'mon, c'mon!"

She pulled his jacket tail, her voice rising in exasperation. "Stop him. He'll be dead by tomorrow if he doesn't get to the hospital."

"Give me my keys," said Mallory, tugging back. "I don't care about tomorrow."

They jostled Haggard. He pounded his hands together shouting, "Sufficient unto the day is the evil thereof."

Rash opened and closed her mouth twice before she screamed, "What is wrong with you people?"

Haggard sputtered and punched his palm. "The Bible says tomorrow will take care of itself."

"My damn bible says *amen* to that, too." Mallory twisted from Rash's hold. "Get out of my way."

She stamped her foot and shrieked, "Pops!"

Mallory coughed into his arm. He panted for breath and handed a crumpled piece of notebook paper from his pocket to Haggard. "Call this number for me. My battery is almost dead. Tell her to call me to confirm she will meet me at the cemetery, or you call me if she can't." He fingered a pencil and paper off a desk and wrote. "Here's my number."

Haggard dug deep in his cardigan pocket, jangling a janitor key chain. "I should drive you."

"You will stay right the hell here." Rash grasped Mallory by his lapel and shoved him. He toppled out the door. "Get in your crap car. I'm driving."

Haggard yelled, "You'll find God in the fight, champ."

Mallory staggered through the heavy, parking lot air muttering, "The old boxer feinted and slipped a punch." He flopped into the seat while Rash started the car. His heel kicked a spread newspaper through another rotted hole, this one on the passenger's side.

Rash scowled, reading through both floor holes, "*VISITOR*," on the blacktop.

"Hurry up," said Mallory, toeing the cavity outline.

Rash mashed the clutch into a whining, herky-jerky reverse.

The church office lights dimmed. Flares from the stove illuminated the room. A shadow hurried between the fire and the desk.

Mallory's third eye watched as they drove away.

HERMES' GIFT

M isfiring valves rattled the car to highway speeds as it climbed over the Petaluma Slough Bridge. The coffin-narrow interior left little room to separate Rash and Mallory. When the road curved, their shoulders rubbed together.

Mallory leaned forward and rummaged in the glove compartment. Cassette tapes clattered under a sheaf of typed papers. He fumbled a Pure Prairie League album into the tape deck and hit reverse. While he waited for the tape to begin, he removed his notebook and draft, tucking the notebook into his jacket pocket. The loose pages stacked on his lap. His cell phone propped against his knee and under the papers. It waited for the confirmation call from De la Cruz that she agreed to meet them at the Presidio.

The dashboard tape deck clicked. A band strummed a chord before the lead vocalist asked, "Ready?"

Mallory closed his eyes. His buttocks teetered to relieve sensations of burning bones. At the end of a lighted cigarette, an ember drooped from the corner of his mouth. It rose twice in the dark on the beat—a somber conductor's baton marshalling a requiem.

"Yeah. I'm ready," he said, opening his eyes. He punched the metal ceiling for emphasis. Balancing the cigarette on the armrest, he sat up straight and flipped on the dome light. His pencil scratched across an unmarked top sheet. He yanked from under it his earlier draft. Holding each precious sheet to the dim light, he marked them with tight cursive squiggles. Knowledge he had reaped at the church filled between the page lines.

Except for an occasional gruff request from Mallory to spell a name, he had not exchanged a word with Rash since they left the church campus. Country rock ballads filled the cabin.

The car passed the Sonoma-Marin county border marked by San Antonio Creek, the low point in the freeway where winter deluges flooded. In his time, Juan Miranda had herded cattle at that spot with his sons for the late summer *matanzas*. Now only gentle hills remained where their rancho had watched over El Camino Real. Even in daylight, a passerby could not have seen evidence the Miranda family had ever thrived. Dairy cattle had trampled into dust whichever of their adobe structures squatters had not ransacked.

Halfway to San Francisco, Mallory placed his pencil across the papers. He closed his eyes. Lurches from pounding uneven road seams bobbled his head. He flopped toward Rash, legs shifting. The pencil rolled from the papers and off his lap. Its yellow shaft flickered down the floor hole and onto the asphalt dark blur.

Rash saw Mallory's cell phone placed in a precarious position. She removed it from his knee, placing the case on his seat. She extended her arm to turn off the dome light. Her wrist brushed his clammy forehead.

The unlit highway bisected hills and tidelands until the road widened to a ten-lane freeway crossing the crowded city of San Rafael. Rubber and burned motor-oil smells seeped through the floor into the cabin. City streetlights illuminated Mallory's lips mouthing the words "pirates" and "gold." Rash stared at him as if he had moved to a far-off point, sliding from her in distances not measured by rods, to a place not geographical in space.

Ten minutes later, the car strained up a grade to where the jewel of the bay, Alcatraz, appeared. Rash rocked forward through each gearshift, coaxing the car forward.

Lights on the former prison floated as if the island paraded on a basilic barge in a pageant of navigation beacons. Behind Alcatraz, a full moon rose over the Bay Bridge. The lunar spectacle bled a silver chiffon runner across the gray water.

First sighting of the Golden Gate Bridge lay beyond the next rise. The car picked up speed on a hard downhill turn that bore through the headlands tunnel. Seductive drafts entwined Rash's ankles. She dared not move from the floor pedals for fear the asphalt whizzing beneath her legs might grind her feet to stumps. Her hands cramped from clinging to the spindled steering wheel.

Other drivers in the tube honked their horns to hear their merry lives echoed before they passed. A rising vista glowed at the tunnel end: the Golden Gate Bridge back-scored by San Francisco's white-lighted avenues and hoop framed by the tunnel.

Mallory slumped lifeless. Rash nudged him with a sharp elbow. "Mick, are you okay? You're scaring me. Please. Wake up. We're almost on the bridge." Her arm relaxed seeing he moved in protest.

His eyelids stretched to focus on the cable-suspended highway. It curved from the Marin headlands to the San Francisco anchorage. Art deco beacons flooded through the windows with a carnival-orange glow. Steel guardrail barriers, which could not hold back Griff Feldman's compunction, flickered by the car. Blurs among their vertical slats resembled an old-fashioned zoetrope that projected images of evanescing ships sailing the gate below. Bow waves plowed bioluminescence over slow rollers. Mariners pushed their ships westward—until they vanished into the Pacific—as had countless voyagers before them.

"It's so beautiful," Mallory mumbled. "Do you hear me, Siobhan?" His chin fell. Breaths flowed through his mouth. "When New York reads this story I wrote.... Oh, Babe, I'm so sorry. It *is* beautiful."

"Come on. You need to stay awake."

Scales of a dream weighed on his eyes. "I'm awake." He glowered back at the horizon. "Don't let Chesebrough say I'm a fisherman."

"Sit up straight. You rant as if you're half-asleep. Roll down your window. Take in the cold air. For God's sake, be careful of that—that—your floor hole."

"Right. I'm an asshole."

"I didn't say that. And you know it."

He ignored her rebuke, leaving the window closed. "Did you ever look up defenestrate?"

"What now?"

"De-fen-es-trate. I told you my lede self-defenestrated."

"Mick, I said sit up." Rash lowered her window. "You're talking nonsense again."

Ocean salt scents rushed in with a gust blown from the headlands. It stirred top pages of the manuscript. Papers swirled into the air.

"Oh, no." Mallory lunged for the sheets. They deflected off the dashboard and fluttered to the car ceiling. His legs twisted. The movement pushed his phone forward. Unaware Rash had rearranged his cell phone to the side of his seat, the clatter surprised Mallory. The phone knocked against the stick shift. For a moment, it balanced at its base, tottering above the floor.

Mallory's hand extended forward, opening wide, and struck. Fingertips pinched the phone edge, retrieving it before it fell through the jagged maw and shredded on the highway pavement.

"Jesus, Mary, and Joseph," he shouted.

Rash joined him with a high, nervous laugh and turned up the open window. "Whoa!" she said.

Mallory twisted from her. A sound zippered the air, as if a vacuum hose sucked up facial tissues. He knew what he heard—what the riffle meant. The soft buzz nauseated him the way faint chemo dispenser beeps turned his stomach.

"*Zipth!*" Blurs of his typewritten draft leapt from his lap and through the open hole.

Mallory tightened his stomach. He yelled at the crevice, beseeching someone as if he stood before the gates of hell. "Stop!"

Rash pressed on the accelerator. "I can't stop in the middle of the bridge."

A squall of papers reflected in the side view mirrors. They scudded over the railing.

Mallory slapped the dashboard with his palm and thumped it harder with his forehead. He couldn't save the papers, or ever type the words again.

As his head throbbed, Siobhan's apparition materialized from the ink of night. Other spirits he did not recognize: Dean, Henriette, Luz, Vallejo, Ida, Hoku, and an albino bear floated within the darkness surrounding Siobhan. They watched. Then, in an instant, they nodded from his awareness.

The car cabin narrowed. He no longer sensed a world beyond its interior. Cool glass pressed against his cheek. Mallory panted condensations on the window.

"My third eye." He kneaded two fingers around his brow creases. "I can't see from it. Hermes! I can't see."

"Who—What?" Rash blurted.

Mallory's face screwed into a pained knot.

"*Shhh.*" A low whistle blew across Rash's lips. She squeezed his knee. "You don't have three eyes."

As a fourteen-year-old stringer in Vermont, Mallory's first newspaper editor had explained to him he slept like a dog, because he had a gift. Mallory saw beyond rooms where others could not. They called him the Argus, referencing the giant of

Greek mythology. An editor had told him, "Argus had so many eyes, some always stayed awake. One day the god Hermes blinded them all."

Though the editor exclaimed he and Argus had a gift, Mallory never agreed. The gimlet eye had first opened the night he crossed the linoleum hall line into his parents' tumultuous bedroom. The third eye saw evil and its violence and he couldn't ever turn from its specter. Future visions provided the grist that catapulted his career. Their revelations also cursed him.

On the bridge, his extrasensory eye went dark. Ugly *what's* of the outside world disappeared, leaving him to concentrate on the personal *why's* that confounded his lifetime.

He sighed and stared at the west-side bike path. "That's where he did it."

"Who did what?" said Rash.

"He did it."

"Are you okay?"

"Self-defenestrate. This is where my lede jumped off the bridge. That's what happened."

Rash's eyes flitted from the road, to the holes, to him, and to the bridge railing. "Oh, my God. This morning?"

"Life happens and I don't know what it is I'm looking at. But I write as if I do." Mallory spat phlegm into the floor hole. "Cheesehead told me to write he drowned while fishing."

"Who?"

"*Eddie* told me." Mallory poked at the button on the glove compartment door. "Like the story would make whatever he said real. Eddie should've been a better friend to his buddy, Griff Feldman—and you."

Rash scratched red furrows on her cheeks until tears chased her fingers. "Did you imply Griff Feldman was your lede?"

The car drifted toward the railing. Mallory covered his eyes. "No longer."

Rash cried, "Eddie didn't tell me." She pushed a speed-dial button on her cell phone for the private line of Edward Chesebrough III.

"He should've." Mallory nodded at the bridge railing.

The car approached the south tower where Griff Feldman had torqued his Audi into a violent U-turn. With the same hand she held her phone, Rash slashed the stick shift from fourth gear to third. She yanked the handle back to second gear, as if she slashed a butcher knife with a lethal sweep.

A chirp came from her phone. She pressed it to her cheek, screaming with vehemence that shocked Mallory.

"Who the hell are you to tell Winkle I'm your whore? ... Winkle! Yes, he did. ... Is that right? You sick creep—Creep! ... Yeah, that's right. As for your little venture, are you insane? ... Oh no, trust me, he told me lots. ... Really? ... No. *You* shut up. Does scrip mean anything to you?"

Rash shot a glance at Mallory and mouthed, "*Yes.*"

"Sure did, Eddie, he sure did. ... Then I'll ask Winkle again. I'm meeting him at the Presidio with Mallory. You're in the city? Meet us there. ... No, Mallory's right here with me. ... I couldn't care less. Go ahead. Call him on his phone if you don't want to believe me."

Mallory shook his head. He raised his cell phone high and dropped it through the hole onto the bridge.

Rash kicked the corroded floorboard, bending a metal wedge. The edge scraped the hissing roadway. Sparks jetted below the car, twinkling on Rash's tears. The odor of flint, and a faint blue smoke wafted exotic patterns throughout the cabin.

Mallory mumbled, "Wow."

"That's him," she snapped into the phone. "I told you he is with me. ... Oh, no? Well, listen again."

Rash held out the phone, stiff-armed, to Mallory's face. "Say something." If he didn't respond, she might ram it through his skull.

Cupping his hands on the sides of his mouth to make a megaphone, Mallory strained to shout over the metal scraping on the roadway, "Eat my shorts, Cheesehead!"

A tiny, high squeak, "*Bitch*," peeped from the phone.

Rash hung up and tapped the phone over her cheek. "Eddie asked me whether you talked about Alcatraz."

"What's done is done," said Mallory. "It doesn't matter what I talk or write about. Never did."

"Hold on." Rash paid the toll collector and stomped the combination of clutch and accelerator in one swift motion. "Now you're a quitter? Damn you and damn those stupid pills. You said your life depended on you writing one more big story. Here's your chance."

"Someone else wrote all the stories before I came on this planet."

"I don't care about whatever planet you're orbiting. I do care, and I do *need*, to have my name on this story. If you have no intention of making sense, just be quiet a minute."

"Fate's one storyteller you can't talk over," said Mallory.

"My career—my *life*, is on the line. I need to think," said Rash. "And you need to stop your foolish chatter."

FORESTS OF THE NIGHT

The Karman Ghia creaked through the open Presidio cemetery gate. Farther up the hill, a pickup screened Dean's gravesite. A silhouette stepped into the backlight of the truck high beams. The figure, dressed in wide hat and overalls, carried a tall pry bar pointing toward the side. Rash defied the signal to pull over to the perimeter wall. The car kicked and stalled before she turned off the ignition. It sat parked in the middle of the access road.

"Let's go," she said.

Mallory shimmied forward in the bucket seat. "I'll kick Bear's nuts." He gripped a door handle resisting his slight exertion. Dizziness further weakened his hold, and his hand dropped into his lap. Rash scurried around the car and opened his door. She lifted him under the arms, hooking his chin over her collarbone. His body, folded heavy in her embrace, pushed the sharp-edged hyacinth brooch into Rash.

Mallory muttered against the comfort of her breast, "Gotta stop him."

Shifting his weight off the jewelry, she said, "I don't see Winkle. If he's not here, he will be soon."

Mallory's arm dangled to where his typed draft had jettisoned through the floorboard. "Take it," he whispered.

"Nothing to take. The notes are gone."

"Wait." He reached into his jacket pocket, retrieving his note-book of quotes and observations. "Here. Find our *why*."

"Don't worry. I'll put a story together after I speak to this cem-etery person." Rash clutched the pad while she struggled to keep Mallory from slumping. Her arms ached. She set him on the fend-er, easing his weight back across the hood.

The truck headlight beam blinded Rash, forcing her hand in front of her eyes while she addressed the long shadow. "His name's Mick Mallory. I'm Louise Rash. Reporters. We came to see some-one he met here this morning. Who are you?"

A voice responded from within the glare, "Juana De la Cruz, cemetery technician." She moved from the headlights to stand near the Dean grave. "Mick, meet me over here."

The top monument stone, the tallest of the three sections, rest-ed on its back. Two lower base-pieces lay askew. An open copper box slanted on its lid near the slabs.

"I have to talk with him alone," said De la Cruz to Rash. "Is he asleep again?"

Mallory rose from the hood, imitating an agitated roar. "Hell, no! Have you seen Winkle?"

Rash gawked the way a tent revivalist stared at a crutch-tossing cripple. "Lay down."

"No one else is inside the grounds," said De la Cruz, "I've been here since before your friend called me."

Rash shook her head and stepped around De la Cruz. "I'll be a second. Watch Mick."

"Stay over there, please."

"No."

"You're not authorized to come here after hours. I represent the cemetery and I insist I speak with Mr. Mallory alone—go back to your car."

"I'm going over there." Brisk steps brought Rash to where De la Cruz had moved the stones.

"Hey. That's a trespass." De la Cruz set the heavy bar against a tree and hurried in front of Rash. She sat on the slab inscription, stymying Rash's closer inspection. Hat removed, her head tilted. "I want to talk with Mick."

"Talk with me. Mick is not well. We're collaborators."

Mallory struggled with the foil packet containing his pills. His hand trembled. After slipping one under his tongue, the last of the drugs dropped to the ground. If he leaned to pick them up, he risked a fall, and if he fell, he might never get up again. He spat on the tablets and rubbed the sputum under the sole of his shoe. Dull energy suffused his body enough to stumble to the women.

"Looks like the jackals have been looting the cemetery bronze again." Mallory winked. "Did you find your father's buried treasure?"

"There's nothing more in here than an empty box." De la Cruz took him in with a brokenhearted smile. "Just an empty box. I came here hoping to find something else."

"Haven't we all?" Mallory scooted her to the side of the stone and sat next to her.

Rash flipped opened Mallory's leather notebook. The cover, supple as an old shoe tongue, comforted her hand. Selecting the first clean page that came after swollen sheets filled with jots and diagrams, she squinted at De la Cruz. "How do we know you're not doing this for Chesebrough?"

"Never heard of anyone named Chesebrough."

"Somehow, I doubt that." Rash wrote her responses. "Feldmans? Mick said your father associated with them. Do they pay you?"

De la Cruz's eyes darted to Mallory. He turned away. "I get paid by the San Francisco National Cemetery, but I work for the heroes buried here."

"Don't deflect, honey," said Rash. "Do the Feldmans pay you?"

De la Cruz's chin flexed. She nudged Mallory with the outside of her knee. "Does she need to stay, Mick?"

"She works for me."

Exhaling, Rash tapped her pencil tip on the notebook page. Dots clouded the sheet. "We need some straight answers and we don't have much time. Mick is tired, so I'm asking for him. What did you think is worth stealing here?"

"I came here looking for answers, too." De la Cruz lifted her face to Rash. "I'm not a thief. I'm worried people might mistakenly think my Father once did a very bad thing. There was nothing other than a post hidden in the grave last night—nothing to steal. Mick saw it."

"That's the truth," said Mallory. "No need for guilt. Nobody is guilty."

"But, Mick, if valuables remained in the box—whatever they might be—that would be enough evidence for me that Tatay wasn't a grave robber. I could forgive him if he just saved for himself a token of sentimental value. But what I see tonight has me fearing he did something much worse."

"So you're implying he *did* enrich himself on the graves of the war dead," said Rash.

"No—I don't know. I didn't mean to say that. How could it be? The De la Cruz family's not wealthy. I've lived my life in Colma with my parents. I wear men's overalls to work. I have a two-dollar lottery ticket for this weekend's drawing. And look, I use the Presidio's truck for personal transportation. Do the math. My family's not rich. Any little, extra money my father had saved in his green MJB can he sent to an orphanage on Mindanao. He donated our family's savings in my grandmother's memory."

"Good for his generosity." Mallory nodded toward Rash.

De la Cruz reached over and pulled up Mallory's corduroy collar. "Maybe good for Tatay, and maybe not." Her voice lost its cross tone. "I had to know whether there was more to this gravesite then I could see from above ground. I cut the seal on the cemetery archives."

"The grave files are government secrets," said Mallory. "You told me that yesterday. You said even the grave dimensions are a privacy issue."

"This was more important. I looked at the monument design."

"That's why you expected a hidden compartment," said Rash. "You broke the law *and* you broke your trust with the deceased and their families. This is not getting better for you."

Mallory snapped in a reedy voice, "Back off, Lou."

"What we're sitting on here today wasn't the original stone from 1899. Are you happy, reporter-lady? There, you got a story." De la Cruz clenched her jaw. She pulled on her hat. "Just know if you write about that, I'll go to federal prison."

"She won't—"

"Maybe I will. My guess is Feldman came here last night to retrieve what was left of his family's property before someone walked off with it." Rash wrote without watching De la Cruz. "Or it's also possible your father stole for Chesebrough."

"I said I never heard of Chesebrough." She turned from Rash to Mallory.

Glazed eyes looked back. Mallory said, "This morning you wanted me to answer you straight-up in the presence of your Filipino mysticism and my Irish intuition."

"Yeah."

"I did. Now it's your turn. Tell me the whole story. The *real* story."

De la Cruz stared at Rash. She rolled her hat from brim to brim, wishing she wrung her neck. "I will do it for you, not for her."

Her lips reset into a sad smile. "Tatay once told me he removed *something* from this grave. I thought he was talking in Filipino mystic-gobbledygook—that he referred to some sentiment or inspiration. It flew right over my head. He promised I would understand when I was older. At worst, if he physically took something, I hoped he stole a stupid item, like that post, something with sentimental value to him. But I have feared that whatever he took must have been worth plenty."

"Why?" said Mallory.

"Every year, a Filipino orphanage sends us pictures of children born of American GI fathers. Their letters thank Tatay for establishing and sustaining the mission. He never could have afforded to give away enough money to deserve all their praise. When years passed without visitors ever paying respect to the Dean grave, I no longer worried the Feldmans might accuse my family of burglary."

Rash said, "What's the Tagalog word for nonsense?"

De la Cruz stood and pointed at Rash. "That *friend* of yours will report the meanest possible untruths about Tatay. Or that *Bullwinkle* detective will come back and he will make something up to disgrace my father and earn himself a promotion. I just know it."

"Lou." Mallory's voice trembled. "Go kill the truck lights. Hurts my eyes."

Rash slogged to the car, sidestepping to clang De la Cruz's pry bar to the ground.

Mallory tugged on De la Cruz's overalls. "For me, not her. Other than to play Robin Hood, why would your father steal from a grave?"

"I don't know. I don't know. I don't know." De la Cruz glared at the Karman Ghia and pivoted on her buttocks toward Mallory. "I may not have the answers for why or what. And neither does she, but I think I can give you an idea for *who* Tatay stole.... She may be right."

Mallory leaned closer to her whisper.

"Last night a man phoned my family's home. I answered. He demanded the cemetery gravedigger. 'The boy would remember who this is,' he said. I said he spoke to the cemetery technician. He hesitated. Then he said I sounded like a girl on the phone. The guy wouldn't identify himself, so I wouldn't either. I assumed he was a crank caller. Then he insisted that I meet him here to empty the rest of the Dean grave at midnight—"

"That was Feldman."

"I didn't know that then. But empty it! Empty the Dean grave of *what?* He hung up just before my knees buckled."

"Did you tell anyone else? Anyone at all?"

"I called the Presidio park police to watch for a possible crackpot in the cemetery. They're spread thin. So, even though they offered to have a patrol car drive by a few times, I headed to work. I hid in the parking lot over there."

She pointed to a Spanish Colonial chapel built in 1931. Stuccoed bluestone rubble separated the church grounds from the cemetery. Fallen tree trunks had breached the length of the wall, leaving easy to step through gaps.

"When I saw a man in a tuxedo scramble over a low wall section, I called the San Francisco police."

Rash yelled from the car. "You shamed Griff so much he jumped off the bridge."

De la Cruz murmured to Mallory, "He killed himself?"

"And he murdered my story."

"She's wrong. I shamed nobody. I stayed hidden so he wouldn't see who I was. I watched the cops, you, and then that Winkle guy arrive later. The detective poked around after everyone left. I don't like him. You were sleeping."

"I know he did—"

Tires squealed. A powerful automobile made a hairpin turn in to the cemetery. Headlights raced from the gate and up the hill.

Rash recognized the low-slung convertible as one Chesebrough never allowed his wives to drive. She shouted, "That's Eddie's car."

Mallory snapped to De la Cruz, "Pick up your bar."

The high-performance engine snarled to a purr when the automobile spun over the wet grass. It slid to a stop among the outer graves. Chesebrough smiled back at them, his face cinched in a loose-fitting hooded sweatshirt.

Until now, Chesebrough had remained confident that no one knew what he planned to do with the scrip, except Griff, Winkle, and the communist financiers in Macau. If Winkle had told Rash, or worse, if he had told that contemptible lowlife Mallory, and he had to assume he had, then Chesebrough must discredit the story before they published it.

"Thank God you're okay," he said, his arms spread wide as he exited the sports car. "I knew you guys would pull through for me."

The women and Mallory passed glances.

"Wait—what?" Rash scrambled toward Chesebrough. "Griff's dead, Eddie."

"Awful, isn't it? … Suicide."

"Didn't you think you should have told me about this after *twice* speaking with me on the phone?"

"I was too fragile to talk about it."

Rash slapped him, driving the side of his hood over his nose. Her palm tingled as if she had scraped it on sidewalk concrete. "He's dead, Eddie. Griff is dead. You had something to do with it. I'm sure you did."

Chesebrough twisted the hood off his face and sniffed at Rash. His lips knotted away from a weal spreading on his cheek. He took a confident step toward Mallory. "My girl here doesn't understand that this big dog's neck has been on the block while I tried to nail that radical Winkle. You're a pro. You'll appreciate what I have been going through. I couldn't succeed in pursuing this story without making my good friend Griff, or the newspaper, look bad. But

I knew if I gave my Pulitzer-man Mallory enough time he'd get the story, and he'd keep my name far from it."

Mallory waved his finger at Chesebrough and De la Cruz. "Know her, *Eddie?*"

A supercilious smile frosted De la Cruz. "No," said Chesebrough. "Who's the *overalls?*"

De la Cruz smirked at Rash. "I'm the cemetery technician. Second generation."

"She and her father before her have been the Presidio grave-diggers," Mallory said.

"Don't listen to him," said De la Cruz. "You're in my cemetery."

Mallory grabbed a granite chip and tossed the sharp-edged stone at Chesebrough. "Who told Winkle I traveled to Petaluma?"

"Hey, Eddie. Why don't *you* go kill yourself?" said Rash. "Take your buddy Winkle with you."

"Cut it out you two. I sandbagged this story for you. C'mon, you realize that. Don't get wobbly on me." Chesebrough pulled his hands toward his chest. "I'd never ally myself with that con man. Listen to the sleaze he conjured up about Lou. Winkle put words in my mouth. No wonder she's upset. Don't underestimate him. The man's dangerous, and he's no friend of mine. Mick, that's why I asked you for that smokescreen about Griff's fishing accident nonsense."

"You never told me it was a smokescreen," said Mallory.

"You're damn right it was. We needed time to prove Winkle plotted all this."

"That cop is a walking centograph," interjected De la Cruz.

Rash squinted, writing the word *centograph* with an exaggerated question mark after it.

"See. It's clear even to her," said Chesebrough. "Have you seen him here?"

"This morning." De la Cruz nodded. "Sure was angry for a guy named Wink."

Chesebrough circled his finger in the air near his temple. "A raging maniac obsessed with white man conspiracies."

"A big liar," said De la Cruz. "I wouldn't believe what he says. Winkle told me we're on Indian land. And the liar said he saw Indian words on the Alcatraz water tank from miles away. Don't trust him for anything he makes up. He's a liar."

"That's nothing, Mick," said Chesebrough. "Though it fits what I already know about him. His Indian cronies were in Chicago today trying to extort the city—the whole city. And not just Chicago, but San Francisco, too."

"Chicago," said Mallory. "With Chicago Indians?"

"Yes. Here's another four-bell bulletin that'll knock you on your keister. The renegades offered to back off their blackmail threats if the United States surrendered to them Alcatraz. What nerve! That was Winkle's grand scheme this whole time. He and his Indian tribe want to take over Alcatraz and make it an independent nation."

"Impossible," said Rash. "They failed trying before."

"I'd think it was very improbable," said Chesebrough, "but not impossible, once you've heard the wild details of his plan. But they lack something they thought Griff had hidden."

Mallory mumbled, "Another center court takeover."

"Center *what?*" A quizzical glance from Chesebrough met Mallory's scowl.

He repeated, in slow monotone, "Another center court takeover, but this time the Indians are using Valentine Scrip to disrupt a bigger game."

"Scrip." Chesebrough raised his open hands. "That's right! That is what they required. How'd you learn about that?"

"I'm a reporter."

"Not just a reporter—a damn good, old-fashioned newshound. I knew of the scrip legend when I hired you, but I promised Griff never to tell anyone. Now, with Griff's death, we can run a feature about Winkle's deceit. I won't take any credit. This is *your* story, Mallory. *Your* byline—*your* next Pulitzer."

"Of course, scrip doesn't really exist," Rash said. She wrote as fast as her hand could move: *MY story. MY byline. MY Pulitzer.*

"I'll bring you on as my full-time columnist. And Lou, you've earned a place back on my executive staff."

"Please make him stop talking." Mallory hugged his ribs. "Shut up, *Eddie.*" A sharp stab electrified him, as if a metal probe hooked under his skull. Gnarled fingers kneaded his forehead. "Just—shut—up."

Chesebrough's mouth spread in a wide, taut smile. He sputtered, "No, listen and understand. I couldn't let Winkle know I was on to the plot. I played him."

"Stop." Mallory extended a palm. "*You* took the scrip."

"Didn't you hear? Rash said scrip doesn't exist. Besides, the Indians are the ones who wanted it. Not me. If he hadn't jumped, those bastards would have murdered Griff for that paper. That's what's central here. If the Indians had Valentine Scrip, they would have executed their conspiracy and been rich." Chesebrough's hands dipped through the air. "But we broke a great story for the Press-Republican. Headline to Winkle: Alcatraz is not for sale and Valentine Scrip is as extinct as the California grizzly."

Mallory didn't breathe and bent over at the waist. "What if it wasn't?"

"What if the *grizzly* wasn't extinct?" said Chesebrough. "Who cares?"

"The scrip."

"What if scrip could still be acquired?" Chesebrough locked on Mallory. His voice hushed. "Then the answer is Valentine Scrip would be worth many, many millions to anybody. The last thing you would want, if you had it, would be to write that secret in a newspaper."

De la Cruz's phone rang. "Juana," she answered, standing and turning from the others. Her head swept from side to side, searching along the dark perimeter wall. "Hello. Hello?" The call ended. She leaned to Mallory. "Winkle can see us."

Mallory nodded to Chesebrough. "Your pal, Winkle, is here."

"Where?" He raised his eyebrows. "If he's here, we're all in danger. That man's crazy."

"You lie," said Rash.

"Don't be an idiot. He could be after you next." Chesebrough checked the shadows for movement. "This is the truth. Winkle heard about the scrip legend because Griff wanted to help the Indians get some stupid village restoration at Crissy Field. He had a ludicrous idea his grandmother hid the scrip in the cemetery. The whole story smacked of a nonsensical family fable."

"Eddie, you're dirty." Rash pointed her pencil at him. "Winkle might have stolen the scrip from Griff, but you were in on the plot."

"How would I—or anyone—have the scrip if it doesn't exist?" Chesebrough blinked his eyes. "That's our breakup talking again. The jilted wife bit is getting old. I said there was nothing to get in on."

"This empty box proves somebody stole it," said Mallory.

"There probably was nothing in it to steal. Even if there were, you couldn't ever prove somebody stole Valentine Scrip. Those beauties were like bearer bonds. Anyone who held them could claim ownership. Finders keepers is the rule with bearer bonds *and* scrip. No questions asked. If you hold them, you own them. But this is ridiculous speculation. Valentine Scrip doesn't exist."

Mallory turned toward Chesebrough. An involuntary shudder rattled his head. He placed his hands in his pockets and pushed his jacket back. "We got it." A small bump from his necklace protruded between the words *Montauk* and *The End*. The gold ring under the fleece softened, its warmth melted across his chest. He grinned. "We have the scrip."

Chesebrough's glare ricocheted off Mallory to Rash. "He's lying."

Rash nodded at him. "I want my toys, Eddie."

De la Cruz interrupted. "Why did Mr. Feldman call my house?"

"Silence!" shouted Chesebrough. He looked hard at Rash and spit out, "Prove to me you have the scrip."

"Answer her question first," said Rash. "If you were Griff's good-buddy, you know why he called the gravedigger."

"Tatay," said De la Cruz.

"If Winkle's here, we don't have time for this," Chesebrough said.

"I do," said Rash.

"*Overalls* knows the answer. I wouldn't fall for her fake innocence. Her father worked at the graveyard. Right? He must have been the fellow whose name old man Feldman kept in his vault."

"Vault?" said Rash.

"Griff's father filled his safe with plans and junk." Chesebrough sneered at De la Cruz. "The Feldman family sent your father a rather large stipend each year to a PO Box overseas. Didn't they? He must have done special jobs for them. Or your gravedigger family blackmailed the Feldmans. Maybe your *Toot-Toot* Daddy has a girlfriend in the Philippines. But I'm supposed to believe you don't know about that, either. Or do you, little Miss Innocence? You know very well why Feldman called your house. He wanted *Toot-Toot* to deliver his property to him."

"Tatay." De la Cruz let the heavy bar slip from her hand. She pulled her hat brim over her eyes and shuffled to the solitude of her truck cabin.

Chesebrough rubbed his reddened cheek and turned to Rash. "That's all of it. Winkle had this mad conspiracy, and I played along. I'm on your side. If you're for real, you should show me the scrip without further delay. I may need to get you protection."

"My rules, Eddie," said Rash. "First tell me who my partners will be if I include them."

"It's a fantasy."

"Okay then. Winkle could tell me. Do you want me to ask him, instead? If I do, he won't keep you in his circle any longer."

Mallory pointed his hand at Rash. "You're the one on a short choke-leash now, *Eddie*."

Chesebrough's left eye twitched and his lips tightened. He shoved his hands into the hooded sweatshirt muff. "Winkle has to complete his plan today, or the opportunity is dead forever. If anyone revealed it, Washington politicians would change the rules so he could never use Valentine Scrip again. No one could. I've just said a lot, and that's all I'll say until you produce the certificates. If you do—right now—I'll lay down my hand. Otherwise, this very influential newspaper publisher has merely whiled away his time with two bitter, former employees. They have zero credibility, and neither will ever get a media job again."

Rash said, "We'll show the scrip to you later."

"Did I scare you, Lou? This is the same slack-jawed way you looked when I left you after our divorce. You didn't have squat then, or now."

Mallory beckoned Rash. She whispered to him first. "Mick this farce isn't worth it. He knows you're bluffing. I gathered what I needed for a story from De la Cruz. You look terrible. Please let me get you out of here."

Her eyes widened when Mallory withdrew from his pocket the certificate corner-scrap he had found earlier on the ground. Chesebrough saw it and his lips parted.

"Hang this on Eddie's nose," Mallory said. "I'm better at hellos than good-byes. I have to go back to my car to sleep."

She pulled him to his feet. He handed the paper to Rash, re-buffing her offer to help him walk to the perimeter road. Mallory shuffled by Chesebrough. "I cover crooks. I don't *work* for them."

Sharp pain racked his chest. He gathered his sweatshirt at his neck, squeezing Siobhan's wedding ring.

"There's more." Rash offered the bait. "My toys, Eddie?"

Chesebrough knew fine printing. He rubbed the paper margin, assessing the cotton bond, age, and quality. Pads of his fingertips brushed the raised words, *"For the Relief of Thomas Valentine."* He stretched the material with his fingers and inspected the type. "My God, Feldman showed me the other piece of this certificate from his father's vault. It's real. It's Valentine Scrip!"

A copy editor had once taught Mallory, "When you can reduce a story to a headline, you've got the story. Straphanger readers like their news personal, spoon-fed, and with a hot sauce kick. Your job is to give it to them. Keep it punchy. Start with a strong headline."

Mallory capsulized a banner for an imagined New York pressroom. It described a plot to heist the Alcatraz National Landmark: *Rich Rats and Righteous Redskins Ruminate Ripping Off Rock.*

Though the alliteration flair pleased him, he fretted the three-syllable word might throw his most loyal readers. He had no more to report. As he staggered to his Gethsemane, his eyes sparked when Rash responded to Chesebrough, *"Mallory* is real."

Chesebrough raised his arms over his head. His shirt drew up, exposing a pale-gray belly mound. "Come to Daddy." He leered at Rash. "We must move fast. This is what we'll do with that beautiful Valentine Scrip. In Chicago there's a defective title—"

"Explain defective," snapped Rash, making note of every detail.

With Chesebrough's Alcatraz plot revelations forthcoming, Mallory had uncovered the reasons that motivated Griff Feldman to jump off the bridge. He had Feldman's *why.* Mallory would never know his own *why;* why destiny entwined his sorry life with the fate of these strangers.

He would never be well enough to write another prose line. Caprice had blown the last of his paper-thin talent out to sea.

Along with its flight, blew his hope the public would ever again question: *Did you read what Mallory wrote?*

And for eternity, he would not find the safe line to cross back to his life where, even if in a dream, he could bid Siobhan good-bye.

Mallory would not herald his final testament, a love letter written in the guise of his best work—as he had hoped—on a million newspaper broadsheets. He died murmuring wordless expressions of love for Siobhan to a host of guardian angels. They descended to him in slow, protective circles.

A lone meteor raced to the horizon. Mick Mallory skitched on its tail.

At the Petaluma church office, far from the angels, Haggard rechecked the unlocked front door. He doddered to his office space. Firelight rounded the sharp corners of the room. He slung the empty casket from the cluttered desk toward the stove, stamping his foot down on its dried wicker. Willow twigs snapped where it creased the weave. Haggard moaned an old man's protest and yanked on the edges, breaking the container into smaller pieces. Fire inhaled through the open stove.

An automobile rumbled to silence in front of the office, a sound for which Haggard had an expectant, cocked ear. The feed of scattered sticks quickened into the fire. Hellacious glows reddened the ceiling as papers, which Rash had read earlier, were tamped into the stove. Sepia news clippings tottered on hot air drafts. They lighted among the embers. Haggard paused to pray over the remaining handwritten entries he had not shown to Rash or Mallory.

On those papers, the diarist had written of how during World War II: *I agreed to cache the Valentine Scrip for Mrs. Henriette Feldman. She justifiably feared her son, Arthur Dean Feldman, intended to steal the scrip from her secret hiding place.*

After the war, a young Filipino conveyed written instructions from Mrs. Feldman for me to exchange a specific quantity of certificates (that I still held in custody) with an antiquarian dealer for a large sum of money. Mrs. Feldman graciously allowed me to spend ten percent of the proceeds at my discretion. For the remaining proceeds, as directed, I distributed the funds to a Philippine orphanage as American war reparations in the name of the courier. Unsold scrip I kept hidden for her eventual blood heirs, as she had requested.

The office door latch clicked. Floor joists sighed. Haggard glimpsed up, hearing measured steps move across the adjacent room. He threw the minister's diary into the stove, and turned from the blaze. His face cooled. Fire backlit his battered ears with a rose quartz glow.

Behind the planted palm, on which Mallory had rested his feet, a framed photograph cast an elongated shadow on the wall. In the picture, Filipino children skipped down chapel steps. Above the chapel door, a sign read, "Herald Home."

Haggard bent the plastic frame off its nail mount. He stared back into the fire sparks. Dancing red constellations burned from the diary. He laid the photograph on the fire. Its glossy edges curled inward. The image bubbled.

"If someone's out there come on in," said Haggard. No one answered.

Glints refracted on the stained glass outside the room. The crackling fire hushed. Embers consumed the last small sticks and dried papers. A bluish haze floated above the lamps.

"Hello?" Haggard called out.

A garment rustled and a heavy object thumped on a desk. Haggard swung the stove door closed. "I'm alone."

The floor creaked. A voice from the other room said, "You are not alone, you are with your brother."

Winkle entered. His shoulders spanned the doorway width.

"The steeple?"

Winkle nodded. "It's out there."

"Please bring it to me."

He returned with the post, handing it to Haggard. "I would still prefer you destroy it with the other evidence."

Haggard cradled the relic, tracing the outline H-E-R-A-L-D with his fingertip. "We'll keep this beacon at the church."

"It's a signpost pointing back to Feldman and the cemetery," said Winkle. "Why risk our destiny for an old post?"

"Because, Mrs. Feldman deserves our respect." Haggard turned to his desk where he'd laid a neat stack of certificates. "Besides, the steeple belongs here."

He handed the documents to Winkle. "These papers are the Valentine Scrip. They don't belong to the church. If, as you say, Griff Feldman is dead, then the church has fulfilled its commitment to Mrs. Feldman. Her grandson was the last of the Dean-Rosenthal bloodline who could claim them. The Holy Spirit must want these returned to the Indian nation who lived here."

"The *Great* Spirit will let the white man have his worthless paper back after he returns our birthright," said Winkle. "I'll take these to Chicago tomorrow."

Haggard removed the cross entangled in the dreamcatcher, laying the ornament on his desk. "Gather them all and go quickly. I wash my hands of them."

Winkle seized his offering. He pressed the engraved certificates to his nostrils, inhaling their complex odors.

"Many years ago, Apache shared their meat and wisdom with a scared and hungry boy. Tonight, my new Apache brother feeds me a feast that will allow our Indian nations to take Alcatraz. The circle of our fathers bends in our direction."

Low, rhythmic hums rose from Winkle's chest, forming words of a benediction.

"What was meant to be is now done. The reporters may be back soon," said Haggard. "You must hurry."

From behind the stiff papers, Winkle said, "They did what I told you they'd do. They think I'm at the Presidio."

"No. Not both reporters. Mallory's wily." Haggard scraped sweat from his hand with a twig broken off the casket. "He left anyway. I'm not sure why."

"You can forget him. He's over." Winkle lowered his hands, placing the papers back on the desk. Fine red vessels netted his eyes.

"Remove them." Haggard motioned at the stack. "They belong with the caretakers of the land, not here."

Winkle picked up the top certificate and aligned its rigid edge perpendicular to his fingers. With a flick, he sliced a deep paper-cut across the middle of his palm. He shuddered, gasping from the pain. Bending, he drew his knife from its ankle sleeve. Its sharp blade glinted from the fire. His fingers wrapped around the blade top, pressing the cutting edge hard into his palm along the line of the paper-cut. A white cleft seared his brown flesh. Blood, reincarnated from generations before him, inundated the slash. Winkle spit on the wound and turned his wrist. He smeared the pulse of Indian spirit across the thirsty fibers of Valentine Scrip.

THEN FACE TO FACE

The next day in San Francisco, a Press-Republican editorial lauded the Arguello Trust for donating land at Crissy Field for a Native American cultural center. While San Franciscans read the editorial with cursory glances, in New York City printers laid out the afternoon city edition. They trimmed a story that had been set on an old Linotype. Rash had faxed the copy to a major New York newspaper from Petaluma. A gritty photograph showed pelican strings gliding by Alcatraz Island in the middle of the bay. The front-page article carried a single reporter's byline.

Four rows of declining-sized headlines blared:

California Demon!
Frisco Paper Pub and Pol Pals in Bed with Reds
Brazen Plot to Heist USA Landmark
Mick Mallory's Last Column

Before sundown the next day, from the Atlantic sweep of the Montauk lighthouse to where Pacific foam hemmed the Golden Gate, readers asked one another, "Did you see what Mallory wrote?"

And for one miraculous moment, an absolute stillness hung in the air.

Nothing stirred on Earth.

Nothing moved in time.

The immortal hand had paused.

All waited for the orb to roll once more, and to hurtle unsuspecting souls toward their destinies.

The End

AUTHOR'S NOTES

This novel is a work of fiction constructed from my fantasy. Events that occurred in Northern California and elsewhere inspired the narrative. The characters' words, their interrelationships, their thoughts, and their physical descriptions, are speculative literary devices of my imagination. Below, I have listed historical and fictitious characters and miscellaneous notes of possible interest.

Chapters CALIFORNIOS through ASSISTENCIA
The Miranda family, Generalissimo Mariano Guadalupe Vallejo, Leonito Antonio Duque de Ortega, and Juana Briones are historical characters.

The Miranda family occupied the land grant for Rancho Arroyo de San Antonio. Vallejo's motives for granting the land to Ortega and Ortega's later abandonment of the rancho are imagined, but plausible with my interpretation of historical records.

Juana Briones, the inspiration for several books and the subject of an excellent California Historical Society exhibit in 2015, which included a wall from her adobe, married Apolinario Miranda, brother of Juan Chrisostomo Miranda.

Kanakas worked Vallejo's Rancho. I invented the islander characters and the English trapper. Vallejo's brother-in-law, Captain John Bautista Rogers Cooper, brought Sandwich Islanders to Alta California's Northern Frontier. Kanakas worked in large numbers for the British Hudson's Bay Company at Fort Vancouver on the Columbia River.

The hacienda at Rancho Arroyo Lema was the United Mexican States' keystone to a chain of interdependent ranchos and pueblos established to secularize Indian lands up to the latitude 42° north, the Oregon/California border.

I encourage you to visit the places referred to in the story. Among them are the lovely city of Petaluma; the Petaluma Adobe; Arroyo de San Antonio, aka San Antonio Creek; Yerba Buena, modern San Francisco; Mission San Francisco Solano in Sonoma; Lachryma Montis, which replaced La Casa Grande, Vallejo's estate on the Sonoma Square; the pulperia, Ortega's saloon-home that later became the Blue Wing Hotel across from the restored mission; the Arroyo Potiquiyomi, now Mark West, where the Hijar-Padres Cosmopolitan Company immigrants intended to build the pueblo, Santa Ana y Farias; Mission San Rafael de Arcángel; Villa de Branciforte, today's Santa Cruz; early residences of Juana Briones at El Polin Springs and El Ojo de Agua Figueroa in the magnificent San Francisco Presidio, managed by the good stewards of the Presidio Trust.

Paso del Estero de Petaluma was an ancient footpath first trodden by Ice Age tribes that hunted mastodons. The trail could have included modern Sonoma Mountain Parkway, Ely Boulevard, and Adobe Road. It passed the Coastal Miwok-speaking, Lekatuit Nation's main encampment. To drive a wagon from the Rancho Arroyo Lema Adobe to the west side of Petaluma entailed traveling northward to the extant Roblar de la Miseria land grant boundary marker. Many rancho's boundaries were marked by ditches wide and deep enough to turn cattle. Large-wheeled carretas forded the slough near Denman Flats. There travelers crossed to the Camino de San Rafael, and drove south, this time on the western shore. The Miranda homestead rested on a hillside near the San Antonio Creek.

One of many theories of Petaluma's etymology is the Spanish adopted it from the Coast Miwok words that described the terrain's soft-rolling hills.

Timothy Murphy is a historical character. I drew from published accounts the Criollo cattle descriptions, the California grizzly activities, and the heinous bull and bear fights, which continued under the American flag. The arena was in the Lakeville Marina vicinity where today a plaque on the edge of a parking lot marks the former location of such a venue.

Thomas Bishop Valentine, emigrated by ship from Eastchester, New York to San Francisco after he deserted a late-winter expedition to cross Northern Mexico with John Woodhouse Audubon's California Company. In later chapters, I mention publisher, J. J. Pennypacker, and Israel Kashow. They were members of the Audubon-led Argonauts. Of them, only Pennypacker completed the journey to California by land.

The United States custody battle for the grant to the Rancho Arroyo de San Antonio is a matter of public record. The case is so much more convoluted; more complex, and involves so many more parties than I described, it's easier to dismiss the real-life incident as nonsensical fiction. It is not.

By 1850, the non-Spanish speaking, "Blond Man's," probate court ordered the Mirandas to surrender the rancho title.

In 1852, Thomas Valentine repeatedly posted this in the Daily Alta:

"THE UNDERSIGNED GIVES NOTICE that he claims to be the owner of the site where the town of Petaluma is situated, and of all the land lying between the creeks of Petaluma and San Antonio,

except about one and a half leagues sold by me off the southern end of the Miranda or San Antonio Rancho; and that my claim to the same is now pending before the Board of Commissioners to settle private land claims in California. Any person, therefore, who shall purchase any portion of the above described tract, except from me, will do so at his own risk. - Thos. B. VALENTINE"

⊶┼┼⊷

Chapters INCUBATOR through VALENTINES DAY
Arthur Lloyd Dean, Leslie Dean, Delia Dean, John Pitts, Lyman C. Byce, Sadie Hinshaw, President William McKinley, Jennie Valentine, Ernest H. Ward, and Earl Osterhout are historical figures. Their described relationships, values, dialogues and physical characteristics, are, for the most part, fiction.

Henriette Elizabeth Rosenthal, Pastor Haggard, and Kevin Corcoran, are fictional composite characters.

Before she died in 2008, I had the privilege to meet Dorothy Crystal Dean Petersen, daughter of Leslie Dean, niece of Arthur Lloyd Dean, and WWII member of the US Women's Naval Reserve (WAVES) at her home in Petaluma. I shared with "Dot" the research I had accumulated regarding her uncle's stained-glass memorial. A wistful memory came to her as we chatted. Her father had taken her to the Petaluma Memorial Day parades. While the soldiers marched by, he held her little hand and wept. My research enhanced her understanding of her father's grief. She remembered her grandmother, Delia, had hung in her dining room a framed photograph of a casket adorned in bunting.

The steamer Ohio and the troops' Embarcadero departure, the Petaluma celebration of Company C's return, the death of Arthur Dean at the same hour as the victory rally, and the town mourning are from historical accounts.

I drew from several documents, newspaper clippings, and archived military records on Dean's military induction and his demise in the Philippines.

Although Pitts' letter to Henriette Rosenthal is fictional, various historical correspondences from that period inspired its composition. Its tenor reflects the times.

The graves of Dean, Pitts, and Osterhout are side by side in the San Francisco Presidio National cemetery. Dean's grave description is exaggerated and enlarged. Sans "HERALD" on the gate, however, their inscriptions are similar.

Pitts and Dean had younger brothers, James Calvin Pitts and Leslie Dean, who served with Company C Militia and survived the war at Camp Barrett, Fruitvale, CA.

▰╪╪▰

Chapter SCRIP
Historical events inspired the White Rock Island (aka Bird Rock) acquisition and the Valentine Scrip land rush. The island is a quarter mile off Catalina's Isthmus Cove. Under private ownership since the 1920s, economic depression and conservationists have thwarted developers from building a casino, and a yacht club on the site.

The characters, except William Wrigley, Jr., who lost his three-year battle for White Rock Island, are fictitious. Chapman University's "Huell Howser Archives" has preserved an online video tour of the island.

▰╪╪▰

Chapter CUSE
Bear Winkle, Mick Mallory, and Siobhan Mallory are fictional.

The life of my former Syracuse University housemate and persistent muse, Pulitzer Prize-winning columnist, Michael McAlary, inspired the Mallory character and inspired me to complete this book. McAlary had a healthy Irish contempt for authorities, liars and the self-righteous. He punched *up*, unleashing his strongest printed opprobrium on the more notorious figures of his time: President William Clinton, George Steinbrenner, Mike Tyson, and then high-society slithering, Donald Trump. His funeral, in 1998, drew disparate New York celebrities, from Paul Simon to Al Sharpton, and the future Governor Andrew Cuomo. New York Daily News columnist Jim Dwyer eulogized McAlary: *"To have been young once with Mike McAlary is to always have a cartwheel in your soul."* In 2013, Tom Hanks triumphed in his Broadway debut portraying McAlary's controversial life in Nora Ephron's Broadway play "Lucky Guy."

Historical events inspired the Saltine Warrior controversy and the Mallory article about the deplorable conditions on a nearby Indian reservation. Modern characterizations and values describing the California, New York, Illinois, and other Native American peoples are fiction. Their enduring stewardship of the land is not fiction.

Chapter BELVEDERE
The San Francisco Press-Republican newspaper is fictitious.

Historical events inspired the claims on the former Fort Dearborn property and Long Beach Harbor. Few legal cases have covered such a wide field of historical interests, as did Thomas Valentine's 19th-century claim to Chicago's Fort Dearborn property. The plaintiff cited the Northwest Territory succession; Fort Dearborn's establishment at Chicago; Illinois's admission to the

Union; the Fort Dearborn abandonment; the Treaty of Hidalgo with Mexico and a half dozen acts of Congress and the Illinois Legislature. They played a part in one of the most complicated disputes argued over a piece of property. Speculators made similar high stakes claims to the Long Beach Harbor and the Seattle Tide Flats.

Each of the 332 Valentine Scrip certificates entitled the holder to acquire 40 acres of unoccupied and unappropriated public lands. Land Sharks, who acquired scrip, identified defective property deeds. They then extorted payments from the presumptive owners under the threat of eviction. Along with White Rock, opportunists scooped up properties from the Great Lakes' shores; to an island on the Sheboygan River in the heart of St. Paul, Minnesota; to Chicken Key in Biscayne Bay Florida.

The Arguello Trust is fictitious.

<hr/>

Chapter EL PRESIDIO through THEN FACE TO FACE
Most of the chapter's characters, events, and the Argus-Panoptes newspaper are fictitious.

A historical event inspired the exaggerated tale of the beach encounter with the fictional gangster Ron Spelotti.

The church minister, the painter, and his accomplice are fictional characters inspired from Petaluma's past. No one carved the old church steeple with initials. However, a worker did carve the construction year into it. I based the clandestine rescue of architectural elements from the church and their later destruction in a house fire on historical events.

The glorious stained-glass windows of Petaluma's First Presbyterian Church are on display inside the church. Their storage and recovery are historical events.

Zionist Benevolent Free Loan Society is fictitious but inspired from the Abraham Haas Memorial Fund. Historical events inspired the telling of the Jewish emigration to Petaluma poultry farms.

If you want more information on the First Presbyterian Church's historical windows, or to donate to their preservation, please send your interests to the following:

First Presbyterian Church
C/o Stained Glass Restoration
939 B Street
Petaluma, CA 94952

ACKNOWLEDGMENTS

Thank you to Charlene, Sarah, Timothy, my 10 siblings, their mates, their offspring, and especially little Baxton for holding me in your circle of love. I am you.

Thank you to my outstanding editors: Copy Editor Katie Watts, Developmental Editor Ellen Brock, and Beta Reader Steven Davis.

Thank you to our underappreciated depositories of culture and civilization, America's public libraries, and archival institutions. I exploited many of them to complete this story, beginning with Petaluma Museum and Historical Research Library; Petaluma and Santa Rosa Historical Annex branches of the Sonoma County Library; Bancroft Library at the University of California Berkeley; San Francisco Civic Center Library History Center; California State Sutro Library; California State Library in Sacramento; Society of California Pioneers; California Historical Society North Baker Research Library; Sonoma State University Library; Belvedere-Tiburon Landmarks Society; Marin County Civic Center Library; Marin History Museum; California Indian Museum and Cultural Center; Public Library of Cincinnati and Hamilton County; Beinecke Rare Book & Manuscript Library at Yale University; Library of Congress; National Archives; San Joaquin County Historic Museum; Stockton Public Library; San Diego History Center; White Plains Public Library; New York

Historical Society Museum; J. Porter Shaw Library of the San Francisco Maritime National Historical Park; Old Sacramento Military Museum; California Digital Newspaper Collection, and the websites of First Presbyterian Church of Petaluma and the Audubon Park Historic District.

Blessings.

Made in the USA
San Bernardino, CA
21 November 2017